Calamity

Knights of Eternity

Book 1

Rachel Ní Chuirc

Copyright © 2023 by Rachel Ni Chuirc

Published through The Legion Publishers Ltd

Editing by Michelle Dunbar

Editing by Faith Williams

Cover by Rashed Alakroka

Typography by May Dawney Designs

Formatting and additional editing by Christine Cajiao

This is a work of fiction.

THANKS

I never thought I'd see the day when I'd be publishing a *whole entire book*. The thing you're holding right now! In your hands! And while we like to think of writing as something we do in a dark tower while a candle flickers and a storm rages outside (very dramatic), there's a bit more to it than that.

Thank you to Brian J. Nordon, Aisling O'Connell, Ilya Voulis, Jack Fields, Maria Leggatt and Ruairí Moore for reading early versions of *Knights of Eternity*. And to the Legion beta readers for their eagle eyes.

To my family, who not only encouraged me to be a bookworm but happily buried me in more books than I could ever read.

To The Legion Publishers: Jez, Chrissy, and Geneva for seeing something in this book.

And thank you, dear reader, for buying up a book I never thought would see the light of day. I hope Zara, Eternity, Valerius, and Lazander become as real to you as they are to me.

Love,

Rachel Ní Chuirc

P.S My last name is pronounced "knee-kirk." If you forget how to say it, picture kneeing Captain Kirk in the face, and you've got it!

Contents

THANKS 3

Prologue...8

Chapter One 21

Chapter Two 26

Chapter Three...29

Chapter Four..34

Chapter Five 38

Chapter Six 44

Chapter Seven...51

Chapter Eight 57

Chapter Nine..63

Chapter Ten 69

Chapter Eleven 74

Chapter Twelve..80

Chapter Thirteen 86

Chapter Fourteen...91

Chapter Fifteen 96

Chapter Sixteen 101

Chapter Seventeen..106

Chapter Eighteen 112

Chapter Nineteen..117

Chapter Twenty 124

Chapter Twenty-One 131

Chapter Twenty-Two 137

Chapter Twenty-Three 143

Chapter Twenty-Four 149

Chapter Twenty-Five 154

Chapter Twenty-Six 160

Chapter Twenty-Seven 164

Chapter Twenty-Eight 172

Chapter Twenty-Nine 178

Chapter Thirty 185

Chapter Thirty-One 191

Chapter Thirty-Two 197

Chapter Thirty-Three 204

Chapter Thirty-Four 210

Chapter Thirty-Five 217

Chapter Thirty-Six 224

Chapter Thirty-Seven 232

Chapter Thirty-Eight 237

Chapter Thirty-Nine 244

Chapter Forty 250

Chapter Forty-One 256

Chapter Forty-Two 262

Chapter Forty-Three 267

Chapter Forty-Four 272

Chapter Forty-Five 278

Chapter Forty-Six 283

Chapter Forty-Seven...................................... 290

Chapter Forty-Eight...................................... 297

Chapter Forty-Nine 303

Chapter Fifty 308

Chapter Fifty-One 313

Chapter Fifty-Two 318

Chapter Fifty-Three...................................... 325

Chapter Fifty-Four...................................... 333

Chapter Fifty-Five 339

Chapter Fifty-Six 344

Chapter Fifty-Seven 349

Chapter Fifty-Eight...................................... 356

Chapter Fifty-Nine...................................... 361

Chapter Sixty 368

END OF BOOK ONE 376

REVIEWS 377

DESECRATE 378

WANDERING WARRIOR 379

QUEST ACADEMY...................................... 380

ARISE ALPHA 381

SOMNIA ONLINE 382

FACEBOOK AND SOCIAL MEDIA 383

LITRPG! 384

LITRPG LEGION 385

Prologue

It moved, slow and languid.

Civilizations rose and fell like the tide. Stars exploded with life then vanished into the Void. Yet the entity remained chained and bound. It took an eternity to shift its manacles even minutely, but the entity was patient—it had time, if nothing else.

The twin suns of Bala and Gaj hung in the sky—the prisons of the entity's former lieutenants. At first glance, impenetrable light bound them, but the entity's keen eye could see cracks of darkness forming—the quiet and inevitable heralds of freedom.

The entity unhinged its gaping maw, greedily inhaling the slivers of power it stole like a thief in the night. It was slow, painful work. Yet the entity was calm. It was determined. It was *patient*.

It would shatter this prison—inch by painful inch.

Soon it would return.

Soon it would be free.

Valerius watched the knights fight for their lives—one hand resting on the hilt of his sword, his expression schooled in calm indifference.

The scenery, on any other day, would be impressive. They were at the edge of a coastal village Valerius had already forgotten the name of. The noonday sun was high and hot, near stifling beneath his heavy ivory armor. Yet, despite the heat, the crashing sea that struck the rock face was cold in its fury, each wave threatening to drag down those foolish enough to get too close.

He smacked his lips, relishing the salty spray. Inhaling the bite of the briny sea, he leaned over the craggy precipice, taking care to remain hidden.

The ground below was treacherous at the best of times—sea-spray and the clinging lichen made the rocks slippery while griffer pods the size of Valerius' palm lay coiled beneath graying seaweed, ready to jam their poisoned needles into unsuspecting feet. While the poison was weak, and the sharpened tip would cause you to stumble at best, a single misstep could be the difference between life or death in a fight.

Especially against a pack of pyrions.

Valerius had always been fascinated by the amphibians. Five large horns curled out from their faces like keratin flowers while their thick, powerfully built legs and whiplike tails made their attacks as vicious as they were elegant. They didn't kill— they *slaughtered,* cutting down those who threatened them with a brutal efficiency Valerius admired.

The light from the blistering sun caught the shifting and twisting scales on a pyrion's body, making him wince. While beautiful, it was their iridescent scales that made them the scourge of any blade. Moving with a pyrion's body, they left only hairline gaps most warriors struggled to pierce.

But the Gilded Knights were not most warriors.

Three of the beasts surrounded Marito, a giant of a man who towered over the pony-sized pyrions. Tightly curled dark hair was tamed by thick braids that trailed down his back. His leather brigandine was cut off at the shoulders, allowing his bare arms free movement as he drew his iconic dual axes.

As the first pyrion lunged for Marito, a purple viscous fluid dripping from its serrated fangs, Valerius idly summoned the Menu. Visible to his eyes only, the translucent interface rimmed by a gold border appeared in the air before him. He mentally skipped past his Inventory, the infinite space nearly bulging at the seams from the sheer wealth of elixirs, weapons, and armor he'd collected over the years. He paused briefly on the Quest tab. A quiet rage flared in his chest at the sight of his current objective, and he had to take several steadying breaths.

He *would* complete his mission, just like all the others. He simply had to be patient.

Finally, he landed on the desired page: the Bestiary.

Bestiary:	Pyrion
A rare medium-sized monstrosity, pyrions are pack-creatures with a strict hierarchy. They are protected by a thick layer of iridescent scales that cover their entire body but for a soft underbelly they guard fiercely. They can easily take down prey twice or even three times their size with the paralyzing venom in their fangs…	

"Ah," Valerius said as the pyrion's fangs clamped down on open air, missing Marito's bare arm by an inch, the venom in question dripping from its jaws. "That explains all the dead mercenary groups before us. Amateurs." He returned to the entry.

Bestiary:	Pyrion
Despite their ferocity, pyrions generally have mild temperaments and will often move onto new territory rather than enter combat to defend it.	

Valerius scoffed, thinking of the fifteen dead men left in the pyrions' wake.

Marito roared, driving an axe into the skull of the snapping pyrion, the blade cutting through the bone like soft cheese. He didn't pause to see the creature collapse, legs twitching as neurons frantically fired in the throes of death. Instead, the giant spun, flinging one of his axes off to his right, far from the pyrions he fought. He grabbed another beast with his bare hand, slamming the creature into the rock beneath. The stone cracked as it gave way, tendrils spreading like cobwebs as the pyrion's skull collapsed.

As the creature's furious shriek cut off, Valerius frowned. Marito was moving quicker than usual…

Valerius blinked, zoning in on Marito. His vision shifted to black and white, the air around Marito turning a shimmering blue as Valerius' interface focused on the giant, trying to break down his fellow knight into a quantifiable measure.

Dissect Activated

scrolled across his vision.

Scanning…

There was a gentle 'ding,' as a pop-up appeared.

Ability detected:	Heroic Strength
This ability allows the user to push their body far beyond human limitations. While exceptionally powerful, it can only be used for a maximum of sixty seconds, before incurring…	

Valerius sighed, dismissing the rest of the text. Were pyrions all it took these days for the knight to use his famed strength? Perhaps Marito was slipping. Valerius returned to the final paragraph of the Bestiary's entry on pyrions. He ignored Marito's grunt of pain as the dying pyrion raked its serrated claws down his arm.

Bestiary:	Pyrion
The exception to this, however, is during the first blooms of spring when the pyrions' young are not old enough to leave the confines of their dens. During this time, the pyrions will enter a violent rage should their territory be threatened.	

"There we go," Valerius said, closing the Menu with a mental flick. His eyes strayed from Marito, following the path of the axe the knight had seemingly thrown at random off to his right.

The thrown axe quivered where it lay buried in the skull of a pyrion that had been creeping forward, using long shadows.

for cover as it stealthily moved from rock to rock. To his annoyance, Valerius had missed the hidden pyrion entirely. The creature had been about to pounce on a slim, sallow-skinned man with ink-black hair and eyes who stood surrounded by pitch-black darkness.

Gabriel was both the only mage and the only member of the Gilded who could use magic—a rare and fickle gift that even spellcasters who'd trained their whole lives struggled with. Unlike most mages, Gabriel's affinity lay in a school of magic usually only found in books of old.

Shadows pooled around the mage's feet, dragging light inward as his magic briefly dimmed the noonday sun. Valerius spotted four pyrions stalking the mage—

their muscles coiled and ready to pounce. Curious as to how Gabriel would handle them, Valerius summoned the Menu once more and used *Dissect.*

Scanning…

The pyrions leaped as one with graceful ferocity—two went for Gabriel's legs, another for his torso while the largest went for the soft flesh of Gabriel's exposed neck.

The downside of Gabriel's magic was that summoning shadows, particularly in the scalding sun, was slow work.

Given enough time, however?

Shadows burst from where they lay at the mage's feet, sharpened points of inky darkness splitting as they shot outward. In a heartbeat, all four pyrions lay in bloodied piles, their limbs and heads an undefinable mess of flesh and bone, their bodies scattered among the rocks they called home.

Magic detected:	Feast of Shadows
A powerful spell that allows the user to solidify and manipulate shadows other than their own. This is a branch of Shadow Magic. Those with this affinity…	

He blinked away the interface, knowing the rest by heart.

Gabriel, eyes closed and unmoving, took a breath—the barest hint of sweat dotted his forehead. The mage's eyes shot open as he turned, yelling, "Lazander!"

Lazander was the last of the Gilded Knights. The red-haired knight had been with the group for less than a year and was both the youngest member and most recent addition. He was struggling with two larger pyrions, his bow abandoned at his feet as the monstrosities closed in. The man had a reputation as an unparalleled marksman but was rarely caught in close quarters. Valerius leaned in, eager to see how Lazander would do in close combat.

The answer? Adequate at best. The knight wielded two short blades that were keeping the pyrions' claws and teeth at bay, but little more. Gabriel's cry was one of warning—Valerius felt the dull static touch of building magic as one of the pyrions' iridescent scales flashed a blistering light meant to blind its enemies.

For a brief moment, the pyrion became a miniature sun on the battlefield, causing even the distant Valerius to shut his eyes tightly and look away, hand instinctively raised.

When he looked back, half expecting to see fangs buried in Lazander's neck, he was surprised to see the two pyrions lying still and unmoving—their throats slashed, soft underbellies slit open.

"BEAUTIFULLY DONE, MASTER LAZANDER!" Marito roared, his voice perpetually at a volume fit for boisterous taverns. The giant casually kicked a pyrion in the side as he wrestled his final opponent to the ground, snapping its neck with one flexed bicep.

"That was all Merrin!" Lazander answered, blushing slightly at the praise. "Her eyes guided me." Valerius' eyes drifted upward, and he spotted the feathered tail and flapping wings of Merrin, Lazander's hawk and perpetual companion.

The celebration, however, was cut short by a bloodcurdling howl. From the depths of a cave up ahead emerged the largest pyrion they had seen yet. It was the size of Valerius' warhorse. Five horns circled its skull like a crown, its scales were a beautiful teal that naturally shone bright enough to stress Valerius' eyes even from this distance.

Marito sheathed his remaining axe, stretching out a thick-fingered hand without looking as a shadow appeared at his side. The inky darkness cradled the axe he had thrown to save Gabriel. He grabbed it, nodding appreciatively at the mage and spinning the weapon in his hand as he went to join Gabriel and Lazander.

"That would be the leader of this scaly band, would it not?" Marito cheerfully called. "How would you handle this, Master Lazander?"

Lazander slung his bow over his shoulder, staring at the monstrosity who snarled, saliva and venom dripping from its mouth—but it made no move to leave the cave entrance. "Given its size, it's best if—"

The beast roared—a bone-shaking barrage of rage and bloodlust as it took off at a blistering speed, charging straight for the knights. Marito leaped forward, axes drawn as he put himself between the beast and his fellow Gilded. Valerius knew that unless Marito managed to pierce its soft underbelly with a single slash, the pyrion would make ribbons of at least one of the knights.

He sighed.

The pyrion lunged, jaw unhinged wide enough to swallow a man whole.

Instead, its fangs bit down on a dragonscale shield—the near-impenetrable metal sending shockwaves of pain to its skull. A sword plunged into the beast's shoulder, narrowly missing its neck, and it shrieked in pain—ice-blue blood pouring from the wound as it scrambled backward.

Valerius lowered his shield, eyeing it for marks left by the pyrion's fangs. Not even a dent, he was pleased to see. He casually flicked his sword, the pyrion's blood splashing all over the graying rocks. Lips curled in a half-smile, he stared the beast down—daring it to try again.

The huge pyrion hissed but backed up toward the cave—its hate-filled eyes locked on Valerius.

"By the Void!" Gabriel swore. "Where have you *been*, Val?"

"I was held up in town," Valerius lied.

Gabriel rolled his eyes but said nothing.

"My lord," Lazander began, ever polite before his leader. "The pack leader is hurt and clearly has no wish to fight any further." He gestured at the pyrion who now huddled at the entrance of the cave, blood pouring from the wound in its shoulder. It made no further move to approach them. "Why don't we retreat for now and return tomorrow? There is every chance it will have left by then."

"It won't," Valerius said. "I'll deal with it."

Gabriel opened his mouth to say something when Marito placed a hand on the mage's shoulder, squeezing gently.

"Very well, Master Valerius," Marito roared, grinning broadly. "Show this beastling the true might of the Gilded!"

Valerius strode forward, ivory cloak whipping about him. He summoned the Menu, scrolling through his spells and abilities.

He couldn't use magic, not with Gabriel so near—the mage would sense it instantly and have questions. Questions Valerius didn't want to answer. But he was the leader of the Gilded Knights, next in line for the throne of Navaros, and had killed more than the rest of the Gilded combined. His abilities, the pillars of any true knight, were all he needed.

Abilities were a knight's bread and butter. Years spent pushing their minds and bodies to the absolute limit meant they could briefly transcend the physical, and sometimes even the material, limitations of this world. Marito's *Heroic Strength* allowed him to break stone with his bare hands while Lazander's *Hunter's Shadow* made the knight seemingly vanish to the naked eye.

These abilities lasted only briefly and carried a physical and mental cost. Most knights only had one or two at most and used them sparingly.

But Valerius was not most knights.

His muscles grew taut as he activated *Swiftness*—his speed and agility more than double what he was normally capable of. *Keen Eye* followed—his peripheral vision expanding as the world became sharper, every blade of grass and whorl of stone suddenly bright and alive with detail. As he readied his sword and iconic shield, he used *Iron Strength*. It wasn't a match for Marito's ability, much to Valerius' quiet irritation, but it was strong enough to deal with a mere pyrion.

The beast, perhaps sensing that the end was near, growled—fangs bared. Valerius had to give it credit—it didn't run. He strode forward, the ghost of a smile on his face.

***

"Gallow's Breath," Lazander whispered as the pyrion's head fell to the ground, eyes wide, tongue slack and lifeless. The fight had taken less than ten seconds—if you could even call it a fight.

More like a slaughter, Lazander couldn't help but think.

"Well done, Master Valerius!" Marito called. "Harlo is safe once more from these savage monstrosities. We should tell the town elders. And who knows," he elbowed Lazander, who nearly fell from the force, "there might even be a celebration! My thirst is mighty."

Lazander smiled back—Marito's excitement was infectious.

Valerius, however, resembled a statue more than a triumphant hero.

"My lord?" Lazander called. "Is everything all right?"

It was only then he heard the mewling.

The creatures were small, their wails as high-pitched as kittens. They emerged from the cave, one at a time. Their eyes struggled with the bright light, tiny nubs of the horns bulging from heads too big for their small forms. They didn't even have scales yet, their bodies a light pink that looked strangely naked next to their fallen alpha.

The cubs sniffed the headless corpse, pawing in confusion—death not yet something these newborn pyrions understood.

"*That's* why the pyrions attacked the town," Lazander said, understanding dawning. "They weren't sick or feral like Harlo reported—they were protecting their young."

"That changes nothing," Valerius said, staring coldly at the small creature that tripped over his sabatons, its claws sliding on his metallic foot. "Fifteen mercenaries died to these creatures. They may be small now, but if they settle here, right at the edge of the village, they'll be the size of their parents in months—and we'll be right back where we started."

He flicked the pyrion alpha's blood from his sword then sheathed it along with his shield. He drew a small dagger from his belt as he knelt, grabbing one of the cub pyrions by the scruff of the neck.

"No!" Lazander yelled, half-starting forward before he could stop himself. Valerius cocked an eyebrow in surprise, and Lazander scrambled his thoughts into something that would convince his ever-practical, some would even say coldhearted, leader.

"I'll take them," he said. "Not to raise, of course—they're not meant to be domesticated. But I'll move them far down the coast, away from Harlo or anyone else they might harm."

"They can't survive alone," Valerius said, shaking the pup slightly. "They'll be dead in days."

"Maybe," Lazander relented. "But their parents are the ones who killed those mercenaries, not them. Let nature decide if they are meant to live."

"I'd also rather not kill them," Gabriel added. "'Gilded Knights of Navaros, protectors of the kingdom!' and 'stabber of adorable pyrion cubs' don't exactly go together."

"Then it is settled," Marito said, striding forward as he slapped a hand on Lazander and Valerius' backs. If the giant noticed the twitch in Valerius' cheek at the contact, he chose to ignore it. "Master Lazander, your affinity for the wilds makes you the obvious choice. Would you mind…"

"Of course," Lazander said, hand outstretched for the pup Valerius still held. "I'll take them, my lord," he said when Valerius made no move to drop the pyrion.

His eyes flickered between Marito and Lazander, but the giant smiled genially as if he hadn't just cheerfully taken charge from under his leader's nose. With a sigh, Valerius released the cub, making Lazander stumble forward to catch it before it hit the ground.

"If they end up butchering civilians, it's on your head," Valerius said, walking away without a backward glance.

***

By the time Lazander returned to Harlo, night had fallen. It had taken time to corral the newborn pyrions. He didn't want to simply scoop them up then and there. Instead, he spent a while sitting with them, sharing out scraps of food until they willingly pressed their stubby horns into his palm, purring.

When Merrin—his ever watchful hawk companion—cried out, he knew she'd found what he'd dearly hoped for. Carefully picking up the six newborn cubs, he bundled them in his arms and began the difficult task of navigating the coastline. While it would have been quicker to stick to the roads, he didn't want to shake the shadow trailing him—instead he laboriously climbed over sea-drenched rocks and strode through waist deep water in parts. He was grateful the cubs had fallen asleep in his arms—a cry of fear from them would spoil everything.

He found a sheltered bay about three hours on foot from Harlo. Carefully placing the sleeping cubs at the mouth of a small cave, he backed away.

It wasn't long before a single female pyrion emerged from the sea—she'd taken to swimming beside Lazander along the way, keeping to the corner of his eye. Her underbelly dragged along the rocks, fat and heavy from the milk she produced. Merrin had spotted her earlier, hiding among the rocks at the edge of the fight.

She lay amongst the cubs, who mewled in excitement at the smell of milk, pushing forward to suckle. Lazander carefully stepped away, beginning the long trek back—sighing in relief.

***

"Another round!" Marito called, slamming his tankard down. A row of empty mugs lay on the table before him, but the knight's eyes were sharp as ever. The same couldn't be said for the villagers who surrounded him.

"Can't believe I'm—I'm drinking with a *Gilded*. You lot rub shoulders with royalty. By the Void, you're *practically* royalty," a bleary-eyed rotund man said, staring at Marito as if he expected the giant to vanish.

"Hah! We are simple knights, my good ser. We fight, love, and drink like any other." At that he brought his tankard to his lips, draining it. The villagers who clamored around him struggled to keep up.

"Mari, could you not give an entire village alcohol poisoning. *Again*?" Gabriel asked, brow furrowed in irritation even as a smile tugged at his lips. The mage sat with Marito at a large table that took up almost the entirety of Harlo's single tavern. The pleasant smell of the fresh straw that dotted the ground mostly covered the warm, fishy musk of too many bodies jammed in too small a space. The villagers still made sure to give the Gilded a respectful berth—though none more than Valerius.

Gabriel and Marito had changed into comfortable tunics and trousers while Valerius sat in the corner, still clad from head to toe in armor. His drink lay untouched before him, and he watched the door with startling intensity.

"Um, Mister Lord Valerius?" a small voice asked. He glanced down to find a child with blonde hair tied in a familiar pattern of braids. He grimaced, knowing what she was about to ask. "My mom says you know Lady Eternity? That she saw you both in the parade last year? My mom says I was there too, but I don't remember. I was only small."

He considered not answering but caught Gabriel watching him from across the tavern.

"I do," he said, deadpan.

"Wow." The girl breathed. "Is she—is she as strong and as pretty as they say? Can she really make people Champions? Could she make *me* a Champion? Oh, I'd be a really really good one. I know all my prayers and everything!"

"Eternity doesn't make Champions," Valerius said, looking bored. "Gallow, the God of Judgment, does." The knight gestured to a darkened corner of the tavern, empty of seats and lit by a single candle. A bird skull was nailed to the wall, a raven's Valerius guessed, and beneath the scoured bone lay a handful of meager offerings—a gold coin, a lock of hair, the first of that season's crops. When the little girl saw what he pointed to, she quickly touched her thumb and index fingers to her eyes.

Valerius rolled his eyes. "You don't get all those pretty powers for nothing though. You have to pass his many, many tests, and then you get the utter *delight* of being his dedicated little soldier. Who wouldn't want a god in their head, watching their every move?"

The girl nodded; his sarcasm lost on her. "Well, um, can you give Lady Eternity this?" The girl pulled a piece of folded parchment from her pocket—he glimpsed what looked to be a flyer for a missing pig on the back. On the front, the girl had drawn two stick figures, one tall and one much smaller, with matching blonde hair and intricate braids. A row of wobbly hearts circled them.

Valerius took the piece of paper without a word, folding it and putting it inside his cloak. It would make for good kindling later.

"Thanks, Mister Lord Valerius," she said after a pause.

Valerius said nothing, merely continued to stare at the door.

As if summoned by the strength of his gaze, Lazander quietly opened the tavern door and was spotted by Marito immediately. "The mighty hunter has returned!" Marito roared to thunderous applause from the drunken audience. Gabriel sighed, shaking his head at Lazander in apology.

"If we leave now, we can get back to the Ivory Keep before dawn," Valerius said, appearing at Lazander's side.

The knight started, glancing back at the messy, crowded tavern in surprise, clearly wondering how Valerius had gotten through it. "Of course, my lord. Let me—"

Marito hurriedly grabbed his tankard and raised it. "To the people of Harlo!" he cried. Someone shoved a tankard into Lazander's hands, and he raised it in answer, silently thanking Marito for his ability to smooth things over. "To the Gilded!" a voice cried from the back.

The Gilded Knights, or the three that remained, drank as one—the tension from their leader's abrupt departure dissipating. It was, unfortunately, something they had grown accustomed to. They spent the night in revelry—Marito loud and boisterous, Gabriel ribbing the giant, and Lazander quietly laughing in return. They had no idea this would be the last time they would celebrate together like this—for something was coming.

Something that would alter the course of not only their lives but the very course of history.

Chapter One

"So, why Valerius?" I asked, leaning gently against the arcade machine. Once bright and vibrant, years of harsh lighting, spilled drinks and sticky fingers had left the cabinet dull and stained. The screen itself was scratched and battered, a hairline crack spreading outward like a spiderweb dotted with morning dew. Cheesy pop music blasted from overhead speakers older than I was, but we barely heard it—there was only myself, Noah, and the world of *Knights of Eternity*.

"Because the last two times I led with Gabriel and Lazander, I got absolutely totaled by the third wave," Noah said, side-eyeing me with a look that *dared* me to question him. He flicked the joystick left and right, hopping between the main characters of *Knights of Eternity*—Marito, Gabriel, Lazander, and my favorite main—Valerius. Black and white pixelated blocks made up his iconic ivory armor and midnight hair while a thin line hinted at the stern expression, I'd always pictured him with.

"You got totaled because you didn't stock up on Fire Resistance potions," I said, doing my best to sound nonjudgmental. "Zara the Fury is tough, but it's her *Inferno* you have to watch out for. And Valerius' armor is only Ice Resistant."

"Yeah," replied Noah. "But Valerius' shield can block her beam."

I resisted the urge to say, "Only if you time it right."

Noah clicked the action button, Valerius' avatar spinning wildly as it was chosen. A pop-up appeared, prompting Noah to choose the rest of his party.

"If Valerius is your main, who else are you taking?" I asked.

Noah paused, his joystick frozen, before he chose two characters in rapid succession. "Two mages and a hunter."

"That's an… interesting party," I said, thinking back on a similar playthrough I'd tried. I was decimated before I'd even hit the Moonvale Mountains—no less than three levels *before* Zara the Fury's punishing boss fight.

YOUR ADVENTURE BEGINS

flashed on screen.

"My mage can cast *Cover of Solace* and hide my party from enemy eyes. That way I can camp, heal up, and kick Zara's head in with full health."

I simply nodded. Noah had a plan and unless he wanted my advice (he didn't), I wasn't going to correct him.

When I first started taking Noah to the arcade, usually after school on a Friday, we played all of the classics: racing simulators, which he loved but quickly mastered. The classic shooters where he developed pinpoint accuracy worthy of a world-class assassin. Then his eyes fell on this—*Knights of Eternity*.

It was an oddity at the arcade, even among the strange mix of machines that spanned decades of gaming. While most dungeon crawlers had a linear progression and one-to-four players, *Knights of Eternity* was a solo campaign with a full party management system, randomized dungeons, permadeath, and a series of increasingly brutal boss battles. The player chose one of four Knights to begin: Valerius, Gabriel, Lazander, or Marito, and then built a party around them ranging from mages to knights, hunters to rogues.

The boss who had annihilated him no less than three times this evening was one of the toughest—a woman with golden eyes who wielded fire with the ease of breathing—Zara the Fury.

"Nice dodge," I said, hovering at his shoulder as he rolled Valerius across the screen, bringing up the knight's shield to block an incoming arrow.

"Thanks, *auntie*," he said with a smirk.

I slapped him gently on the back of the head, unwilling to disrupt his game.

Despite the mere five years between us, I was indeed Noah's aunt—a fact he loved to point out. I was also the youngest of four, a fact my sisters loved pointing out. To top it off, I was the only one who still lived at home—a fact my *mother* loved pointing out.

My sister Clara was married and had one kid—Noah, who was twelve years of age and the oldest of my nieces and nephews. And while I would never say it out loud, not even under pain of torture, he was my favorite.

"I'm almost to Zara!" Noah hollered, hopping from foot to foot, a sign he was either excited or really needed the bathroom—likely both, considering he'd been playing for two hours.

The arcade was quiet on the best of days, but it was a morgue tonight. A couple of college kids were facing off on a dance machine, of which only three of the four arrows worked, and some older guy's sipped beers and argued about whose turn it was on an old-school fighter. Other than that, Noah and I had the place to ourselves.

Well, mostly.

"How's my favorite troublemakers, eh?" a voice growled, a huge meaty palm slapping my shoulder. I jumped to see the broad grin and graying temples of a man who'd been at every Sunday dinner since I was a kid—my uncle and the owner of the arcade, Jacobi. "Shouldn't you two be out on the town, worrying your poor mothers?" He laughed with an easy warmth that made even strangers feel like family.

A pity I couldn't look him in the eye.

My gaze dropped automatically, and I knew the smile on my face looked closer to a wince. "I, ah, promised my sister I'd help Noah with his, um, math homework," I said, looking guiltily at the abandoned school bags at our feet.

"I can see that's going well," Jacobi joked, nodding at Noah who seemed unaware his great-uncle stood towering behind him. Jacobi leaned into the screen, frowning. "You know Valerius' armor is only Ice Resistant, right?"

"I *know*," snapped Noah.

Jacobi merely shrugged; hands raised in surrender.

"Delighted you got Noah into this beauty though," Jacobi said to me, nodding at the arcade machine. "I was so sure it was gonna be a hit back in the day. Now, I bet you'd be hard-pressed to find another in the whole country. A bunch of them were recalled after one of them caught fire, or something—killed the damn series before it could take off. Pity."

He traced a hand lovingly over the words *Knights of Eternity* on the machine's side, and the title's heroes—the Gilded Knights. Gabriel, Marito, Lazander, and Valerius stood back-to-back—armed and at the ready. Beneath the knights a woman knelt, her hands clasped, eyes closed in serene contemplation. Her blonde hair flowed around her in gentle waves but for two slim braids that framed her heart-shaped face. She was Lady Eternity, the "princess" the four knights battled monsters and villains to save.

But something stood between Eternity and the heroic knights. A woman with a smile like knives, her golden eyes vicious and cruel reached for the unsuspecting Eternity—her obsidian talons primed and ready to strike—Zara the Fury.

I shivered. There was something about those golden eyes, how they seemed to follow my every move, that had always made me uneasy.

"He's actually coming up on Zara," I said, hating how small my voice sounded. *Just relax*, I wanted to yell at my brain. *It's Jacobi!*

"You don't say?" Jacobi grinned. "Hey, Noah, you know how there's a little crack in the screen, right over there in the corner?"

"Yeah," said Noah, eyes still fixed on the screen as he mashed buttons.

"Well," Jacobi continued. "Your auntie used to play this game every single day after school. And one day she got *so mad* that she couldn't beat a particular boss, she threw her school bag at the screen and cracked it."

Noah, for the first time in hours, looked away from the screen and stared at me in a mixture of shock and—was that *admiration*?

"Really?" he asked, his eyes almost comically wide.

"It was *one time*," I said, a blush flooding my cheeks. Whatever Noah had been about to say was lost as the arcade machine beeped, and his head swiveled back to the game.

"No, no, no!" Noah yelled. Zara threw a fireball, bright and orange in its pixelated fury, and it slammed into Valerius. He collapsed, body shimmering red as the words *Game Over* flashed on screen.

"Argh!" Noah's hands balled into his hair. "Why?"

Jacobi dropped a meaty paw onto Noah's shoulder in sympathy. "Listen, once you get past her, and you will, the rest will be no bother to you—'cause you'll have the game down pat, you see?"

Noah nodded miserably while Jacobi continued. "If nothing else, you should keep going just to see the endgame. Toughest fight I ever had. Zara the Fury turns into this huge—"

"Don't tell me!" Noah yelped, hands over his ears. "I want to see it for myself, or not at all!"

Jacobi laughed, a booming sound that made the college kids on the dance machine jump.

My chest tightened as half the arcade turned to us, and I had to force myself to look at Jacobi.

Ignore the stares. Just ignore them! Jacobi didn't even notice.

"A man after my own heart. With that kinda attitude, you might be the one running this place one day, eh?" He pressed a bag of tokens, more than double what we had spent that evening, into Noah's hands.

Chapter Two

"No, Uncle Jac," Noah said, his eyes lighting up despite his protests at the full bag of tokens Jacobi had handed him. "You don't have to—"

"Not a word, kid. Try again—kick Zara the Fury's butt! And *don't* tell your mother."

"Thanks, Jacobi," I mumbled, smiling when Noah immediately loaded the machine with three tokens and started anew.

"Not a word to his mother, seriously. I know she's your sister, but she scares the hell out of me," Jacobi said to me as he grabbed dirty glasses from a nearby table, wiping the surface down with a cloth in his other hand. "This one time at a family BBQ, I forgot to bring mustard, and I thought she was gonna—"

"I'll do that," I said, grabbing the glasses from his hands.

Jacobi blinked in surprise, either from my abruptness, but more likely because I was never this forceful. "Nah, kid. I got—"

"I insist," I said over my shoulder, already striding away, arms full of dirty glasses. I caught a glimpse of a confused Jacobi before he shrugged, drifting toward Noah, already offering advice on which of the Gilded Knights would be best suited to taking down his nemesis—Zara the Fury.

I slowed my pace and focused on breathing. My destination, the arcade's center, was mere steps away—at the end of the row of machines where *Knights of Eternity* sat. But I took a circuitous route, ducking between machines as I looped the arcade, picking up glasses, plates, and rubbish as I went.

This was partly to help Jacobi but mainly to calm my racing heart. Jacobi had shown me my first ever video game, he'd been there for birthdays, Christmases, and every celebration in-between. He was *family*.

But he wasn't on the list.

The list was short and not one I had written. My brain had composed it about four years ago, around the time of my thirteenth birthday. It had decided, in its infinite wisdom, that it no longer felt comfortable around 99.9% of the population. Instead, it would send orders to my heart to begin pounding, my cheeks to turn crimson, and my tongue to trip over words. As for my brain itself? Well, it chose to freeze when asked the simplest questions, to flood my body with panic when anyone paid attention to me, but worst of all…

… my brain decided we could never look someone in the eye. Stare at their chins, their shoes, that lovely stain on the wall behind them, but never look them in the eye. Not unless they're on the list.

I loved Jacobi, but for some reason my brain refused to share with me, he hadn't made the cut.

It had hurt him, of course, when I pulled away. I saw it in the way he stopped going for big, crushing hugs, or how careful he was when inviting me to something—he always left me an easy way to decline.

However, I am as stubborn as a donkey with a vendetta.

I shoved the panic down and told my sister I'd start taking Noah to the arcade. It had been a few weeks, and while progress was slow, I was starting to feel more at ease in the loud cacophony that was arcade, and well, Jacobi.

I couldn't help but smile as I weaved my way around arcade machines, my discomfort fading as I remembered the hours I'd spent here as a kid. The arcade boasted about thirty machines, including pinball and a few punching bags. There had even been a high striker at one point. The huge mallet used to hit the target, praying it would be enough to ring the bell and win a month's supply of free game tokens, was still in the attic somewhere gathering dust. But its legacy lived on in a gigantic hole left in the wall.

The hole hadn't come from the mallet. It had been courtesy of a customer who, furious at his loss, had taken a swing at Jacobi. In response, Jacobi had driven the customer's head through the plastered wall.

There was a reason the arcade didn't have much security.

I passed the Racing Hall of Fame where the winners of Jacobi's annual tournament had their pictures proudly displayed. Noah's first win was at ten years old. Usually dark-eyed and serious, he was holding up a tiny plastic trophy and grinning bigger than I'd ever seen. It was a sight that I hadn't seen since.

I'd now done a full loop around the arcade and could put it off no longer. Hands very full of plates and glasses, I approached the arcade's center—cutting through two rows of pinball machines.

The arcade's center was made up of free-standing counters, so whoever was on duty could attend to customers from every direction. There were slushy machines (the blue one was delicious, no idea what was in it), popcorn machines (salted popcorn is superior), and drinks. That wasn't what caught the eye, however.

The first thing I spotted, as usual, were the towering screens—their blue and silver hue visible from every corner of the arcade. One screen, a bright, blistering cerulean, displayed this month's high scores, and the owner's full name or chosen nickname in black. The "Legendary" winners were on the right, on a screen of silver. These were the "True Heroes" of the arcade, as Jacobi liked to call them—people with eternal high scores who had never been beaten. I looked away when I caught sight of my own name.

So focused was I on the screens I bumped into a table, the edge driving into that soft part of your hip that—at the slightest touch—felt like a stab wound. I yelped, dropping everything in my hands.

The arcade filled with the sound of shattered glass.

Stupid, clumsy, idiot! Everyone is going to look at you, they're going to see how useless you are, how—

"Woah, you all right?" a male voice asked.

I froze, wanting the ground to swallow me up, put me in a blender, and then scatter my remains into the wind—never to be seen again. Because the truth was, while I was glad to help Jacobi out, that wasn't why I had grabbed the dirty glasses out of his hands and then circled the arcade like a demented hawk, picking up rubbish and plates like they were prey. The reason I had done it...

"Watch your feet. I'll grab a broom."

... was walking away to find a broom to clean up my mess while I stood there, wishing I had the power to rewind time.

Chapter Three

His name was Adrian, and he was in my year—and for the longest time that was all I knew, or cared to know, about him.

Until Noah's dad died.

We never said it out loud, but Noah could see it—how much weight his dad was losing. How weak and tired he'd become—and the appointments, so many appointments. When he lost his hair and spent his days vomiting in the bathroom, I started to spend more and more time at my sister's apartment.

I moved in after the funeral.

It was supposed to be for a week or so, just to help out. That week turned into two weeks, turned into two months, until one day I woke up, Noah snoring in the twin bed beside me, and realized I couldn't remember the last time I'd slept in my own bed.

I thought my mom would be angry when the school inspector showed up at her house wearing a sharp suit and stern expression to investigate the "home situation." He didn't ask so much as *demand* an explanation for my extended absence and dropped the words "child services" more than once. Mom had known where I was, of course—had encouraged it even. However, I don't think she'd realized *quite* how much school I had missed (an, uh, entire term.)

When I opened the door of my sister's apartment to find Mom there in her nurses' uniform, half-asleep from a night shift, the school inspector's letter in her hand, I flinched. I expected some screaming, the dreaded wagging finger, the classic "I'm so disappointed" that always made me want to curl into a ball in shame. Instead she'd reached out and hugged me tight, fingers gripping my shoulders.

"I'm sorry," she'd whispered into my hair. "For letting you take on so much."

I still stayed with Clara after that but only on the weekends. As soon as Clara found a job with more flexible hours, Mom cut back on her shifts at the ICU, and I, with gritted teeth, returned to hell.

I mean, school.

Principal May gave me a choice, one he said was only being given due to *exceptional* circumstances. I could skip the summer term and return in September to repeat the entire school year (over my dead body), or I could cram two terms of schoolwork into four months and pray I passed my exams with enough luck and pity to graduate.

I chose the latter.

Awkward conversations ensued: "Do you have friends who can catch you up on what you missed?" *Friends? What are those? Can you use it in a sentence?* "Would one of them agree to tutor you after school?" *Would a unicorn let me catch a ride to school on its back?* and so on.

When I stared at my feet, not a single name on my lips, Principal May mercifully got the hint. "I know someone who tutors—he's in your year, in fact. Let's see if we can't arrange something."

Thus entered Adrian.

"Not a fan of Romeo and Juliet?" he asked. We were in my kitchen, the brown-haired smiling guy with his neat button-down and white teeth at odds with the peeling wallpaper and wobbly dining room table.

I shrugged, staring at his faded t-shirt as my heart hammered in my chest. I focused on the barely legible text and was trying to figure out if the third letter was a curvy "g" or an angry "y" when he gently took the play from my hands.

"What if I told you that you can connect every single Shakespearean play to a season of WrestleMania?" he asked, a glint in his eye.

I shrugged, my lips twitching into a smile despite my nerves.

"Well," he said, rubbing his hands together.

What followed was a two hour conversation on leg dropping Montagues, camel clutching Capulets, and how to successfully tie off a high-stakes storyline.

I got a C+ on my next essay on Shakespeare.

Adrian told me Hulk Hogan would be proud. I rolled my eyes, involuntarily lifting the corner of my mouth. It was his follow up of "I know I am," however, that set my heart racing.

Soon my mornings and evenings were filled with catch-up work, and I pushed myself to solve every problem, polish every essay, and memorize every theorem Adrian set for me.

He matched my enthusiasm with his own, making increasingly elaborate presentations. Once, he described law of refraction using some pipe cleaners and a spoon.

Embarrassed at how much extra time he was putting into this, I told him he didn't have to keep tutoring me—I could take it from here.

He put a hand to his chest and looked at me with an outraged expression. "I am not starting my career as the world's greatest teacher by getting *dumped* by my star pupil!" He winked, smiling easily—and I caught myself meeting his bright blue eyes for the briefest second.

"Nice try." He shrugged. "But you're not getting rid of me that easily."

By the end of the term, I didn't even need to tell my mom when he was coming over—she'd have the table set for three instead of two and a cup of coffee waiting for us both (black, two sugars for me, milk only for him).

To Principal May's clear and not at all egregiously offensive surprise, I began to not only catch up to my fellow classmates, but surpass them. My C- grades quickly became B- and then A+.

"I confess, I was sure the next conversation that we had, we'd be discussing your return in September to repeat the year." He shuffled papers on his desk, and I glimpsed a recent chemistry exam of mine—the 98% grade circled repeatedly in red. He stared at it grimly as if expecting it to either vanish or grow teeth and maul him in his office.

We were in Principal May's office, and the end of term was just two weeks away. The walls were a graying white and dotted with the faded photographs of past "star pupils." Judging by how old the pictures were, it had been close to a decade since he'd had a pupil who deserved any wall space. I had a feeling I wouldn't be making the cut either.

"I... have a good tutor," I said, staring at the ink-stained table. Adrian sat next to me, grinning broadly. He had noticed, of course—how uncomfortable I was in front of, well, everyone—but it never seemed to bother him. Instead he bumped his leg up against mine, resting it briefly. A shot of warmth jumped through me.

"She did this all on her own," Adrian said, speaking to Principal May but looking at me. "And she'll pass her final exams with flying colors. I know it."

Pride threaded his voice, and I knew he meant every word. I smiled at him—grateful.

"Maybe. Maybe not," Principal May replied, mouth twisting.

Anger, red hot and indignant, flared in my chest. I'd worked myself into the *ground* for months, and instead of being happy with me, like any decent teacher would, he was going to be prissy about it?

"I'll ace them," I said, surprising everyone in the room, but mainly myself. "*Watch me.*"

Principal May shook his head, dismissing us with a flick of his fingers.

I left quickly before I lost my temper, slamming the door shut.

"'Watch me,'" Adrian repeated, punching the air. "I love it."

"Shut up," I said, secretly delighted.

"Tell you what, *when* you ace your exams, we're getting ice cream. My treat."

Before I could reply, the bell sounded and hundreds of students, sweating and eager to be home and out of the summer heat, flooded the halls. Caught in the tidal wave of bodies, Adrian waved, lost to the crowd as he moved for the exit. I ducked to the side, dodging high-heeled sandals ("Watch it, freak!"), sharp elbows ("Weirdo"), and a football that missed me by inches ("Nice one, man—you almost got her!") to reach the bathroom—slamming the door behind me. I sighed, leaning against it, eyes closed.

Fighting my way through sweaty bodies to make it to my bus on time was my personal idea of *hell*. The thirty minute wait for the next one was a small price to pay.

Splashing cold water on my face, I stared at my reflection.

Things had been hard. Harder than I dared admit. I had cried in the dark when I was sure Noah couldn't hear me. My brain tormented me with visions of watching my whole class graduate while I clapped limply from the audience. The idiot. The weirdo. The *freak*.

But I'd done it. In the process I'd met someone who was nothing but funny, kind, and made my heart flutter with every smile—*and* I was gonna get ice cream with him.

It was going to be okay—*I* was going to be okay.

Chapter Four

"I am *so* sorry," I said, gingerly picking up the larger pieces of glass from the floor—anything to avoid looking at Adrian.

"No worries," he replied easily. "Only one broke, and considering how many I dropped on my first day here, I don't think Jacobi is going to mind."

Be cool—no, be normal! Act like you're talking to Noah—no, that's creepy. Does Adrian think I'm creepy? Ah! Just say something funny.

"I—I dunno," I said, focusing on a spot on his shirt. "You should see what happened to the last assistant." I leaned in, dropping my voice. "You, ah, see the old Donkey Kong game? The one that never works?"

Adrian matched me, dropping his shoulders and leaning close.

"Well," I continued, pitching my voice low, waving my hands for added effect. "At night, when no one else is around, you can hear a voice. Real quiet. Saying— *'Don't forget to empty the ice tray, or Jacobi will shove you in an arcade gaaaaaaame.'*"

"Very considerate of the dead cashier to be so specific in his warning," Adrian said.

"Maybe he's a considerate ghost." I shrugged.

Adrian laughed, and my heart leaped (*I wasn't weird! I did it!*). Together, we swept the last of the broken glass into the pan in easy silence, and I grabbed the bin, dumping the larger shards in.

A couple of guys, now tired of their fighting game, rapped on one of the far side counters, calling for drinks. While Adrian served them, I made a poor show of looking busy, rearranging the table and chairs I had disrupted by being a klutz, and glancing back at *Knights of Eternity* to make sure Noah was in one piece.

"Has Noah beat Zara the Fury yet?"

I rolled my eyes. "Is there anyone he hasn't told?"

"I asked. This is a fight of epic proportions—and I know the little guy can do it."

"Not so little anymore," I said, staring straight ahead at Noah. I noticed his jeans now brushed the tops of his sneakers (when did he get so tall?), and he had to bend slightly to see the arcade screen properly. Jacobi was pointing at the screen, yelling something while Noah was hopping from foot to foot again.

I glanced back at Adrian to see him staring at me intensely. "Sorry," he said, flustered. He grabbed a dirty dishcloth and began wiping a perfectly clean section of the peeling red counter.

"Did I—is everything okay?" I asked, fighting the urge to apologize profusely.

"It's just… you're really good with him," he began, pink edging his cheeks. "Noah, I mean. I'm not close with my sisters. Or my parents. When I was a kid, I just played by myself." He pointed his dishcloth at Noah, who was staring so intently at the arcade screen that the two had nearly fused into one. "It's been nice spending time at your mom's house. Seeing you hang out with Noah—how much you all care about each other. He's lucky to have you. So am I, to be honest."

His flush turned crimson when he realized what he'd just said. He stared at me, watching my reaction carefully while my brain short-circuited like a toaster in a bathtub.

Think of something to say. Come on, anything. How about "thank you"? Thank you is good—nice, neutral. Oh god, why haven't you said it yet. Just say. Say it!

"You get your exam results on Monday, right?" he asked quickly, and just like that the moment was gone. Mortified, I stared at the floor and nodded.

"So… ice cream afterward? I promised to treat you, after all. I'm not working on Monday, so I can go anytime."

"Yeah, sure, Monday sounds good—if it's good for you. I mean, you just said it was, so yeah. See you on Monday," I said, walking away quickly with a wave before I put my foot in my mouth again.

He meant it, I knew he meant it. He wasn't just being nice.

I fought the urge to kick my heels and settled for a subtle air punch.

I was halfway back to Jacobi and Noah when I realized I hadn't gotten Noah a refill of his drink. I froze, caught between the embarrassment of returning to Adrian or listening to Noah beg and plead, saying he couldn't go get it right now because this part of the game was *important*. I decided Noah's whining was the lesser evil and turned, immediately colliding with someone.

"Ah, ow," I said, rubbing my side. The guy stumbled backward, clutching his stomach. I stammered an apology, but he just pulled his hood down and walked off, glancing left and right every few seconds. I had an image of a caged animal as it paced—torn between the fight or flight.

I stopped, staring after him as I worked my side—grimacing. Something heavy had jammed into me when he bumped me, and it *hurt*. What the hell was in that guy's hoodie? A metal ribcage? A shiver went through me—not the good kind. I resolved to tell Jacobi about this guy.

Then a voice cut through the noise and chatter of the arcade, a voice I would know anywhere.

"I'll give you anything you want, just don't—don't shoot."

Adrian.

I ducked down, less caution and more instinct. The thick industrial carpet beneath my feet—graying, moldy, and as old as the building, muffled my panicked steps. I chose a machine at random, grateful for the "OUT OF ORDER" sign slapped on its front—the long shadow of its cabinet hid me from view.

My fingers gripped the cabinet's edges, digging into the cheap wood as I squeezed my eyes shut, counted to three—and forced my head around the corner.

Adrian stood with his hands in the air, face pale, the whites of his eyes showing. The man who'd bumped me stood in front of the red counter. Shorter than Adrian, his hoodie was tattered and gray, holes worn into the wrists worried by nervous fingers. His jeans were in similar condition, his shoelaces undone.

My brain registered all these details before noticing the gun in his hand. Pitch black, it seemed to soak in the overhead light—its metal dark, insidious, and dangerous.

"Don't," he snapped when Adrian dropped his hands.

"Sorry! Sorry, I was reaching for the cash register. What should I—do you want to get it?" he asked, voice high and panicked. The gunman hesitated, then flicked his weapon from Adrian to the register—like a nervous twitch.

"No, you get it. But—but go slow," he said, stumbling over his words. He moved from foot to foot, hopping almost, in a way that would have reminded me of Noah if I wasn't terrified.

As the gunman's head whipped about the arcade in sharp, jerky movements, I realized he had a mask on, one of those cheap plastic Halloween ones that fogs up almost immediately. He became increasingly erratic as he struggled to adjust his mask with his free hand while keeping the gun trained on Adrian, who was slowly punching in the code to open the register. Gaining confidence, Adrian moved quicker, keeping his hands in sight as he opened the register and took out two bundles of notes.

"And the rest!" the gunman barked. Adrian looked at the cash register, terrified.

"That's it—that's all the money."

"It can't be." The gunman abruptly leaned forward, staring at the empty register, and then jerked back, his gun trained on Adrian as if he expected him to lash out. But Adrian remained perfectly still, eyes on the gun, his breath coming out in frantic bursts.

"A bag!" the gunman shouted suddenly. "Gimme a bag!"

"They're under the counter. I… I have to bend down. Is that—"

"Do it. Now!" the gunman shouted. Adrian dropped behind the counter to grab the plastic bags I knew were down on the left—right next to the arcade's panic button. *Don't*, I frantically thought. *Don't be a hero—just give him the money.*

"The hell is that? C'mere!" There was a scuffle as the gunman leaped over the counter, digging his hands into Adrian's hair, yanking him upward. Instinctively Adrian's hands went up, slapping at the gunman.

A shot rang out.

Movies taught me that gunshots were a single, sharp crack—enough to make you jump, but little more. In reality, it was explosive—a burst of noise so loud, it sent echoes of pain ringing through my ears.

But the echoes kept going, despite my hands slapped over my ears, and I realized the sound was Adrian screaming.

He kicked out, his left ear a mangled mess of flesh and gore. Blood spattered the slushie machines, the popcorn, and the fogged mask of the gunman. "I didn't mean—stop. Stop!" the gunman roared, his voice high with panic as he gripped Adrian's hair, shaking him like a dog. "Shut up, or I'll—I'll blow your head off!"

I was on my feet, running toward them with no idea of what I was going to do.

Then Jacobi charged past me.

Chapter Five

O ne of my favorite stories about Jacobi was one he'd told himself at my sister's wedding. I'd been too young to be a bridesmaid, much to my fury, and had to make do with being a flower girl. Frank and Clara had been together for years, Noah was four years old by then, but they put off having a wedding. They said they wanted to wait for the "perfect day"—and it was.

It was absolutely perfect.

Frank's coworkers had come in on their days off to build a stage and a dance floor. Chairs and tables had been decorated by myself and my family under Clara's watchful eye until the outdoor venue looked like something straight out of *The Secret Garden* (Clara's favorite film). My mom had been cooking for what felt like weeks to prepare for the hundred people that attended.

I sat on Jacobi's knee for most of the wedding and saw no reason to move just because he was making a toast. He picked me up easily, cradling me against his chest as he took the microphone.

"Let's give it up for the happy couple!"

The crowd cheered and howled as if it was the first time they'd applauded that day, not the fiftieth.

"I've a story I've been saving," Jacobi began. "For just this occasion—mainly because I know my darling godson Frank," he winked at Frank, who looked increasingly suspicious, "is going to kill me, but the truth is the truth.

"As you all know, I own the arcade in town. And when Frank was but a shy teen, he asked me about one of my employees—a beautiful girl by the name of Clara who happened to be my niece. She'd been with me during the summers for years, and what a trooper she was, but when I threw my back out, even she couldn't manage the huge batch of machines we got in. So, I enlisted the help of my godson, Frank, to help her set up."

Frank and Clara nodded while I yawned, hoping we'd have dessert soon.

"Then wouldn't you know it," Jacobi continued, "I got a bad bout of the flu, and Frank had to come in and cover for me."

Frank's eyes widened while Clara still looked confused.

"*Then* didn't the darndest thing happen—my pipes burst! And I had to spend *all that time* fixing them in the back while Frank covered the arcade floor with Clara."

Clara stifled a laugh as she glanced at Frank, who had buried his face in his hands with a groan of realization.

"I think you all know where this is going," Jacobi said.

"I don't," I replied.

The crowd laughed.

"A confession," he said, raising his glass. "I never threw my back out. I never had the flu. And I wasn't fixing no burst pipes in the back—I was doing crossword puzzles. Because!" he continued, settling the laughing crowd down with a wave of his hand, "I knew the moment that Frank and Clara laid eyes on each other that true love existed. I knew what it meant to see your soulmate and feel like the world was no longer a scary place. And I *knew* that the two of you would bring a little more light into this world and into the lives of everyone lucky enough to know you.

"If it meant I had to tell a little lie or two to help fate get a move on—well, I was more than happy to do it. To Frank and Clara," he roared, grinning madly.

"To Jacobi!" Frank and Clara yelled.

The crowd roared in approval when Frank kissed his new bride and she wrapped her arms around him, holding him tightly.

***

For such a behemoth of a man Jacobi sprinted like someone half his size, covering the ground between him and the counter in seconds. He didn't bother shoving the tables and chairs aside, instead they seemed to leap out of the way as he charged through them.

The gunman heard Jacobi before he saw him. With a panicked jerk, he dropped Adrian, two hands gripping the gun as he turned the cold metal on my uncle.

Jacobi didn't even flinch. Instead, his feet pounded the dull carpet, arms pumping as he picked up speed.

The first shot went wide.

The second didn't.

Jacobi crashed into the counter, his huge body denting metal that had withstood forty years of business. He flung out an arm as he went down, backhanding the gunman before he hit the ground hard. The gunman was knocked clear off his feet, mask skittering across the floor as his head struck a table.

The entire thing had taken less than ten seconds. But I felt like I'd been trapped here for hours—watching two people I loved get shot for a handful of change as I stood by. Frozen. Pathetic. *Useless.*

The gunman lay still, his face turned away from me. Finally, he groaned, curling up on his side as his hand went to his head.

Jacobi lay with his back to me. A spot of red blossomed like a peony in the center of his usually pristine white shirt.

He didn't move.

Someone was screaming, a high sound filled with pain and grief. It was only when I fell to Jacobi's side and ran my hands over his still face that I realized the noise was coming from me. I touched his face with useless fingers—his skin was hot and flushed. He didn't react to my touch.

"Uncle Jac? Uncle Jac!" Noah sobbed behind me, grief piercing the words like a knife to the gut.

Noah? Oh god.

Noah stood, half in shadow from the arcade screen's light—the dramatic, pounding music of Zara's boss battle blaring. I heard the zap sound effect of her *Inferno*, a towering column of fire that destroyed all in its path.

"Do not give up, fair knights!" came a cheerful cry—Marito's generic battle cry. "Do not give up, fair—"

Marito's pixelated voice cut through the white noise of my brain.

Move. You have to move, grab Noah, and get to the exit. Nothing else matters, so move your useless, stupid—

"D-don't move!" the gunman yelled, hood down as he reached out a shaky hand—steadying himself on a plastic chair as he got to his feet—dazed. "Stay where you are."

Noah stared at him, eyes flickering from Jacobi to the gunman to somewhere off to the left.

What is he looking at—oh no.

"Noah, don't!" I cried, but he was already running, hand down, ready to grab the gun that had slid across the floor and come to rest at the end of a row of machines off to the left. The gunman realized what Noah was doing a split second after I did and sprinted after him. As Noah stumbled, breath panic filled, I knew he wouldn't reach the gun in time.

I had never been particularly athletic. I did PE class under duress, and despite years of practice still flinched when a volleyball came near my head. My sprinting times were average at best, and my PE teacher, Mr. Gord, had once jokingly said he hoped I never had to run for my life.

At that moment, I didn't run for my life—I ran for Noah's. My feet ate up the carpeted floor of the arcade center as the distance between myself, the gunman, and Noah vanished.

It wasn't enough. I wouldn't reach the gun in time.

Determination filled my body like heart's blood.

The gunman skidded past the last of the machines, dropping his hand as he grabbed the gun. He spun, turned to face us as he gripped the weapon. Shoelaces undone, he stumbled, and I saw his face clearly for the first time—whiskers of stubble above his lips, soft brown eyes, and a chin that he hadn't grown into yet. He was my age, I realized, if even that.

Noah tried to stop as the gun leveled with his chest, but he was too late. The gunman's fingers curled around the trigger, his eyes alight with panic and instinct. If he had stopped for just a second, if he'd let reason take the wheel instead of fear-induced adrenaline, I like to think he'd have lowered the gun. However, he'd just shot two people, and a third now rushed him—the fact that it was a twelve-year-old kid didn't matter to fear. All fear understood was survival.

He pulled the trigger as I slammed into Noah—shoving him out of the way.

I heard the shot but didn't feel it. In fact, I didn't feel anything at all. There was a strange comfort in the numbness, in knowing it must have been the same for Jacobi. He didn't deserve to be in pain.

The speed from my frantic sprint, coupled with the force from the shot sent me spinning. I slammed into an arcade machine, sliding to the floor as my limbs turned heavy and woolen.

Why am I on the ground? I wondered, sure there was a good explanation. I remembered we'd come to the arcade with great plans to do homework but had been sidetracked by *Knights of Eternity*.

A sound drifted through the arcade, the cheery 8-bit theme song of *Knights of Eternity* blaring.

Did Noah finally beat Zara the Fury? I vaguely wondered.

My thoughts flitted about like fireflies, and I struggled to catch one long enough to make sense of it.

I could hear Noah screaming, but the words were garbled. A guy in a tattered gray hoodie stared down at me, eyes wide, breathing hard. I wondered what was wrong with his face until I realized he was crying.

"I'm sorry," he said, and then he was gone—running through the darkness toward the exit.

"Help is, ah, damnit, help is coming," Adrian said. *Oh, Adrian is here? That's good. We're supposed to get ice cream.*

"Look at me, all right? I need you to look at me." A hand slapped my cheek, and I frowned when I saw Adrian's pale face.

Why'd he hit me? What the hell, Adrian?

He pressed what used to be an off-white towel to his ear that was now bright red and blood-soaked.

Oh, he hurt his ear? That's bad, I should find a bandage... a really big... bandage...

The *Knights of Eternity* music changed, shifting from the cheery opening to the quiet foreboding creep of the boss music. *Is someone playing it? That's cool, I thought no one but myself and Noah...*

My head drooped, heavy with exhaustion.

"Don't fall asleep. Do *not* fall asleep," Adrian snapped.

I stared down at my chest, and the mess that was my t-shirt. "I think... I think I spilled something..." I mumbled.

Noah was crying, and it shook me out of my stupor long enough to notice he was holding my hand. "Noah, s'okay," I said, my tongue thick and heavy. "S'okay. Tell Clara… tell her…"

My mind blanked on what I wanted to tell her, but his small, dark eyes were staring at me so intently I didn't want to leave him hanging.

"Tell her, you didn't get any math homework… okay?"

He laughed, a harsh choking sound that I belatedly realized was a sob.

"Don't cry, it's only… homework."

I was so tired. Why was I so tired? And why was my chest starting to hurt? If I just go to sleep, I'll feel better.

"Open your eyes!"

A slap I heard but didn't feel.

"Wake up!"

"Do-di-do!" *Knights of Eternity* trilled. I could see it as clearly as if I stood in front of the screen—the iconic gold-ridged Menu and the huge lettering in a striking black font.

YOUR ADVENTURE BEGINS.

Chapter Six

It was cold—a bone-deep cold that dragged me from the depths of sleep. My body wanted to wake, but I fought it—squeezing my eyes shut. My tongue was thick and heavy, a stinking corpse in the grave that was my mouth. I smacked my lips, but no saliva came—only a dry, racking cough that made me hunch over, fingers cradling my throbbing skull.

As my brain muddled its way to consciousness, pain followed. It started in my toes, a sharp needling that left my feet numb. It crept up my legs—my skin dry and stretched too thin. My chest burned, each breath slow and labored. None of that compared to my head, which pounded like a hammer on an anvil.

I groaned, the ground beneath me hard and unyielding. I curled up—looking for warmth. For comfort.

Then I heard the chains.

Opening my eyes, I found only pitch darkness. Panicked, I moved too quickly, the world tilting as I struggled to sit up—the sound of metal slithering against stone following my every move.

A sliver of moonlight peeked through a slit in the stone wall, far beyond my reach, but it was enough to see the thick, heavy manacles that circled my wrists and hands, encasing them completely.

My chest tightened, fear pressing on my heart, my ribs—threatening to crush me. Instinctively I yanked hard at the manacles. Huge chains as thick as my forearm slid across the floor in answer. My vision blurred with tears and panic as I pulled harder. Rings of raw, chafed skin circled my wrists from where the metal had cut into it.

What is this? Where am I? What is going on?!

I shook as adrenaline flooded my body, screaming at me to do something, *anything*, or I was going to die.

I dragged myself to my feet, throwing myself to one side as I wrenched on the chains as hard as I could. The metal whined, bending—but it held fast. My limbs felt strange and jerky, like an inexperienced puppeteer teased my strings.

A scream was building in my throat when the singular door of my cell swung open.

I froze—hunched over like a cornered animal.

Two figures lingered in the doorway—one of them held a candelabra, the flickering candlelight doing little to illuminate their faces.

"My lord, you have searched my domain from dusty attic to wine-filled cellar. Unless she has shrunk to the size of a mouse and taken up residence in the walls, she is not here," the candelabra-wielder said, his voice carrying the perfect amount of servility wrapped in sarcasm to avoid criticism.

The other person didn't answer. Instead, they approached me, the soft clank of metal sliding over metal accompanying every step.

"I don't believe you two have met," the voice continued. "This is my betrothed, Zara the Fury, as she is commonly known. Forgive her appearance—she has been misbehaving of late, and some punishment was needed."

Wait, what? What did he call me?

I awkwardly raised my arms, scrubbing my eyes with my forearm to see a knight towering over me.

He was clad in white armor. Delicate filigree crept along every plate, creating a subtle pattern of veins that glinted in the moonlight. Buckled at his waist, a huge sword with a sharp-beaked creature decorated the pommel, and from the ease with which his hand rested on it, I could tell he was prepared to use it at a moment's notice.

A cascading wave of ivory enshrouded him in a cloak that looked soft to the touch. On his chest, the same sharp-beaked creature with outstretched wings decorated his breastplate.

I lifted my gaze and found his eyes—black etched with silver, a stark contrast to his armor. His shock of midnight hair was swept back from his face, a marbled thing of angles and edges that stared down at me.

I had only seen him in pixelated form as he charged across the screen, shield and sword in tow as he blocked fireballs and arrows with ease. Yet I knew his name, despite my brain protesting at the ridiculousness of the idea.

Valerius stood before me—leader of the Gilded Knights, next in line for the throne of Navaros, and one of the four playable characters in *Knights of Eternity*.

"Va-Valerius…" I said, and froze. The low, sultry voice that had echoed in the stone room was utterly foreign to me.

"You know his name?" the voice called from the doorway, surprise and amusement threaded in each word. "Be humbled, my Lord—Zara takes interest in precious few."

Valerius frowned. A gauntleted fist snapped out, grabbing my hair and tugging sharply as he yanked my head back—staring at me intently.

"Help me," I blurted, ignoring the panic I felt at the strange voice that fell from my lips. I lifted my useless bound hands to Valerius, pleading. "I don't know where I am. I don't know what's happening to me. Help me, *please*, I need—"

"Disappointing," he said, staring at me as if I were an abstract sculpture in a museum—one that he didn't understand the point of.

"Wh-what? Please—"

He cut me off, releasing my hair and striding away. Any further pleas for help died on my lips—my hope along with it. Valerius paused by the figure who waited in the doorway, the candlelight casting his face in shadow.

"Let's drop the act, shall we?" Valerius said, his voice a rich baritone. "She isn't here, and we both know it. But Lazander has been… most insistent that we search your estate thoroughly. You know how he gets."

"I cannot blame the knight for his due diligence," drawled the figure.

"I can—for wasting our time. Throw open your doors, show me what you need to show me, and I'll be on my way."

The figure bowed in response to the knight's request. "Of course, my lord. I only pray Lady Eternity is found swiftly and safely."

In response, Valerius simply marched through the open door, not even glancing behind—like he'd already forgotten I was here.

My mind raced with everything I'd heard—a terrible, horrifying thought brewing.

"I see your time here has done you good, dearest." The figure finally stepped into the room, soft shoes making no sound. He wore a crimson silken tunic with gold embroidery over his heart and dark gray trousers that grazed his ankles.

Sleek blond hair fell effortlessly over his shoulder, and he pushed it back, peering at me closely. He would have been handsome if his expression wasn't twisted with cruelty. Gray eyes, as unfeeling as stone, met mine with a curiosity that made my skin crawl.

"I know your magic is dampened, but I was sure you'd bite him, at the very least." He laughed. "You keep this up, and I'll let you out. But I think a few more nights in here will do wonders for your attitude, don't you?" With that he strode out of the room, snapping his fingers. The door slammed shut behind him. I was alone, my mind reeling, my heart thumping.

Fear and confusion bubbled up in my chest, twisting my heart until it hurt. I knew if I didn't find a way to release it I would go mad with it.

So I did the only thing I could do while chained up in the darkness. I screamed. I screamed until my throat burned, begging me to stop. And then I screamed some more.

***

Dawn crept through the slit that served as a window—coating the room in more shadow than light. I lay still, staring at the door.

My eyes burned from lack of sleep, but my mind refused to succumb to exhaustion. I stretched, my muscles aching from their cramped position as I examined my body for the hundredth time—now in the amber light of dawn.

I was filthy. Dirt coated my bare feet and legs while dark brown stains splattered across my rough-spun tunic—stains that looked suspiciously like dried blood.

Even covered in grime, it was clear this body wasn't mine. Limbs, long and elegant, stretched out on the stone floor, and when I flexed I saw a powerful undercurrent of muscle. Hair the color of midnight fell over my shoulders. I knew, even without a mirror, that a delicate scar ran from my forehead to my right cheek and that my eyes were the color of molten gold.

Zara—I was Zara the Fury.

The disdainful blond who had locked me in here was Magnus of Ashfall, my— I struggled to even think the words—fiancé. Together, we were the main villains of *Knights of Eternity*.

There were others, of course—monsters and beasts, servants and fallen heroes. All of them served Magnus, and through him—*me*.

I thought back to the ivory knight who had looked at me with cold disinterest— the character I'd worshipped as a kid, and played hundreds of games with—Valerius. He was here with Magnus for a reason. That reason was the braided, blonde-haired beauty that caught everyone's eye on the side of the arcade cabinet—Lady Eternity.

It had been years since I'd done more than backseat game over Noah's shoulder, but I would never forget the game's opening. Lady Eternity is stolen away in the middle of the night, causing a vicious and bloody war to erupt between neighboring kingdoms, Navaros and Evergarden—each blaming the other for her disappearance.

Am I at the start of the game? No, that can't be right. Zara kidnaps Eternity and then hides out in a forest, ready to do battle with the knights. She isn't chained up in a dungeon—terrified out of her mind.

A slit at the base of my prison's door opened. I caught a glimpse of a graying hand and then a tray slid toward me—contents spilling.

Now's your chance, I thought. *Call out to the person at the door and explain what's going on—but what is going on? That doesn't matter, just ask for help. Maybe ask for Magnus—wait, why would I want to speak to that creep. Who should I ask for? Damnit, just do something, anything! You stupid—*

The door slammed shut and I heard footsteps, an uneven plod, walking away.

"Damn it," I snapped, furious with myself. I raised a manacled fist above my head—wanting to kick, punch, *hurt* something.

CALAMITY SYSTEM INITIATED

The words hung before my eyes—black and vivid. A shiver of something old and ancient whispered in my mind. Text scrolled across my vision, every word a deadly promise.

If the world will not yield, then I will break it.

My muscles expanded as strength flooded my body—a euphoric high washing away the sleepless night. My body was coiled and ready—I was a force of nature, a wild beast. I was *unstoppable*.

Monstrous Strength Activated

flashed in the corner of my vision, but I barely noticed. I needed to do something, to *hurt* something, or my body would shatter from the power that burned through me. I drove my fist into the stone beneath me. It exploded into a shower of dust on impact.

The sudden burst of strength vanished as quickly as it had appeared.

Exhausted, I slumped against the wall, breathing hard. Rubbing my eyes roughly against my forearm, I saw no trace of the text that had appeared seconds before.

I looked down to see a huge hole in the floor—the *stone* floor. While it wasn't deep enough to breach the floor below, it still took up a solid third of my cell.

"What in the hell?" I scuttled backward, staring at my manacled fists as if they had grown heads. But cold iron merely rattled when I shook them, no different than they had been seconds before.

Curious, I pulled my fists back—choosing another spot on the ground. Gritting my teeth I slammed my fist against it as hard as I could.

I hit the stone awkwardly, my wrist collapsing to the side at the poorly delivered strike. My forearm followed, and I fell onto my side in a lump, cracking my elbow against the stone. I hissed, cradling it—wishing harm on the person who came up with the name "funny bone." I glanced at the floor.

Not even a dent.

I sighed, grabbing the contents of the tray, which had spilled all over the floor. I salvaged a couple of mouthfuls of a pale slop that could generously be described as porridge and a bread roll. My stomach rumbled, suddenly ravenous. Even as my mind was still debating whether or not to eat it, I tipped the contents back into my mouth, my bound hands struggling not to spill it. It was thick and viscous, the flavor close to what I imagined burnt cardboard tasted like.

I kicked the tray away, a petty gesture, and sat with the bread roll. My mind turned dark with the text that had flashed in front of my eyes, and the terrifying strength I had used, if only for a second. But I focused on a phrase I'd never heard, not in all my years playing *Knights of Eternity*...

What the hell was the "Calamity System"?

Chapter Seven

Hours of staring at every inch of my prison had left me three theories as to what the hell was happening to me. I was either:

1) In a coma. This was my brain's way of coping with the trauma.

2) On some incredibly powerful medication in the hospital, and this was a hallucination.

3) Or…

I didn't even want to think about it, but I had to.

I was dead.

It's a strange feeling—thinking you're dead. It causes panic, but the body can only handle so much fear, so much adrenaline. After a night filled with both, I was exhausted. My chest felt empty, but my head was clear—and I realized that regardless of which one it was, it didn't change the fact I was being held prisoner by a man who looked at me like I was dirt on his silken slippers.

In the real world, I had battled Magnus of Ashfall plenty of times—usually with Valerius as my main. Magnus was the endgame boss, and one of the toughest fights—especially when Zara the Fury showed up to fight by his side. With magic that could freeze the world with a touch and a maniacal laugh that would be the envy of any cartoon villain, I'd always thought he was one of the cornier characters in the game. The fact that Zara and he were supposedly "engaged" had felt like a random storyline insert.

Sitting here, chained and filthy, I no longer thought Magnus was corny. I turned the chains in my hands, remembering the cold calculating way he mentioned punishing his betrothed for "misbehaving" of all things. Like a child to him. Or a *pet*.

"You fear him too?"

The voice echoed in the room as clear as a struck bell.

"Hello?"

I felt the faintest touch on my skin, and I shuddered. Something glided over my arms, hesitating on my manacles, and then cradled my face gently. As strange as it was, I didn't feel scared. The presence felt warm and gentle, if a touch uncertain.

"You are not alone—not anymore."

The feminine voice echoed in my head as something brushed against my manacles. *"Break them. Find me. And I promise you safe haven. Please."*

"Wait!" I called out. "Where are you? Hey!" But it was gone.

I didn't know what the voice meant, or where it was, but suddenly the world didn't feel quite so large or terrifying anymore. Someone in here needed help—more than me from the sound of it. Resolve burned in my chest, banishing all hesitation— I could sit in this cell feeling sad and pathetic, or I could *do* something about it.

The next few hours I spent testing the limits of my chains, yanking and twisting them with calculated movements as I searched for a weak spot.

Finding none, I resorted to brute force. I'd dented stone earlier without even thinking about it—the words *Monstrous Power,* or something like that flashing before my eyes. I leaned back, teeth bared and *pulled.* I dug deep, trying to find the spark of strength, of power, I'd glimpsed earlier—imagining the chains snapping, and the joy I'd feel when I left this damn room.

The metal didn't so much as strain. I may as well have been a child trying to push a car uphill for all the good it did.

Breathing hard, I changed focus—deciding the manacles themselves might be my way out. Turning them in the noon-tinged light, I saw the iron was engraved with strange runes I didn't recognize.

I wonder if I can't understand the runes, or if it's the real Zara who can't read them. How does this even work? Do I know what the real Zara knows? Probably not, since I don't remember how I ended up in here. Or does that mean—

"Why do you linger in your cell?" I jumped at the voice's return.

"Alone he may punish us, but we are not alone—not anymore."

"I did as you said—I tried to break them," I said aloud. "Do you know another way out? Please say yes."

My mind flashed with an image of a room, similar to my own, but lit by torches. A tray of fresh fruit and meats lay untouched on the left. Strange symbols similar to those on my manacles circled the floor. However, while only a few etchings marked the metal around my wrists, most of the floor in this room was covered in them.

"*The sigils on the floor of my prison are powerful—they prevent me from using my magic, well, mostly.*" I heard the slightest hint of a soft smile in the voice. "*As the ones on your manacles prevent you. I will do what I can to halt yours, but it will only be for a moment. Ready your magic.*"

"Wait," I said. "I don't know how to use magic, what are you—"

A rush of heat shot through my body from my head to my toes as words flashed across my eyes.

My fury is but a whisper of the flames to come. I gasped as power flooded me, sharp and furious—begging to erupt. In that moment I could conquer cities, burn the world to the ground, and stand atop its ash-filled corpse as its ruler. I was vicious. I was *glorious*.

Blazing Whisper Activated.

The feeling vanished as quickly as it came. I opened my eyes, breathing heavily.

My manacles were gone, melted into puddles of quickly cooling metal at my feet. Scorch marks surrounded me, staining the floor and the walls. My tray and empty bowl were reduced to mere ash.

I stared at my hands. My fingers were long and elegant, tapering to midnight-blue points the same color of my hair.

Woah, was the only thought I managed.

I took a step, stumbling when a wave of tiredness hit me. It wasn't as overwhelming as the rush of exhaustion I'd felt in the wake of the strength I'd somehow summoned. I instinctively knew that fire was a willful mistress, and to underestimate it, or use it thoughtlessly, would leave me more than exhausted—I'd become the ash that crunched beneath my feet.

Approaching the smoldering door, I gingerly pressed my fingers against it. The metal was scorching to the touch, but it didn't burn—in fact it felt somehow comforting. Then the door slowly and precariously fell forward, its hinges reduced to ash, and crashed into the hallway beyond with an explosive thud.

I winced, scanning the hall, sure that a guard, or worse, Magnus would appear to shove me back into the cell. However, no one appeared to sound an alarm.

Breathing a sigh of relief, I reached out for the warm presence. "I'm out," I whispered. "Thanks to you. Where are you?"

Silence echoed in response. I repeated myself but got no answer.

Head low, I chose a random corridor—resolve overcoming uncertainty as I set off, determined to find the source of the voice.

***

The castle was designed to infuriate me, and only me, I decided as I ducked around the corner of yet another identical corridor.

It was always the same—pale walls of an indiscriminate beige, iron wall sconces each bearing two candles, and the same three pieces of decoration: a huge vase, a painting of a bland landscape, and a twisted sculpture of metal that was probably "art." Every single corridor was painted and designed the exact same way.

It was maddening.

I crept forward, keeping my back to the wall and glancing back and forth until I reached a corner. Poking my head around the side, I sighed when the same bland, beige corridor I had just left greeted me.

Am I losing my mind, or is Magnus' idea of interior design this boring?

Thump.

My chest tightened at the sound I heard in the distance.

Thump.

Thump.

I ducked behind the twisted sculpture that was all metal and edges—pressing my hands over my mouth. Someone, or *something*, was coming down the hallway.

Thump. Thump. Thump.

A rasping breath accompanied each thump. I tensed every muscle in my body, trying not to make a sound.

It passed by my hiding place, visible for just a moment, but that moment was enough to haunt me for the rest of my life.

It was a twisted graying thing with too many limbs. Two arms sprang from its left side while a singular arm on its right dragged along the floor. One leg was shorter than the other, forcing it to swing itself forward as it walked—the source of the noise. It leaned back as it passed me as if the weight of its upper body was too much for it.

But that face… I only caught a glimpse of its profile, but that was enough. Eyes, alive and pleading, swiveled about its multiple eye sockets. *Human* eyes trapped in a monstrous face, begging for release. I looked away, my skin crawling.

They were called "sucklers" in the game. The first round of Magnus' defense. I still remembered looking them up in the game's Bestiary, delight and growing horror at the description—" the former inhabitants of Ashfall. Needing servants empty of disobedience and loyal to a fault, Magnus transformed his own people using magic dark and forbidden."

The first time I saw them on screen as a kid, I'd been terrified. Seeing them in real life, knowing it was once a real person, was worse—so much worse.

Once the thump of its strange walk had faded, I told myself to go. That I needed to leave before it came back.

My body wouldn't move.

I braced my palms against the floor and tried to force myself up, but my legs were as unyielding as the stone beneath my feet. My heart hammered as my mind flooded with images of the suckler—of it coming back. Its uneven gait and many eyes swiveling, focusing on me.

Its scream as it charged at me.

Shut up. Shut up!

I berated my mind, telling it this was *not* helping, and we needed to leave to avoid exactly the thing it was terrified of.

My pleas were useless. Image after image of the suckler reaching for me, of what it would do to me, flickered through my mind like a torturous movie reel. I looked around for something, anything, to focus on as my mind and body rebelled against me.

The flickering of a candle flame in one of the wall sconces caught my eye. It was one of many, but the sight of the fire shifting, twisting as if a breeze floated by, made my brain calm for just a second.

The flame grew larger as I watched, engulfing a nearby candle—its wax dripping. Still I stared transfixed—my eyes watering as my lids refused to close.

"Your lies are shadows—my eyes the flames," I said, words falling from my lips unbidden. **"You cannot hide from me."**

Piercing Sight Activated.

The corridor shimmered, my eyes drawn to a thin band of shadow that lined the floor, walls, and ceiling right where the hallway joined the next corridor. The shadow receded as the flames expanded, splintering into sparks that erupted, scattering across the passageway. I felt nothing but a gentle kiss as they landed on my skin, fizzling gently.

The fear and panic subsided, my body relaxing. While in my cell, the power I had felt was explosive. This felt peaceful and gentle, like the comforting warmth from a crackling fire. I felt at ease for the first time since I'd woken up in this body.

I felt like me.

I examined the candle I'd been focusing on. What was left of it at least.

It had melted entirely, taking part of the iron wall sconce with it. Soot and ash marred the wall behind it from where the flames had grown tall, licking the ceiling above.

I looked for the shadow I had seen, the one at the entrance to the next corridor. Finding nothing but more beige walls, I rounded the corner and stopped dead—a smile lighting up my face.

Chapter Eight

The large ugly vase and bland landscape painting were still there as were the wall sconces, but gone were the never-ending beige walls. It was a corridor lined with doors, heavy and metal. A corridor that looked just like the one where I'd been kept prisoner.

Which was exactly what I was looking for.

While the castle was an endless maze, I wouldn't have left even if I'd found the exit. The voice was the reason I'd gotten out of my prison, and I wasn't going to leave the owner behind.

There were no windows in the prison doors, so I had to get on my hands and knees and open the food slot of each one to peer inside. Most were empty, but for one that had a pile of bones with too many limbs to be human.

Frustrated, I stood, wondering how many of these corridors I would have to search when something shifted in the corner of my eye.

I turned, staring at a patch of wall. Something dark flickered, and I blinked, unsure if I saw something or if my mind was playing tricks on me.

Curious, I ran my hands over the stone, finding it smooth to the touch. It was only when I stepped back, however, that I realized the wall was perfect—too perfect. The stone on either side was nicked and marked with age—this however, was completely clean and even.

Closing my eyes, I thought of the candle and the gentle flow of power I had felt when I concentrated on its flame. Since I'd woken in this world, black text had hovered in my vision right before I'd become impossibly strong or used Zara's infamous fire. I tried to picture the words I'd seen right before I pierced the shadowy illusion that had trapped me in a maze.

Nothing happened.

"What was it? Your words… no. Your shadows—that wasn't it. Damnit. Oh! **"Your lies—"**

Power flooded me, gentle and warm. I stumbled over the words, and the power disappeared—a vanishing spark when I needed flames. Focusing, I started again, forcing myself to finish the phrase.

"Your lies are shadows—my eyes, the flames. You cannot hide from me."

My voice at the end was unrecognizable. Every word was a command, tinged with a rage that sent shivers down my spine.

I opened my eyes and found a shadow in front of me, twice my height and width. It covered the stone wall in front of me in a perfect rectangle.

Piercing Sight Activated.

"Yes!" I punched the air at the sight of the door in front me, then immediately regretted it as the world grew soft and muted at the edges. Taking a breath, my vision sharpened once more—the dizzy spell passing.

"No more magic for a while, I think," I muttered aloud, rubbing my temples. I stared at the door I had revealed and couldn't help but smile.

I had finally done something in this world, in this *body* without the help of anyone else. Flexing my taloned fingers, I looked down at my new form with fresh eyes, seeing how much stronger, how much more *powerful* I was.

Maybe there were worse characters to be than Zara the Fury.

A handle appeared as I reached for the shadowed door. I gripped it, pushing it open.

***

"Magnus of Ashfall is a liar," I said aloud. "Who could have guessed?"

The room was exactly as it had appeared to me in the vision—lit by torches, a plate of food (nicer than mine, I might add) lay untouched on the floor. Row upon row of sigils spiraled out from the room's center where a figure lay unmoving.

Her long blonde hair was tied in complicated braids that framed her face—cascading down her back. The woman wore what I thought was a simple blue dress until I noticed the thousands of sky-blue flowers embroidered on every available inch of fabric. Curled up on her side, head resting on her arms, she looked to be asleep. I knew her eyes would be the color of sapphire. Just as I knew she was the reason I and every character in this world existed.

She was Eternity, and the purpose of the entire game was to rescue her after a war breaks out between the neighboring kingdoms of Evergarden and Navaros over her disappearance. However, something wasn't right—Eternity only appears in Magnus' hideout at the end of the game, not at the beginning.

Is the game Knights of Eternity *just one version of events, and this world doesn't follow that sequence? Or maybe this happens in the game too, but players never see it?*

Eternity winced, a sigh escaping her. I could philosophize about this bizarre world later—I had to get us out of here first.

I stepped forward, my bare feet touching one of the floor symbols, and gasped—muscles locking into place as blazing knives of pain erupted along my skin.

I leaped back, breathing heavily from both the sting and the shock. The sigils I had just touched flared a bright blue that spread, spiraling out from the floor in a deadly domino effect. I flexed my toes, the pain already an echo that left behind a pleasant tingle.

I didn't know if that was proof of how strong Zara was or a sign of how used to pain she was—likely at Magnus' hands, if his words back in my cell were anything to go by.

I shook the thought off as I gingerly held a hand over the markings, but there was no pain. I leaned forward, bending at the waist, trying to shift as much of my body over them without letting my feet touch them.

No pain.

Next, I crouched low, letting my hand hover above them once more, but this time, I slowly let my hand drop, coming steadily closer to the floor, and the sigils.

It was only when my palm was about five inches away that they flared bright blue once more, forks of light erupting from the floor, reaching for me. I snatched my hand back, shaking off the pins and needles of pain running up my hand and arm, greedily searching for flesh.

"Right—so you only activate when I'm in *very* close proximity. Got it," I said aloud, glancing at Eternity. She didn't move, but I considered her silence a hearty agreement.

While I couldn't read the sigils on the floor, I knew this from the very beginning of the game. The solution was simple—well, it was when I had a joystick in hand and my finger on the action button.

Let's see what it was like in the flesh.

The room was about twenty-five feet long with markings carved into almost every inch of the floor but for the small circle in the room's center where Eternity lay—about five feet of empty space surrounding her. Ten feet of symbols, and the promise of burning agony, lay between myself and Eternity, and another ten feet of pain lay behind her—reaching as far as the prison's windowless wall.

I backed up, through the prison door and into the hallway.

I'd seen what my magic could do—it was powerful enough to reduce metal into mere puddles and gentle enough to reveal hidden illusions. I'd even split stone with my bare hands. However, these things carried a cost—in *Knights of Eternity* I had a handy little bar in the corner with my mana.

Here I could only guess. Judging by the wave of dizziness I felt after using *Piercing Sight*, I couldn't keep using it, not unless I wanted Magnus to find me drooling and unconscious on the floor. I crouched slightly, placing one foot in front of me. It was time to see what this body could do.

I pushed off the ground, throwing myself forward as I ran at full tilt.

I PE class, it would take a couple of seconds of running before I could build up to my (pathetic) top speed. In this body…

… in this body, I was a goddamned runaway train.

My old PE teacher Mr. Gord was always banging on about the "joy" of moving, of pushing your body to its limits. I had never understood it—hating every moment I was forced to exercise in front of my entire class. Thoughts of falling in front of everyone and how embarrassing it would be, or how I would definitely come last in any race, would plague my mind until all I could do was hide at the back and wait for class to be over.

But now—alone and free from these thoughts, I felt it. I felt *free*.

The markings flashed blue as I leaped, just missing the curl of electricity as it reached for me.

I couldn't help it, I laughed. It was so easy, so effortless.

My joy was brief, however, as I realized midair, I had overshot my jump.

I sailed past Eternity, and the safe, symbol-free circle she rested in, heading straight for the sigils on the other side of the room.

I turned, twisting my body midair in an impossible arc, landing with one foot on the smooth gray stone of the center.

The other landed smack bang in the middle of the sigils. They lit up, the room flashing bright blue as pain flooded my body, my brain screaming at me to run to fight to do anything to get away. Gritting my teeth, I pushed past it and threw myself forward.

Collapsing in a heap on the gray, agony-free stone, I let out a shuddering breath. The pain faded as quickly as it appeared, but it still *hurt*.

That'll teach me not to get cocky.

"You came," a small voice whispered.

So focused had I been on making that jump I had almost forgotten why I was here.

She lay curled up on her side, deep shadows under her eyes. Her eyelids fluttered—she could barely keep them open. Lying on my back, I turned my head to face her.

"Hi," I said.

Really? You're talking to the most important character in your favorite video game as a kid and that's the best you could come up with? "Hi?"

"I knew… the stories weren't… true…" she whispered, eyes closing.

"Eternity?" I sat up, hesitating only a moment before resting a hand on her shoulder. "Eternity, are you okay?" I shook her gently, but her eyes remained closed.

I dropped an ear to her face, closing my eyes.

Her breathing was even, if a bit shallow. I pressed my index and middle finger to her wrist as my mom had taught me and measured her pulse. It was steady.

Deciding she must have fainted, and was not, as my panic suggested, on the brink of death, I stood. Brushing myself off, I admired the distance I had leapt—remembering how easy it was. Remembering how good it felt.

I stared at my hands, at their midnight-blue tips, and clenched my fists—feeling the strength in them. Zara the Fury and I couldn't be more different. In the game, she'd kidnapped Eternity, almost started a war, and would happily burn the world to a cinder if it meant getting what she wanted.

She was angry, cruel—*evil*.

But I wasn't Zara.

I glanced at the sleeping Eternity, noticing how pale she was. Who knew what it had cost her to reach out to me, to free me from my prison? She had done it without even knowing if I would come to help her. I couldn't leave her here—*wouldn't*.

That didn't mean I wasn't scared—of the sucklers, of Magnus, of whatever was happening to me. But helping Eternity, getting us both out of here—this was something *I* could do. Not Zara the Fury—*me*. Game or not, what was happening to me right now was real—or as real as it could be. This was my new life.

And I was going to do something about it.

Chapter Nine

I tested the jump several times—first, without carrying anything. Then, confident I could judge the distance accurately each time, I grabbed the huge ugly vase from one of the hallways and practiced using that.

I was glad I had because I dropped the vase the first time, I made the jump. Not only did it miraculously not break, it also didn't set off the sigils—perhaps only organic matter did? Either way, Eternity wouldn't have been so lucky.

I briefly considered trying to cover the sigils and simply walk across but quickly discarded the idea. I'd have to run back the way I'd come to grab enough vases and tables and paintings to make that happen, which would increase my chance of getting caught. Plus, I had no idea if they'd be able to take my weight plus Eternity's.

I bent low, pushing one hand under Eternity's head and scooping another under the bend in her knees. She didn't make a single sound as I lifted her, nor had she woken again. I pushed my worry to one side. There was nothing I could do for her except get out of this hellhole and run.

I considered the manhunt for the woman in my arms that was part of the *Knights of Eternity* plot. Right—run very *very* fast.

I couldn't tell if Eternity was very light, or if I was just extremely strong now, but she weighed as much as a feather in my arms. The problem was her length. While standing she probably barely came up to my shoulder, cradling her like a damsel in a movie poster was going to make leaping across pain-filled symbols awkward.

"Sorry about this," I said, flinging her over my shoulder like a sack of potatoes.

I apologized again, this time mentally. I didn't think she was listening, but I felt a little better anyway.

I backed up, one arm hooked around Eternity's legs, holding her tightly—praying she wasn't going to fall off.

You've done the jump, you even practiced with a vase—a vase! You're not going to drop her. On the ground. On the electric-chair sigils that cause pain so intense you thought you were going to pass out. Nope. I definitely won't think about how weak Eternity seems right now, and how if it hurt that much for you, how bad would it be for Eternity who looks like a stiff breeze would be the end of her?

Maybe this isn't a good idea. Maybe—

I charged forward, knowing if I didn't do it now, I never would.

So focused was I on psyching myself up that I mistimed the jump, and right as I was about to leap, my toes brushed against a sigil—the entire floor lighting up in blue as sharp, needlelike agony ran through my whole body.

By some miracle, I cleared the symbols, my knees hitting the unforgiving stone floor as blue light crackled against my skin. I turned, pulling Eternity from my shoulder to my chest as I fell, my back hitting the ground—hard.

"Ow, ow, owww," I said uselessly. I lay wheezing on my back for a few seconds, my confidence at my new body getting a smack in the face from reality.

I bet the real Zara the Fury wouldn't have stubbed her toe and landed in a heap on the floor.

I looked down at Eternity, who was cradled against my chest, and noticed her breathing was a little quieter—and a lot shallower.

Picking her up in my arms, I made sure her head was supported by the crook of my elbow.

"I'm going to get us out of here," I said. "I promise."

With that, I—no, *we* set off.

***

"My lord," Lazander said as he packed away his bedroll, strapping it to the back of his horse. His red hair, a rebellious bundle of curls at the best of times, was particularly unruly after weeks of hard riding. "I believe we should search the premises once more."

Valerius said nothing as he mounted his warhorse, a beautiful white beast that pawed at the ground—eager to leave. Noticing the horse's agitation, Valerius dropped a hand to his steed's neck, rubbing an armored hand in small, soothing circles.

As Valerius hadn't told Lazander to be quiet, his usual response, the knight took this as a sign to continue.

"We've heard rumors of Lord Magnus of Ashfall's activities for months now—he's been hiring mercenaries from every corner of the kingdom. Yet his outgoing orders for grain, fresh fruit, and other supplies are exactly the same. How does one increase the hungry bellies of his land by at least a third and yet not need any extra food?"

Valerius sighed. "Magnus' shopping list is hardly my concern."

Lazander smiled tightly. "The point, my lord, is that something is afoot. Regardless of Lord Ashfall's bootlicking, I firmly believe Lady Eternity is here."

"Lazander, you would drive a monk to drink," Valerius said, dark eyes flashing. "We have already stayed another night at your insistence. Your continuous, *irritating* insistence. I'm not wasting any more time here when Evergarden's armies flank our borders."

"The king has managed to stall them thus far," Lazander argued.

"And who knows how long that will last," Valerius snapped. "This isn't some petty dispute over grain, Lazander—we've been accused of violating the peace treaty."

"Which is exactly why we must take care to search every estate thoroughly—Gallow's Chosen must be found." Lazander's thick brows were driven together in a rare frown, and Valerius gripped the reins at the knight's words.

"We both know what this is really about," Valerius said. "You despise Magnus—you took against him the moment you met. And" he continued, raising a hand when Lazander opened his mouth to argue. "I will not allow a school yard dispute to get in the way of finding Eternity—sorry, 'Gallow's Chosen.' You're a Gilded Knight—act like it," Valerius said, ending the conversation as he kicked his steed in the sides, setting off at a trot.

The rest of their troop, who had very clearly been listening to the exchange while feigning nonchalance, followed. It was a small but experienced collection of knights, squires, and servants who could keep up the punishing pace Valerius and Lazander set.

A couple of knights gave Lazander a sympathetic nod. He knew he wasn't the only one who mistrusted Magnus of Ashfall. The lord was ill-liked and had become increasingly eccentric and withdrawn over the years. The last time he'd been seen in public was at the yearly gala the queen threw for the nobles of Navaros.

Held at the Ivory Keep, the kingdom's capital, it was the social event of the year. Or it had been until a few years back when Magnus downed an entire barrel of wine and had to be pulled from the ballroom. Describing the smell of the bandits his betrothed had burned alive was not a polite conversation starter.

It had been a strange thing, his engagement to a falsling—and one from the Moonvale Mountains at that. Stranger still to speak about the flames she could wield with such pride in his voice.

Lazander stood to one side as the troop picked up speed, the clank of metal armor and the thrum of hooves starting out quietly. It built to a crescendo of noise as they charged down the dirt road that would lead them out the Ashfall estate. They would search the next estate, and the one after, until they'd turned the kingdom upside down—all in the hopes of finding Lady Eternity.

Lazander sighed, mounting his own horse, a beautiful mare with a chestnut coat he called Mabel. She whinnied, sensing her rider's irritation—a rare event from the steady warrior.

"I'm all right, girl." Lazander rubbed her neck, but she snorted in disbelief. He didn't blame her.

He'd wanted to join the Gilded Knights all his life—they were the heroes of Navaros, the stuff of legends made real. A glimpse of one of the knights would be the topic of gossip for weeks, never mind the precious few who *met* them. None were more famous than Valerius—the prince who'd given up his title to serve his kingdom, who'd fought giants and faced down armies with nothing more than his sword and shield.

The day he'd finally done it—when the queen had pressed her hand to his forehead and said the words he'd dreamed of, "Rise, Sir Lazander, Gilded Protector of Navaros," he'd thought his heart would burst with joy.

He hadn't expected the cold stares and calm indifference. Hadn't expected he'd have to watch every word with a leader who only cared about finishing the mission quickly, efficiently, and often brutally.

The Valerius he knew, and the Valerius of legends couldn't be more different.

Lazander looked back at Magnus' castle. A towering behemoth of cracked black stone. Valerius was right—Lazander had never enjoyed visiting it on the Gilded Knight's yearly tour of the kingdom or meeting its owner. His skin crawled the moment he laid eyes on it, and he had taken to turning down Magnus' offer of a soft feather bed—claiming years on the road made it impossible for him to sleep anywhere but under the stars.

During their weeklong investigation of Magnus and his castle grounds, Valerius had actually joined him for the first time, rolling out his bedroll alongside Lazander's.

Lazander knew they had to move on, of course. There were other nobles to investigate—other estates to visit and search.

That didn't mean he couldn't leave behind an extra pair of eyes.

The knight took a deep breath, the sigil on his left wrist glowing beneath his gauntlet as he opened the connection between him and his eternal friend and companion.

There was a sharp cry and flap of wings, and then talons dug into his armored forearm. The hawk was beautiful—soft plumage in shades of gray and white covered her wings and chest. Her tail feathers ended in a startling white with threads of silver akin to starlight.

"How was the hunt, Merrin? Catch anything?" Lazander asked.

The hawk chirped, nuzzling against Lazander's neck. The knight chuckled, then bent his head, resting it against Merrin's. They stayed like that for a long moment, the dusk-tinged air silent—their bond, both magical and familial, past the need for words.

"You know what to do," Lazander said, throwing his arm to the sky as Merrin flapped her powerful wings, shooting off into the sky.

Lazander had seen her do it countless times, but the sight of her soaring so effortlessly while he remained on the ground below always filled him with a strange mix of joy and sadness. He sometimes wished he could join her in the sky. To forget all his worries and simply become one with the wind.

The knight sighed, pulling on Mabel's reins gently. He clicked his tongue, and they set off at a trot that turned to a gallop—eager to catch up with the rest of the troop.

***

I was slowly finding my way through this maze-like prison, thanks to my new ability *Piercing Sight*. I used it sparingly, but each spell of dizziness lasting longer and longer—clearly I had some kind of limit.

At the entrance to a new corridor, a black shadow ran along the walls, ceiling, and floor—just like the one I'd seen the first time I used *Piercing Sight*. It was a curious darkness edged with fraying tendrils that seemed to pull in the flickering candlelight. It wasn't wide, perhaps five inches across, and formed a type of frame.

When I stepped through it, I would end up back at the beginning of the previous corridor. Because the change was so subtle, and the decor had been designed to look the same, I hadn't noticed it earlier. It was genius, in a way. Even if a prisoner like me managed to leave, they would end up stuck in a boxed maze of repetition.

"Your lies are shadows—my eyes the flames. You cannot hide from me." Though I whispered, the same righteous fury spilled out with each word—my voice rife with command. Eyes burning, the shadow at the corridor's edge dispelled easily. Expecting yet more beige walls, I grinned when a staircase appeared.

"Now we're talking," I said to Eternity, who hung limply in my arms. "See? Told you I would get us out—no need to break out the cake and balloons, a simple thank you will suffice."

While she hadn't so much as twitched since we'd left her cell, I swore for a second that I saw her smile—or maybe that was just a trick of the light.

Chapter Ten

U nfortunately, the staircase ahead was going up, not down, but having found no other exit I didn't see much choice.

My thighs burned as I walked up the stairs, and I shifted Eternity, wincing. My arms were starting to ache, but I didn't want to throw her over my shoulder… again. It was illogical, but I worried if I took my eyes off her face for longer than a minute, she'd vanish—or worse, stop breathing.

She'd grown paler since we left the prison, and I stopped to study her.

Light freckles dusted the bridge of her nose, and she had a slight dimple in her cheek that likely deepened when she smiled. There was kindness to her face that spoke of a person who loved to laugh. I found myself trying and failing to guess her age—her face seemed to shift in the light, moving from my age to a woman in her thirties. Right now she seemed closer to mine—maybe nineteen or twenty at most.

Despite having played *Knights of Eternity* more times than I could count, I knew very little about Eternity. Her lines of dialogue in the game consisted of things like, "Over here, knight!" and "Unhand me, you villain!"

I dearly hoped I would get the chance to talk to her. Or at the very least, thank her for getting me out of that prison.

A *thump* stopped my train of thought, one I recognized instantly.

I knew I should quietly back down the stairs and hide from the suckler.

Rationally, I knew this. My feet, however…

The thought of its eyes, of them swiveling and focusing on me, made me spin and charge down the stairs, the burn in my thighs forgotten.

I had made it only a few steps when I heard an answering *thump* from farther below and the sound of metal banging against stone over and over. I thought of the sucklers I'd beaten in the game and immediately knew what it was—a cudgel, heavy and deadly, clipping against the steps as the suckler carried it in its longer arm.

"*Shraaaaaa,*" one screamed, the incoherent sound high-pitched and painful. The noise acted as a signal to the others, each answering with their own animal like noise of pain. The *thump* of their feet blended into a cacophonous roar that echoed around the narrow staircase as they charged.

A part of me, a very small part, was grateful when the first suckler suddenly appeared on the stairs below, a cudgel raised above its head—shrieking.

It meant I had no time to panic.

Cradling Eternity to my chest, I turned sideways, instinctively kicking my leg out.

"**If the world will not yield, then I will break it**," I hissed, anger sharpening each word.

Monstrous Strength Activated.

There was a sickening crack as my foot sank an inch deep into the suckler's flesh. It gasped—a pathetic mewling sound that made the hair on my arms stand to attention. The suckler shot backward, hitting the stone wall of the staircase, and kept going.

It burst through the stone wall—leaving rubble and a sizable hole behind. Its scream echoed even as it fell—stopping only once it hit the ground below.

Holy crap.

I caught the barest glimpse of the world beyond the castle—a river curved lazily about the estate, looking silver in the moonlight, and a thick forest lay just beyond the border. Then another suckler appeared on the steps above me, eyes swiveling to focus on me as it opened its jaw—jagged yellow teeth gnashing.

Don't think. Just move.

I crouched, focusing my new strength into the balls of my feet as I gripped Eternity tightly.

"Hang on," I whispered to her.

The suckler swung its heavy club at me—aiming straight for my head.

I jumped directly up, twisting midair to rest my feet against the ceiling, light as a whisper. A split second later I kicked off, landing behind the suckler. Its cudgel cracked against the stone where I had been less than a second earlier.

I had the briefest moment to admire my acrobatics before my leg shot up above my head—my body moving on pure instinct. It came down in a graceful arc, the elegance of the movement undercut by my heel slamming into the suckler's head— the skull cracking open like a raw egg.

I gagged at the sound, like a soapy sponge squeezed too tight. I spun on my other heel, fleeing up the staircase—refusing to look at the bloody carnage Zara had—no, that *I* had left behind.

My eyes burned, either from too many uses of *Piercing Sight* or from almost two days of no sleep. My thighs ached, my stomach caving in on itself as I ran, fueled by fear and stubbornness. I twisted my body around the tight staircase as I leaped, using every ounce of my newfound strength.

I began to falter, my strength fading as I reached the top of the staircase where a latched wooden door stood. Teeth gritted, I dug for the last shred of power as I kicked it—the door flying off the hinges. I winced at the shattered wood and then immediately chided myself—Magnus deserved many things, but my guilt for breaking a door was not one of them.

Another door lay ahead. Decorated in striking reds and golds, it was the most extravagant thing I'd seen in the castle. I slowed, panting as my vision blurred.

Don't stop. Don't think. Just move.

Stumbling to one knee, I hooked the handle with an elbow, pushing it open. I stopped, my exhaustion forgotten as I stared—eyes wide, heart hammering. There were no corridors on this floor. No beige walls or prison bars. Huge and sprawling, the room took up the entire floor of the castle. Luxurious furnishings, beautiful paintings of blonde-haired women, and a thick white carpet inches thick dominated the room—or would have, if not for the giant bed that lay in the center of the room.

"Shraaaa."

The suckler's scream made me jump, almost dropping Eternity.

Stupid, stupid! Why did you stand there gaping like an idiot?

Sucklers burst through the remnants of the wooden door I'd kicked down and charged, their twisted flesh colliding as they pushed and shoved one another in their eagerness to reach us. Thick tongues lolled out of their mouths as their jaws dropped and they whined—a crying chorus akin to the screams of children.

My heart hammered, my determination to escape, my resolve to save Eternity gone—a mere wisp blasted away the hurricane that was fear.

A small part of me, one I liked to pretend didn't exist, whispered to leave Eternity behind. That she would slow the sucklers down long enough for me to get away. I wanted to escape. I wanted to *live*. Then I thought of my uncle Jacobi—of how he'd faced down a gun with nothing more than fists and a defiant roar. I shifted Eternity to my shoulder, raising my free hand in a poor mockery of a fighting stance. The sucklers reached the red and gold door—mere seconds from me. I roared, half from fear, half from fury.

The monsters abruptly skidded to a stop. They screamed, crawling on top of one another as they crowded the doorway, their undulating flesh filling every open gap— but they made no move to enter.

At first I was still—every muscle tensed and ready. I wiped terrified tears from my eyes, but the sucklers stayed where they were.

I backed up cautiously. While their many eyes followed my every movement, they made no move to follow me. Something was stopping them from entering— and I doubted it was me.

I backed up, aiming for the gigantic monstrosity that was the bed. My muscles burned from carrying Eternity and that last burst of *Monstrous Strength*. Eyes always on the sucklers, I set Eternity down gently on the lilac sheets, keeping her within arm's reach as I stretched.

My shoulders clicked and I groaned in relief. I pressed one hand to my chest, feeling my thudding heart begin to slow.

Realizing I likely wasn't going to be eaten by a suckler anytime soon, I surveyed the room.

On the one hand, it was beautiful—the kind of beauty that only money and decadence could buy. The walls were blood red and embedded with tiny gold rocks. Shaking off the thought the walls were decorated with *actual gold* I moved on to the furnishings—no less than seven armchairs and two couches were scattered about the room. Atop each, thick blankets and puffed-up cushions were artistically placed— each matching the red and gold color scheme.

And the bed—the bed! Ridiculous was the only word that came to mind. Lilac sheets embroidered with gold were surrounded by pillows in silver, teal, and burgundy. The mattress itself was huge—no less than five people could comfortably starfish on it without touching each other.

The entire room was the type of thing rich people thought signified taste, but all I saw was something a ten-year-old would draw when asked what their dream house was.

I looked down at the pristine white carpet, my feet sinking in so deeply I could barely see my toes. My bare feet left filthy gray footprints with every step. I snickered, imagining Magnus' face at the sight of his precious carpet.

Then my eyes caught one of the many paintings that dotted the room—each with a blonde woman as its subject.

"What the hell?"

Chapter Eleven

The woman in the painting was beautiful. With flaxen hair draped over one shoulder—her bright blue eyes an invitation. A promise.

On the far side of the room, another stared adoringly at me. Her blonde hair was partially braided on one side, her silken nightgown clinging to her skin as she held a candelabra in one hand—posing on shadow-cloaked stairs.

The wall behind me—another blonde. Hair piled atop her head in an elaborate bun. Party dress. Midnight-blue eyes sparkling, capturing her mid-laugh. Peeking over a fan. Riding a horse. Strolling by the beach. Every painting a snapshot of different women who could all have been sisters—beautiful, blonde, their blue eyes whispering with longing. My eyes moved between each portrait, coming to rest on the woman I'd just laid down on the bed.

Every single one of them looked just like Eternity.

I scrambled, searching the room for an exit, a window, anything that would get us out of here. My relief at finding this room, at avoiding the sucklers had vanished. My skin wanted to crawl from my bones and flee.

The game never specified why Magnus had orchestrated Eternity's kidnapping—nor had I given it much thought. I'd always guessed it was to start a war, then take over the kingdom in the wake of disaster—the usual moustache twirling of villains.

However, this room, with its gaudy decadence and near endless paintings of Eternity look-alikes spoke of something far darker. We all have instincts—some sharpened from experience, others just gut feelings that might fly in the face of reason but prove to be true. Right now, every single one I possessed was screaming to run, to get Eternity out of here—because whatever flame Magnus carried wasn't love, it was *obsession*. One I doubted Eternity would survive.

The room had two doors and no windows—the sucklers' graying bodies filled every inch of space in the open doorway. Their cries had diminished into dull whines, their many eyes swiveling to watch me intently. On the far side of the room, near a crimson couch that could hold ten people, lay the second door. It was simple in comparison to the rest of the room—a pleasant maple with a golden handle.

"Stay here," I said to Eternity. She didn't move or show any sign she'd even heard me, but the words were more for my comfort than hers. The thought of being alone in this weird shrine to Eternity, let alone *sleeping* in it… I shuddered.

I made for the maple door, ignoring the sucklers. It was only when I reached for the handle that I notice the silence. Frowning, I glanced back at the monsters. They no longer looked at me with ravenous hunger—instead they focused on something just beyond me, their eyes shining with the dull light of adoration.

I realized my mistake a second too late.

The maple door swung open, clouds of steam enveloping the room. My nose stung from the overwhelming scent of lilacs, the smell sticking to the back of my throat. I leaped back, fists raised as a figure emerged from the steam. One hand massaged a towel into his damp hair while another clutched his waist.

"What a pleasant surprise," Magnus of Ashfall said, mouth twisted in a grin as he draped the towel around his shoulder. "My darling Zara has come to pay me a visit."

The sight of Magnus' smug face made my stomach turn. Something rose from the shadows of my mind, and a terror not my own gripped me.

He strolled past me, completely at ease with finding me dirty and barefoot in his private chambers.

"You were right, you know. I'm probably tempting fate by putting beeswax in my ears—I didn't even hear the door open." He laughed, a self-deprecating tinkle. "But it's only you, after all."

He casually dropped the towel from his shoulders onto the floor, running his fingers through his damp hair. Tilting his head, he removed the wax from his ears with a pleased sigh. "Don't you love the solitude of an uninterrupted bath?"

I said nothing—my body shaking as fear turned my blood to lead, my muscles to stone. I was *scared* of him—had been since he'd taunted me in my cell. This fear, however, was like the anger that edged my words when I used *Monstrous Strength, Blazing Whisper,* or any of my other abilities—it wasn't simply my own.

It was Zara the Fury's. He pressed his hand against a panel on the wall I had completely missed. A hidden shelf noiselessly slid out. I glimpsed rows upon rows of neatly hung silken robes. Confidently offering me his back, he selected one seemingly at random and slipped it on. It was, of course, bloodred and patterned with gold.

"So, what is it now?" he asked, sinking into an armchair. He leaned back, rolling his shoulders as he relaxed against the cushions.

"Did you kill one of my prized horses? No—you did that last time." He tapped a finger to his chin. "Perhaps you gutted some of the mercenaries I hired—the expensive ones." Magnus nodded. "You wouldn't simply kill them though—that's far too boring. Did you string them up by their intestines? Spell out a rather crude word in their blood?" He laughed. It wasn't a pleasant sound.

"I was rather vexed when you did that to my old minstrel, but I must confess— it *was* creative."

I tried to ignore his words, to focus on getting the hell out of here, but my mind clung to each word—and the truth of them. I looked down at my hands, at the sharpened tips of my midnight-etched fingers, and imagined driving them into someone's stomach, clawing at their insides as I pulled. My gut twisted as nausea hit.

Magnus sighed, a loud drawn-out sound. "Don't keep me in suspense. We do this song and dance every *single* time. You disobey me. I punish you. You have a petty tantrum and ruin something I spent good money on."

He stood, spreading his arms wide.

"Then what happens, my darling? You calm down—as you always do. I know it's difficult, and I know I push you—but that's because you are no mere spark. You are a forest fire, an inferno—one that could destroy the very world if left unchecked."

He stepped forward and I flinched, backing up. He frowned in surprise, but continued. "But I will not falter, my darling. I will not stop until you see the truth— that your place is here by my side."

Was this cycle of punishment and cruelty all there was to Zara's life? She could burn this man to cinders—why would she stay and play this awful game of cat and mouse with a man who thrived on torment?

The sucklers chattered, a horrible gnashing sound that made Magnus bark, "Quiet!" He rolled his eyes. "Did a cat get in the castle again? That usually riles them up. For however long it lasts, that is."

Closer. He'd moved closer to me, and I hadn't even noticed. Magnus rested a palm on my shoulder. He smelled of lilac, but beneath that I caught a hint of something putrid—like raw meat that had been left in the sun.

"Valerius and Lazander have finally left, so I'm feeling a smidge more patient than usual. Tell me what of mine you've destroyed, and I'll let you sleep at the end of my bed tonight, hmm?"

I was sure he was smiling, but all I could stare at was the edge of his robe. His feet were bare, a stray golden thread brushing the tops of his toes. I focused on the thread, trying to slow my breathing—my heart was hammering, and dark spots clouded my vision.

Don't pass out, do not *pass out alone in a room with this psychopath.*

"Get away… from her." Her voice was barely a whisper, but Magnus flinched as if he'd been struck. Eternity had pushed herself up on one arm—I'd completely forgotten about her. The other stretched out, fingers splayed, pointed directly at Magnus.

"Why," Magnus hissed, an icy rage in his voice. "Is. Eternity." The hand that gripped my shoulder flexed painfully, accentuating each word. "*Here?*" A silver glow enveloped Eternity's fingers, and she gritted her teeth, forcing herself into a sitting position. "Get away," she said, a note of steel entering her voice. "From her."

Magnus laughed, a high-pitched sound that made Eternity wince. Her hand didn't waver. "No," he said, simply clicking his fingers.

Eternity flew backward, her neck nearly snapping as an invisible force grabbed her by the hair, flinging her across the room. She crashed into the opposing wall, knocking down a painting of her look-alike picnicking in the sun. It followed her limp body as she hit the ground with a muffled thud, coming to rest on her unmoving form.

"Oh, dear." Magnus sighed. "That may have been a *touch* too rough."

Help her. You have to help Eternity. Move damn it. Move.

The hand that gripped my shoulder grew ice-cold to the touch—burning my skin. I looked down in horror to see a layer of ice erupt beneath Magnus' fingers, spreading over my shoulder and chest. A split-second later ice exploded around my feet, covering my shins, thighs, and creeping up my waist. I gasped at the pain.

"This, my dearest, is your best one yet." He slapped my cheek gently, almost fondly. "I thought you would kill a mercenary, how small-minded of me. You think so much bigger than that."

He pressed his other palm against my shoulder, leaning in. I flinched but couldn't move—ice holding my neck in place. "What was the plan, hm? You bring her up here, cut her up a little bit, make me watch? Did you hope I'd beg for you to stop, knowing that I need Eternity alive, or all will have been for naught?"

My teeth chattered as the initial burn of the ice began to fade, leaving a freezing numbness in place.

Magnus idly brushed my hair over one shoulder, tracing the line of my neck. "Bravo. What I did not expect, however, was for her to defend you. I can only imagine the lies you told her. I forget there is a shred of intelligence in that brain of yours.

"However," Magnus said, his geniality falling from his face like a mask, "as brilliant as this was, you have gone too far. The Gilded have only just left my grounds. If you had pulled this little stunt mere hours earlier, you would have risked everything for nothing more than a temper tantrum.

"You have overstepped yourself. And must be corrected…"

His hand snapped out, gripping my middle and index fingers on my left hand. Ice burst from his hands, encasing them. Abruptly all feeling left that hand. Panicked, I tried to clench my fist, but my hand didn't so much as twitch. Tears blurred my vision.

"Did you know that frozen flesh shatters? It's the most beautiful sound—like the crunch of morning snow beneath my boot."

A sharp pain in my right hand cut through the panic. Looking down, I saw I'd driven my nails into the soft flesh of my palms, leaving crescent moons etched in crimson, dripping blood falling onto the pristine white rug.

I was terrified of Magnus—of the sucklers he had created, of the callous way he spoke to Zara, of the cruelty that pervaded every inch of him. In that moment, however, I shared another emotion with Zara. I was angry. Angrier than I had ever been.

Angry at the pain he caused Zara, how he thought her little more than a stupid animal.

Angry that he'd hurt Eternity—flinging her across the room like she was a doll. Angry that I was trapped in this body. Angry that any of this was happening to me.

Deep in the recesses of my mind, I felt something uncoil. Something ancient and powerful, something *furious*.

For a moment I *was* Zara the Fury, and that power we shared came with a phrase, a threat—a *promise*.

Everything that I was had suddenly distilled into a single word as fire erupted from me—my body a volcano of fury and vengeance.

"Burn."

Chapter Twelve

Inferno Activated.

The blast of fire that erupted from me was all consuming. Cushions, armchairs, rugs, even the bed with its expensive silk sheets and sturdy wooden frame burst into flames.

Part of my mind pushed back, whispering about Eternity, and I reined the flames in, focusing them into a single point in front of me. Focusing them on Magnus.

He raised his right hand as if it could ward off the flames, the movement pure instinct. Hungry for kindling, the flames accepted his offering, twisting around his flesh—igniting his robes, hair, and skin.

He screamed, but the fire snatched the sound from him, his face a silent portrait of fear and pain as the inferno engulfed him. The flames rose, building until they pressed against the ceiling—tendrils of fire chasing each other as they fanned outward. I thought the stone would blunt its fury. That the fire would dissipate once it found something it could not burn so easily. It didn't.

There was a crack, the smallest of sounds—like that of a snapped twig during a winter walk. Then the ceiling split into an angry line—cutting the room in two.

Rock and stone fell in huge unwieldy chunks, crashing to the floor. The inferno that surrounded Magnus blazed even brighter. I pushed, imagined it burning through his flesh and bone, annihilating his body until not even ash remained of his sorry, pathetic self.

As quickly as the fury consumed me it left. I gasped as I collapsed, falling to my hands and knees. Something blinked behind my eyes, red text that faded in and out of view, obscuring my vision.

WAR...NING...WARN...ING.

CALAMITY... SYS... TEM... COMP... ROM... ISED.

MA... NA... DEPLE...TED...

PEN... ALTY... PENALTY...

I gasped—a lightning bolt of pain striking my brain's center. Magnus. Eternity. The castle. Everything faded away as I curled up in a fetal position, breathless with pain.

PENALTY... PENALTY...

Time passed, minutes that felt like hours, until the pain faded to a dull ache. I unlocked my arms from where they had gripped my knees, my limbs weak and brittle. Where anger once burned, a hollowness lay in my chest—echoing with the pain I'd wanted to cause Magnus.

Before this, I thought I'd known exhaustion, but the slow throbbing ache that pervaded every inch of my body was like nothing I'd ever felt. My mind spun with the words I had seen, "Calamity System," "Penalty"—and the crippling pain that followed. Was that the price to pay for burning through my mana?

A large piece of stone crashed to the ground next to me, barely a hand width from my head.

Now is not *the time—you can figure this out later. You have to move. The ceiling is going to collapse.* Move you useless idiot!

I raised my head to see the inferno still wrapped around Magnus. I prayed with a newfound viciousness that he was burned to a cinder at its center. Gritting my teeth, I forced myself to crawl.

Eternity. I had to get to Eternity.

I kept my head low under the thick layer of smoke that filled the room. Coughing, I pulled my tunic over my mouth, the rough fabric doing little to filter out the smoke as I crawled on all fours, praying I was heading in the right direction.

I would have missed Eternity if not for the fallen painting. It had protected her from some of the debris that fell from the ceiling but would have done little against anything sizable. Her hand, small and unmoving, poked out from beneath the frame.

I took a deep breath, holding it tightly as I forced myself to my feet. Smoke burned my eyes. I braced my shoulder against the painting and pushed—the frame barely moved. The immense power and strength of this body was now a distant memory. Teeth gritted, I shifted the frame inch by inch until it fell to one side, revealing a blonde form, her dress tattered, and smoke tinged. "Eternity? *Eternity!*"

A trail of blood trickled down her forehead, covering her right eye and trailing down her cheek. Her eyes were only half open. "The flames," she whispered. "Magnus. What... what did you do?"

"I—I don't know. But we need to get out of here. Can you stand? I'm not sure I can carry—"

A huge crack sounded above, and my body moved of its own accord, covering Eternity. A shower of stone pelted my back—each strike a painful sting. I heard screams, awful rasping cries, that quieted almost as soon as they began.

I peered through the black smoke, praying we hadn't been buried, and saw the main doorway had collapsed—taking the sucklers with it. A graying hand reached between the rocks, twitching for a second, before falling still.

I remembered their eyes—eyes that had seemed to scream out for release. Death, no matter how horrible, must be better than being stuck in those mindless bodies.

Light pierced the smoke, gentle against the burning flames. A huge chunk of the ceiling had fallen in, revealing stars and a half-moon, hanging in the sky like a beacon of hope.

That was it—that was our way out. "Eternity, can you stand?"

"The fire—I'd heard the stories, but I thought them a lie. I've never seen..." A tear fell from Eternity's eye, trailing down her smoke-tinged cheek. I thought she was shell-shocked, that the trauma of everything she had been through and was still going through had caught up to her.

Seeing her wide eyes fixed not on the falling stone and flames around her, but on *me*, made me realize I was wrong. She was afraid—of me.

"Eternity," I said, deciding to simply tell the truth, or at the very least as much as I could explain right now. "I don't know how I summoned that fire—I'm terrified and feel like I'm gonna puke. All I want to do is lie down and cry." My hands tightened on her shoulders. "But we need to go. Please."

She hesitated for a long second, then nodded—holding out her hand. Breath shaky with relief, I grabbed it, hauling her to her feet. Slipping her left arm around my waist, I jabbed my right hand under her armpit—hoping it would be enough to catch her if we fell.

Eyes stinging, we pushed through the smoke, stumbling over smoldering furniture and fallen rocks. The smoke had dissipated slightly, curling upward through the gaps in the roof. Once we reached the fallen doorway, my heart sank. The stone that buried the sucklers had created a path up and onto the roof. To reach it though, we'd have to jump onto a ledge that was head and shoulders above me.

Untangling myself from Eternity I reached up, but not even my fingertips could brush the ledge. I jumped, banging my knees against the stone and stumbling. Less than thirty minutes ago I could have easily leaped upward and cleared the ledge. Now everything hurt—a bone-deep pain that no amount of gritted teeth and berating myself could overcome.

Eternity knelt before the stone, bracing her hands against it as she slid to her knees. "Use my shoulder as a springboard to reach it."

I hesitated, and she frowned at me—the steel I'd seen when she told Magnus to get away from me flashing in her eyes. "I used to do this with my brothers. *Go.*"

I took a step back and jumped, bringing my left foot down onto Eternity's shoulder and then pushing upward with all my weight. I felt her collapse beneath me but didn't dare look down while my fingers struggled to grip the ledge. Scrambling, I hauled myself up.

Behind me, I saw the inferno curling in on itself, pulsating as it struggled to contain something within. Flashes of white and blue exploding with its center. Magnus was still alive.

"Eternity!" I cried, dropping my hand down. She lay on her side—unmoving.

My gaze flittered between Magnus and Eternity, the explosions of icy blue magic growing larger. Frustration made me slap the ledge—we were close, so *close* to getting out of here, if only—

"**Get up, Eternity!**" I roared, a thunderous cry that commanded respect. My voice promised fang and claw if I wasn't obeyed—a cousin of the fury of my *Inferno*, if not a sister.

Vicious Command Activated.

A pop-up appeared, the same as the one that had flashed before my eyes when I first used my strength in my cell.

CALAMITY SYSTEM REINITIATED.

Eternity's eyes flew open. I jerked as my skull throbbed, the world shuddering into a sharpened focus. She groaned, forcing herself to her feet. Shakily she reached up, eyes on mine as she reached for my hand.

"Your magic fails, you treacherous harlot. I am coming. You will get down on your knees and scream for my forgiveness before the sun rises—I swear it."

Magnus' voice echoed in my mind as clear as the night sky above, and I made the mistake of looking back at him. I caught a glimpse of his blond hair through the flames, his features obscured by smoke—but I knew what I would see in his eyes.

Death.

Squeezing my eyes shut, I pulled Eternity up onto the ledge, fear screaming at me to run, to hide, to beg, to plead—anything to stop Magnus from getting us. He had been toying with me earlier, his voice trimmed with violence and amusement. If he caught me now—if he placed those icy hands on me…

I shook my head, pushing the thought aside. If I stopped to think about it for even a second, I would collapse onto the ground—comatose from fear.

Eternity had barely gotten one knee onto the ledge when I grabbed her, unwilling to give her time to recover. She stumbled but fell in step with me as we hobbled up the makeshift path that led away from the smoke and fire and to the night sky above.

***

Eternity's deep shuddering breath was cut short by a coughing fit that made her whole-body shake. She braced her hands against her knees, and I patted her back uselessly.

I looked over my shoulder at the deep hole leading to Magnus' chambers. The flames that engulfed him had faded even further. I squinted and realized he only used his left hand—the other was pressed against his side. Yet even one handed, every pulse of ice-blue light from his fingertips dimmed the flames even further. We didn't have long.

I surveyed the roof. Almost nothing remained of the ceiling, baring the rim of the gaping hole from my flames. It was a miracle we hadn't been crushed beneath falling rock. I searched every corner of the roof, looking for something—weapons, ropes, *anything* we could use to stop Magnus or flee.

Nothing.

I looked over the side. The drop below took my breath away. A river wound lazily about the castle, vanishing into a dark, luscious forest that swallowed the moonlight whole. The forest stretched out endlessly, disappearing into mountains that looked like mere smudges in the background of a painting.

I stared downward, but all hopes of flinging myself from the battlements and landing in the river were gone. It was too far from the castle walls—we would never make it.

We were trapped.

Chapter Thirteen

"You wouldn't know a spell that could make us fly, would you?" I asked Eternity, only half joking.

"I know one that could slow our fall," she said, joining me at the battlement as she looked down. She wiped her eyes, which only further smeared the blood from her seeping head wound into her skin. "But it's a powerful spell. I doubt I have enough mana left for us both."

I looked back at Magnus, who was surrounded by mere embers now.

"Once he makes it up here, jump," I said, hoping I sounded braver than I felt. "I made the roof collapse. I dragged you up here. I'm the one who pissed him off."

Eternity shook her head. "I hear enough of that nonsense from Lazander and the other Gilded. We escaped together; we shall leave together."

Before I could reply, a blast of ice-blue light erupted out of the gaping hole in the roof, hurtling toward me. I pushed Eternity to one side, instinct taking over as my body bent into a roll. The magic collided with one of the battlements, freezing it solid.

While I didn't feel as strong as I had hours before, I was grateful Zara's instincts remained.

"How dare you." Magnus' voice echoed in my mind, ricocheting about my skull. He was behind me, above me, all around me—his voice taunting me from every side. I looked down into his chambers, searching for the flames that had once engulfed him—but I could see only smoke-tinged shadows.

"You were a rabid animal when I first brought you here—all teeth and fury. Your power threatened to consume you—you needed to be controlled. Restrained. I gave you what you needed."

I swiveled, frantically looking for that shock of long blond hair and smug expression. My heart hammered as every muscle in my body tensed up—adrenaline demanding I fight or flee, anything to get away from the voice. The smoke was finally clearing on the floor below, and I peered into the darkness, searching.

"Was I not patient with you over the years? I punished you, of course—but only when needed. Never out of spite. Never out of malice."

My mind flashed with images of endless nights in the dungeon, Zara shrieking and howling as she fought against the manacles around her wrists. She snarled, biting at the chains until her lips tore. *"You stand here because of me, and only me."*

My mind flipped through a scrapbook of images, no—*memories* until it settled on one. Zara lay in the dungeon once more, but this time blood dripped from her nose and mouth. A large bruise blossomed over her right eye. Her spark of rage and stubbornness from the previous memory was gone—instead a glaze settled over her eyes as she stared at the floor. Moving her chained hands as best she could, she curled onto her side—knees to her chest. The shadows in the room lengthened and shortened as the room shifted from day to night, yet Zara did not move—her golden eyes locked on her prison door, pupils dilated.

"When you retaliated after your punishment, I accepted it—knowing that you needed to feel some measure of control."

I slapped my hands over my eyes, but it did nothing against the images my mind painted in stunning color—the minstrel gasping for mercy as Zara drove her fingers into his stomach. The horses who whinnied in fear when Zara approached, midnight-blue fingers splayed.

By the time she left the stable, blood flowed into the courtyard like a small river.

She used her hands when it was personal, I suddenly knew. A blade never felt satisfying enough.

Trapped in the mental onslaught of images, I was only dimly aware I was on the roof of a castle—smoke from a fire I had summoned curling about me as it drifted into the atmosphere.

Warm breath against my neck brought me back to the present—a moment too late.

"You made me do this," Magnus whispered.

I gasped as something cold and sharp pierced my back.

"Zara! No!" Eternity cried.

I spun, flinging a handout in a wild swing, but Magnus dodged it easily—the blade of ice in his left hand already evaporating. My knees went weak as the world tilted, my vision spinning as I grabbed the battlements for balance. The wound in my back was a single point of ice so cold it burned. I could feel it spreading, its tendrils digging into my muscles—paralyzing me.

As much pain as I was in, Magnus looked worse. Gone was the all-knowing expression. Instead, his mouth twisted in a snarl that could rival Zara's in its fury. His hair was shorn, burned to the scalp in parts, his face and skin darkened by smoke and ash…

His arm. Dear god, his arm.

A charred hunk of blackened meat was all that remained. "Yes, my love, look—look at what you've done."

A wisp of smoke curled upward from what was once his shoulder. His flesh was still burning, I realized in horror.

Magnus grabbed me with his remaining arm, yanking my head back viciously, tearing strands of hair from my scalp.

"Your family was once safe as I promised. But no more. They will pay the price for what you've done here."

My family? Zara has a family? The stray thought was lost in fear as he bent forward, pressing his forehead against mine. The smell of meat left on the grill for too long filled my nostrils. I could barely see, barely think—all that I could focus on was Magnus.

"We will start with your aunt. She will die screaming—at *your* hand. "

A monstrous roar, fierce and guttural, echoed through the night. I heard the snap of wings, and my hair fluttered about me as something sailed past the castle at a blistering speed, soaring into the night sky above.

Magnus leaped backward, releasing my hair, and I slumped over the battlements, gripping them with the little strength I still had.

I caught only the barest glint of gold as the monster twisted in the air above, wings outstretched. I thought I saw two figures atop the creature, but my mind was still scrambling to comprehend what I was seeing.

I had seen them in countless movies and books—from four-legged beasts built like tanks to long, slender creatures that whipped through the sky like snakes. My mom had pretended to be one more than once as she chased me about the room—

flapping her arms wildly as she roared. I, at the fearsome age of eight years old, did battle with a cardboard sword.

Never in all my daydreams did I expect to lay eyes on one.

A dragon, my mind insisted. *That's a dragon.*

Magnus snarled, his left hand glowing an ice-blue.

"*Valerius.*"

A silhouette stood against the night sky, balancing easily on the dragon's neck. The clouds in the sky parted for a moment, revealing the gleaming white armor of Valerius, leader of the Gilded Knights and heir to the throne of Navaros.

Despite how comically small he appeared next to the huge beast, my heart still constricted—whether from fear or relief, I didn't know.

Another knight knelt by his side; his hand pressed against the neck of the dragon whose wings cut through the air like a knife as it hovered effortlessly above us. The knight's hair was a startling shade of red that seemed to glow in the moonlight, outshining the golden armor he wore. Armor, I realized, that was the exact same shade of gold as the dragon he rode.

Even if the armor hadn't given it away, I recognized his red hair the moment I saw it. He was Lazander, hunter and Master of Beasts—another of the playable characters in *Knights of Eternity.*

I glanced at Magnus, wondering if he would strike at them as he had at me. To my surprise, he simply watched—his face twisted in anger.

Lazander stood, his hand on his sword, but Valerius held out an arm—blocking him. I couldn't hear what was said, but it was clear they were arguing. Lazander seemed to relent and sheathed his sword, kneeling on the dragon once more—his hand returning to its neck.

Valerius turned his gaze to Magnus. I didn't have the time to wonder how he was going to get down here, it was easily a distance of thirty feet, before he simply stepped forward into the open air.

I gasped as he fell, cloak extending behind him like a single white wing.

He landed hard; knees bent. The roof shuddered beneath him but held. The metal plates of his armor clanked gently as he stood, the full force of his dark-eyed gaze on Magnus and me.

"Something is different about you, Magnus," he said, gesturing with his sword to Magnus' ruined arm. "New haircut?"

Magnus hissed, a noise of pure rage. A shock of blue magic leaped from his fingers, lighting up the night sky, and shot straight for Valerius.

Chapter Fourteen

Valerius barely moved, simply stepping to one side as the bolt of magic closed the distance. It shot past him, grazing his face. A spattering of ice crystals formed on his cheek, and he brushed them aside with a flick of his fingers.

"Attacking a Gilded, Magnus? You know that's treason," Valerius said, raising an eyebrow. "But then again, this isn't your first treasonous offence, is it?

"A war brews on our borders," Valerius continued. "A war caused by Eternity's disappearance. And wouldn't you know it—there she is." He nodded at Eternity, who was a mess—the blood from her head wound streaming freely. I doubted she could even see much. At Valerius' words she edged closer to me.

Magnus sighed, a dramatic gesture. Slipping his hand behind his back, his fingers glowed as he moved them in a complicated gesture. "Would you believe, my lord, that I forgot she was staying with me?"

The glow about his fingers died. In the distance, I heard the barest whisper of a scream.

Valerius smiled. "Joke and bluster all you like, Magnus. You know I could cleave your head from your shoulders with a single stroke."

There was lightness to Valerius' smile, one that grew brighter with every word. It made me wonder—was he *enjoying* this?

Magnus hissed. "You arrogant child, do you think this a game? I took Eternity for good reason. One day you will thank me for it on bended knee—as will the king, queen, and every man, woman, and child in the kingdom."

"So, you *did* kidnap her," Valerius said. "Thanks for the confession."

A scream cut through the night. And then another. And another. Eternity's hand slipped into mine. Valerius didn't so much as blink. Magnus stared the knight down, teeth bared.

"You are a drab, self-serving, piss-poor excuse for a knight who has spent his life cowering beneath his mother's skirts," Magnus snarled. "Every moment spent in your company has made me long for the bottom of a bottle of wine, and your fellow knights are little more than boys your mother has forced to listen to you." Valerius smiled. He *smiled.*

"Did that feel good?" he asked.

"No," Magnus said, hand erupting in sparks of ice-blue. "But this will."

Magnus threw a blistering barrage of magic at Valerius as a pack of sucklers erupted out of the floor below—swarming the knight.

"Valerius!" I cried out, struggling to my feet—and then immediately collapsed, hanging onto a battlement for dear life as ice-cold agony gripped my back. I gasped, struggling to breathe.

Valerius raised a brow at my outburst but said nothing as he spun, his right hand unsheathing his sword as he reached smoothly behind with his left. His blade was a blur as it flashed upward, cutting off the arm of a club-wielding Sucker at the shoulder. The suckler shrieked, slamming into another in its pain and confusion as Valerius drew a huge silver shield from his back.

Knights of Eternity, in its limited pixels, had tried to do Valerius' shield justice. A graying blur with a swirl of barely visible sigils, it had nevertheless looked impressive every time I shoved the joystick to the left, hammering the action button as Valerius brought up his shield—blocking almost any attack, magical or physical, that someone dared throw at the knight.

But seeing it now was nothing short of breathtaking.

It was huge, covering Valerius from shoulder to knees, yet he held it as easily as if it were made from paper. The sigils that the game depicted as black smudges were engravings of ferocious monsters and twisted eldritch symbols that chased each other across the shield's surface.

I blinked, looking away after I swore one of the... monsters, a sharp-beaked creature like the one on his breastplate, turned its head toward me.

The ferocious blasts of Magnus' magic collided with the shield, sputtering into small, harmless cottony puffs—like a poorly thrown snowball.

Ice. Valerius' armor and shield is Ice Resistant, I recalled with delight. Which was all I'd seen Magnus use...

The mage gritted his teeth as shards of ice formed in his hand. Valerius drove his sword through the heart of a suckler. It screamed, shuddering before falling still.

Another suckler charged. Valerius brought his shield down with a sharp jerk—driving its edge into the creature's skull. It split like an overripe watermelon, the contents bursting forth in a pustulous spray.

Killing sucklers on a pixelated arcade game screen where they were little more than graying blobs with flailing arms did little to prepare me for seeing the real thing. From what I could tell, they were semi-conscious beasts who obeyed Magnus' every whim.

All I could think of though was the Bestiary's entry on them, "the former inhabitants of Ashfall." A few lines of glaring green text against a black screen that carried a significance I didn't understand until now. I didn't know their names or even what they looked like before Magnus' magic turned them into these horrible, twisted forms, but I forced myself to look as Valerius cut down suckler after suckler—quietly hoping as each one fell, they found peace.

They deserved that at least.

For every suckler Valerius killed, two more took its place. They were swarming, pushing and shoving each other, gray, putrid tongues lolling as they charged Valerius.

"You're hurt," Eternity said. So focused was I on the fight, I jumped at her voice, looking down to see that not only was she staring at me with intense concern, but that our hands were intertwined.

I squeezed hers, intending it to be comforting, but she flinched. "Sorry, sorry!" I said, releasing her fingers. It seemed some of my waning strength had returned. "I'm…" I trailed off. What could I possibly say—I'm not used to this body yet? I have no idea how strong I am?

"It's fine," Eternity said, reaching down and gripping her blue dress. She pulled at it once, twice, twisting it in her hands, but the fabric held. Realizing what she intended, I gripped the fabric and pulled, tearing a strip off it easily. I moved to press it to the wound on her forehead, but she stopped me.

"It's not for me," she said, a white glow enveloping her fingers as she trailed it along the fabric.

"But…" I trailed off awkwardly as I gestured to her still bleeding head. I felt tongue-tied, unable to meet those piercing blue eyes.

She frowned at me. "You've just been, quite literally, stabbed in the back. Turn around."

Her voice commanded obedience in a way that was at odds with her delicately embroidered dress and wide blue eyes. I smiled despite myself and showed her my back—deciding not to protest. She pressed the fabric to the ice-cold wound, and I bit my lip, holding back a whimper.

"**Judgment awaits**," she whispered, and the hairs rose on the back of my head as her magic coiled around me. "**Rise, so you might carry on His fight**."

To my surprise, the wound instantly began to warm, and I felt my muscles relax as a feeling of comfort and ease spread throughout my body.

It wasn't fully healed by any stretch, but breathing no longer hurt. Well, it didn't hurt much, at least.

"The sheer *amount* of magic Magnus poured into this," she muttered behind me, "you shouldn't even be standing."

My mind struggled with a reply. Thankfully Eternity didn't seem to need an answer.

"You'll need more than a simple ward," she said. "Once we reach the Ivory Keep, I'll ask Liddy to treat this—she's worth twice any other healer. You'll see."

Her words, though well-intentioned, left me feeling awkward and unsure. Since I had woken up in the body of Zara the Fury, I'd been consumed with just trying to escape, and then survive. I hadn't thought about what would happen in the next minute, let alone hours or days later.

I looked at my midnight-blue fingertips—recalling the images Magnus had shown me of the people she, that *I*, had killed. To my knowledge Zara had never set foot in the capital and royal family's personal home—the Ivory Keep. I doubted they'd welcome the right-hand woman of Eternity's kidnapper.

"You *rescued* me," Eternity said suddenly as if reading my mind. "You will be treated as my savior and nothing more—I swear it."

"Thank you, Eternity," I finally managed, glad she couldn't see my face.

I felt her smile behind me. "My name isn't actually Eternity, you know," she said. "It's just a title. Use it, if you wish, or you can call me—"

A scream brought me back to the fight ahead, and I stepped in front of Eternity, pushing her behind me.

Dozens of sucklers lay dead before Valerius, their gray blood congealing about his feet. Yet the knight wasn't even breathing hard. Far from being pushed back by their numbers, he had moved farther from Eternity and me, navigating the crumbling stone left by the inferno I had summoned. Magnus too had moved away, but in the opposing direction. Now he stood, facing Valerius across the cavernous hole that dominated the roof.

After flinging several ice-bolts, Magnus would stop—waiting for Valerius to drive his blade into a suckler before attacking once more. It was a cowardly tactic that relied on Valerius being distracted enough to fall prey to Magnus' magic.

Sweat gathered on Magnus' brow as he unleashed yet another barrage of magic—teeth gritted in effort.

Valerius was startlingly fast, yet precise—every movement flowing from one to another. His rebuttal to Magnus' cheap shots was no different. Valerius would shift his body ever so slightly as he brought up his shield, the magic fizzling uselessly against it, and then he would return to cutting down the sucklers like it was merely another step in a familiar dance.

Valerius had no snappy comebacks during the fight like he did in the game. No calls for justice or oaths to save Eternity and restore peace. Instead, his lip would twitch, and he'd smile ever so slightly at Magnus before returning to the next enemy.

Valerius was winning, I realized, looking up at the dragon above. *We* were winning.

The dragon had risen slightly to about fifty feet above us. Lazander leaned over the neck of the beast, watching Valerius intently.

I thought of Eternity's words, of her invite to the Ivory Keep, and for the first time I felt the stirrings of hope in my chest. Lazander and the dragon hadn't even entered the fight. It seemed Valerius alone could beat Magnus, which meant I—*we* could leave this hellish place.

Chapter Fifteen

Magnus clenched his remaining hand as Valerius easily blocked another magical bolt, smiling at the mage. Magnus' attacks had become less tactical and more erratic, and while he didn't have a convenient mana bar floating above his head, even I could see he was almost out of magic.

Magnus snarled and abruptly backed away from the battle. I thought he was going to retreat back toward his chambers, that this would all finally be over, but instead he made a beeline for Eternity and me.

I stepped forward, bringing my leg up for a kick, but the wound in my back flared once more—ice-cold tendrils causing my muscles to spasm. I cursed as I froze—paralyzed. Magnus took advantage and charged—backhanding me. The rage in the blow carried as much force as the slap, and I fell to the ground in a heap—cheek stinging.

He grabbed Eternity, yanking her hair back.

"Valerius!" he roared.

Abruptly the sucklers stopped their frantic onslaught. Valerius, shield and sword at the ready, cocked an eyebrow at the mage and the squirming Eternity. His armor was stained, dripping in blood that looked gray and putrid in the moonlight. A couple of flecks spattered his face and neck, but he didn't wipe them away. Instead, he locked eyes with Magnus, staring intently.

Above, Lazander stood up sharply—his sword drawn. Valerius raised a hand without glancing upward, and the red-headed knight stayed put but did not sheathe his weapon.

Eternity looked on the brink of collapse—her movements haphazard and limp as she tried to twist away from the mage. Magnus abruptly let go of her hair, then pulled her against him. She froze as he wrapped a forearm around her neck, a blade of ice crystallizing around his twitching fingers and trailing down his arm.

"You will let myself and Eternity leave. Or she dies—here and now." The tip of the blade dug ever so slightly into her soft flesh, and a trickle of blood slid down to her collarbone, making a point better than words ever could.

"I imagine you expect me to protest—to negotiate even," Valerius called out. He didn't look even the slightest bit concerned, not even when Eternity whimpered, her hands reaching back uselessly to push at Magnus.

Magnus watched Valerius intently, his body tense—ready to drive the ice blade in at any moment.

"But," said Valerius, raising his voice, "I won't risk Lady Eternity's life." Valerius sheathed his sword and slipped his shield onto his back. "You may go."

What? My mind spun in shock and growing outrage. I stared up at Lazander, seeing a similar expression on his face, and for a brief moment we locked eyes before I looked away. His gaze was furrowed, no doubt surprised to see his enemy, Zara the Fury, sharing his sentiments.

Magnus looked just as surprised but said nothing as he slowly backed away toward the gaping hole in the roof and his chambers below.

I struggled to my feet, but Valerius held out a hand in warning, flashing eyes of darkened silver that spoke of harsh consequences if I didn't stand down.

I thought of my frantic dash through endless corridors, poor Eternity limp in my arms, of the steel in her voice when she commanded Magnus to get away from me, of her concern when she tended my wound and comforted me with my welcome in the Ivory Keep.

Most of all, I thought of her voice when it first called out to me in the prison.

"You are not alone—not anymore," she had said, her voice a plea for help as much as it was a comfort. I saw it again in her eyes now. Saw it as Magnus dragged her away, and the knight who was supposed to save her stood by and did nothing.

But Eternity wasn't looking at Valerius.

She was looking at *me*.

"You will stay here until morning—my sucklers will inform me if you dare move," Magnus called, frantically snapping his gaze back and forth from the rocks and uneven terrain beneath his feet to Valerius. His movements were stiff and awkward as he struggled to hold Eternity with only one arm, the blade of ice nicking her skin when he stumbled, leaving thin red lines across her throat that trickled with blood.

Magnus didn't even look at me. Neither did Valerius. The Gilded Knight had told me to stay put, and it didn't even dawn on him that I would do anything but obey.

Like I wasn't worth their attention.

My mind flashed with images of Zara as she cut down Magnus' minstrel and butchered the animals in his stable.

Like I wasn't a *threat*.

A burning sensation started in the tips of my fingers and spread to my palms and feet. I yearned to scratch them but dared not move.

I looked at Valerius, willing him to do something. Even if Magnus didn't intend to kill Eternity, all it would take was him stumbling on a loose rock for his blade to slash across Eternity's throat. Yet he leaned back against the battlements like he was chilling at a pool table in the arcade.

He had meant what he said—he was going to let Magnus leave with Eternity.

"Stop struggling!" Magnus snapped, squeezing his forearm against her throat. Her eyes bulged as she gasped, nails digging into his arm.

The itching in my hands grew, becoming pinpricks of pain. Words, unbidden, flashed before my eyes. I whispered them, my fingers splayed, power flowing through me.

"I am death's mistress—bow before me."

Fury's Claw Activated.

Hands tingling, I looked down to see that the midnight-blue tips of my fingers had elongated into vicious talons, curved and deadly. I risked a glance at my feet and saw they had increased in size, talons digging into the ground below. I dragged a foot across the ground, quietly gasping when my talons left deep grooves, cutting through the stone like butter.

When Magnus had bombarded me with images of Zara's viciousness, he'd shown me how deadly she was. How fast.

How the only weapon she needed were her hands.

Magnus and Eternity reached the cusp of the collapsed roof, their bodies slowly disappearing out of sight as he made his way through the rubble.

I slowly leaned forward, bracing one foot against the battlements behind me.

They were about twenty feet away from me. The distance looked huge and was growing with every moment, but Zara could make it.

I could make it.

"Don't!" Valerius cried, his hand going for his sword as I pushed off.

From the moment I had woken up in this body, I knew it was strong. That it was fast. I'd felt it as I'd carried Eternity and leaped with ease out of the circle of sigils that trapped her.

This, however, made my previous strength and agility feel like a slug crawling through a garden on a hot summer's day. I was vaguely aware of the pain in my back, which suddenly felt days old instead of minutes.

Valerius, ironically, was the reason I made it to Eternity.

Magnus' head whipped about when Valerius cried, "Don't!" He raised his dagger away from Eternity's neck, holding it out toward the knight as if expecting him to rush toward him.

He didn't even look in my direction.

The stone beneath my feet cracked as I charged forward. A single bound covered ten feet. A second step and another ten feet disappeared behind me. Then I was in front of the startled mage.

I brought a clawed hand down, dragging it viciously across Magnus' outstretched arm. His blade of ice vanished instantly as he howled, falling backward. I grabbed Eternity, who didn't make a sound as I scooped her into my arms—slower than I'd like, but I was terrified of accidentally slashing her with my claws.

Magnus shouted at me; his eyes wild. "You little b—"

I pulled Eternity close, spinning as I kicked Magnus. Every scrap of pain, rage, and hatred went into that kick. My foot connected with his chest, a loud crack cutting the mage off.

He shot backward at speed, disappearing down the hole and into his chambers below. I heard his body hit the stone again and again as he tumbled down.

"Stop!" Valerius cried, sword and shield at the ready. He crouched from his position at the edge of the hole where suckler bodies surrounded him and leaped—aiming for where Magnus had stood moments before. He planned to cut me off before I made it to the floor below.

I pivoted on one foot, Eternity in my arms, and bounded back toward the battlements that surrounded the castle roof.

One step—I was almost there. Two steps, and I was at the roof's edge.

I heard the rattle of armor as Valerius charged after us, but I dared not look back. He closed on us with astonishing speed, and I realized with no small amount of surprise that if I had much farther to run, he would have caught up to me.

Good thing I was done running.

I dug my clawed feet into the ground. Valerius realized what I planned a second before I did it.

"**Wait!**" he roared, and I felt a thread of magic in his words—similar to my own voice when Eternity had collapsed in the fire below, and I'd commanded her to get up. I shrugged it off, batting the spell away as if it were nothing more than a fly, but not before a thought struck me.

Valerius shouldn't have been able to do that—to use any spells whatsoever, in fact. Everything about his build in *Knights of Eternity*—from his shield that specialized in ice resistance to his powerful armor that could repel mid-tier magic, focused on him being the antithesis to magic, not a source of it.

It was only a passing thought as I pushed off, leaping from the castle's battlements—and into the open air.

Chapter Sixteen

I had grown up in crowded streets and tall buildings. We moved a lot when I was younger, hopping from apartment to apartment. It never bothered me because everywhere felt the same—screeching car alarms, smoke-tinged staircases that stank of urine, cheap furniture stained by previous tenants, and a skyline so crowded by apartment blocks I stopped looking up.

When I jumped, that world fell away.

The moon was huge and full, dominating the sky and filling me with a quiet sense of calm and strength. The air was fresh and cold, and my lungs greedily inhaled a deep breath. I was shocked by how many stars lit up the sky—a thousand lights that twinkled with warmth.

I forgot about Magnus and Valerius. I forgot I was trapped in the body of an arcade game villain. I even forgot I had just leaped from a castle rooftop.

The world felt quiet and peaceful—it felt safe.

Then I started to fall.

"Eternity!" I yelled, the air whipping about me, threatening to snatch my voice away. I yelled louder, carefully pressing the length of my clawed fingers against her shoulders as I shook her.

"The spell!" I roared. "Use the spell to stop me falling! I'll carry you down!"

Eternity hung limp in my arms. "Eternity!" I screamed again, shaking her.

She didn't move.

Oh, crap.

My tunic snapped about me as we picked up speed.

"Eternity!" I roared, threading my words with the spark of *Vicious Command*. She didn't even stir, her head lolling back as she hung in my arms—white-blonde braids raising upward to create a strange reverse waterfall as the wind caught them.

Crap, crap, crap.

The ground beneath me, which had initially looked like an inviting sea of green, began to sharpen with detail as we sped toward it. I frantically looked for something

I could grab, something I could use to halt our descent, but I'd leaped too far from the castle—my claws were useless against a stone wall I couldn't reach.

Below us, I saw nothing but rocks and trees that grew larger every time I blinked. I had a mad idea—maybe I could grab a tree branch, slow my fall before I hit the ground? Even if my arm wasn't wrenched out of its socket (unlikely), and I survived the fall (doubtful), what about Eternity? I glanced at her, fervently praying she'd choose this moment to dramatically wake up and save us.

However, I might as well have been carrying a corpse.

My frantic planning felt like it had taken minutes, but barely five seconds had passed since I'd jumped. That was all it took to realize my leap into the unknown had killed us both.

"I'm sorry," I whispered to Eternity, holding her close.

I heard a growl as something both huge and fast sped past me like a golden bullet.

Lazander's fiery red hair looked like a bloodied speck on the dragon's neck as they flew straight for the ground below. The knight leaned to one side, and the dragon followed until the two were directly beneath us. Without warning, the dragon snapped its wings wide—abruptly braking.

The leathery membrane of the dragon's wings shook at the force of the air resistance, but held. I didn't have time to think—the dragon was suddenly right below me, its back offering a narrow landing. Lazander sat at the neck, so I aimed for right behind him—between the dragon's shoulders. I bent my legs slightly and hit the beast hard—my knees collapsing beneath me. The dragon growled at the force of the impact, dipping slightly.

"Steady, steady!" Lazander cried, but it was too late, the dragon had tilted to one side, taking me with it. He shot out a hand, desperately trying to grab me, or more likely Eternity, but it came a second too late. We slid down the side of the dragon's neck into the open air beyond.

Without thinking I shot out a clawed hand, desperate to slow our fall.

We stopped with a jerk, my shoulder wrenching in pain as my talons found purchase, sinking deep into the gap between the beast's neck and shoulder.

The dragon roared, snapping its head back and forth as it bucked. I swung wildly, cradling Eternity with one arm as I was slammed face first into rough scales that dragged along my cheeks and arms—taking skin with them.

I heard Lazander calling out frantic reassurances, trying to calm his steed, but the dragon would hear none of it as it snapped and roared. I hung on for dear life as I rolled back and forth, the dragon's golden scales digging into my arms, back, and legs.

I knew if this kept up, I would fall—and I would take Eternity with me.

I silently offered up an apology to the dragon and leaned both my feet back—building up momentum as I drove my talons forward—deep in the dragon's chest.

The dragon screamed, flapping wildly as it shot upward. By now my claws were so deep in its flesh I barely shook—solid and secure.

I'm sorry.

I lifted my left leg up, digging it into new flesh as I hauled myself up.

I'm so sorry.

Gritting my teeth, I took a deep breath and yanked my right hand out of the dragon's side, reaching up farther as I pulled.

Suddenly an armored hand gripped my wrist. I looked up to see a furious Lazander staring down at me—his sword drawn and pointed straight at me.

"You're hurting her!" he roared.

I panicked, staring at the limp Eternity, who I'd tucked under one arm. As near as I could tell, she had no clear wounds or no more than when I'd leapt from the castle.

It was only when I looked back at Lazander and saw him wince at the dragon's cries that I realized he wasn't talking about Eternity.

My heart twisted with guilt. Blood, a stunning azure that would have been beautiful in any other circumstance, poured from the deep wounds I'd left in the dragon's side—coating myself and Eternity. Lazander wasn't angry, I realized as the knight's gaze flickered from me to the dragon. He was *upset*.

"Take her!" I yelled, struggling to lift Eternity, who with every sway threatened to fall from my grasp. "Now!"

Lazander's eyes widened, but he sheathed his sword. He unceremoniously shoved a gauntlet hand under Eternity's armpit and lifted her up with a grunt, pulling her to his side and safely onto the dragon's back.

My relief that Eternity was no longer in danger dissipated when Lazander gripped my wrist tightly and stood—dragging me with him.

The dragon roared as my claws pulled free, blood pouring down my fingertips. I feared she would buck once more, but Lazander called out a command to steady and she did so—her wings no longer beating frantically as she slowed.

I waited for Lazander to pull me onto the dragon, but he held me at arm's length like I was little more than a ragdoll. My legs dangled over open air, and I made the mistake of looking down.

We had shot up into the sky in the dragon's frantic dash, and I could no longer make out the trees and rocks on the ground below. The river, forest, and even the castle, looked far away.

We were high up. Very, very high up. Panic settled in my chest like a leaden weight, and I forced myself to look at Lazander.

While Valerius' white armor and midnight hair made him look both cold and fierce, Lazander was the opposite. His golden armor complemented his bronze skin while his curly red hair spoke of a tempestuous wildness—a direct contrast to Valerius slicked back locks.

Up close, I could see that animals and birds of all shapes and sizes covered Lazander's armor. I spotted things that looked like tigers with several tails and fangs the size of my forearm, birds with four sets of wings, and a host of other beasts I couldn't even begin to name.

"Sheathe them," Lazander said, bringing me back to the present.

"Don't drop me," I sputtered, ignoring what he'd said in my fear. "Please."

"Sheathe. Them," Lazander said, his grip tightening around my wrist enough to hurt. I whimpered, flexing my fingers in pain—and then I realized what he meant.

Talons, long and deadly, still sprang from my hands and feet. I glanced down, catching sight of at least four places where I'd punctured the dragon's side as I frantically held on—digging into her for dear life. Blood dripped into the air below.

I didn't blame him for refusing to let me on board, I just had one problem.

"I-I don't know how," I said. "I promise," I added when Lazander frowned in disbelief.

"I can only hold you for so long," he said. "You saved Eternity—you have a place on Galora. But not at the price of her pain. Sheathe them, or I drop you. Choose."

Chapter Seventeen

This is a trick, my mind whispered. *He's lying. He's going to drop you regardless of what you do—you're going to fall. You're dead, dead,* dead.

The panicked thoughts didn't slow, each promising a horrible and painful death—and there was nothing I could do about it. The wind felt sharp and cold, every snap of the dragon's wings sending my hair spilling about my face.

"My arm wavers," Lazander said. "Sheathe your claws, and you may board Galora."

His voice was neutral, his face still—a far cry from the upset look he'd given me when he first grasped my wrist, his sword drawn.

He meant it. He would let me board. I just…

I stared at the gauntleted wrist that circled my wrist, holding me over the open air. Since waking up in this world I'd summoned fire, pierced illusions, and broken rocks with my bare hands—my words summoning Zara's abilities with an ease I didn't feel.

None of that meant I had any idea how they *worked.* Nor did I know how to stop them once I'd activated them. My talons flexed in my panic, claws glinting in the moonlight. I kicked uselessly, my feet searching for purchase where there was none. At this angle, if Lazander dropped me, I wouldn't be able to reach any part of him, or the dragon, when I fell.

I would die.

Breathe. Don't think. Not about Lazander. Not about falling.

I closed my eyes, but my mind kept picturing what would happen if he dropped me. How I'd hit the river below, my bones shattering, my neck snapping—killing me instantly, if I was lucky. How I'd sink into the depths below like a ragdoll, broken and forgotten.

Think of something else. Anything else.

The memory that sprang to mind was a recent one.

***

"Make a worse one," Adrian said, leaning against the arcade counter. "I dare you."

"I'll do it. Just remember. You wanted this," I warned in a dramatic, menacing tone.

"No. I refuse to believe there is a worse dad joke than 'Did you hear about the man who tried to catch fog? He *mist.*'" Adrian made a show of rolling his eyes, but his lips twitched into a smile he could never hide. Not around me.

"You ready?" I said, schooling my face into a serious expression.

Adrian nodded solemnly.

"Why don't skeletons go trick or treating?" I asked.

"I don't know," he replied. "Why don't skeletons go trick or treating?"

I sighed dramatically. "Because they have no *body* to go with."

Adrian groaned, cupping his face in his hands as I laughed. He kicked me gently but didn't move his leg away after—pressing it against mine.

"You," he said, dropping his hands, smiling widely as he leaned against the arcade counter, "are simply the worst."

I was with Adrian. It was a Friday night and my uncle laughed behind me, handing Noah a basket of fries he barely acknowledged as he battered the controls of *Knights of Eternity*.

Everything was all right.

***

I opened my eyes.

Everything was all right.

I looked up, breathing a sigh of relief when I saw only midnight-blue fingertips wiggling in the moonlight.

I did it!

Lazander carefully pulled me inward, dropping me gently onto my feet next to him.

"I'm so sorry," I said, nearly tripping over the words in my haste. "For hurting her—for hurting Galora."

Lazander blinked in surprise but said nothing, merely nodding as he cradled Eternity in his arms, pushing her hair back from her face. She hadn't so much as twitched during our mad escape, and for a second I thought she was dead. I breathed a sigh of relief as I saw her chest rising and falling as Lazander settled once more into his place at Galora's neck.

She was alive—for now at least.

I stood awkwardly as Lazander murmured words of comfort to Galora. I didn't know if I should try to sit where I stood, with nothing but rough scales to grip, or try to scoot behind Lazander—where the knight might push me off for having the sheer *audacity*.

"That was foolish," Lazander said suddenly, his back to me. "Rushing Magnus like that—leaping into the night's sky without so much as a word. You almost killed Lady Eternity."

"Sorry," I mumbled, bowing my head—feeling like a child being chastised by a stern teacher. The dragon turned, cutting through scattered clouds as we slowly made our way back to the castle. I stumbled at the change in direction and decided to neither sit where I stood nor next to Lazander—instead settling into a crouch, my balance instantly improving. I'd be damned if I was going to survive imprisonment, sucklers, and a knife in the back only to have the shame of *falling off a dragon*.

Lazander sighed heavily.

"It was also brave. You, rather, were brave," he said, casting a glance over his shoulder at me. "I know we've not met before—Magnus likely hid you away every time we visited. But I am not your enemy."

I nodded, unsure of what to say.

"Your master has committed crimes against Navaros. Evergarden is mere days away from declaring all-out war with us over Lady Eternity's disappearance. Regardless of your role in her kidnapping, you will be judged and likely punished as Magnus' accomplice.

"But," he continued. "You have my personal oath that you will not be harmed. You will endure a trial and likely have to suffer a thousand cross-examinations. But you are the reason Lady Eternity is alive and well—and I *will* testify to that fact."

His gaze returned to face forward where the castle grew larger with each of Galora's wing beats. I noticed, in the space between his words, he didn't mention Valerius.

"That inferno you sent into the skies was quite the distress call. I owe you my thanks, though my hawk, Merrin, might feel differently—you singed her feathers."

I couldn't tell if I should apologize for hurting *another* of his animals or if he meant it as a joke, so I focused on Eternity instead. "Is she going to be all right?" I asked.

"My medicinal knowledge is limited to staunching wounds and binding broken limbs, but she is strong," he said. When the silence stretched between us, he glanced down at Eternity and quietly added, "One of the strongest people I know. She will recover, and knowing her, she will come out all the more resilient for it." The knight sighed sadly. "Though I wish none of this had ever happened to her". The warmth of his voice gave me hope, even though I knew that last line wasn't meant for my ears.

Galora growled, and Lazander looked forward, rubbing his hand down her neck.

I carefully shuffled forward, curious as to why he kept touching the same spot.

Runes glowed blue up the side of Galora's neck. Noticing my look, Lazander raised a hand, pushing back his armor just enough to expose his wrist—a corresponding symbol glowed there.

"A bonding," he said. "While others bend their animals to their will, I prefer to enter into a partnership with them. Galora and I are bonded for life—I feel what she feels and vice versa."

"So when I hurt Galora…" I said, my guilt doubling in size.

"You also hurt me—correct," he said. His lip twitched into a wry smile. "Your talons are impressively sharp."

That was a joke! Lazander just joked around with me.

I smiled, relieved, as a fraction of tension left my body. I stretched out a hand around Lazander and Eternity. The knight tensed for a second but said nothing as I gently ran my fingers over Galora's golden scales. They changed slightly at my touch—becoming a deep amber. Whether it was a trick of the light or some physical reaction, I didn't know. To my surprise, despite being essentially a giant reptile, she felt warm to the touch. "Then I'm sorry, to you and Galora both."

Lazander raised his brows in boyish surprise—the expression making him seem years younger. He stared off into the distance.

Galora huffed—making the air around her steam.

"She says as a fellow claw-wielder she will forgive you—just this once. But if you do it again, she'll eat you."

I laughed, half at his words, half out of nerves. "That's more than fair."

"Hold on to my shoulder," Lazander said. "We're coming in."

Even now that the fire had died down, the castle's upper floors were a smoking ruin. Almost all of the roof had collapsed, and I had a clear view into the Magnus' private chambers. Stone had crushed most of his furniture, and the bed was a charred mess. I saw no sign of Magnus himself.

I remembered the viciousness I felt toward him when my flames had engulfed him—how much I wanted him dead.

I could lie to myself and say that feeling was a by-product of the magic I'd summoned, but my hand on Lazander's armored shoulder gripped tighter than necessary as I stared at the castle below.

I hope he's dead.

A part of me was upset at the violent thought but only in passing. After seeing Zara's memories, how he'd treated her like a caged animal, he deserved it. I didn't linger too long on my fervent hope I was the one who killed him.

Galora dipped suddenly, dropping past the castle roof, hovering at a height of the floor below—approximately where Magnus' chambers were.

"Aren't we landing on the roof?" I asked. "To get Valerius?"

"No need," Lazander said. "Look up."

I did as he suggested and gasped when I saw Valerius flying toward me.

Not flying—*falling.*

I flinched, instinctively raising my hands to shield myself. Valerius' cloak snapped in the wind as he sped toward us. A split second before he landed he slowed, cloak spreading around him as invisible hands cradled him—gently guiding him onto Galora. His armor didn't make a sound as he landed with knees bent, dark head bowed.

The small petty part of me told myself I could have had a badass superhero landing like that if Eternity had managed to cast that spell to slow our fall.

Catching the wind, Galora turned away from the castle—snapping her wings briskly as she flew low, drifting over the tops of the forest.

"You will return, Zara."

I gasped at the sound of Magnus' voice. I looked back toward the castle, eyes darting to every window, searching for the mage.

"You will bow. You will beg. And you will be grateful." I spotted a figure, a mere shadow, at one of the windows of the third floor. I blinked and it was gone—if ever it was there to begin with.

Magnus was alive. My fists clenched and my teeth ground into one another. I had trapped him in an inferno, burned his arm to a mere crisp, and broken at least several ribs when I kicked him in the chest, and yet he lived.

Hate blossomed in my chest. Mine or Zara's, it no longer mattered.

"What?" Valerius asked, rising to his full height. He drew his sword and pointed at me. "Is *she* doing here?"

Chapter Eighteen

"I—" I started, but Valerius merely flicked his wrist, pressing his sword against my throat. There was so little room on Galora I could do nothing but freeze—my hands raised in surrender.

"I didn't ask you," he said. "What is Magnus' personal lapdog doing here, Lazander?"

Zara was tall, Eternity barely came up to my shoulder, but Valerius dwarfed me. I had to tilt my head back to meet his gaze—his stony eyes glared at me with open contempt, daring me to move.

Confused, I stayed silent, my hands raised in surrender as I stood between the two knights.

"Peace, my lord," Lazander said. He turned awkwardly, keeping an arm around Eternity and his other hand on Galora's neck. "Lady Eternity is safe because of her."

"She tried to kill both herself and Eternity," Valerius said. "Why else would she throw herself from the roof?"

"Wait, no!" I said, wincing when steel cut into my neck—a not so gentle warning.

Determined to make my case, I continued. "I'm-I'm the one who broke her out of her cell. She was in some kind of trap. Symbols were drawn onto the floor—they messed with her magic."

"A binding?" Lazander asked, eyes flicking to Valerius. "Gabriel would know for sure."

I shrugged, turning ever so slightly so I could keep both knights in view. Valerius' blade followed me but didn't press any harder into my neck. Taking this as a good sign, I continued. *Just explain, and everything will be all right.*

"Magnus found us—he hurt Eternity, threw her at a wall. After that I..."

I thought back to the fury I had felt, how ancient and powerful it was. How intoxicating.

"I-I summoned fire. Trapped him in it." The two knights shared a glance. Lazander's brows raised, impressed, but my words only seemed to make Valerius angrier.

"Magnus hurt Zara—*me*," I corrected. "Locked me in a cell. Beat me more times than I can count."

Lazander, at least, had the decency to look concerned.

"All I wanted was to find Eternity and get out of there."

"While I've never kidnapped anyone," Valerius began, "it's strange to steal them away, only to change your mind and rescue them."

See? They don't believe you. None of them will believe you. You may as well just throw yourself off the dragon for all the good—

I slammed the door on my brain, knowing I couldn't afford to panic—not now. The door wouldn't last, my thoughts always found a way to weasel in, to break me down, but I could stall them.

"I think Za—I mean, *I* was at my breaking point. Magnus wanted to make me his… his personal lapdog. And it almost worked… until Eternity helped me. She's the only reason I got away from him. She saved me as much as I saved her." I winced at the cheesy expression, but I had no other way to explain it. Even now as Lazander cradled Eternity, I felt a strange feeling of protectiveness toward her. "I couldn't leave her behind," I finished lamely.

As a child playing *Knights of Eternity*, Valerius was my favorite character. To me, he was exactly what a knight should be—brave, composed, and willing to help all those who needed it.

Valerius scoffed. "How conveniently noble of you."

Clearly things weren't so black-and-white in this world. This man wasn't the Valerius I'd adored as a kid—the knight I knew wouldn't have left me in Magnus' cell or stood aside and done nothing when Magnus threatened to take Eternity. Still—seeing him look at me with distrust and scorn, I was glad my ten-year-old self wasn't here to witness this. Her heart would break, even more than mine was right now.

"What happened after you trapped Magnus?" Lazander asked." We-we made it to the roof, but he snuck up on me," I said, shoving down my shattered hero-worship of Valerius. "Stabbed me with a blade of ice. Eternity did something to the wound— used a bit of her dress and some magic on it."

"Lies," Valerius hissed, his sword biting painfully into my skin. "A drop of her magic is worth half the kingdom—she would never waste it on you."

"Face Lord Valerius," Lazander said.

I did, feeling unsure as he pressed a gentle hand to my back.

Aware that the full weight of Valerius' gaze was on me, I looked at his feet—his stance slightly wide as he balanced easily on the dragon. His boots had been polished to a dull shine that reflected my face. I focused on that instead—anything to avoid the weighty judgment in his eyes.

One of my mom's favorite phrases suddenly popped into my head. *The truth holds power.* She'd say it at every opportunity—from when I came home crying because kids at school claimed she was sleeping with my teachers for my good grades to when I came with bloodied fists after some kids mocked Noah. *When you tell the truth, good people listen.*

It had worked for me back then—I could only hope it would now too.

I winced when Lazander touched the wound left by Magnus' blade.

"Look," Lazander said. "The same material as Lady Eternity's dress."

I turned a fraction to see Lazander held a piece of blue fabric stained with my blood in his hands. My knees shook as ice-cold tendrils began to spread throughout my back. I hadn't realized how much pain Eternity's magic was keeping at bay.

Lazander moved to return the makeshift bandage to its place on my back, but Valerius held out a hand. The knight leaned forward, carefully keeping me at arm's length as he took the embroidered fabric from Lazander.

"Perhaps she *is* lying, and her story is but a fabled construction," Lazander said, and I had to force myself not to argue. "But this is proof Lady Eternity helped her— that alone is reason enough to take her back to the Ivory Keep for cross-examination."

Valerius took his time examining the makeshift bandage, holding it up in the moonlight, turning it this way and that.

Sweat began to bead on my forehead from the effort of standing.

"A ploy," Valerius said, tossing the fabric over his shoulder.

I gasped, watching the little pain relief I had drift away into the wind—gone.

"Unlike you, Lazander, I know what she's capable of," Valerius said. "She'd happily slit the throats of half a battalion before you could even draw your sword. Lies and murder are the tools of her trade."

I fell to my knees as my vision blurred.

"I won't let you or anyone else be bitten by this viper."

I knew Valerius was fast, but I neither saw nor heard him move—I was simply in the air, his gauntleted fist bunching my tunic as he held me aloft.

"Valerius!" Lazander barked, struggling to his feet with Eternity in his arms. Even if he hadn't been weighed down, however, I doubt he could have stopped what came next.

Exhausted, I hung limply in Valerius' grasp, the seams of my tunic tearing from the tightness of his grip. I clung to his wrist, staring up at him. I tried to put what I was feeling into my eyes—that I was telling the truth. That I didn't want to hurt Eternity, or him, for that matter.

That I needed *help*.

He stared back at me, eyes dark and impassive. His gaze made me feel colder than the magic that crept along my spine, freezing my limbs. To him I was small. Insignificant.

I was nothing.

"Plea—" was all I managed before he bent his arm at the elbow ever so slightly.

And flung me from the dragon—out into the open air.

"No!" Lazander roared. He made an instinctive, almost comical move to save me, one arm cradling the unconscious Eternity as he reached for me. Even if he'd moved at the same time Valerius had, the knight had thrown me with such force I flew several feet away from Galora—speeding through the air almost as quickly as the dragon.

Just like that, I was falling.

I can't believe it, was all I could think, over and over again—shock blocking out any other reaction. I thought of the countless times I'd played as Valerius, the dungeons we'd conquered together, the enemies we'd defeated. The shiver of joy I'd feel when we'd beat a particularly difficult boss.

I can't believe he did that.

I stared at the sky, feeling the air press against my back as I picked up speed, my long hair tangling about my face.

Magnus' magic, now free of Eternity's influence, filled my body—my muscles stiffening, hands reaching for a rescuer who would never come. Mouth opens for a scream I couldn't unleash.

I closed my eyes, aware I was going to die. I cleared the tops of the trees, wood snapping from the speed and force of my fall, my body unrelenting as it slammed into branch after branch.

Words, bright red and bold, flashed behind my eyelids as I hit the ground—hard.

TUTORIAL.

FAILED.

Chapter Nineteen

Queen Firanta Abigail Alexandria Najar the Third was known for three things. One: the treaties and trade agreements she had negotiated since taking the throne thirty years ago. She had been a mere eighteen years of age, yet her diplomacy was unmatched, ushering in an era of prosperity and peace. Two: a childhood illness had left her blind in one eye and unable to walk without the help of a cane. Three: she hated, loathed, and utterly *despised* one thing more than any other—tardiness.

"You're *late*," she said, lips pursed as Valerius strode into the throne room of the Ivory Keep. While on paper it was the seat of power of Navaros, the throne room in practice was a spacious room decorated for comfort. Carpeted floors had been removed; an even surface was easier for the queen to walk on while extravagant furniture was kept in the guest hall for more official events.

The queen sat on a simple wooden chair that had been lined and stuffed with sheep's wool and goose feathers. A fur-lined blanket covered her legs, and her most loyal companion, a beast of a dog named Thaddeus sat by her feet. Thaddeus' specific breed was unknown, but judging by his huge black paws and elongated front teeth, Valerius had always guessed bear and saber-tooth tiger were mixed in there." Forgive me, Mother," Valerius said, bowing low. Gone was his heavy armor. He now wore a dark tunic and matching boots. The colors made his pale skin look almost ghostly.

"Forgive me, my *queen*," she said, and Thaddeus growled—not that the queen needed the added menace. Her arched brow had brought many a stuttering noble to bended knee as they babbled apologies.

Valerius, however, was impervious to his mother's infamous stare. "I'm here before Lazander, surely that counts?"

"No," a voice came from behind him. "You're not." Lazander sidestepped the knight and approached the queen, a pair of thin wire frame glasses in his hand. He bowed low, handing them to her.

"Thank you, Zander," the queen said, the warmth in her voice at odds with her stern expression. "These eyes aren't what they used to be—bless the mages for their optical trickery." She slipped the glasses on, adjusting a dial on the side as she focused on one of the many sheaves of paper on her lap.

She held one up to the light, frowning at its contents, then slipped it behind the stack and began on the next.

Valerius' foot began to tap impatiently against the stone floor. He forced it to a stop. "Has Fath—has the king sent word?" he asked.

The queen ignored him, moving on to the next page.

Valerius tried not to fidget as the silence stretched on.

Lazander stood off to one side, looking as at ease in the throne room as he was on horseback beneath an open sky. Thaddeus, unhappy no one was paying attention to him, gave a huff that sounded more at home on a vast savannah and wandered over to the red-haired knight. Lazander broke into a wide grin, bending low as he scratched the huge dog's chin. The behemoth rumbled happily and rolled onto his back, delighted when Lazander obliged with tummy rubs.

At long last the queen removed her spectacles, folding the papers on her lap in half and placing them on a small side table.

"As a courtesy, I am going to give you a single opportunity to explain," she began, staring intensely at Valerius. "What possessed you to throw our single informant *off the back of a dragon.*"

"The king has taken half our armed forces to Evergarden's borders. War is set to break out at a moment's notice, and you have less than a third of your usual protective retinue. She would have been within arm's reach of you, Mother." Valerius bowed his head, weaving a note of worry into his voice. "I couldn't risk it."

In return, the queen rolled her eyes. "Yes, because I share my bed with every prisoner of war you knights show up with. We have prisons for a reason."

"It's not just that," Valerius began, changing tactics. "You remember Helena of Vagra? She was the lord of Magnus' estate before Father gifted it to him some ten years ago."

The queen cautiously nodded.

"She was found dead in the middle of a field," Valerius continued. "Her neck was broken—apparently thrown from her horse. But Helena was a prized rider, and her horse a mare she'd raised since birth."

At the queen's skeptical frown, Valerius ploughed on. "Ambassador Kal from Freley—found dead from poison in a brothel just on our border. It took you weeks to talk Freley down from war. Frederick Mahon—a minor lord from the south who tried to bring in a registry for mercenary guilds."

"I remember," the queen said. "He washed up on the southern coast."

Valerius nodded. "His vessel, a small fishing boat, was found drifting days later with no supplies or even a spare change of clothes. Strange for a man who apparently drowned while taking an afternoon swim."

"Make your point, Valerius."

"Helena of Vagra, Ambassador Kal, and Frederick Mahon all visited Magnus the week before their deaths."

The queen's eyes widened, and Valerius could almost hear his mother doing the mental calculations he knew she would. While Valerius was pretty certain Magnus had killed Helena of Vagra, he'd had his eye on her lands for years, but the link between the other two were tentative at best. At a push Valerius could argue the influx of mercenaries Magnus had hired was reason for him to want Frederick Mahon and his mercenary registry out of the way. The Ambassador of Kal was a harder sell—why would Magnus want war with Freley?

Regardless, Valerius knew he wouldn't need to explain further. His mother's greatest strength was that she considered every possibility.

It was also her greatest weakness.

"Zara the Fury is the reason we no longer have a bandit problem on our western borders," the queen said.

"She's also the reason the wind stank of charred human flesh for weeks," Valerius countered. "You read the reports: heard of the scorched earth she left in her wake, of the men who begged for mercy while she melted their flesh from their bones. We made a mistake thinking she was simply an exotic choice of a fiancée for Magnus. I believe her to be his personal assassin."

"Zander disagrees," the queen said, eyes drifting to the knight.

"You heard what she said—Magnus beat her, *tortured* her," Lazander argued, brow furrowed. "If Zara hurt others at his command, it wasn't by choice."

"So she claims. But you've never met her—*I* have. In fact, I ran into her while searching Magnus' castle for Eternity. She was curled up on his lap like a cat with cream, staring at him with sickly adoration," Valerius said, lying easily. "If he hurt her, as she claimed, she could have left at any time. Instead she's clung to his side for a *decade*. No—this woman is no victim. She's a swindler who thrives on lies and manipulation."

Valerius looked to the queen as he gestured to Lazander. "The fact that Zara managed to convince Lazander she wasn't a threat only strengthens my case. That she did so after *slicing his dragon to shreds* is nothing short of miraculous."

"What about Lord Magnus then?" snapped Lazander. He rarely raised his voice, but now his fists were clenched, his cheeks flushed. "You were going to let him leave with Lady Eternity."

"Of *course* I wasn't," Valerius said calmly, cocking a brow as if the very thought was absurd. "Why do you think I ordered knights to the front and back entrances of his castle? If I rushed him with his guard up, he'd have slit her throat. The fact that Zara was able to do so leads me to believe this was all planned."

Lazander grimaced, but the queen raised her hand—silencing him.

Valerius resisted the urge to argue further. He'd already taken a risk pushing his mother as hard as he had on this—if he didn't tread carefully she might turn her single-eyed gaze onto him. That was the last thing he needed.

"What do you think, Imani?" she called out.

A whisper twisted through the windowless room. The back of Valerius' neck prickled, his body tensing as he felt eyes boring into the back of his skull. A quickening of his breath was all that betrayed the knight's surprise as a woman appeared at his shoulder.

Imani was the tallest woman he'd ever seen, taller even than Zara the Fury. With skin as dark as night, and midnight armor to match, she moved like a shadow made flesh. Her head was shaved to the quick, and her blue eyes locked onto the queen as she strode past Valerius without a word.

He hadn't even felt her enter the room.

Imani bowed to the queen—in a sense, at least. She tilted her body forward to the absolute minimum requirement and then straightened it.

"Lady Eternity is safe—that is all Gallow required," she said—her voice a soft velvet at odds with the corded muscle Valerius knew lined every inch of her body.

"I didn't know Gallow had blessed us with the presence of one of his Champions," Valerius said, unable to stop himself. "How convenient that you show now—and not when Eternity was kidnapped, or say—when we were *scouring the kingdom for her.*"

Imani ignored him entirely, and Valerius squashed the urge to brain her with the pommel of the dagger he kept hidden in his boot. He detested Gallow and his little soldiers. Followers of the God of Judgment bleated endlessly about "honor," "sacrifice," and "obedience"—their cries as pompous as they were exhausting. Yet they would at least bow to him—he was the Prince of Navaros and leader of the Gilded.

Gallow's Champions, however, would no more bow down to him than they would a cockroach.

They traveled across the kingdom, always alone, always unburdened by food or drink, carrying out missions secret to all but themselves. They refused allegiance to any kingdom or war effort.

They were unpredictable. Inscrutable. *Dangerous.*

"Lazander—any further insight into how Eternity was taken in the first place?" the queen asked. Valerius inwardly sighed in relief at the topic change—he'd bought some time. For now, at least.

"None," Lazander said. "But we've moved her from the Gallowed Temple to one of the Keep's towers, and the palace mages have spelled every inch of its interior. Unless she willingly leaves the tower, she is safe."

The queen sighed, rubbing a hand over her tired face. Valerius felt a rare pang of guilt that he quickly dismissed.

"Are you content with Lady Eternity's new abode?" the queen asked, shifting slightly as she eyed Imani.

If Valerius hadn't known better, he'd have said she was as uncomfortable as he was in the Champion's presence.

"We are," Imani replied.

"Then convey our apologies to the God of Judgment for our misstep. You have my word this will never happen again." The queen inclined her head, and Imani followed—her nod slightly shallower than the queen's.

"Now, out—all of you," the queen said, not unkindly. "Evergarden ambassadors are due to arrive in a few hours, and I've not even begun to prepare."

Lazander bowed low. Imani simply turned sharply on her heel, dark eyes catching Valerius'. She winked at him, lips curling into a hint of a smile, and Valerius knew she'd felt his discomfort. He desperately wished for his sword. He pictured the joy he'd feel as he drove it through her chest, wiping the smug look off the Champion's face.

"Was there something else, Valerius?" the queen asked sharply as he stared after the vanishing Champion for a beat too long. He came back to himself, rearranging his expression into one of concern as he looked back at his mother.

"You're meeting with Evergarden ambassadors?" he asked, grabbing the last thing she'd said. "Weren't they threatening to coat the Ivory Keep in oil and burn every soul in it to ash—you included?"

"Yes. They do have a way with words, don't they?" she said, smiling ruefully. "Thankfully Eternity's return has guaranteed they will at least speak to me before they do so."

"You will have them backing down from our borders and returning home by tomorrow." Lazander grinned with unabashed confidence.

Valerius wanted to roll his eyes.

The queen gave a rare, sincere smile. "That, my dear Zander, is the plan. One I am only able to execute because the two of you brought Eternity back—*mostly* safe and sound. We will end this war before it's even begun—and ensure both our kingdoms' safety."

She waved a hand. "Now go. I have much to do and little time to do it in."

Valerius bowed low, grateful that the movement allowed him to hide the look of frustration and disappointment on his face. He'd come so close—the closest he'd ever managed.

As he backed up into the hallway, he turned—walking briskly away. He wanted nothing more than to be alone in his chambers where he could scream, howl—do whatever was needed to vent this building resentment.

However, the long strides that echoed after him, easily catching up, had a different idea.

Chapter Twenty

The queen waited until Valerius and Lazander's footsteps had disappeared into silence. She was alone—a rarity when you help rule a kingdom.

Or at least, she appeared to be.

"What do you think of Valerius' theory, Thaddeus?" she asked, flexing stiff fingers.

The canine cocked his head to one side, considering, before answering. "We initially investigated Helena of Vagra's death as a potential murder, but we lacked the evidence to levy a case against Magnus."

"What of the other two, Mahon and Ambassador Kal?"

Thaddeus sighed heavily as he hauled himself to his feet—trotting over to the queen. "My personal theory is that Kal's murder wasn't political—I believe his brother poisoned him over a petty dispute involving inheritance. Mahon is more difficult to pinpoint. We found a significant amount of alcohol in his system, but the lack of supplies and placement of his fishing vessel is suspicious. There's every chance Valerius is correct, but as of now it is just that—a theory." "I need you to investigate the veracity of my son's claims. Did Magnus and Zara have anything to do with their deaths, and what might he have stood to gain? If it's even the smallest possibility, we need to explore it."

Thaddeus dipped his shaggy head. "It shall be done, my queen."

"And Zara the Fury—what do we know of her?"

"Precious little." The dog growled, a low sound brimming in frustration. "She was driven out of the Moonvale Mountains a decade ago alongside every other falsling not of the Xi'an clan. Their takeover was as abrupt as it was violent. She appears to have had no contact with her kindred since. Since her arrival at Magnus' estate she's left only a handful of times. One of which was to deal with the bandit troop who'd been murdering and pillaging their way along our borders."

"I remember that. Fifty men strong she killed, wasn't it?"

"At least that, although she left so little of the bodies it was difficult to measure. Her ability to wield fire is… unprecedented. I wouldn't face her without every mage of the Ivory Keep at my back."

"Is she alive, do you think?"

Thaddeus shook his head. "From the distance Valerius threw her, she's either dead or crippled beyond saving."

"What of Magnus himself? Has he been found?"

"No, my queen. But if I were an optimist, I'd say he died when his castle collapsed."

The queen cocked a knowing eyebrow at the dog. "I look for many things in my spymaster—optimism isn't one of them."

The dog huffed—an approximation of a laugh. "I'd bet my left paw he's alive. We're searching for him as we speak. He will be dead before the week is out for his treachery—you have my solemn vow."

The queen paused, a hand on her chin in consideration. Then she sighed. "As much as the thought delights me, we need him alive. So much of this makes little sense: Eternity is Gallow's Chosen and the only being capable of wielding his magic—what use does he have with her? Unless his goal was not Eternity, but to trigger war?" Her voice grew louder with every word.

Thaddeus placed a meaty paw on the queen's lap. She sighed again, scratching the beast behind his left ear—his favorite spot. "I know," she said. "One problem at a time."

The dog whined; eyes closed in pleasure. The queen smiled. "If only poor Zander knew who he was really scratching."

"This coat is inches thick, my queen. *Inches*. I need all the scratches I can get." Thaddeus huffed.

"Speaking of…" the queen said, lips pursed.

Lost in the joy of an ear scratch, it took Thaddeus a moment to register the queen's words.

"You felt it too?" he asked.

The queen cocked an eyebrow, inviting him to continue.

"It isn't unusual for reports to differ slightly—regardless of how keen the eye or sharp the memory. But Lazander and Valerius' may as well have been on two different rooftops. Perhaps Valerius is right, and Zara's actions were pure theatrics—but throwing her to her death? That is extreme—even for him."

"Then again, Lazander is young and has a soft heart—especially for creatures with fangs and claws. You recall the pyrions?" the queen asked.

"I do, but that's what makes me all the more confused. Did you see the scars Zara left on Lazander's dragon? I'd have killed Zara myself in his shoes… something doesn't add up."

"I know you are stretched thin, but I would like you to keep an eye on Lazander and my… and Valerius," the queen said with a heavy sigh. "Since he fell… ill some years past, Valerius has been different, as I'm sure you've noticed. Gone are the days he would greet me with a kiss on the cheek after every mission. I put it down to my being so hard on him—I can hardly expect the affection of a mother when I demand he speaks to me as a queen." She spoke matter-of-factly, but Thaddeus felt her fingers stiffen in his fur—his withdrawal from her had hurt her more than she would admit.

"You demand the same of the king, yet his affection for you is as clear as a blue sky," Thaddeus said, nudging her hand with the top of his head.

The queen waved a hand in gentle dismissal at her spymaster's words. "Make sure you examine Lazander's report—thoroughly. He went to lengths to describe everything Valerius did wrong, yet spoke little of his own actions. And nothing smacks of guilt like a pointed finger."

Thaddeus dipped his head. "If one of them is lying, my queen, I will uncover it. You have my word."

***

"Tattling to my mother," Valerius said, lip twitching in a forced smile. "How could you, Lazander?"

The red-haired knight drew up by Valerius' side—their outfits startling in their contrast. Valerius dressed in darker tones while a rich forest green highlighted

Lazander's fire red hair, and the worn leather boots on his feet spoke of many a morning mucking out his personal stables. It was a job Lazander insisted on doing if he was present on palace grounds, refusing many a confused stable boy—he claimed taking care of his horses brought him as much joy as camping under the night sky.

Valerius had no such inclinations.

"Respectfully, my lord, I did no such thing," Lazander said. "I filed a report. One you failed to submit."

"I found no need. Eternity is safe—that's report enough."

"We still have no insight into who kidnapped Lady Eternity—Magnus, Zara, or a third party, nor how they accomplished it. If someone is aiding Magnus, especially someone powerful enough to infiltrate the Gallowed Temple—a place guarded by enough magic to keep an army at bay—we need to find them. Who knows what we might have missed that the queen—"

"Bloodied Void, Lazander, do you ever tire of getting down on bended knee and kissing my mother's feet?" Valerius snapped. He immediately wanted to take back his words—he had been careful for so long. He needed to keep his temper in check.

Lazander pressed his hand to Valerius' chest, and the knight stopped in place—more from surprise. Outside of training sessions, Lazander had never laid a hand on him.

"You should have consulted with me before throwing Zara to her death. Who knows what we could have learned."

Valerius shook his head—he needed to quash this, *now.* "You saw her at the castle—her power, her viciousness. She would have eaten us both alive before we made it back here."

"I think you and I saw very different things, my lord." Lazander's voice was cool, but a rare flicker of anger lit up his eyes. Beneath that something smoldered closer to the bone.

Disappointment.

"Then it is good I lead the Gilded Knights and you do not," Valerius snapped, breaking eye contact first as he pushed Lazander's hand aside. Head bent; Valerius did not look back as he strode away. Nor did Lazander follow him.

***

Lazander watched his leader walk away without a backward glance—his every step laced with anger. Anger Lazander didn't understand.

With a sigh, he began to pace as he ran through the events of the previous night once more—anger stirring in his chest. How Valerius refused to let Lazander fight on the roof, claiming he needed to stay flying above with Galora. How Valerius spent his time cutting down sucklers, enemies he could have felled with a single blow while Magnus was mere feet away. How Valerius had been prepared to let the mage leave with Lady Eternity—a death sentence in Lazander's eyes.

It was maddening, watching such a blatant disregard for their mission, for Lady Eternity's *life* from afar. When he'd written his report, he'd done what he could to be factual—hoping the queen would see the pattern he did. Yet she'd been sidetracked by Valerius' unfounded theories of personal assassins. He couldn't blame her. While she made a point to give Valerius a hard time, nothing could change the fact that he was her son—of *course* she was going to investigate his claims. Not to mention with war threatening, all her energy was focused on resolving things peacefully with Evergarden.

That didn't make this any less frustrating.

He should just leave it, he told himself. He'd written his report and made his arguments. He had to trust in his queen, and in her spymaster—whoever her mysterious right-hand might be—to see the rest of this through. His job in this was done.

So why were his instincts screaming that something was wrong?

It had been just over a year since he'd donned the armor of the Gilded, but from his first day in the Ivory Keep, he'd thought the dark-haired knight very different to the hero he'd once idolized. The leader of the Gilded was aloof and at times cold— he bunked separately from the other knights and was prone to disappearing for days on end, something Gabriel and Marito had assured him was normal. Yet despite these oddities, Valerius had never done anything to make Lazander question his loyalty.

That word "loyalty" stuck in his head. With it came questions he'd been trying to push aside. Questions about whose side Valerius was really on. And what, if anything, could Lazander do about it?

He could speak to his fellow Gilded, Gabriel and Marito, and see if they'd noticed anything. While Gabriel was clearly frustrated with their leader at times, Marito was harder to read—the joyful, booming knight was never anything but cheerful.

He sighed, rubbing his temples. He was a knight, not one of the spymaster's shadows—and for good reason. Who was he to go against the darling of the Gilded?

"Are you well, sir? Can I get you something from the kitchens?" a small voice asked.

Lazander looked down to see a servant boy, no older than ten years. "No, I…" He frowned, looking out the window at the sun as he approximated the time. He glanced back at the boy, his brow furrowing.

"Shouldn't you be in school?"

The young boy immediately looked away, guilty. "I, uh, I had some jobs I didn't get done in time yesterday, so…"

Concerned, Lazander bent down to his level. Voice low, he asked, "If your duties are affecting your school work, I can speak to the head servant?"

"No, no, sir!" the boy said, turning pink. "I-I…" Flustered, he finally managed, "I took a nap in the barn yesterday instead of finishing my work. I'm sorry. Please don't tell anyone."

Lazander felt a smile tugging at his lips, but he schooled his expression into one of gentle admonishment. "Did you know I used to be a servant?"

The boy's eyes went comically wide. "What? Here?"

"No," Lazander said. "In Freyley, a neighboring kingdom. As part of a peace treaty we signed many years ago, my family, among others, agreed to settle here in the capital. Freyley welcomed some of your civilians and even nobles too. I grew up in a castle just like this and joined your army when I moved here."

"But you're a *Gilded*."

"I am—the first from outside Navaros. And despite the fact that I wasn't born here, or I'm not a prince, or a noble, or anything like that, I was able to become a knight. Do you know why?"

The boy shook his head.

"Because I worked hard to get both my lessons *and* my castle duties done. And while there's nothing wrong with the occasional nap in the barn—I did it myself." Lazander smiled as the boy finally met his eyes, astonished at the knight's confession. "The castle makes time for your schooling for a reason—try not to skip it again, all right?"

"Yes, sir. I won't, sir."

"Good. Now, go on."

The boy nodded but made no move to leave. He wrung the end of his tunic to near shreds with nervous fingers. "Sir, I…"

"Yes?"

"You're my favorite knight."

Before Lazander could reply the boy took off at a blistering pace, tearing around a corner and disappearing out of sight.

Lazander smiled, his heart feeling warm and full. It was such a small thing, the boy's words, but they chased away his lingering doubts.

He was a knight, that boy's favorite knight in fact. A knight who had followed orders and merely watched as Valerius fought Magnus—ignoring Eternity's cries for help. Who had allowed Zara the Fury to be thrown to her death.

Who was tired of turning a blind eye to Valerius' strange, and increasingly bizarre, actions.

He had a duty to protect Navaros, the kingdom he called home. And if that meant investigating the heir to the throne, then so be it.

Fresh resolve in his heart, he left to speak to Gabriel and Marito.

Chapter Twenty-One

The mirror shattered beneath Valerius' fist, shards splitting the skin of his knuckles. With a roar he spun, grabbing a beautiful ceramic vase, a gift from a noble for saving his son, and threw it at the stone wall—shattering it instantly.

It wasn't enough. Not nearly.

Valerius drove a fist through his armoire, a piece carved over a hundred years before. He easily punched through the ancient wood, yanking boards out with his hands as he reached for tunics, shirt, and trousers—tearing and ripping them wildly.

He didn't stop until his private chambers were a broken mess—not even his bed survived his fury. He'd drawn a small blade from his left boot, stabbing the mattress until feathers covered both him and every available surface in the room.

At last, long exhausted, he lay on the floor—panting.

He'd hoped the destruction would make him feel better, but all it had done was leave his knuckles bruised and bleeding, his chest heaving, and his eyes prickling with tears of rage.

He'd come so close—so painfully close.

He closed his eyes, easing into the Calamity System as he summoned its Menu.

It was never far, the Menu. When he'd first arrived in this world, he'd needed to fall asleep in order to summon it. Now all it took was a stray thought and it appeared. Like it was pasted to the inside of his eyelids, always watching—always waiting.

Even after all this time, the System still amazed him. His fellow Gilded had to push their bodies and minds to the absolute limit to improve themselves. The years of training it took for Marito to use his famed ability *Heroic Strength* had left deep scars on the giant's back and torso and was done in service of a precious few minutes in which he was strong enough to tear metal.

Valerius had to suffer no such training.

The Calamity System gifted him a similar ability, *Iron Strength,* after he'd killed a group of falslings from the Moonvale Mountains at its behest. An ability he had complete and instantaneous access to in mere seconds.

While Marito had to be careful not to overexert himself, relying on instinct and experience to navigate each fight, Valerius had a stamina and mana bar in the corner of his screen that told him everything he needed to know.

Then came the Inventory. He'd collected so much since he'd arrived in this world—from weapons to elixirs—that it needed almost endless scrolling to reach the end. His fellow knights had to pack carefully for each mission, using intel from the spymaster to gauge what they might need.

Valerius could summon whatever he needed.

His class was displayed on another tab. He was a knight—technically speaking, at least. Knights relied on the physical in order to fight and spent years building up a resistance to magic. Valerius recalled watching Lazander step into Gabriel's shadows. The mage would try to crush Lazander's body through an overwhelming force of mana, only stopping when Lazander called out—pushing every time to last longer. Marito would simply sit in the shadows until Gabriel's magic expended—a contest of wills between the two friends. Occasionally Marito would bring a book of poetry with him, spouting his favorite lines from the darkness to the increasingly frustrated mage.

The upside of this was that knights could withstand magical spells and abilities that could kill a regular human. It did little good to send a troop of knights against a mage if a single spell could explode them from the inside out. The downside was that they could use no magic—and healing potions and spells were much less effective on them.

The same was true of Valerius. When he'd first arrived, at least.

He'd been here so long, had finished so many quests, reaped so many rewards, that he was no longer bound by the rules of this world. The Calamity System and its branching skills allowed him to wield magic knights could only dream of. He would never be any match for a true mage, but he didn't need to be. His opponents never expected him to shove a flame-etched hand in their faces—and their surprise cost them. Dearly.

The System was a tool. A guide. A shortcut.

One that had a price. A price Valerius paid all too often.

He sighed, a fresh wave of dread punching him in the gut as he reached the Quest tab.

"*Summon Eternity,*" was all it read.

He'd turned those words in his mind over and over again. What did this blasted game want him to do? How could he finally get out of here? How could he get home?

When he'd figured it out, he didn't leave his chambers for three days. Marito had appeared with hot soup and a big speech about how a knight had a duty of care to his mind as much as his body, and how he applauded Valerius for taking this time. Gabriel had stuck his head in and said, "Let us know when you're done." Even Lazander, despite having only been with the knights for a few months, had shown up with a traditional Freylen stew and an offer to come riding with him some evening.

He didn't tell them, of course. How could he? He was supposed to follow the *Knights of Eternity* opening scene and help orchestrate the kidnapping of the realm's darling—Lady Eternity, Gallow's Chosen, the voice of the God of Judgment, the creator of Champions. And then…

Valerius dug his hands in his hair. Even after all this time, he could barely think it—let alone say it aloud.

The fact at hand was that if he wanted to leave this world, he had to do it. If that meant choosing between himself and Eternity…

Well, he chose himself.

Then Zara the Fury turned traitor—and ruined everything.

On the night Eternity was kidnapped, it had taken him time to disable the Gallowed Temple's spells and intricacies. Killing the guards was child's play by comparison (Eben, who loved feeding the temple's stray cats. Fyodor, who always smelled like baked goods fresh out of the oven. Triana, who barely spoke but always had a smile for Valerius). The stone bloodied, the temple silent and defenseless, he had stood at its doors—waiting.

The wind picked up, becoming hot and suffocating as it whipped around him. He felt a whisper of violence on the wind—a threat. When she stepped out of the darkness in front of him, she stood as if she'd been there the whole time.

Zara didn't even pause—she simply smiled that vicious little grin of hers, eyeing Valerius' blood-spattered armor as she sauntered toward him. Her dark hair was nearly lost against the midnight sky while her golden eyes shone with deadly promise.

His hand had instinctively drifted to his sword, but she made no move to unleash her infamous talons. Instead she leaned forward, kissing him gently on the cheek.

"Good boy," she whispered. Her exhalation was hot on his skin, and she smelled like the night itself.

It had taken his breath away.

They'd never spoken before this. Neither Magnus nor Zara knew he was planning to help them, yet the Fury took it all in her stride. When Zara left the temple with an unconscious Eternity under her arm, giving him a little finger wave as she vanished into the night, he was shaken by her confidence. Her *ferocity*. He saw in her a kindred spirit—someone who rebelled against their fate. Someone who was willing to fight to the death for what they were owed.

Yet she stayed with Magnus—a slimy toadstool of a man who, if he hadn't been so pivotal to the game's success, Valerius would have killed long ago.

When the door to her cell had opened in Magnus' castle, and Valerius met her once more, he saw a very different Zara the Fury. Gone was the beautiful, tempestuous force of nature. Instead a begging, weeping bundle of fear cowed before him.

Just like that his admiration for her vanished like smoke in a strong wind. She was weak like everyone else. *Disappointing.*

He dismissed her—and it had cost him dearly.

Hovering above Ashfall estate on Lazander's pet dragon, Valerius could scarcely believe his eyes. Magnus, his arm burned to a crisp, looking fit to murder the world while Zara and Lady Eternity stood—side by side.

It was confusing, at best, as were the tears in Zara's eyes as she pleaded her innocence. But she'd survived years at Magnus' heel—that would make anyone a hell of an actress.

Throwing Zara to her death had been a last-ditch effort to mitigate his failures. The Calamity System wouldn't care—Eternity was safe. The queen would restore peace to Evergarden and Navaros. Everything was in ruins.

Failure had a price. One the Calamity System was quick to remind him of.

When *Knights of Eternity* hit the arcade scene, it was renowned as a punishingly difficult game. Nothing he'd experienced playing it, however, could have prepared Valerius for the harshest part of this world.

The penalties.

He had suffered many, from minor irritations such as items being deleted in his Inventory to being stripped of his armor and dumped in an alien desert.

He still had nightmares about the heat and the sand and being so thirsty he could *hear* his blood moving through his body. No doubt the price for failing this—his most important quest to date, would be even greater.

Covered in goose feathers, collapsed on the floor, exhaustion tugged at him.

He could fight it no longer, he knew. Better to give in now and pray he had the strength to survive whatever the Calamity System had in store for him.

Fists clenched, he let himself fall into a deep, fitful slumber.

***

A thud pierced the darkness of an unpleasant dream. It was the same he had every night. He was burning, flames flickering along his skin as he sank into darkness. A voice screamed in the distance, and he kicked out—frantically trying to reach it.

He awoke, as he always did, just before he could reach it—drenched in a cold sweat.

"My lord, are you all right? I can't—I can't open the door. Is something blocking it?" a panicked voice called out.

Valerius rubbed his palms over his eyes, the sunlight piercing his windows befuddling him. He looked down to see he was still in the Ivory Keep—albeit fully dressed and covered in goose feathers. He ran his hands over his body—two hands. Ten fingers. Two feet. Two ears. Ten toes. Two eyes.

If the System had taken a body part, it was nothing he was aware of. He opened the System Menu, scrolling through his tabs—everything seemed to be accounted for. The Quest tab, and the words *"Summon Eternity"* remained unchanged.

"My lord?" came the voice on the other side of the door—a servant. Which servant, Valerius didn't know—he had long stopped trying to keep track of them. The smashed armoire had collapsed to one side, blocking the door. The servant rattled the handle, twisting the knob frantically. "I'll summon the palace guard—hold on."

"I'm fine," Valerius called out as he stared around the room in confusion.

"But—"

"I said I'm fine! Leave, now."

A weighty silence greeted his words. He heard a shuffle as footsteps hurried away from his door.

"What in the hell?" Valerius muttered, scrambling to his feet.

He'd failed the quest—he knew he had. So why hadn't the System punished him?

A jolt shot through him as text, bright red and bold, appeared before his eyes in a pop-up he'd never seen.

A NEW PLAYER HAS ENTERED THE GAME.

"*What?*" he barked, but the text simply faded—leaving an afterimage of light against his lids.

Thoughts chased each other around Valerius' mind—the who, the what, the why of it all simply overwhelming. But he knew, even as he tried to sort through it all, that one thing was indisputable.

This changed *everything.*

Chapter Twenty-Two

Fragments of dreams drifted before my eyes. I vaguely recalled the words "Tutorial Failed" and boxes of text with a gold border. Did I see the word "Menu"? I frowned, grimacing as something pressed against my cheek. Something pointy and increasingly irritating.

The light blinded me as I cracked an eyelid.

"Why are you on the ground?" a singsong voice asked.

I tried to hold a hand up to block the sun, but my right arm wouldn't move. Panic setting in, my eyes shot open—immediately closing again as noon day sun flooded my vision, burning my retina. I groaned.

"Why are you making that sound?" the voice asked. Something poked my cheek, and instinctively I growled—a low sound that warned of teeth and claw.

I heard a shuffle of feet, and then silence.

"Are you kin?" the voice asked, only slightly less singsong than before.

I tried to move my left arm. A painful burning sensation started at my shoulder and shot through to my fingers, which twitched feebly. I tried my legs next, they were stiff and frozen. The burning in my shoulder moved from my chest to my hips, then settled in my legs, tiny, red-hot needles pressing into my flesh.

"Hel—" I started, but the sound ended in an agonized hiss. My brain could barely function in a fog of pain, but I knew one thing.

I was hurt. I was hurt very, *very* badly.

A face appeared above mine, blocking out the sun. It was covered in freckles with a shock of curly black hair. Eyes, brown and wide-eyed, stared down at me. A kid—likely eight or nine. He held a stick in one hand—ready to poke me in the cheek again.

"Are you hurt?" he asked.

I managed to twitch in a passing of a nod.

He looked around, uncertain—clutching his stick to his chest like a weapon. Frowning, he looked into the distance, suddenly looking much older, before turning back to me with a decisive nod. "Wait here," he said, vanishing from view.

I desperately wanted to call out—to beg him to come back, that I didn't want to die alone, but the words caught in my throat, choking me as my vision blurred. In seconds, his muffled steps were mere echoes.

I must have passed out again because when I awoke the light had dimmed, my eyes more at ease in the creeping dusk. The pain was still there, holding my limbs in a vicelike grip, but it had dulled slightly, lingering on the edges like a threat. An image lingered in my mind, tugging at the familiar.

That word again: "Menu." A blocky black font at the very top of a screen. Tabs that said "Inventory," "Spells and Abilities," "Quest," among others. Each was edged in a distinctive gold trim that finally clicked in my fog-addled brain.

Why was I dreaming about the *Knights of Eternity* pause screen?

A howl in the distance, sad but fierce, broke me out of my reverie. A primal fear shot through me, my heart speeding up as adrenaline flooded my broken body. I felt a whisper of recognition at the sound, but the fear overrode it—instinct screaming I needed to hide, to get away, but I couldn't run. I couldn't even move.

Slowing my frantic breath, I tried to reason with myself.

Whatever howled isn't close. Figure out where you are, then make a plan. A plan that needs to make sure you don't get ripped to shreds by something huge with claws that—

Wincing, I forced my head back—pain sidelining panic.

I was lying on a bed of leaves that had grown to mulch beneath me, cold wetness creeping through the thin cotton of my tunic. Every inch of me touching the ground, from the back of my head to my legs, was completely soaked through. As I shifted, I felt something hard and cylindrical pressing into my lower back, lifting my stomach and chest off the ground. I grimaced, wincing as I turned my neck to one side, ignoring the creeping numbness up my spine.

A branch the size of a small tree was wedged underneath me. One side narrowed to a fine point, small branches splitting off it into crimson-tinged leaves. The other side was twice as wide as I was and splintered from where it had snapped off at the trunk.

To break one that big I must have…

The thought trailed off as I looked up.

The trees above were gigantic, some the size of twenty-five-story skyscrapers. They were a deep, nutty brown, their branches ending in crimson and violet leaves that had grown so thick, they had formed a roof above the forest floor. Tendrils of the night sky broke through the canopy above, but a hole directly above me allowed an unimpeded view of the stars. The hole was large—like a giant's fist had punched through.

Or a video game villain had blasted through it after being thrown from a dragon—by the knight she had desperately wished would save her.

Broken branches and snapped twigs dotted every tree I must have hit on the way down. It was a clear line of destruction at the end of which I lay.

When I had leapt from the castle walls, Eternity passed out in my arms, I'd had a brief, mad idea to grab a tree and slow our fall. It had been ridiculous, I knew, but that was because I'd thought I couldn't save us both. Looking at how far I had fallen now…

I should be dead.

I took a deep breath, more to calm myself, but the action made my nose come alive with the scents of the forest. As if on cue, my ears tuned in as well, and I was suddenly flooded with information.

Tithe of Beasts Activated.

I could hear a small six-legged animal scurry mere feet from me, its tiny claws gripping the soaked leaves for traction. My nose caught an acrid scent as it cocked a leg, urinated on a nearby tree—the words *"warning" "stay out" "territory"* zipped through my mind at the smell.

A staccato snap of feathered wings made me flinch, the sound impossibly close. When nothing crashed into my face, I cracked open an eye—the night sky remained quiet and still. Focusing in on the noise, I realized the bird was about twenty feet southwest of me.

All this information came to me in an instant, my mind nearly overwhelmed with the hundreds of sounds and scents pouring over me like a tsunami.

Something huge and heavy cut through my confusion. The sound of its footsteps, the snort of its breath in the cold of the night demanded my attention— my *fear*. My nose wrinkled at the unfamiliar stench. Blood, fear, and urine clogged my nose, making me gag. The beast howled, the tinge of sadness I'd heard earlier gone from its cry. Now, I heard only a warning.

Stay away.

Despite its size it moved gracefully, paws pressing against fallen leaves with the barest crinkle. My heart sped up as it edged closer to me. Lost in the darkness of the night, I frantically scanned the shadows.

Stay away, it growled, coming closer.

Stay away.

I could hear nothing else. No snap of wings, no scurry of claws. The forest was deathly quiet, aware that a predator walked among them.

I couldn't breathe, couldn't think—I could only stare into the darkness, eyes jumping at every dark outline, every twitching leaf.

Then I saw it.

Eyes.

White. Staring. Unblinking.

"There!" a voice called out from behind me, the same singsong from before. "I told you, I told you!"

The thud of hooves, the snap of reins—in an instant, the deathly silence of the forest was broken, and it came alive. Wings snapped, claws scurried, and the eyes vanished—bleeding into the shadows.

"Gallow save me," a woman's voice called out. A horse neighed as she yanked on the reins, stopping some distance behind me. I couldn't see them, but I could smell them. They both smelled of a harsh, almost antiseptic stink of soap that made my nose wrinkle, the scent blocking out everything else.

I heard the woman's heart beat as she jumped from the horse, a child's small feet running toward me.

A freckled face filled my vision, smiling. "Are you dead?"

"Hrrrk," I managed.

The child beamed in delight. "She's not dead!"

"Waylen, of all the stupid, reckless—get away from her, now!"

There was a scuffle of fabric, and I managed to turn my face just enough to see a woman pulling Waylen back. I stifled panicked thoughts, my head whispering that they were gonna leave, that the monster was going to return. I could only imagine what I looked like to her, lying half dead in the leaves.

Be calm—show them you're not a threat. Do not *panic and make claws erupt out of your hands. Stop thinking about your claws. Stop. It.* The woman was pale, her face lined by exhaustion but not age. At a guess I'd put her in her late twenties. Her dark hair was tied up in a loose bun on the top of her head, tendrils falling around her ears. She had large, brown eyes, the very image of the boy Waylen's, and a smattering of freckles. One look told they were related, a sniff of the air confirmed it—the same soap, the same household.

"I'm not…" I grunted, every word was an effort. "… gonna hurt…"

It was all I could manage before my head dropped of its own accord, exhausted.

"See? She's a friend," Waylen said, gesturing to me like I'd made the most convincing argument he'd ever heard.

"Use your nose, Waylen! You ever smelled anything like her? Her scent is all over the place. She isn't right—not by a long shot."

"So?" Waylen countered. He gripped her hand, and although he was looking in my direction, his eyes had glazed over—lost in a memory. "Lukas wasn't right either."

I didn't understand the argument, but the boy's words clearly had an effect on her.

"Waylen, you are your father's son, and it's going to be the Gallow-damned death of me." She sighed before narrowing her eyes at me. Pushing Waylen behind her, she stepped forward cautiously. "Who are you?"

I opened my mouth to say Zara but stopped. I had no idea if she'd heard of the Fury, but if she had, she would go running into the night.

I didn't have to go by the name Zara anymore, I realized. I could go by my own name—my real name.

"I'm…"

I froze. A white, blank space in my mind.

"My name is…"

I searched wildly for it—hoping for a hint, a shadow of who I was.

I found nothing.

I ran through everyone else—Noah, my nephew. Clara, his mother and my sister. Our mom's name was Margaret. Mr. May, my principal. Mr. Gord the PE teacher. Jacobi. Adrian...

Neighbors from dozens of apartments, classmates whose eyes I never met, teachers who barely glanced my way—all of them came to me one after another. Their faces clear, their names visible.

So why couldn't I remember mine?

"Tell me who you are, or I'm leaving—now," the woman said, already backing away.

"I don't..." I called out feebly.

What was my name? What was my name?

"I don't know."

"She looks scared," Waylen said. He didn't mention the tears that were running down my cheeks.

The woman paused, looking from the horse and cart behind her to where I lay.

"Please," was all I managed before she blurred with fallen tears.

"Damn it all," she muttered. With a start, she faced the forest. "If this is a scam, or some kind of ambush, you lot should know two things. One: I haven't two coppers to rub together, so this is a waste of your time. And two: if you lay a finger on us I will rip out your throat with my *teeth*."

The forest was silent at her fierce proclamation. She nodded—satisfied. "Waylen, grab the tarp."

Chapter Twenty-Three

It was dark—the glowing darkness of an arcade screen in a poorly lit arcade. I saw the golden box of the Menu—clearly this time. I hadn't been mistaken before—it really *was* the pause screen of *Knights of Eternity*.

The Menu shifted, moving to the Spells and Abilities tab. I was struck by the sheer number listed there, even though most of them were hidden behind a black box. I realized with a start the name at the top of the screen—Zara the Fury.

Wait, was this me? Were these Zara's spells and abilities in the game itself—something I could never see as she wasn't a player character? Or were these what I could do while in Zara's body?

A pop-up menu appeared, the text red and flashing.

TUTORIAL FAILED.

PENALTY INCURRED.

A tutorial? Penalty? What in the hell was…

As quickly as I read the pop-up, another appeared. The text was half the size and white against a black background. It began to scroll through a series of bullet points so quickly I only caught snatches.

Escape Magnus' prison without assistance—FAILED.

Leave unnoticed—FAILED.

Trigger no magical traps—FAILED.

And countless others. Soon all I could see was the word "FAILED" over and over again.

"PENALTY INCURRED" flashed on the screen once more as the Menu shifted back to the Spells and Abilities tab.

From the list of abilities, *Blazing Whisper* was selected—the controlled explosion that had let me escape my cell.

A box with the word **DELETE?** appeared, the words **YES/NO** flashing beneath it.

YES was selected.

"No! No, stop!" I cried out, but no words sounded.

ABILITY DELETED.

The screen repeated the action, selecting *Piercing Sight.*

ABILITY DELETED.

I watched with growing horror as several more flashed, all fire-based skills I hadn't heard of, let alone used. Each time they were selected for deletion, the cursor chose **YES** with painful deliberation.

Until finally it rested on *Inferno*—Zara's infamous tower of flame and rage. It had trapped Magnus in its center, burning his arm to mere kindling with barely a thought.

DELETE?

"Please, stop—stop!" I silently pleaded.

ABILITY DELETED.

The cursor finally stopped its slow annihilation of Zara's Spells and Abilities tab, and I could only frown in confusion at the screen. What was going on? Was this a dream? What did—

A bright gold box appeared, making me jump. Trumpets sounded—a pixelated noise that echoed as if through ancient speakers. Golden balloons dotted with sparkling confetti bordered the new pop-up.

NEW QUEST AVAILABLE.

WOULD YOU LIKE TO PROCEED?

Beneath it were the words **YES** and **NO**. I froze, unsure of what to do. I tried to reach out, trying to touch the Menu, belatedly realizing I had no hands. Or body.

Instead I thought the question, *What happens if I say no?*

The screen flashed its answer.

TERMINATION.

I flinched—that wasn't much of a choice.

Yes—proceed.

NEW QUEST!

STOP AERZIN.

No other text appeared. No explanation or option for further clarification.

What? What does that mean?

STOP AERZIN flashed on the screen.

Who is Aerzin? I thought.

The quest flashed again, more rapidly. If I'd had hands, I'd have dug them into my hair in pure frustration.

The edges of the screen began to fade into darkness.

What's going on? What is this? Who—who am I! No, wait!

***

I awoke with a gasp—flinging a handout as I reached for the Menu. A blanket immediately engulfed me, thrown in the air by my sudden movement. Pathetically I became tangled in it, thrashing madly.

Suddenly the blanket was plucked from my head, and I looked up to see the woman from before staring down at me, head cocked to one side.

"Bad dream?" she asked, eyebrow cocked in wry amusement.

I nodded, embarrassment cutting through the panic at waking up in a strange place.

The woman turned away without a word, snapping the rough-spun blanket out, then folding it in half as she crossed the room. She didn't even glance back at me, seeming completely at ease with having a random stranger sprawled out on her floor.

I subtly pressed my fingers onto the ground beneath me—feeling the rough crackle of straw. I pushed harder until my fingertips touched hard wood.

It's real. I breathed a sigh of relief, crushing a piece of straw in my fist. *This is real. You're alive. Breathe. Just breathe.*

Feeling slightly calmer, I looked around. I lay on a bundle of straw, the tarp from the wagon folded into a pillow for my head.

Above me was a thatched roof held up by thick wooden beams spotted with stray cobwebs. The woman, her back to me, tended a fireplace that had been roughly carved into the stone wall on the far side of the room. With one hand, she easily hefted a huge copper kettle from its depths, the bottom blackened by flame.

A copper pan and pot hung above the fireplace—polished to a dull shine. In the center of the room lay a battered wooden table with two chairs. Cups and plates, all chipped, were neatly stacked in its center.

I was in a cottage, a very small but homey cottage—one clearly well-loved. A sudden whiff of decay made my nose wrinkle, which I tried to hide by wiping my face. In the corner, I spotted several sacks of what must have been some type of flour and corn drooping to the floor—the crumbs within stinking of mold.

The gone-off food was at odds with the neat and tidy cottage. The stray thought vanished when I realized my straw bed had taken up at least a third of the cottage's small space. I looked around the room, searching for a bed—nothing. If I had slept in here, where had she slept? What about the boy, Waylen?

Guilt washed over me. This woman had dragged me half dead out of a forest and given me the only space she had in her cottage to sleep. She'd probably slept outside in the cold while I dreamed of arcade game menus.

"Thank—thank you," I said, eyes on the floor, wishing my tongue wasn't so useless.

She ignored me, popping the cork on a small vial and shaking a small amount of its contents into two cups. With the other, she dipped the copper kettle, hot water pouring into the two cups. "I packed the wound in your back with jesper root and bandaged it as best I could. When I checked it this morning, it had nearly healed overnight."

I shrugged uselessly, mind blanking on any possible explanation. She set the kettle on the table with a thud, glaring at me as the silence stretched on—her hand drifting to her pocket.

The air hung with a tension I didn't understand. She suddenly sighed, dropping her hand.

"Let's get a few things straight, all right?" She held up a finger. "One: I'm not the one you have to thank—that'd be my son, Waylen. I didn't want you here—he did. Don't get me wrong, I'm glad you're still breathing, but that's mainly because I don't have time to bury a body."

A slight twitch of her lip hinted that she was joking, but the steel in her eyes said otherwise.

She held up a second finger. "Two: I haven't been dubbed a saint for good reason—I didn't help you for free. I expect you to work in return for saving your skin. Is this fair?"

I thought it was a rhetorical question, but she made no move to continue. I nodded vigorously—anything to stay out of that forest with the white, staring eyes.

"Good. Can you stand?"

A good question. I started with my fingers, flexing them gently—all good so far. Tentatively I shifted to my knees, using the wall to steady myself as I stood. The room spun, ever so slightly, but slowly righted itself.

Good news—I could stand. Bad news—I felt like I had been hit by a truck… then another truck, and then tied to some tracks and run over by several trains. But I could move—just about.

Arms crossed, she nodded in approval, ignoring my audible grimace.

"That'll do. Drink up," she said, handing me a steaming cup of what looked to be tea. I took it, sniffing the contents—fruity with a hint of zest, as she grabbed her own cup, knocking it back like a stiff drink. Not wanting to be rude, I quickly followed suit. While piping hot, the tea slid down my throat with a soothing warmth. I instantly brightened—this stuff was almost as good as *coffee*.

She took our cups, setting them on the table before pointedly holding up a third finger. "And three: you've clearly got your secrets. Keep them. But if you so much as look crooked at me or my son, I *will* slit your throat. And Gallow will thank me for it." She pointed at one of the only pieces of decoration in the cottage—a creepy bird skull that had been nailed to the wall. Beneath it, a copper coin and what looked like a cup of flour lay. The woman pressed her index finger and thumb to her eyes, dipping her head to the skull.

"Got it?" she asked.

I nodded—vigorously. Who Gallow was, or what they had to do with a bleached bird skull that gave me the creeps, I had no idea. But I knew now wasn't the time to ask.

"Good. By the way, I searched you while treating your wounds and discovered we have something in common—we're both broke. So if this is some elaborate ploy to rob me, you've got the wrong mark."

The logical, rational part of my brain knew it was only fair this woman would search a complete stranger. The larger, louder, and far more dominant part flushed crimson at this woman seeing more of me than anyone but my doctor, mother, and one awkward encounter in the bathroom of a burger place (long story).

With military efficiency, the woman had washed and dried both our cups by the time I'd finished the thought and flung an apron at me. My hand snapped out of its own accord, catching it instantly. This earned a raised eyebrow from her.

"My name's Lenia by the way. Now come on—Didi is waiting for you."

Chapter Twenty-Four

Noon's sun crept across the wooden floor, banishing shadows, but Eternity hardly noticed. She knelt in the center of a small, circular room, surrounded by scraps of parchment with crudely drawn symbols. A writing desk lay beneath one window, a behemoth of a thing with a chair to match that made her back ache in minutes. Wooden shelves lined the walls, almost entirely empty of books, and a four-poster bed that could fit three of her dominated the room.

It had been decided that the Gallowed Temple was no longer "suitable" as Valerius so succinctly put it. Instead, one of the Ivory Keep's iconic towers would be her home until "further notice."

She had laughed when he had first pointed out the easterly tower, shaking her head at his raised brow. As a child, she'd grown up reading about princesses locked in towers where they spent their days waiting to be rescued by a daring knight. She'd never thought the leader of said daring knights, with his cool indifference and taciturn demeanor, would be the one locking her away.

Marito, Gabriel, and Lazander had tried to make her new home more welcoming. A haphazard selection of books lay on the writing desk, covering everything from the magical properties of Void-touched magic to springtime poems to "soothe the soul." Lazander had gifted her a stock of dried meats she had barely touched, and even Merrin, Lazander's "better half," as Marito jokingly referred to her, had joined in.

The hawk made a point to drop by when she could, proudly bearing a dead rodent in her beak. Eternity always made a show of gratefully accepting the hawk's gifts before flinging it out the window the second Merrin flew off.

She appreciated it—she really did. But it didn't change the fact she now spent most of her days in crushing, lonely silence.

With a sigh, Eternity straightened her back for the first time in hours, stretching her shoulders with a satisfying crack. Rubbing her eyes, she told herself Gallow was simply, in his infinite wisdom, testing her patience.

Patience that was steadily wearing thin.

She flipped over the parchment she'd been drawing on and started anew on the other side. The paintbrush she held was too thick for the delicate symbols she needed, but she didn't want to ask for another. Everything, from hair ribbons to prayer scroll, had to be requested and inspected before Valerius begrudgingly handed it to her. She told herself it was necessary, but that didn't make it any less humiliating.

When asking for a paintbrush and ink, she'd said it was so she could draw the Ivory Keep in all its glory. The army barracks below her—with their endless drills and sparring. The gardens beyond, which the queen still personally tended. And the Gallowed Temple nestled against the northerly wall—the towering behemoth of stone and magic that was the closest to a home she'd had in years.

It would help her feel less lonely, she'd told Valerius, making her voice small and sad. He'd gruffly returned the next day with a paintbrush, two types of ink, and half the paper she'd asked for.

Brush in her right hand, she clasped her forearm with her left—steadying her arm.

Dipping the brush in red ink, she wiped the excess against the inside of the glass jar and then carefully pressed it against the page.

The symbols were sharp and demanded precision—cutting through one another as she struggled with the thick, horse-haired brush. Her knees ached from the hardwood floor, but she sank into the pain, welcoming it even. She served the God of Judgment—it would take more than aches and pains to stop her.

She leaned back to admire her work—wincing. It was better than her last, but that wasn't saying much.

Magic was a difficult, tempestuous thing—even for Eternity, who'd been using it since she could walk. Those gifted with magic had a natural attunement to a specific art, or even a sub-division of magic. Someone talented in the elements, for instance, might only have an affinity for ice-magic. That didn't mean they couldn't summon a brisk wind or mold the earth beneath their feet, but it would be much more difficult and would drain their mana significantly.

It was why she had struggled for days with a divination spell—an area of magic she had no attunement for and only rudimentary knowledge of. Yet she was stubborn, something her mother had always chastised but secretly commended her for. And she wasn't going to let herself be defeated by a *spell*.

A thought crossed her mind, one that had lurked beneath the surface for days. If her divination spell failed, should she use her power? Should she wield the power of a god—the power of Gallow?

Eternity's life had been defined by duty. Or as the Elders of the Gallowed Temple proclaimed—destiny. Eternity was more than human—she was Chosen. She could reach across the Void and wield the power of a god.

Gallow was not the easiest god to serve. His followers could recite hours-long prayers at the snap of fingers, followed a strict diet of only a handful of accepted meats and plants, and adhered to a moral code that accepted no deviation. Eternity had followed this with ease and no complaint—for Gallow was the God of Judgment.

It was through her, and therefore through Him, that the Champions would rise—and protect the world once more from the evil that lurked along the fringes of their very existence, waiting for its moment to strike.

It was why Evergarden and Navaros had been on the brink of war when she'd been kidnapped. Evergarden accused Navaros of trying to keep Gallow's power for themselves and threatened invasion if Eternity wasn't found. Since the queen's landmark treaty a decade ago, she had been passed back and forth between the two kingdoms like a parcel at a child's birthday party. The queen had smiled warmly at her, telling her she and her Champions had been the "defining asset" of the treaty.

She'd smiled back brightly as she always did, even as her heart twisted at the thought of "her" Champions, of her life being distilled down to a mere "asset." Only a handful of the people who'd knelt before her, begging for Gallow's judgment, had passed the god's tests and become Champions. Yet she'd tried a thousand times and would a thousand more—hoping this time it would work. That this time it wouldn't fail as it so often did.

She shivered at the thought. Each failure hurt, chipping away at her soul like an artist's chisel on marble.

Annoyed at herself, she dragged the brush downward—the brush stroke thicker than she'd intended. Duty had a cost—she knew this when she'd become Gallow's

Chosen. It was a cost she gladly paid to keep millions of people safe from a monster who would crack the world in two with a smile.

Screams. Claws digging into sockets as eyes puncture. Bodies, small and large, bleeding as the sky darkens and—

Focus, she chastised herself as she touched the fine tendrils of magic, her *own* magic, that wrapped around her soul. A feeling of warmth spread through her as she pictured dark hair and golden eyes. The scar that ran down her face, one that would make anyone else look ferocious but only enhanced her awkward smile. The blush that rose up to her cheeks. The way she wouldn't meet Eternity's eyes.

Pressing her hands against the still drying paper, Eternity focused on the image of Zara.

The symbols on the page swirled, and Eternity bit back a cry of joy.

She's alive! I knew it—I knew she was all right!

The ink chased itself around the page, forming the rough shape of Zara—her hair was tied up in a loose bun. She had something in her hands and was driving it downward.

Eternity squinted, struggling to make sense of the rough, inky details. Zara drove the object downward, then made a throwing motion over her shoulder.

A shovel! Eternity realized she was using a shovel.

Wait, was she shoveling—no. That isn't possible.

Zara the Fury, the monster beneath the bed for children and bandits alike, the demon who wielded fire with the ease of breathing, who she'd seen burn a man's arm like it was kindling… was mucking out an *animal* pen? She caught a flash of a rotund creature with a curly tail near Zara's feet.

A pigpen?

Magic spent; the ink wavered—returning to the crude symbols Eternity had drawn.

She laughed aloud; she couldn't help it as she leaned back against her bed.

Eternity had spent much of her life alone. People tended to either place her on a pedestal or treat her like she was made of glass, but few and far between treated her like a person. Treated her like someone who could be as scared, lost, or hurt as anyone else. Fewer still who understood her.

Until she met Zara the Fury.

When she'd sensed the woman in Magnus' prison—a captive, like her, she'd debated reaching out. This was the Fury—Magnus' fire-wielding betrothed. It had taken days to make a crack in the *Fazim Binding* that imprisoned both Eternity and her magic. If she reached out, and Zara betrayed her, who knew what Magnus would do to them both?

However, Eternity had felt it—how scared Zara was. How alone she felt. It made Eternity's heart ache with familiarity.

Freeing Zara had taken its toll—the *Fazim Binding* had flared to life, snapping Eternity's magic back on her and leaving her drained of mana. Her last thought before she'd passed out was that she'd made a mistake—that she'd wasted her one chance of freedom.

Yet it was Zara who saved her, time and time again. Who smiled at her with awkward gentleness. Who held her hand atop the castle's barracks. It was Zara who charged her tormentor and captor with unyielding ferocity while Valerius stood back—content to let her be taken. Again.

Eternity shoved down a rare spark of anger that bordered on betrayal—the Gilded were her protectors. While she might find Valerius… difficult, he would *never* turn on her, or Navaros. She was sure of it.

So why was Zara mucking out a pigpen when Valerius had told her the Fury had refused to ride home with them, instead choosing to go back to Magnus?

Something had happened, she knew. But as usual no one told her anything—it was infuriating.

It was why, when her repeated requests for an audience with the queen had been denied, the letters she'd sent explaining Zara was an ally returned, she'd spent days trying to cast a divination spell that felt like slapping her head against a rock. The spell only worked if you'd spent a lot of time in that person's presence—and apparently being unconscious and carried around by them had counted.

There was more to Zara than people claimed—Eternity had seen it. While she might be trapped in a tower for her "protection," she was determined to figure out a way to help Zara.

It was the least she could do for a friend.

Chapter Twenty-Five

"**S**queal!"

"Look, if you just stop getting under my feet—"

"Squeaaal!"

I yelped in surprise as I jumped out of the way of an angry, scared, and very panicked pig. Sliding in the mud, it took much flailing and zero dignity to keep my balance—but I managed. Just about.

"Didi doesn't like youuuu," Waylen said in a singsong voice. He leaned against the pigpen gate, watching me intently as he had been since I'd emerged from the cottage. The way he stood and how much older he appeared when he didn't think you were watching him reminded me of my nephew Noah.

Noah… his dark hair and sad eyes. Too sad for a twelve-year-old kid. Where was he now? Was he by my side as I lay in a hospital, gripping my hand as he thought of his dad, dead only a year past, and wondered if he was going to lose someone else?

Or was I already gone—eyes glazed over on the floor of the arcade, my blood pooling about me? For the rest of his life, was that what Noah would see when he thought of me? Dead from a bullet meant for him?

My heart constricted and tears welled in my eyes. I gripped the shovel, rubbing my eyes.

"You smell funny," Waylen announced. "Why?"

He'd either missed my tears or was choosing to ignore them. Either way, I was grateful.

"I don't know—what do I smell like?" I asked, curious.

"Like one thing, but then another thing—it's weird," he said, looking thoughtful. "Lukas smelled like that too."

"Who's Lukas?" I asked, distracted. Didi was cowering in the corner of the pen, and I didn't want to waste my chance.

"My friend—he was practically a grown-up, but he didn't treat me like a little kid. He was funny. And really good at telling stories. Oh! He showed me how to skip rocks. I could only do five or six, but he could do a hundred!"

I smiled at the clearly exaggerated number. I liked kids. They were easier to talk to than adults—and definitely had wilder stories. "A hundred? That's a lot."

"Yeah. He did it with a tree once when he was mad—but it was only like two or three skips."

I laughed—this kid had some imagination. "I hope he didn't get mad very often."

"Oh, no! Only one or two times when my uncle said mean things about his mom, or the others told him he should go back to the Moonvale Mountains even though we're not allowed to go back there anymore."

I blinked at the sudden influx of details. The Moonvale Mountains? That was a level in *Knights of Eternity*—one where vicious beasts who served Magnus lived. What was this kid doing talking about it?

"Ah, Waylen—what do you mean go 'back' to the Moonvale Mountains? Did you used to live—"

His dark eyes widened in panic, and I immediately shut up. "You have to promise not to tell Mum about the tree, or she'll be mad. It was one of her favorites down by the lake—the big blue twilight blossom one."

"What? What tree?"

"The tree Lukas ripped up! The big blue twilight blossom."

"Oh," I said, thrown by the subject change. "Of course—your secret's safe with me."

"Good," Waylen said, swinging his legs over the fence. He was balanced precariously, and I had to fight not to hold out a hand to steady him.

"I miss Lukas. Lots," he said quietly. "But you're nice too."

Warmth spread through my chest. "I like you too, Waylen. But the way you're talking about Lukas… is he okay? Did some—"

Didi tore past, her hooves digging into my bare feet with a snort. I cursed, dropped my shovel, felt guilty for cursing in front of a kid, and immediately began silently ripping the pig a new one.

The pig neither knew nor cared for my cursing. She reached the edge of her small pen, skidded to a halt, spun around, spotted me, and let out a squeal of terror as if I'd just magically appeared. She tore toward me in a mad dash until she reached the other side of her pen. Thus began her cycle of spotting me, squealing, dashing with terror, repeated. Again. And again.

I was going to murder this pig.

"You done?" Lenia called; her arms full of clean clothes as she moved from the cottage to the washing line in record time. Did that woman ever get tired?

"Al-almost!" I called out, embarrassed at the sheer amount of muck and straw still left in the pen. I gripped the shovel, diving into my job in earnest. Once I'd gotten past the gag-worthy, putrid stink of the pen, I began to enjoy the chore—the rhythm of it loosening up my sore and bruised body.

Then I felt something warm and familiar brush up against my mind.

An image flashed, Eternity kneeling on a wooden floor, surrounded by papers with strange, curling symbols. She wore a white summer dress, the kink of unraveled braids left her hair curly and soft. All that remained of the deep cut on her forehead was a tiny, pink mark. A bandage on her forearm was the only sign of the fight that had nearly killed them both.

"*Eternity?*" I called out, feeling shock and relief and a surprising amount of joy at the sight of her. She was all right! I had so many questions—where was she? Was Galora all right after I clawed her? And Valerius...

I blinked and Eternity was gone—leaving nothing but an empty space where I'd felt her. Despite the suddenness of the vision, I felt no fear. Her touch against my mind was akin to when she first spoke to me in the castle—a gentle warmth framed by concern. I had the feeling that, wherever she was, she was safe—and she was checking up on me.

My relief quickly faded as doubts crept in, each sharper than the next. What did she think of Valerius throwing me from Galora? Did she agree with him? My hands tightened on the shovel's handle. And why wouldn't she? I was the personal assassin of her captor, after all.

"You all right?" Waylen asked.

I nodded, brushing my eyes roughly. I didn't know if I could stand it if Eternity looked at me the same way Valerius did—eyes narrowed in cold disgust.

Didi ran over my feet once more, her hooved feet digging into my big toe with enough force to make me shriek. Frustrated, I dropped the shovel and crouched low—hands outstretched. My feet slid in the mud, but I didn't care. I was filthy and disheveled, and my life was a mess.

But I wasn't going to let a *pig* get the best of me.

When Didi began her frantic dash once more I tackled her, sliding in the mud as she thrashed and flailed. She squealed in alarm, a piercing sound that made my sensitive ears wince, but I held her as gently as I could while still stopping her from escaping. Her heart beat frantically against mine.

"Shhh," I whispered. "I'm not gonna hurt you. Shhh."

I continued murmuring softly until Didi stilled.

Sensing victory, I brought a hand up to scratch between her ears. "There you go, that's a good girl. See? I'm not so bad."

I released her and tentatively stood, not wanting to scare her. Didi looked me up and down—snorting. She clearly wasn't happy with me being in her pen, but she was no longer terrified. Kicking a hoof into the air, she pranced into a corner I had just cleared.

I turned to Waylen, expecting applause and cries of victory, only to find Lenia instead. Her washing lay abandoned by the side of the house, the basket turned over—fresh sheets in the grass. Her cheeks were flushed, teeth bared as she pushed Waylen behind her, staring at me as if I had a machete in hand and a mouth full of steel teeth—ready to attack at any moment.

"Is…" I dropped my eyes, completely taken aback by the anger and suspicion in Lenia's face. "Should I, uh, not have done that?"

My words hung in the air, tension crackling.

Lenia shrugged, stepping away. "Once the pigpen is done, we'll have lunch." I saw a flash of something silver in her hand before she slipped it into her pocket, heading back to the cottage. My chest constricted.

A knife. She had a *knife*.

I looked down at Didi, who looked at me with wide eyes—as confused as I was. What did Lenia think I was going to *do*? I turned back to Waylen, who looked away guiltily.

"Waylen, what just hap—"

"Do you want to see my rock collection?" he said, eyes bright, singsong voice back in full force.

I nodded, knowing I wasn't going to get an answer out of him. He smiled as he pulled rocks out of seemingly endless pockets and explained he'd found this white one in the river and this one inside a bigger rock that broke and so on. The comfort I'd felt at doing chores, things I had hated back home, but were now a welcome escape, vanished.

Did it not matter what I did, or how hard I tried to help—was everyone going to look at me, look at Zara, with distrust? Suspicion?

Everyone but Eternity that was—and who knew when, or even if, I'd ever see her again.

Feeling lost, I finished mucking out Didi's pen—a much easier task now that she wasn't tearing around like a lunatic. Lenia took one look at me when I approached the cottage and handed me a bar of soap and a rough towel. "There's a river not two minutes' walk from here. Wash up. I'll have lunch ready when you're back."

She disappeared into the darkness of the cottage before I could say a word.

The awkward urge to run in after her and apologize, despite not knowing what I should be apologizing for, was soon replaced by excitement at being *clean*. It had been days since I'd seen the inside of a shower—the very thought made my skin crawl. I was suddenly aware of how itchy I was—layers of sweat, mud, and blood covered me. I took off at a quick pace in the direction Lenia had pointed.

I'd talk to her once I got back, apologize if I needed to. Mom always said there was nothing that couldn't be fixed with a chat and a cup of tea. She'd been right so far.

Lenia and Waylen's cottage, and the small enclosure it lay in, had been cleared of trees and undergrowth, but everything beyond that was a wild and tangled forest—at least until you cut through to the other side where the village of H'tar lay. Waylen told me about it, saying that was where his uncle, cousins, and even "Chief" lived. When I asked why he and his mom lived alone out here if there was a village close by, he'd simply shrugged and told me about a cloud he once saw that looked like a sad horse.

A dirt path born from use led me through a path of overhanging trees, different to the ones I had woken up beneath. These were tall and slender with vines trailing down covered in flowers stained lilac and pink. They smelled familiar, annoyingly so, but I couldn't figure out where I had smelled them before.

I slowed my pace and stood beneath the lilac-dusted branches, trailing a hand up their leaves. A peace settled in my heart. Breathing in the fresh scent, I pressed on—eager to feel clean again, knowing it would clear my head.

As I pushed through a thick curtain of lilac I gasped, my mouth stretching into a grin.

Chapter Twenty-Six

The "river" that Lenia had directed me to was actually closer to a lake. A beautiful, idyllic lake that looked like something straight out of nature documentary.

The water was as still as a mirror, broken only by the gentle splash of what I dearly, dearly hoped were just fish swimming beneath the surface. Grass gave way to stones, smoothed by the water. They pressed into my feet as I made my way to the water—refreshingly cold. At a squint, I could see the opposing side of the lake, the edges lined by a mixture of yellow and red-leaved trees (*I needed to ask Lenia what all these plants and trees were called.*)

A rush of water made me cock my head. Closing my eyes, I realized the sound of a river came off to my right where it was likely feeding into the lake. With a start, I realized I'd reached the water—my toes flinching from the icy cold. I was surprised there weren't ice cubes floating in it.

Getting in was going to be… interesting.

I looked around, straining my eyes and ears—but there was neither sight nor sound of anyone else here.

As desperate as I was to be clean, I didn't know the next time I'd be alone. I had to try something—or risk it running through my head day and night.

I thought back to Magnus' castle where I'd used flames to see through his illusions, to the towering inferno I'd summoned to trap him. To the fire that sprang from my hands, flickering into life with a stray thought.

Dropping my towel, I shook my hands off—jumping a little on the balls of my feet.

I'd dreamed of the *Knights of Eternity* Menu. I'd watched as it deleted all of my, or rather all of Zara's, fire-wielding abilities.

Time to see how real it was.

Closing my eyes, I focused on the delicious anger of the flames, how powerful I'd felt—how unstoppable. I thought of the flames that had let me burst out of my cell—*Blazing Whisper.*

"My fury is but a whisper," I said aloud. "Of the flames to come."

Silence.

I cracked open an eyelid. I stood hands outstretched, feet shoulder-width apart. I looked and felt like an idiot.

Maybe *Blazing Whisper* was too difficult—I'd never used it consciously before. But I had used *Piercing Sight* repeatedly. This one would work. For sure.

"Your lies are shadows," I intoned. "My eyes, the flames. You cannot hide from me."

I opened my eyes.

Nothing. I pressed my hands to my eyes—my skin was no warmer than the rest of me. Was it true then? Had I been stripped of the fire that had saved myself and Eternity?

A hole seemed to settle in my chest, widening with every spark I failed to conjure. I knew what that hole meant. I felt it when Noah's dad died and again when Jacobi was shot.

Grief. Though whether it was mine, or Zara's, I didn't know.

But Zara was more than her fire magic—I'd seen it. Felt it. Had shivered in awe and amazement at her strength and at the brand new world her senses had opened up to me. The scurry of claws, the snap of wings, and the chatter of animals were as deep as the words I spoke.

And just like that—the world opened once more.

Tithe of Beasts Activated.

I grinned in delight as sounds and smells rushed through me—the careful step of hooves, the crunch of greenery by teeth made for grinding, the scent of fresh water—even the acrid pong of animal droppings. Each was as unique as they were comforting.

When I had awoken in the forest and the world had opened, it felt like I'd been handed a thick, heavy-bound book, the information dense, indecipherable, and overwhelming. Now, I realized all I had to do was skim the pages to find exactly what I needed.

I blinked, and the world narrowed once more.

I let out a laugh, relief tinged by fear. The inferno I had summoned and the ancient fury that had erupted in my very soul had scared me. Terrified me, if I was being honest. The fact that my dreams were not just my imagination working overtime didn't help.

Yet knowing that not everything had been taken from Zara—from *me*, was a comfort. A small one, but still—at this point, I'd take anything.

Shaking my head, I slipped off my rough tunic and stepped into the water.

"Argh!" I cried out. The water was cold enough to *hurt*, my back arching as my arms bent at the elbow as if to ward off the ankle deep water. The thought of merely splashing some water on me and calling it a day crossed my mind. Then I looked down at myself—at the mud, and sweat, and blood—mine and Magnus'.

I charged forward before my mind could protest, diving into the depths.

Underwater the freezing pressure gripped my head, making it pound. I pushed through, eyes open as a school of fish, tiny and silver, scattered around me. I swam until my head felt like it would explode, then kicked upward, bursting through the surface—shrieking loudly.

Knowing I wouldn't get back into the water if I got out now, I did a couple of breast strokes, swimming in a small circle close to the shore. The exertion and repetitive motion warmed my body, and in a few minutes the once freezing water felt warm and comforting.

I swam back long enough to grab the soap Lenia had given me. To my surprise, it lathered in the cold water, and I eagerly scrubbed my arms, legs, and face. My skin turned red from the force of it, but I wanted it *gone*—the fear when I awoke in a prison cell. The Menu that haunted my dream—the word *FAILED* endlessly repeating. The mournful human eyes that stared at me from the sucklers' twisted faces. The blade of ice Magnus drove into my back.

Valerius—how trapped and alone in a cell, I'd *begged* him for help, this knight I'd worshipped and adored as a kid. How he'd looked at me with cold indifference and said:

"Disappointing."

The disgust on his face when he'd thrown me from Galora. Like I was small.

Like I was nothing.

I wanted it gone. I wanted it all gone.

The world blurred with tears but still I scrubbed. It was only when the soap bar in my hand had disintegrated that I stopped. I ran back into the lake—diving deep.

I swam underwater until my lungs screamed for air and then I swam some more. My arms hurt from the frantic pace, and the wound in my back ached, but still I pushed.

When I finally came up for air, gasping and crying, I was halfway out on the lake. I turned, floating on my back as I cried, shrieked, and howled—letting out everything I felt since I had awoken scared and alone in this body. The fear, the panic, the anger, all of it. My tears vanished into the lake that carried me and still I cried.

***

The sun had dropped low in the sky by the time I came back to myself, my tears exhausted. My body spent.

I floated in the lake, my fingers wrinkled and pruned but found I couldn't move. I knew I had to go back to Lenia and Waylen and that she was going to be furious with me for disappearing for hours, or worse, annoyed that I had returned at all. But while I was dreading it, my chest didn't feel like it was being crushed beneath a boulder for once.

I thought back on my time here—how I was able to speak to Eternity and even Lenia, who kind of terrified me, despite the fact they weren't on "the list." How it took mere minutes to feel comfortable around Waylen—something I couldn't have imagined back home. I still felt as awkward as an arctic seal in a desert, but I was handling this better than I could have imagined.

Well, other than the whole "having a breakdown in a lake" moment.

Was this because I was in Zara's body? Or had something else changed?

A flash of movement among the trees caught my eyes, and I turned in the water—my musings forgotten. My eyes strained for the shadow I *knew* I saw, and I dearly wished *Tithe of Beasts* made my eyes as good as my sense of smell and hearing.

The blue-leaved trees by the lake rustled, and my eyes opened wide at the monsters that lumbered out of the forest.

Chapter Twenty-Seven

The first was *huge*. Its paws were flat and wide, each the size of my head while its long talons bunched together to form pointed claws—the kind made for digging. It was covered in a reddish brown fur but for a black streak that began at the top of its head and continued down its back. Its fur looked thick and coarse, even from this distance.

It trundled along on four—no six—legs and had no tail I could see from this angle.

It stopped by the shore, shoving a long pointed snout into my dirty tunic. Abruptly it stepped back, growling low, and two more beasts emerged from the shadows of the trees, smaller than the first.

One of the shorter ones followed suit, sniffing my abandoned clothes. It barked once, a surprisingly high-pitched noise for something bigger than a bear. In a flash, it dug short, stubby teeth into the tunic, snapping its head to the side as it ripped easily.

My breath froze. I stayed utterly still, holding my body taut as I struggled to float upright. I had no idea what these things were, but they clearly had no love for me, judging by the ribbons they were making of my tunic.

One of the smaller ones stopped, raising its head as it sniffed the air, turning toward me.

I ducked underwater, instinctively squeezing my eyes shut as if that could protect me.

The breath I had taken was shallow, but I stayed underwater until my chest was on fire, my lungs crying out for air as I prayed they hadn't seen me. I tried to gently breach the surface, but my lungs were greedy. I burst upward, gasping, water stinging my eyes. I wiped them with one hand as I spun in the water, looking for the monsters, but the lake was quiet—empty.

Cautiously I paddled to shore—prepared to swim back out at a moment's notice. The beasts, while bigger than anything I had seen in my world, somewhat resembled a badger, and I prayed that meant they preferred land to the water.

Stepping cautiously I tiptoed to shore. A glance at my tunic, and I knew it was past saving—there wasn't enough cloth left for a bikini, never mind a dress.

Feeling quite literally naked and vulnerable, I crossed my arms over my chest and went to grab my towel from where I'd left it warming on a rock.

It was gone—a set of six paw prints and turned up pebbles where it should have been.

What the hell?

I was stark naked in a strange world where giant angry badgers ripped my clothes and stole my towel.

This was less than ideal.

The forest loomed behind me, the comfort I'd felt walking through it earlier all but gone. Now I saw deep shadows, perfect hiding spots, even for huge badger-monsters. I debated staying in the open, but the sky was already streaked with red and orange. If night fell, then I'd be naked, alone, *and* in the darkness.

For once, it was an easy choice.

Taking a deep breath, I let the world expand.

Tithe of Beasts Activated.

Ears trained for the footfall of a heavy step, I entered the forest. I was so focused on the darkness I completely missed the cluster of trees with trailing blue vines to my left, their petals slowly opening in the encroaching twilight.

And how, in the center of this cluster, lay a huge gaping hole of twisted roots as if someone had simply ripped one of the trees out of the ground with their bare hands.

***

There is a tension to the dark—an inky expectation. I felt it back in my real body when walking home alone at night. I felt it more keenly now with my hearing tuned to every skitter of claws, every thump of a tail.

I smelled fresh turned dirt and heard the scrape of talons as animals who thrived in the sunlight buried deep, bunkering for the night. Birds flapped, dropping insects and seeds into hungry mouths before flaring their wings, covering their younglings from sight. All around me, the forest shifted from day to night as things with claws and teeth emerged blinking—howling, cackling, cawing. Ready for the night. Ready for the hunt.

I wasn't afraid as I would have been in my old body. I felt calm, at ease even, despite my fear of the badger-monsters.

I felt at home. Or maybe Zara did. It was hard to tell.

I was halfway to Lenia's when a scent overwhelmed me—the lilac flowers from earlier whose familiarity had itched at my mind, but I couldn't quite scratch. My sense of smell now heightened by *Tithe of Beasts,* I couldn't believe I hadn't made the connection. It was the soap I had smelled on Waylen and Lenia when they'd found me half dead beneath the stars. The same as the soap I had just scrubbed myself raw with.

Bending closer to the tiny, purple petals I realized the flower's scent wasn't just overwhelming, it was actively *blocking* all other scents. While near it I couldn't smell the bark of the tree it hung from, nor the damp earth from which it sprang.

I had to back up several feet, sniffing the air in short bursts before the woody musk of the forest finally burst through. Sniffing my arm and still damp hair, I realized the soap overpowered my own natural scent too.

"Ahhhoooo."

A howl cut through the forest. One I recognized instantly.

Fear was a crackling static electricity that caused every hair on my body to raise. I focused on my hearing—the snap of wings as something sped up, flying away. The scurry of tiny feet as they hid in the high branches of a tree. The chitter of a warning.

There, the trod of something large. Something vicious. The same I'd heard as I lay, body bruised and broken. Had seen its milk-white eyes staring at me from the shadows. My muscles tensed—fingers itching.

I looked down to see my nails had lengthened a fraction—fingers not yet full talons, my body a hair's breadth from transformation. The creature in the distance growled. The same throaty call. The same warning.

Stay away.

Stay away!

My heart sped up, my claws ready to erupt. I crouched, readying to fight for my life if I—

"Mom!"

Waylen's voice brought me back, my sharpened hearing honing in on the fear and panic in his voice, despite him being on the other side of the forest. Branches whipped across my body like the lashing wind and just as easily forgotten. Charging through the forest, I abandoned all attempts of stealth. Far from the lilac flowers, I could smell the badger-like creatures. They had come down this path.

Waylen and Lenia could be in danger, and here I was standing around and sniffing the damn forest?

Furious at myself, I doubled my pace, my injured back aching, the packed wound dripping with what I hoped was residual water from the lake.

I burst out of the forest and skidded to a halt. Didi's pen had been ripped open, the gate hanging from a single hinge. The pig was nowhere to be seen. The door of the cottage had been torn clean off.

"Waylen!" I yelled. "Lenia?"

"Here!" Waylen cried. I charged toward him and the cottage.

At the door, my sigh of relief at seeing Waylen alive and unharmed vanished when I spotted Lenia curled up on the floor—her head in her hands. Waylen knelt by her side, his back to me.

"Mom? Mommy, say something!"

Lenia's laundry lay abandoned on the floor. I grabbed a sheet, wrapping it around me and tying it in a rough knot as I jogged toward them.

"She—she told me to hide," he spluttered, tears and snot clogging his nose. "I waited until they were gone but—but she won't get up."

"I just…" Lenia gasped. I could hear her grinding her teeth as she struggled to keep the pain from her voice. "I just need a minute, Waylen."

"What happened?" I asked.

"Uncle told her to come, that she was in big trouble! They said Chief needed to—"

"Enough," Lenia hissed. Waylen shut his mouth, looking distraught.

"There's… Jinny balm mixed in the cupboard. Bandages in… the one below," she managed, each word forced through gritted teeth. I rushed to the cupboard, throwing it open. I stared in indecision at the multiple jars and bottles—all brightly colored, none labeled. I hesitated, wondering which was Jinny balm when the pixelated image of a yellow jar popped into my head.

I bit back a smile as I began opening jars at random, rushing back once I'd found one holding a thick, yellow paste that stung my nose. Jinny balm—of course. In *Knights of Eternity* it was a salve from the earlier levels used to treat minor injuries. Its icon was a clay jar with a yellow top.

I grabbed a rolled up piece of cloth that would serve as bandages and knelt by Lenia's side.

"I need to see," I said, gently pulling her hands from her face. I bit back a gasp.

The entire right side of her face was already swelling, the skin shades of purple and red. A cut on her cheek welled, a trickle of blood sliding down her cheek. I knew a punch when I saw one—Mom's kitchen was a conveyor belt of neighbors and injuries, especially on a Sunday morning after a night out. This wasn't a simple punch—this was a *beating*.

Lenia tried to take the Jinny balm from me, but as soon as she got up on one forearm, she swayed. I caught her with one arm, laying her gently back down.

"Lie still," I said.

Eyes closed, Lenia had to bite her lip not to argue. With a sigh, she nodded.

***

It didn't take long to coat the wound in Jinny balm and wrap a bandage around Lenia's head. I quietly thanked my mom, who as a nurse had insisted I know basic first aid. I tied Lenia's bandage neatly, making sure it was tight enough not to unroll but not too tight to cut off any blood flow.

I picked her up easily, asking Waylen where they usually slept. He wouldn't meet my eyes as he shrugged. I looked at the straw and tarp that had been my makeshift bed. *Don't tell me I'd been right, and they'd slept* outside? The heat of the sun was warm and pleasant, but I couldn't imagine what it would be like in the dead of night.

Guilt, familiar and wearing, rose up. I lay Lenia down on my "bed," covering her with the blanket she'd just neatly folded for me that morning. I had no idea what the treatment for a concussion was—Mom's advice had always been to take the injured to the hospital at the first signs. If Lenia began vomiting or seemed in distress, maybe I could take her to the village Waylen had mentioned—H'tar. But what if the person who had done this was hightailing it back to H'tar as we spoke? Dragging her there might just make everything worse.

"Does your mom have any, uh, clothes I could borrow?" I asked Waylen, fervently hoping the answer was yes. It was either that or I would suddenly have to get very good at tying knots in sheets.

"My auntie gave her a dress thing. She doesn't really wear it. One second..."

He rooted through a small chest in the corner I had missed earlier, pulling out a forest green dress. I touched it, feeling how soft the fabric was, admiring the beautiful, embroidered flowers around the neckline and sleeves—this was clearly a gift. It definitely wasn't something I wanted to wear without Lenia's permission. I was about to ask if there was anything else when I glanced inside the chest.

A shirt and trousers clearly meant for Waylen remained. Two larger sets of trousers and two shirts were in the corner, but they had been tied with a black ribbon. Poking out beneath them was a piece of blue fabric. I lifted the shirts to find a baby-blue dress stained with tiny droplets of dark brown that looked like blood.

"Not that!" Waylen said, hurriedly. "That's mom's favorite."

I replaced it carefully, checking the rest of the chest. Nothing but scraps of fabric and undergarments were piled in the center and little else.

I hesitated, holding the green dress in my hands. I didn't want to take it, but I could hardly run around in a towel.

Waylen knelt by his mom's side with his back to me, and I changed quickly, pulling the dress over me. It fell to my knees and was soft and warm—a far cry from the rough spun tunic Magnus had dressed Zara in.

"Waylen?" I said gently. "Why was your uncle here? Why did he say your mom was in trouble?"

"If I tell you, Mom will be mad."

I nodded, sitting with my back against the wall as I closed my eyes. Taking a deep breath, I let the scents of the room take me.

The Jinny balm was overwhelming, a citrus smell that threatened to obliterate everything else. I sniffed the air, focusing on the underlying notes in the room. There was Waylen and Lenia and the soap they used.

Then other scents drifted in of two, no—three men. To my surprise, I once again smelled the same floral scent. The assailants used the same soap, but the scent was fainter and tinged by sweat as if they hadn't washed in a few days.

Something else lay underneath it all, but I couldn't distinguish it.

"There were three of them," I said to Waylen.

His wide eyes confirmed I was correct.

"Your uncle hit your mom?"

He nodded, eyes flickering to Lenia, whose eyes were closed—her breathing deep and even. "Uncle... uncle was *mad*. He thought..." He curled inward, head bowed. "Animals have been going missing. In the village."

"And he thought you two had something to do with it?" I probed.

Waylen shrugged.

I thought of the cottage door that had been ripped off its hinges and Didi's empty pen—the gate torn open. The fact that I'd seen three monsters by the side of the lake, and moments later three men had kicked down Lenia's door.

I desperately wanted to ask more questions, to confirm my suspicions, but Waylen was fidgeting with his fingernail and looking like he wanted the ground to swallow him whole.

"What happened to Didi?" I asked instead, choosing a safer topic. I'd chosen wrong. "Didi is gone? Did they take her?"

He said, eyes welling with fresh tears. "What if they hurt her? What if they *eat* her?"

"Hey, it's okay, she's going to be okay!" I said, squeezing his hand. "I promise." When he nodded tightly, I stood, brushing myself down. I had an inkling of what was going on, but Waylen wouldn't tell me anything. I didn't blame him—he was clearly scared, but I wasn't going to find out anything by sitting here twiddling my thumbs.

"Keep an eye on your mom," I said, trying my best to smile. "I'll be back soon."

Chapter Twenty-Eight

Didi was a pain in the backside when trying to clear out her pen, but she was a breeze to track. I'd rightly assumed Waylen's uncle took her—the hoof prints vanished out of the pen, and then a set of three human tracks began. But then their paths diverged, and Didi's appeared in the dirt once more. My best guess was she was carried for a while before she kicked up such a fuss that she either escaped or was simply let free.

I smiled at the thought of Didi kicking Waylen's uncle in the face before running off. It was the least he deserved.

Even if I hadn't found her tracks, her scent was easy to follow. I was taken aback by how pleasant she smelled, now free of straw and muck. It was only when I'd been on her trail for a while that I realized why—she smelled like unsalted pork. I thought guiltily of how much bacon I had eaten with relish and hoped Didi wouldn't hold it against me.

For such a small pig, she had run a hell of a distance—heading deep into parts of the forest thick with trees both ancient and fragile. Their leaves and branches intertwined to create a dappled twilight in the setting sun. I spotted crimson and ochre leaves above my head and wondered if I was close to where Waylen and Lenia had found me.

To some, the heavy trees that surrounded me might have been ominous, but I breathed in the air, feeling relaxed and at peace. The silence was one of quiet solace.

The trees grew gnarled and crowded, and I despaired of ever catching up to the tiny pig, but I finally spotted a blob of fleshy pink with pointed ears. Didi stood with her back to me, her tail rigid.

Not wanting to risk a repeat of her frantic dashes around the pigpen, I crouched low—stepping carefully toward her. A not insignificant part of me enjoyed feeling like a hunter of old, creeping up on her prey. There was a tension to the stillness of the air as I moved on all fours, my eyes hyper focused on Didi. I grew closer and widened my arms, waiting for the perfect moment to *pounce*.

"Got you!" I yelled, scooping her up in my arms—triumphant.

I expected a squeal of protest, but to my surprise, Didi buried her head in my shoulder. Confused, I ran a hand down her back and found her trembling.

"It's okay, I'm here," I murmured quietly.

What had scared her so…

I had my answer when I looked up and saw a nightmare made flesh.

It was smaller than the creatures I'd seen by the lake, but they looked like cuddly toys next to the monster that stared me down. It was long and sleek, its fur a glossy black that blended with the lengthening shadows of the forest. Fangs too long and too large for its face jutted out awkwardly from a narrow and misshapen jaw. A single line of saliva, thick and viscous, dripped from its lip.

I could hear it. Hear every breath rattle like sandpaper against flesh. Its milky eyes stared at me, empty lanterns in the encroaching darkness.

It sniffed the air once. Twice. Twisting its head left and right while it breathed deeply, nostrils flaring. It was blind, I realized as it tilted its head toward me, staring through me. But I knew it had seen me. It had smelled me. Any chance of escape had vanished the moment it had drawn breath and caught my scent.

It extended one paw, pressing it into the ground with cold deliberation as it stepped toward me. While its face was misshapen, its body carried a graceful fluidity, its inky fur seeming to draw in the little light that pierced the canopy.

Fear, primal and deep, crawled over my skin, burrowing deep into my soul. Yet beneath that I felt a spark of the familiar—of recognition. Zara knew what this monster was.

And recoiled from it.

I took a step back and it froze, growling.

Stay away.

That same growl, that same warning. But as I stepped back, Didi silent in my arms, the monster stalked forward—matching my footfall perfectly.

Stay away. Stay away!

The monster's growl grew louder, vibrating through the deathly quiet forest. I froze mid step, fear and confusion jostling for position. What did it want me to do? Stay? Go?

My legs backed up of their own volition, blood pounding in my ears with the need to flee, to hide, to pray the monster wouldn't find me. I could feel dozens of eyes of animals large and small watching us, hoping the predator would be satisfied with its new prey.

I gripped Didi tight, heart hammering as my muscles tightened and my body and mind screamed in unison.

Run.

I turned, dirt flying as I took off at a blistering sprint, praying the monster was not as fast as it looked. A roar echoed in the forest behind me, a cacophony of flapping wings and frantic claws as birds and animals alike fled.

I heard the monster take off but dared not look over my shoulder, my heart sinking when I struggled to build up speed to put enough distance between myself and the monster—I was not as quick as I had been back in Magnus' castle. Whether that was the wound in my back or the abilities that had been taken from me as a penalty, I didn't know, nor did I have time to think about it.

Instinct kicked in and I ducked to one side, jaws snapping the air where I had been a moment before.

It was faster than me. Much faster.

I spun on my heel, kicking up dirt as I charged back the way I'd come. The monster's claws skidded in the soil, snapping fallen branches as it skidded to face me—I'd only gained half a second at best. Frantic, I spotted a clump of trees planted closely together. Years of overcrowding had left them curled around one another, some bent at the middle as they struggled not to collapse—creating a small cage of fallen branches and broken trunks.

There. Run you idiot, run!

I made the mistake of looking back, nearly tripping when I saw how close it was—its eyes had rolled back in its head, jaw nearly unhinged as if it meant to swallow me whole. It snapped, near rabid, its fangs an inch from my elbow as I slid beneath a fallen branch, vaulting over another as I leaped into the heart of the overcrowded circle of trees, gripping Didi with everything I had.

It howled, driving its head between two trees as it rammed them, spittle flying from its foaming mouth. If it had simply backed up and gone to either the right or left, it could have easily caught me.

But it was too far gone in its rage.

There was a crack as a tree trunk broke, falling toward me. I dodged it easily, stepping to one side. I prepared to sprint, not willing to lose the precious few seconds my mad plan had bought, when a splash of red caught my eye.

Blood dripped from the monster, a shaft of wood from the broken tree rammed into its chest. Still, it drove forward, snapping and clawing at me—driving the branch into its chest like a wooden spear.

My talons inched out of my skin. I felt Zara's anger rise.

Strike. My fingers itched with whispered need. *Strike it down. Slit its throat. Butcher the beast for raising fang and claw against you.* The voice, the instinct, the desire—whatever it was, was nearly overwhelming.

Time seemed to slow as the monster thrashed and flailed, driving the makeshift spear deeper into its chest. Either I killed it now, or it would kill itself—either way, death was a certainty.

But then I saw its eyes, those white eyes, and stopped. I expected to see hunger, bloodlust—*rage.* I didn't expect fear. Grief.

Pain.

I didn't expect to see a human staring back at me.

I had a sudden memory of Zara chained up in Magnus' cell, ripping at her manacles with bloodied lips as she fought and kicked. How small and scared she looked.

"Stop," I said, unthinking—horrified at the blood that gushed from the monster's wound, inches from its heart.

It roared, thrashing now as it drove the shaft deeper.

"**Stop**," I roared—my voice loud and thunderous. It commanded submission and a swift death if not obeyed. I was no longer prey and he was no longer predator—he was a creature to be commanded. *Dominated.*

Vicious Command Activated.

The monster froze, panting. Its muscles trembled as if unseen hands dug into its limbs, holding it in place.

"**Get back**," I growled, focusing on the feeling of command, on the belief I had to be obeyed. My voice shook, ever so slightly, but the creature blinked its sightless eyes, backing up a single step.

Blood poured freely from the wound—far from its first. Scars and cuts crisscrossed the monster's body, creating a maze of scar tissue. Did they come from fits of rage like this, or had someone hurt it? I was surprised by the jab of pity I felt for the creature that had come so close to killing me.

"**Stay**," I said, holding up a hand as if it was an unruly dog. It crouched, bowing its head, eyes locked on me. *"Stay!"* I barked as I backed away, Didi silent in my arms. The monster whined. Then the growl began anew.

Stay away. Stay away.

I kept my eyes on it as I shuffled backward, terrified that whatever spell or trick I had managed would break, and it would charge after me once more.

A thready hope rose in my chest. It stayed put, crouched low, milk-white eyes wide and baleful as it watched me disappear into the forest.

***

I didn't show my back to the monster even after it had faded into the darkness. It was only when I stumbled through the cover of the forest and into Lenia and Waylen's small enclosure that I dared face forward.

I don't know how I'd found my way home—my nose and instinct had done all of the work. All I knew was I had just stared down a real-life nightmare and told it to "stay"—like it was a disobedient puppy. And it had *worked*.

I gently placed Didi in her pen, surprised when she nuzzled my leg. She even let out a whine when I propped her gate up against her pen.

I knew she wanted company, I desperately wanted a cuddle myself after facing down that monster, but I had to check up on Waylen and Lenia. I brushed down my new green dress, taking care to dust off the hoof-shaped dirt prints. I knew it was likely the last thing Lenia would care about, but it meant a lot that I had this to wear. It made me feel less like Magnus' puppet and more like myself.

Who that was, exactly, I didn't know. That was something I was still trying to figure out, but it was a comforting feeling nonetheless.

The cottage door still leaned against the doorway where I had left it. I picked it up, setting it gently to one side before stepping into the shadowed darkness of the cottage.

"Waylen? I found Didi. She was fine."

I deliberately left out the part about her nearly being a monster's appetizer, figuring now was not the time. No one answered, but I didn't panic. I could hear two even sets of breathing inside. One, however, was surprisingly deep and rumbled a little.

Curious, I squinted, trying to make out shapes in the darkness as I stepped over the threshold.

As my eyes adjusted, I could make out Lenia's dark head and her sleeping form still curled up on her side. But something the size of a Doberman lay next to her, it's fur coarse and thick.

I froze when I counted six legs with talons bunched together, like they were made for digging.

Chapter Twenty-Nine

The knife glinted on the table, shadowed in moonlight. The flash of silver I'd seen earlier in Lenia's hands was actually streaked with threads of blue, the wooden handle etched with symbols I'd never seen. I gripped it, feeling the spark of heat I'd come to associate with magic.

The threads of blue glowed and I turned the knife in the light, struck by both how beautiful it was and how my heart thrummed with fear at the sight. I didn't understand the reaction—I'd held knives before, well—the cooking variety. But something in me instinctively recoiled at the sight of the runed blade.

Curious, I reached out with my other hand, pressing a finger to the threads.

I nearly dropped the knife, hissing in pain. Sticking my finger in my mouth, I winced as it slowly cooled. Examining my fingertip once the pain had dulled, I saw tiny burn marks were etched into the flesh that had touched metal.

I thought of Lenia, how twice that day she'd gripped that knife, a hair's breadth from using it on me. If it burned this badly just at a touch...

I twisted it in the light, making sure to hold it just by the wooden handle. Why would she even have something like this in her house? Then I remembered the huge creatures that had ripped my tunic to shreds, and the monster out in the forest. Even something as large and as powerful as them would recoil from this, especially if it ended up buried in their necks.

A snore made me look back at Lenia, or rather the creature curled up by her side. Its six legs twitched, lost in a dream. The soft downy fur around its eyes and neck made me want to reach out and pet it—a thought that proved that even after days in this world, I had zero survival instincts.

I was debating what to do, wake Lenia or return later, when she sleepily cracked an eyelid, eyes darting to the knife I still held in my hand.

"No, don't!" she screamed.

The creature's eyes shot open as I opened my mouth to explain. It yelped, a high barking sound, paws scrambling as it caught on the tarp, struggling to find purchase. Straw flew into the air as its talons tangled in the blanket, shredding it. I backed up in surprise when it barreled past me. Lenia struggled to her feet, grasping the windowsill for balance while I held my hands in the air, knife in hand as if in surrender.

"It's okay!" I said, dropping it with a clatter. "I'm not going to hurt him!"

The creature stood in the doorway, trembling from head to toe. Unlike the red-coated beasts I had seen earlier, this one had no black stripe going from its snout to its tail. Its fur looked soft, a beautiful shade of auburn while its eyes were small and pale. I frowned. I had missed that earlier with the creatures by the lake—was its eyesight poor? Like the monster in the forest?

The creature quivered, letting out a whine as it sniffed the air.

"I'm here, peanut. I'm here." Lenia pushed past me before I could protest, wrapping her arms around it.

It whined as it cuddled her.

"It's all right, Waylen," she whispered into one of his small ears, tucked neatly into the sides of his head.

"So it's not just the men who attacked you…" I said, my guess sinking in.

"No," she said. "We're all molger, and you weren't meant to see this."

***

Waylen took some time to settle down. Lenia gently asked him if he wanted to change back, but he'd taken one look at me and shaken his head. Guilt prodded my chest—I'd scared him. Badly. He turned in a circle, taking care not to catch his claws in the shredded blanket as he lay down, Lenia whispering gently as she stroked his back.

Once he was asleep, she stoked the fire and hung the heavy copper kettle above. She said nothing as she took two chipped cups from the center, added some dried leaves from a jar, and filled them with hot water. It was the exact same way she had started the morning with me, and yet things couldn't have been more different.

"I will give it to the humans," she said, wincing slightly as she sat down. "Tea is a wonderful invention."

I was keenly aware she didn't say "you humans."

With a heavy sigh she sipped her drink while I focused on the cup in her hand, watching the steam gently twist and vanishing into the air. To say I had questions would be an understatement, but I didn't want to rush her—not after the day she'd had.

It took time, the full story, and even then I'm sure I only got a version of it. The badger-like creatures I had seen from the lake were molger and members of H'tar village—just like Waylen and Lenia. Unlike the rest of the community, however, Waylen and Lenia kept to themselves on the outskirts—maintaining several pigs for a yearly sale at the Ivory Keep.

When I asked where the rest of the pigs were, I had only ever seen Didi, Lenia waved a hand, saying it didn't matter.

The village on the other side of the forest was the molger's attempt at a safe refuge. She didn't say where they had come from, or what they were fleeing, just that this was the safest they had been in years. After all, no one could find them if they couldn't smell them.

"The soap," I said, things clicking into place. The smell of the men who'd attacked Lenia, the overpowering floral scent that curled about Waylen and his mother even now—it was all the same. My fist tightened, balling the edges of my dress. Her own *people* had hurt her.

"It's done wonders," she said, smiling sadly. "It was my husband's invention— a brilliant man when he had his head on straight. The *salily* flower is potent—it almost completely smothers any other scent. If we wash with it often enough, it makes us all but invisible. A pity he didn't live to see the good it did."

She looked sadly at the sleeping Waylen. One of his paws twitched as he dreamed. I hoped it was of pleasant things. "We're not prey, but we're far from the top of the food chain. We thrive in darkness—our eyes are weak to light. And our claws are built for digging, not fighting. We briefly tried living underground, but it's easy to spot the signs of a molger den if you know what to look for. Ironically, living out in the open has been the best place to hide."

"But who would want to hurt you? And why?" I asked.

"Kin who would kill us for territory. Or fun. Not to mention *humans*." Her fingers tightened on her cup, a flush creeping up her neck. Her words were even, but every syllable throbbed with anger. "We hide from the same monsters' humans do, but they tar us all with the same brush—calling us all skin-stealers. Corpse-hunters." She looked resolutely into my eyes, and I gripped my cup as I forced myself to meet them.

"They might try to hide their judgment behind the nicer human term, 'falsling,' but it all means the same thing—*not one of us*."

Whether Zara was human or not, I still identified as one. Ashamed, I dropped my eyes, examining my tea—cold and untouched.

"It's clear you don't want me here. So why did you save me?" I asked instead.

"I didn't—Waylen did. He's his father's son—can't look away from someone who needs help. Even if it lands him in trouble," she said, her lips turning into a sad smile. "There was an… incident in H'tar recently. A kid called Lukas was in the thick of it—only a little older than you, I reckon. Good kid—if a bit mouthy at times. The whole thing broke Waylen's heart. Nothing he could have done about any of it, mind you, but I think he hoped saving you would make up for it."

The silence drew itself out. I shifted uncomfortably, unsure what to say until I spotted Lenia studying my dress.

"Making yourself at home, I see."

"I-I'm so sorry. I wanted to take something else, but—"

Lenia chuckled, shaking her head. "I'm kidding. Besides, she'd approve. It suits you better than it did me."

"… Who?" I said, keenly aware I was wearing the nicest clothes this woman owned.

"My sister-in-law. She said that every good wife deserved a good dress. I haven't worn it since—" She winced, pressing her fingers to her temple. I moved before thinking, reaching out to her, but stopped myself—my hands returning to my tea.

"Waylen said his uncle did that to you," I said quietly.

"Enough," she snapped, eyes narrowed. "It's my turn. I caught a scent when we first picked you up, one I haven't smelled in damn near a decade. Who are you? Any hint of a lie, and I'll toss you out."

I hesitated. What should I tell her? That I was Zara? I had no idea how close or far I was from Magnus—she might kick me out the second she heard my name. And then what would I do? Where would I go?

I stopped, a wave of shame brushing aside all thoughts. Here I was thinking about how to save my own skin, when her harboring me could bring Magnus, Valerius, and half the kingdom down on their heads.

"Have you heard of…" *Why was it so hard to say*? "Have you heard of Zara the Fury?"

Lenia gasped, the chair hitting the ground as she stood up—backing away.

That was a yes, then.

"I knew it. You're a vaxion."

I blinked at the unfamiliar term. "I'm a what?"

"Why didn't you kill Didi? In the pen?"

I frowned, more confused than hurt. "You thought I was going to *kill* her? But— you asked me to muck out her pen. Why?"

Lenia looked at me like I'd asked her what color the sky was. "Because of your scent. When we found you I smelled vaxion, just for a moment, but then you begged for help. You *cried*. No vaxion would have done that—hell, they'd have slit their own throats before admitting they'd stubbed a toe. You being half dead and bawling was the only reason I took a chance. But I wasn't going to risk my *son* on a gamble."

I thought of the knife Lenia had in her hand when she pushed Waylen behind her. "It was a test—to see if I'd hurt Didi. And if I had…"

"I'd have driven my moonblade through your eye socket, straight to your brain," Lenia answered without hesitation.

"But if I'm a va—a vaxion, why haven't you kicked me out?" I asked, hating how small my voice was.

"Because nothing about you makes sense," she half-yelled. "I've heard of Zara the Fury—who hasn't? She's one of the most powerful vaxion in the world, and probably the most hated—which is a high bar, let me tell you. Hell, her own people kicked her out. She sold her soul to a mage, debased herself to his every whim. She would have ripped Didi apart and likely me too." Lenia shook her head. "And yet here you are—helping a molger with her chores. Wearing my clothes. Sitting there as meek as a mouse while I roar at you. I don't understand."

"Something... happened to me," I said awkwardly. "I've changed. A lot. I'm not that Zara anymore." I shrugged, hands raised uselessly. What little grace Lenia had given me would be gone if I tried to explain I was from a different world or I was in the body of one of a game's most terrifying villains.

"I don't know if you're spinning a lie, or if you're genuinely her—the Zara who could burn this place down with a snap of her fingers." She laughed, a low unhappy sound. "If you are, you're certainly different from the stories."

I wanted to ask so many questions—who and what were the vaxion? If a molger could change into a badger-like creature, did that mean vaxion could transform too? That *I* could? But my questions would reveal my ignorance, and Lenia already distrusted me enough.

"Morning," Lenia said finally, turning and heading back to the sleeping Waylen. She lay down, curling up on her side—facing away from me. "You're gone by morning. I'm on thin ice with H'tar as is, and the last thing I need is to be strung up for harboring a vaxion."

I nodded, then realized she couldn't see. "I understand."

I knocked back my cold tea and went outside, carefully replacing the broken door with as little noise as possible.

Settling in the grass, I leaned back against the stone cottage. The cold of the blocks was refreshing, helping clear my head as I closed my eyes, trying to sort everything I'd just learned.

Vaxion.

I rolled the word around in my mind. I'd never heard it before, yet somehow it made sense. It felt right.

I had learned a little bit more about who Zara was—who *I* was in this world. I'd known nothing about her in the game—she was there to throw fire and laugh maniacally. I'd also never given her much thought beyond trying to figure out ways to kill her.

I felt strangely guilty now at the thought.

As I closed my eyes, nodding off, I couldn't help but wonder what had happened to Zara. Why had she left home to be debased by a mage who thought her little more than a dog to be leashed?

And why had no one stopped her?

Chapter Thirty

When the Menu appeared, gold-tinged against the dark background, I wasn't surprised. Not this time.

I knew now I could only access it when I was asleep. Now was the time to take advantage—to see if I could figure out what I was doing here and how I could get home.

Home.

The word ached more than I thought it would. I thought of my mom, tired after a night shift at the hospital but insisting on having a cup of coffee with me before I went to school. Noah, eyes lighting up every time I suggested we go to the arcade.

Adrian. His name was harder to summon than the others—like he was farther away. Distant. I knew he tutored me, and I had spent many a class daydreaming about what it would be like to go on a date with him—a real date. Maybe get ice cream. But it felt like it had happened to someone else. Not to me.

I shook the feeling off, needing to focus.

Inventory—Empty. Not surprising. The tab raised questions though. What "items" ended up being counted by the Inventory—clearly not the dress I was wearing. Did the items have to be physically on my body, or could I use a type of "magic pocket" like in *Knights of Eternity*? Likely the latter, but how could I access it if I could only use the Menu in my sleep?

Another question that was part of an increasingly long list.

I scrolled to Spells and Abilities. *Tithe of Beasts, Monstrous Strength, Vicious Command* were neatly ordered at the top with several more beneath, but they were hidden by a large black bar. Frustrated, I mentally tapped on them, even tried commanding them to "Open," "Reveal," and "Show." But the black bar remained stubbornly in place. Clearly Zara had more than three abilities, but how was I supposed to *use* them if I didn't know what they were?

Annoyed, I scrolled aimlessly, struck once again by how similar it was to the *Knights of Eternity* pause screen. Then a tab caught my eye—" Help".

The Help tab in the arcade game had tips for combos and a very defunct hotline to call if you were struggling with a level. I had tried it once, and ten-year old me was gutted to discover not only was it disconnected—it hadn't been in operation for more than a month before most *Knights of Eternity* machines were recalled. The company who made them went quietly bankrupt, vanishing into the ether, despite some very dedicated internet browsing on my part.

I don't know what I'd been hoping to find in the Help tab. A way to access home? To call for help? My mind raced with the possibilities as I mentally clicked on it.

A pop-up appeared.

WOULD YOU LIKE TO SPEAK TO THE OPERATOR?

That was new. Mentally shrugging, I agreed.

I gasped as pain coated my skin like gasoline set aflame. I was in my body once more—the Menu gone. My skin burned as symbols, alien and twisted, slithered all over my skin—every breath agony as they burned me. Branded me.

I was naked, my hands and knees sliding across vermillion sand. Every breath burned me from the inside out, sandpaper on my lungs, but the symbols that melted my flesh were worse. I slapped at them frantically, trying to get them off me, but I couldn't touch them. I could only feel them sinking through my skin—straight to the bone.

I screamed, a wordless cry for help, frantically searching for anyone, anything, that could stop the pain.

The scream died in my throat when I saw where I was.

Two suns, black and burning, hung in the sky above me. I was in a desert, miles of red sand stretching in all directions, the occasional rock puncturing the otherwise flawlessly smooth plane. Even through the pain, I could feel a cruel and alien essence whispering. What was this? Another world? Another *planet?*

YoU MAy SPeak aS LoNG As YOU Can BEar thE pAIn.

A harsh, cold voice echoed throughout the desert. The burning on my skin worsened. I gasped, grinding my teeth as I fought to remember how to speak.

"Who..." I ground out. "Are you?"

ThE OPerATOR.

That was a useless question. I tried again. "Why am…" A burning began on my neck, and I slapped a hand over it, pinching the flesh tightly in my hand, trying to focus on it. "Why am I… here?" I gasped.

YoU AsKED tO SPeaK TO ThE oPERatOR.

I wanted to cry. I struggled to phrase another question, darkness edging my vision.

"Why am I… in the world of…" I hissed as the fire engulfed my cheek, creeping toward my eye. "Of the arcade… game. *Knights of… Knights of Eternity?"*

There was a long pause, and I prayed I wouldn't have to repeat the question when the voice said.

tO sUMMon EtERNITy.

I fell to the ground, cradling my head as something crawled from my cheeks to my eyes. I slapped my hands over them, gasping as my flesh bubbled, my retina frying in a pan of hot oil. I couldn't take it. But I had to ask.

"Am I… dead? Back in the real…" *Focus, focus on the question.* "Real world?"

yOu—

***

Birds were chirping. In the distance, something splashed in the lake. Tiny claws dug for grubs in the earth by my head. Didi snuffled and snorted as she rummaged in her pen.

I heard it all. Smelled it. But I couldn't move. Not yet.

I cracked open one eye, then the other. Taking a deep breath, I rolled onto my side. I had fallen face first onto the ground during the night, and imprints from blades of grass pressed into my cheek. I gingerly looked at one arm, relieved my skin was clean and unblemished—no sign of the burning marks from the Operator.

I pulled my legs to my chest, wrapping my hands around them. That world— that horrible red dessert. I had thought I'd known pain—the sigils I accidentally stepped on when rescuing Eternity, the blade of ice Magnus had stabbed into my back.

But that world, feeling my eyes cook in my sockets—my empty stomach heaved at the thought of going back there.

The Operator—another mystery to add to an ever growing list. While the voice was useless at answering my questions, one thing was clear—the Operator was the reason I was here. It had summoned me and stuck me in this body.

More importantly, it told me why it had brought me here—to *Summon Eternity*. I didn't know the specificities of it, only that it clearly had something to do with Eternity herself. But the words themselves, *Summon Eternity*, the Menu, the penalties for failing the tutorial, all of it finally clicked for me.

I had to play the game. I had to *Stop Aerzin* (whatever that meant) and move on to the next quest. There was no other answer. If this was a game, then the Operator was the designer. I had to play by its rules until I could figure out how to leave.

What other choice did I have?

I got to my knees, wincing. While the Operator had left no mark, I felt like I'd been pummeled by a cement truck.

There was a *thunk*, and a small cloth bag dropped to the ground in front of me. It was tied neatly at the top.

"We don't have much in the way of food—we tend to forage until the winter months. But that should be enough for a meal or two," Lenia said.

I nodded, shifting into a sitting position. "You didn't have to."

"I know."

"Mom, can't she stay? Didi really likes her now." Waylen ran out the door, looking from me to his mother. I smiled at his protests, happy he seemed back to his old self.

"No. She's…" Lenia paused, and I knew she was debating saying the dreaded word out loud. "Vaxion." "She has to go home—her family is waiting for her. Right?"

"Right," I said, getting to my feet. "I'm sorry for scaring you last night," I said to Waylen.

He shrugged. "I wasn't scared."

I smiled at his lie, and then turned to Lenia. I met her eyes, my heart still, my chest relaxed—my mind calm as I held her gaze. I knew Lenia held no animosity toward me—she was just doing what she needed to do to protect her and her family.

"Thank you," I simply said.

"Ivory Keep, the capital, is west of here—about ten days walk if you push yourself. Well, if *you* push yourself, you might get there in three days for all I know. Nothing about you would surprise me."

She shrugged. "Someone at the Keep is sure to be able to help with your…" She gestured vaguely to her head. I was glad at least she hadn't called me "crazy." "Push through the forest and you'll hit the main road. There's not much signage, but if you keep due west you can't miss it.

I wasn't about to tell her I had absolutely no idea which way was west, so I nodded sagely as if I knew exactly what I was doing.

"While you're in the forest though," she said, pointing at the bag, "make sure you keep using the soap."

I nodded, waving. "Bye, Lenia. Bye, Waylen." Waylen crossed his arms and refused to look at me. I tried not to smile—he reminded me of Noah when he was mad.

"Bye, Didi!" I called out as I passed the pen.

She snorted in reply.

I paused by the edge of the forest, my back to the cottage. This was the first time in this world I wasn't simply rushing from one thing to the next, that I could *choose* what to do. There was a weight to it, an expectation I hadn't been expecting.

There was also an undercurrent of fear as per usual.

Still, every day here in this new world I'd grown a little more used to this body. I'd used abilities that bordered on magic, had faced down sightless monsters—even saved a pig.

I took a deep breath as I stepped into the forest.

I can do this.

A sharp whistle sounded.

I glanced backward to see Lenia pointing to my left. "West is that way," she called.

Mortified, I raised a hand in thanks and turned sharply left.

Yeah, I can totally do this.

Chapter Thirty-One

Lazander smoothed down his dark green tunic, hands fluttering with nerves. It was just Gabriel and Marito, his fellow Gilded. They had sparred countless times, fought everything from bandits to rabid falslings. In fact, it was Marito who had first put Lazander's name forward to become Gilded, and Gabriel had seconded the nomination. Despite being here for only a year, they were brothers in all but blood—he could come to them about Valerius and his suspicions. Of course he could.

So why was his heart hammering?

He shrugged the feeling off and pushed open the library doors. A servant had pointed him here after he had checked the training grounds, stables, and the Gilded's private chambers. The three of them were housed on the same floor while Valerius had left some three years previous—requesting separate accommodation.

The library was a place Lazander spent precious little time in, but whenever he stepped into its dimly lit corridors, it took his breath away—the scent of time and knowledge enveloping him.

The walls were stacked floor to ceiling with thick spines bound in shades of wine red, sky blue, and that particular shade of yellow leaves turn in autumn's breeze. Free-standing shelves filled front to back were organized in neat rows, tiny plaques signifying their area of interest: "botany," "hippology," "runes and sigils," and more caught his eye as he passed.

He stopped instinctively by a long corridor. It stood out from the rest of the open plan library, which was dim but warmly lit by small magical fires encased in wall sconces of blurred glass. A breeze tickled Lazander's cheeks despite the fact not a single window was open. It was a quiet and shadowed place that seemed to suck in all light and noise—swallowing it whole.

A plaque simply reading "Gallow—Disciples Only" was nailed above a cordoned off entrance. He stopped, hair raising on the back of his head as he recalled the stories of Gallow he'd grown up reading.

A thousand years ago, an evil god known only as the "Tyrant" ripped the skies open and descended—flattening an entire continent with a single step. The Tyrant wanted one thing and one thing only—complete and total subjugation. When the people of this world refused, it intoned in a voice that reverberated in the skulls of every living creature.

"One year. In one year, you will bow. And you will be *grateful.*"

And thus it began.

What followed was not death, but pure, unadulterated carnage. Cities vanished overnight—a single footprint left in its wake. Seas boiled. The skies clogged with ash, blood, and decay. And at the end of one year, its proclamation came true—the world bowed, from humans to falslings, all swearing undying loyalty.

All but one woman—Eternity.

The Tyrant tried to break her. It made her watch as it murdered her family, bursting them from the inside out. It took her eyes. Her tongue. Her hands. It ripped her open piece by piece, but still she refused to submit.

Furious, the Tyrant cried out, ripping out her heart.

As she lay dying, a single star fell from the pitch black sky. It cut through the darkness and settled inside her heart—flooding her with power and light as it healed her.

A god, so impressed by Eternity's strength and courage, had descended in order to save the young woman.

Gallow was the god's name. Together, they pushed the Tyrant back, granting those brave enough to fight by their side immeasurable power. Their soldiers. Their *Champions.*

Ten years it took, but finally in a battle that nearly split the world in two, Eternity and her Champions trapped the Tyrant in the black Void from whence it came. But their victory was not without cost.

Eternity sacrificed her life for the second time—giving up her light in order to bind the god. After that day, when Gallow chose another to seek his Champions, she too took the name Eternity in honor of their savior. As had every Chosen since.

At least, that was the version Lazander was taught. He'd heard different versions—in some, the Tyrant was a towering behemoth. In others, a column of darkness. In one, it wasn't a star that fell from the sky, but a creature made of light that had been trapped in the earth—a god long hidden. However, all versions had one thing in common.

The Tyrant was not gone—merely contained. And one day, it would return.

It was a proclamation followers of Gallow took seriously. Almost militant in their faith, Lazander had always felt uneasy around the masked apostles and dead-eyed disciples. They were quiet as ghosts and nothing but polite—at times painfully so. When it was Navaros' turn to host Lady Eternity, he'd expected Gallow's Chosen to be much the same.

What he hadn't expected was a short blonde woman who was quick to smile and laughed easily. Who remembered the names of everyone in her retinue—from knight to servant girl.

Lazander smiled at the memory of her very first night in the Ivory Keep. All the Gilded (except Valerius, of course), had toasted her arrival in Navaros beneath the stars. Her blue eyes had widened as Gabriel made colors and sparks burst from his fingers, and Marito had made it his business to make her laugh until she cried. It was a delightful sound, high-pitched and contagious, and soon they were all joining in until their sides hurt, tears streaming from their eyes.

While he was happy Eternity was different to what he had expected, it had made seeing her wield Gallow's judgment all the more difficult. The first time he saw her wield his power, he hadn't been able to look her in the eye for weeks.

He shuddered, dismissing the memory as he strode deeper into the library. He was procrastinating—he had to find Gabriel and Marito.

Lazander poked around until he discovered his fellow Gilded at a table backed by windows, partially hidden by the mounting stacks of books that surrounded them.

He spotted Marito first, but that was hardly surprising. A giant of a man, he stood head and shoulders above Lazander. His twin axes were strapped to his back as always, and even from where he stood Lazander could see they were polished to perfection. Marito wore a shirt cut off at the shoulder, his huge biceps straining as he hunched over a book, the light of the window silhouetting his dark skin.

A bright smile, teeth white in the soft lighting, split Marito's face.

"Master Zander, how farest thou?" he called out dramatically. He stood, clasping the surprised Lazander in his arms as if it had been years since they had seen each other as opposed to mere weeks.

Lazander smiled and squeezed the giant back, wondering if he even felt it.

"It's a library, Mari, not a damn tavern. Keep it down," a voice called from amongst the books.

"Master Gabe is most irked," Marito said conspiratorially. "A darling mage turned down his invitation for a *rendezvous*."

"Mari, we're working on a new technique to extend the reach of my Shadows, and she asked to reschedule," Gabriel said, his dark head appearing above his books. His sallow skin was flushed, brow furrowed as he rolled his ink-black eyes at Marito.

"Your temper is short, your patience shorter, good ser. It would do you well to read less of your magic texts," Marito said. "And more poetry—poetry is the way to any heart!" Marito flipped his book closed, showing the title to Lazander—*Spring Calls in Twilight: Poetry and Prose of the Romantic Era.* "A classic, Master Lazander. I cannot recommend it enough," Marito said sincerely.

Gabriel huffed and sat down abruptly, muttering darkly to himself.

Lazander used every ounce of training—from the constant grind of the army to the hellish trials required of a Gilded—to keep the smile off his face.

It was always like this with Marito—the laughing giant who could break a person in two and the bookish Gabriel who commanded shadows with the ease of his own limbs. The two argued constantly and yet were rarely apart. Traveling with them made any excursion, no matter how dangerous, light and entertaining—if a little loud.

"Well done on saving Lady Eternity, Master Lazander. A dashing tale of knights rescuing a beautiful damsel, if ever there was one," Marito said, clapping a hand on Lazander's shoulder with enough force to make his knees buckle.

"Kindly do not refer to Gallow's Chosen as a 'beautiful damsel,' Mari. She could make you explode from the inside out," Gabriel said, eyebrow cocked as he poked his head up from his books.

"Why?" Marito asked, winking at Lazander. "Do you not think she is beautiful, Master Gabriel?"

Gabriel flushed, a bright red that began at his neck and crept up his cheeks.

"That is what I wanted to talk to you about, actually," Lazander interrupted before an argument could break out.

"About how beautiful Lady Eternity is?" Marito joked. "Happily—I thought it past time you courted the Lady. I have seen how you look at her. Although perhaps the tavern is better for such talk—we wouldn't want to embarrass Master Gabriel any further."

"N-no! It's not that," Lazander said, surprised at how flustered the idea made him. "I wish to discuss Lady Eternity's rescue. And some… unusual behavior I witnessed."

Sensing the seriousness of Lazander's request, Marito nodded, moving a stack of books from one of the many chairs Gabriel had conquered and gestured for the red-haired knight to sit. Gabriel said nothing, merely closing his own tome—waiting silently for Lazander to begin.

Lazander took a breath and began from the beginning. He described how Valerius had insisted Lazander take the estate grounds, and how he had slept, for the first time, outside the castle alongside Lazander. How he refused to search the premises further despite Lazander's insistence. Valerius' behavior during the fight—how he had wasted time on the sucklers and was willing to allow Magnus to leave with Lady Eternity. He spoke of Zara—how desperate she seemed to flee Magnus. How she was the one who risked her own life to save Eternity from Magnus.

He ended with how Valerius had thrown her to her death without an ounce of hesitation.

At least Lazander hoped she was dead. A fall from that height, if survived, would leave even the strongest man shattered in body if not mind. It was not a fate he wished on anyone.

Gabriel frowned, and Lazander could almost hear the gears of his keen mind turning.

"You may be a Gilded, but a repeat search of Magnus' castle would have yielded nothing if the magic hiding Lady Eternity was as powerful as you believe," Gabriel said, leaning back in his chair as he crossed his arms. "I likely would have been the only one who could have sensed her presence."

"So why did Valerius insist he and I search Lord Magnus' estate and not you?" Lazander countered. "Lord Magnus' prowess as a mage is hardly secret."

Gabriel's dark brows furrowed, a hand on his chin.

"Lady Eternity's safety is paramount," Marito began. "Unless I could have guaranteed I could reach her in time, I too would have likely allowed Lord Magnus to leave with her, only to ambush him at a later date. It is not an uncommon tactic."

Lazander wanted to pull his hair out. Why could they not see what he saw? Or was he simply paranoid, seeing shadowed motives in Valerius' actions where there were none?

"That said," Marito reluctantly continued, "casting Zara from your mighty steed without a word of warning is… unbecoming of a knight. We are Gilded—it is our duty to offer help to those who need it, even if they are an enemy."

"This isn't the first time Val has gone off the rails," Gabriel said quietly. He looked meaningfully at Marito, whose mouth twisted in disapproval.

"Digging up skeletons is hardly useful," Marito said.

Gabriel cocked an eyebrow. "Not if they were never buried to begin with."

Lazander desperately wanted to ask what was going on, but he sensed if he interfered now they'd both change the subject. He kept his peace as the two Gilded stared each other down. Marito broke first.

"Something… happened to Valerius a number of years ago," he relented. "Something *unsettling*."

Chapter Thirty-Two

G abriel's voice dropped to a whisper. "About three years ago we were tracking down a group of bandits. 'Brothers of Blood' they called themselves. They were soldiers from Evergarden, Navaros, and even Freyley who'd been dishonorably discharged."

Lazander nodded. "I remember them. They sacked half the county. Zara the Fury killed them when they came close to Magnus' lands."

"That's right. But what you might not have heard is that Zara wasn't alone when she found the Brothers of Blood," Gabriel said. "*We* were there."

Lazander felt his eyebrows raise.

"At first we thought it was a forest fire," Marito said. "We knew there were casualties—the scent of burnt meat on the wind was proof of that, but we'd no idea of the source. We followed the smoke, planning to help tame the fire until we could reach out to Lord Magnus' estate for assistance."

The giant winced. "It took hours for us to find them—and it was a sight I dearly wish I could scour from memory. Zara had corralled the Brothers of Blood into a valley, trapping them in a ring of fire. Eighty men must have been there—or what was left of them."

Lazander grimaced. He'd passed that valley on his way to Magnus' estate. The earth, even years later, was black and twisted—a deathly silence carved out.

"Did you help Zara?" Lazander asked, having never heard this version of the tale. "Or try to stop her?"

"Neither" Gabriel said, grimly. "Val had an—"

"Attack, of some sorts," the giant jumped in.

"Val's eyes rolled back in his head, and he fell to the ground—convulsing," Gabriel said, lips pressed tightly at the memory. "I had one of Liddy's stabilizing potions on hand, but the attack stopped almost as soon as it began. After that, even the hardest slap wouldn't wake him—and I watched Mari give it his all."

"A full night he slept," Marito continued. "And when he awoke…"

The two looked at each other, uncomfortable.

"He was a different man," Gabriel said.

"Confused," Marito countered.

"He didn't know who you were, Mari. Or me," Gabriel said.

"And did he not remember? It took some time, yes, but the queen called forth those gifted in healing magic—a rarity as you know, Master Lazander. And even they could find nothing wrong with him." Marito shifted, clearly unhappy with the conversation.

"I've never heard of this," Lazander said, shocked that something as monumental as the heir to the throne losing his memory, even temporarily, was kept this quiet.

"The queen is excellent at stamping out rumors," Gabriel said grimly.

Marito frowned. "That is not very charitable of you, good ser."

"That doesn't make it any less true," Gabriel replied.

"But what does this have to do with Lady Eternity? And the mission?" Lazander asked.

"Val wasn't what I'd call a soft hand before this," Gabriel began. "But in no time it seemed the sword was his answer to everything. He killed more in that first six months than in the two years previous."

"You make him sound like a vicious killer, Master Gabriel." Marito frowned. "His sense of mercy… waned, but he was not brutal."

"Mari, do I need to remind you of the vaxion who fled the Moonvale Mountains?"

Marito shifted, uncomfortable. "Master Valerius said they were spies."

"They didn't live long enough for us to find out." Gabriel turned to Lazander. "Val burst into our rooms one morning, yelling about intel on a rebel group of vaxion. Claimed they were planning an attack on the Ivory Keep. In less than an hour, he had us and some ten strong packed and ready to go. We rode day and night to find them. How he knew they were in some Gallow-forsaken cave near the edge of Navaros, I'll never know. But he ordered us to wait outside and make sure none of them escaped."

Marito and Gabriel stared each other down, neither willing to finish the tale.

"What happened to the vaxion?" Lazander asked. As far as he'd known, the reclusive falslings hadn't left Moonvale since they'd driven out every non-vaxion a decade ago. Borders closed, they kept to themselves—he'd never heard of an incursion into Navaros. Nor of a planned attack.

"Val entered alone," Gabriel finally said. "We heard screams, but held our posts as ordered. Several women and children tried to flee. We captured them, of course. They would be questioned back at the Keep."

"When Master Valerius left the cave, he was covered in blood." Marito sighed heavily. "He ordered the women and children lined up."

"He didn't…" Lazander began, horrified.

"No, because I held his shadow in place and told him I'd knock him out cold and drag him back to the queen by the ankles if he laid a hand on them," Gabriel said, locking eyes with Lazander.

The red-haired knight knew he'd have done it too.

"He apologized," Marito argued, but even Lazander could tell his heart wasn't in it. "And he's never done anything like that since."

"What happened to the vaxion? The ones you captured?" Lazander asked.

"Dead," Gabriel said, that one word echoing a sorrow Lazander had never heard in his fellow knight's voice. "We camped under the edge of a cliff. A rock fell during the night—crushing them and the carriage we had locked them in."

Lazander's blood went cold.

"Did you bring this to the queen?" Lazander asked.

Marito shook his head. "Master Valerius asked us not to—he said a red mist had descended and a fury he'd never known overtook him. He was ashamed."

"Or so he said," Gabriel whispered. "He's been distant with us ever since—disappearing for days on end, showing up with weird cuts and bruises. I don't even know where he *is* half the time anymore."

Marito shook his head, dreadlocks sliding over his large shoulders. "Master Gabriel, we discussed this years ago—it is not very knightly to dredge up a past put to rest."

"What we *discussed* is that we would make sure nothing like it ever happened again," Gabriel replied, a finger jabbing the table. "Doesn't this crap with Magnus and Eternity seem weird to you? Everything Val did is just on the right side of questionable, but when you put them all together the whole thing stinks. I felt it with the vaxion, and I feel it now. Tell me I'm wrong."

Marito crossed his huge arms. "If we begin doubting one another, good sers, then we may as well hand the keys of the Ivory Keep to Navaros' enemies and tell them to make themselves at home."

"Valerius wanted Lord Magnus to succeed," Lazander said quietly. "I have no definitive proof, but my instincts are screaming that I'm right. Instincts that guided me from Freyley to the trenches of Evergarden to sitting here—with two knights I consider my brothers. But if you tell me to drop it, I will. No questions asked."

A look passed between Gabriel and Marito that was indecipherable to Lazander. Marito sighed heavily. "If you had come to me with such suspicions about any other knight, I would recommend a suspension of their knighthood until the matter was thoroughly investigated. It is the fact that it is *Valerius*—my brother. My friend. That makes me hesitate." The giant rubbed a hand over his eyes, and Lazander was surprised at the raw emotion he saw there. "My heart breaks at the thought that the best of us might be a traitor, but to bury our heads in the sand is to fail in our duty as Gilded."

Gabriel paused, letting Marito's words seek in. "What do you suggest we do, my friend?"

"We do what we have always done—we serve Navaros and its best interests."

Lazander opened his mouth, but Marito held up a meaty hand. "Lazander might be right. He might be wrong. We do not know. What we *do* know is that if we go to the queen with this, we will be accusing the leader of the Gilded, her *son*, of treason—and that needs more than the wild theories. We will watch Master Valerius. We will listen. And most importantly we will gather hard evidence—is that understood?"

Lazander nodded, more quickly than Gabriel who looked as if he wished to argue. But the mage knew better than to push his old friend when he was stirred up like this.

"Fine," Gabriel relented. "How do we do this?"

As the knights spoke, heads low, voices heated as they hashed out their plan, a whisper of a sigh drifted past their table. The sigh drifted around the corner, far from the knights, and floated into the cover of two towering bookshelves.

The air shivered, a form coming into clarity as if a hand had wiped away the fog of a steamed up mirror. Valerius stepped into existence, taking care to make sure he was well-hidden.

The invisibility spell, *Whisper of Darkness*, left him sagging against the shelves. It was a powerful spell that cloaked not only his presence but the very magic that powered it—ensuring that not even Gabriel would sense him. Unfortunately while the Calamity System allowed him to break the natural rules of this world and wield magic, that didn't make him a mage. His spellcasting ability was limited, and *Whisper of Darkness* had pushed him hard—he'd been a hair's breadth from draining his mana entirely.

He couldn't afford to let it drain—not when the Calamity System would cripple him with pain, sending shockwaves through his body as punishment. The sight of their leader writhing on the floor, caught hanging on their every word, would only confirm what the knights had guessed.

That he was a traitor.

Valerius sighed, sinking to the ground.

He remembered waking up in this world, seeing towering flames twist through the sky long after the bandits had turned to ash. He thought the flames from his last moments on earth had followed him, chasing him to this new world—this new body.

Marito and Gabriel had been kind in their retelling of the story—he had to give them that. In truth he'd turned his blade on Marito, screaming and delirious with fear. When Marito had easily bested his clumsy sword thrusts, Valerius had turned a dagger on his own throat—convinced if he simply ended things, he would awaken.

Gabriel had to wrap him in shadow magic, binding him tightly until they dragged him back to the Ivory Keep.

It had taken him days to realize that he was trapped in the world of an arcade game. Once he crossed that gut-wrenching hurdle, however, he'd quickly realized the most important rule of this world:

The Operator's word was *law*. To ignore it was to suffer consequences—painful ones. But if you obeyed?

The rewards were near endless.

So he focused on decoding and finishing the Operator's cryptic quests— adapting to the Calamity System's strange turns of phrase. The game didn't seem to care *how* you interpreted the quest—so long as you did it, awarding bonuses and striking you down with penalties with equal ease. Soon he was clearing quests as quickly as he was receiving them, his abilities and power growing at a hundred times the pace of his fellow knights. He would be out of this world in no time, he thought.

Until the vaxion.

Valerius' fingers dug into his hair as the memory rose—unbidden.

Silence the Vaxion Defectors.

Four simple words with endless possibilities. He spent three days skirting the Moonvale Mountains, and several near misses, to discover that a group of vaxion had fled. A week of tracking led him to the falslings where he spent several nights hiding downwind. Using *Whisper of Darkness* when he could, he eventually discovered why they had fled.

They had planned to plead with the Ivory Keep for safe harbor. In exchange, they were willing to tell the king and queen everything they knew about the secret inner workings of the vaxion—including why falslings had conquered Moonvale. And why the Ivory Keep's very own Lord Magnus of Ashfall had struck a deal with the Mi'xan clan.

Valerius didn't want to kill the vaxion defectors—not at first. He tried diverting them with mudslides and broken dams. Summoned illusions of vaxion eyes in the dark. Even killed one or two of them in the night—hoping they'd abandoned their mission.

They didn't.

It became obvious that the one way to *Silence the Vaxion Defectors* was with the end of his blade.

He refused.

Then the penalties began. His equipment vanished. His mana halved. For one terrifying day his sight was taken—but still Valerius refused.

That night as Valerius slept, he didn't dream of the Menu. Instead the Operator brought him to its alien plane of twin suns and red sand.

And left him there.

He didn't know how long he lasted. Didn't know how long it took his flesh to melt from his bones as blades of fire dug into his eyes. How long the Operator's omniscient voice repeated those words over, and over, and over.

sILEnce tHe vaXiON DEfectORs.

sILEnce tHe vaXiON DEfectORs.

sILEnce tHe vaXiON DEfectORs.

He gave in eventually—as the Operator knew he would.

When he drew his sword and slaughtered the vaxion in that cave, he hoped killing the men would be enough.

But the Operator visited again that night, and the pain began anew.

And so Valerius pushed that boulder from the cliff, aiming it directly for the vaxion carriage. The last of his sentimentality died, along with the women and children whose bones were now crushed into a fine paste.

This world wasn't real, he told himself. These people weren't real. All that mattered was finishing the game and getting out of here.

The Operator hadn't visited since, nor had it needed to.

He thought of the child he once was, who dreamed of becoming a knight just like Valerius. The countless hours he spent playing *Knights of Eternity* in his parents' basement—enraptured by Marito's strength, Gabriel's magic, and Lazander's skills.

To hear them turn on him now…

It cut deep. Deeper than it should.

An icon flashed in the corner of his eyes, a new quest courtesy of the Operator. He opened it, laughing bitterly.

He should have known this day would come.

Hating himself, he clicked accept.

Because if it was him or this world, he chose himself.

What other option did he have?

Chapter Thirty-Three

I didn't get far into the woods before I stopped—Lenia's advice to go to the Ivory Keep ringing in my ears.

I knew the Keep from *Knights of Eternity*—it was the starting area of the game, a pixelated background of twin ivory towers I sped past every time, eager to get that session going. It was where the king and queen lived—nameless royals who thanked you for saving their nameless kingdom in the game's finale. Valerius would stand by their side if he wasn't in your main party and commend you for bringing honor to the Gilded—the image of a heroic knight.

The wound in my back twinged, a dull throb that made my whole body tense.

And what a "heroic knight" he'd turned out to be.

Despite my countless hours playing *Knights of Eternity,* every day here proved I knew painfully little about this world. Some of the characters, enemies, and items were the same, but it felt like dipping my finger into an ocean and thinking it a puddle—ignorant of what lay beneath.

What proof did I have that the eternally smiling king and queen of the game wouldn't take one look at a vaxion and lock their doors. Or worse.

Then I thought of Eternity. The concern in her eyes. Her warm smile. Who knew what Valerius had told her about what happened, likely nothing good, but she'd still reached out to me. Eternity, who was one of the most powerful characters in the game, who had every reason to hate Zara, had been one of the kindest people I'd met in this world.

My hands tightened on my little cloth bag—my only possessions in this world. I'd go to the Ivory Keep, I'd be honest with Eternity—about my world, the Operator, *Summon Eternity,* everything.

I could trust her, my gut insisted. I just had to figure out how to get to her.

Noon's light pierced the thick red and yellow foliage, light dappling along my skin. The towering trees I stood beneath were just like the ones I'd crashed through before Lenia and Waylen found me. All I had to do was climb one of them, right to the top, then I could poke my head above the canopy and figure out where I was. Maybe I would even see the Ivory Keep from so up high, and then—

Valerius flashed in my mind. The look on his face when he threw me from the dragon. The whistle of the wind as I fell. Hitting the ground. The pain. The fear.

My hands trembled. *If I climb up there, a branch could snap. I could slip. I'll fall. I'll be paralyzed. I'll die. I'll—*

Dropping my bag, I grabbed the lowest branch of the huge, twisted trunk, yanking myself up with just the strength in my arms. I reached for the next branch, focusing purely on the physical movement, knowing if I didn't do this now, I never would. I would fear heights, trees, and who knew what else for the rest of my life— and I refused to let Valerius do that to me. The smug, condescending *jerk*.

Spite, it turned out, was one hell of a motivator. Healthy? Probably not. But it worked.

My back, even after a night of sleeping on nothing but grass, felt stronger. The Operator's penalties didn't seem to have affected Zara's healing—a small blessing. I quickly gained speed and confidence, relishing the ease with which I climbed. Apologizing to something with two legs and black fur that squealed as I passed, I slowed only when the branches thinned—testing my weight on each before resting on them fully.

I hesitated when I reached the canopy—the urge to look down almost overwhelming. I knew if I did, every anxious fear would come crashing around me. Shaking my head, I pushed through the canopy, the leaves tickling my face like trailing fingers.

The sun was blinding and viciously hot. I realized the canopy had created a shaded refuge from the dry, crackling heat. It took several heartbeats for my eyes to adjust, my hand shaded against the sun as I blinked.

My heart sank as the world sharpened.

Endless forests, from the red and yellow treetops that surrounded me to coiling trunks topped with purple, stretched in every direction. This wasn't just a forest— this was a damn *continent*. How was I ever going to get out of here?

Squinting, I looked for the dark stone of Magnus' castle. Some smudges in the distance could be them, but that might just be the panic that spiked my heart every time I thought of his smug expression. The blue-green mountains I saw from the castle roof were also visible but as blurry as they were before. I'd no idea if I was closer or farther from them.

I spun, trying to see if I could pinpoint anything that remotely looked like a landmark, seeing nothing but trees. I was about to give up, wishing *Tithe of Beasts* expanded my sight as well as my hearing when I spotted a smudge of white nestled in mountains of purple and dark gray.

I strained my eyes, making out the slightest two-pronged bident of towers.

The Ivory Keep—that must be it!

Elated, I braced myself for the descent when the hair rose on the back of my head. My nostrils flared as my blood pounded. On instinct, I activated *Tithe of Beasts*.

Instantly my nose flooded with a familiar, soapy scent.

I ducked beneath the canopy, sniffing the air in rapid bursts as the rumble of many pawed feet reached my ears.

A pack of molger came into view seconds later, led by a gigantic beast with six legs, its claws kicking showers of dirt behind it as it charged forward in an odd, stumbling gait. Two smaller ones trailed it. I recognized them instantly—the molger from the lake.

I crouched low, trying to make myself even smaller in the shadows of the tree, thinking of the vicious bruise on Lenia's face and their growls of fury when they'd ripped my tunic to shreds. A part of me whispered that it was pointless, that all they had to do was look up and they'd spot me.

Fighting sucklers, flailing creature's half my size, was one thing. But a molger?

I was suddenly cold despite the sun's warmth that had kissed my skin only seconds ago.

Keeping deathly still and waiting for them to pass, I spotted something in the largest one's mouth—something long and slender. I gasped, stifling the sound with a hand over my lips when I realized what it was. *Who* it was.

Lenia hung limp and lifeless, her head and arms facing the ground, the tips of her fingers trailing the dirt as she bobbed up and down in the molger's mouth—her head dipping dangerously toward the ground.

They have Lenia! Did they find out she hid me? Did they hurt her? Is she—is she dead?

Crap—none of that matters! Just get out of this damn tree and stop them. So what if they're three times the size of me? And have teeth. And claws. And—and—

And just like that the molger passed me by, charging ahead—in the opposite direction of the Ivory Keep. The forest rattled at the intrusion, wings and claws fleeing. The noise lasted for mere seconds before the forest settled once more—the silence intensifying the shame that flooded my body.

Stupid, useless coward. Same as back home, same here. Zara would have stopped them in an instant. But not me—no. I was busy hiding in the shadows like a pathetic, insufferable idiotic—

I called myself every name I could think of, increasing in ferocity and cruelty. At home, this would briefly make me feel better, like I had been punished enough that I could move on—but here, it just felt pointless. Even in this body, I was afraid. Helpless.

A squeak broke the freshly settled silence, and I spotted a tiny, auburn shape with six legs stumbling through the forest—hot on the trail of the molger. Next to the others, this one was so small it looked almost comical—like seeing a Chihuahua next to a Doberman.

My heart swelled at the sight.

Waylen.

Panting and clearly terrified, he raced forward nonetheless, disappearing into the undergrowth after them.

Wood cracked beneath my hands as I gripped the branch I clung to, splintering—but I felt no pain.

If a little kid could be brave, then so could I.

Taking a deep breath, I let myself fall.

My hands reached out of their own accord, grabbing a thick branch as I twisted my body in the air. My touch was light as I leaped from branch to branch, staying just long enough to slow my blistering fall to the ground.

I hit the dirt with my knees crouched, barely making a sound.

Then I was off at a full sprint, away from the Ivory Keep and Eternity.

And straight for the molger.

***

Eternity sighed, twisting her braid in her hands.

"It's been difficult, you see. *Lonely*," she said, making sure to keep her smile soft and sad. "While I appreciate the lengths you have gone to keep me entertained—" Eternity gestured at the desk with magical theory she already knew and romantic poetry she had no interest in, "I need to get out of this tower—just for a few hours."

Lazander shifted, looking uncomfortable. When Lady Eternity had asked for him specifically, and not her very own Champion, Imani, he'd rushed to the Ivory Keep's second tower, hoping she'd recalled something about her kidnapping. He was not expecting big blue eyes that locked with his as if he was her only hope in the world.

"Lady Eternity, I know this is uncomfortable, but we still don't know how your kidnapper managed to breach the defenses of the Gallowed Temple. This is the safest place for you."

Eternity smiled even brighter, blazing like a sun in the darkness, and Lazander felt his resolve crumble. "I would have thought the safest place in Navaros was by the side of a Gilded Knight?"

Lazander sighed, knowing he was beaten. "The Gallowed Temple is the best I can do. But you are not to leave my side, understood?"

Eternity nodded, pushing down the need to clap her hands in delight. She didn't like lying, especially to Lazander—who seemed like he didn't know the meaning of the word. But she had to get out of this infernal tower—there was little she could do to help Zara from here.

"Is there something in particular you wish to—" Lazander began, but before he could finish the sentence, Eternity grabbed the dark gray cloak of Gallowed disciples, swung it over her shoulders, and stood beaming at him.

"Ready."

Sensing he'd been had, he smiled nonetheless. He'd been so caught up in dealing with Valerius, he'd forgotten Lady Eternity must be going out of her mind with boredom. He made a note to try to visit her more often.

"After you, Lady Eternity," he said, bowing dramatically as he opened the door. Eternity curtseyed deeply. "Gallows mercy upon you, esteemed knight."

The pair smiled as they left the tower, Eternity feeling lighter than she had in weeks.

Chapter Thirty-Four

The noise took Eternity aback. "Nock!" and "Loose!" bellowed the drill sergeant, roaring at full volume as if her bow-wielding cadets were not mere feet from her. Mares neighed from their stables as their foals pawed the paddock ground nervously, their trainers slacking their ropes as they called out in encouragement, trying to get the young foals to trot in a circle. The clatter of wooden swords on wooden shields as soldiers sparred. The jeers and banter of those who looked on. The area surrounding the tower's base was nothing short of a cacophony.

It was further proof of the power of the magic that protected her new home—she hadn't heard so much as a whisper from her room.

The noise made Eternity's chest unexpectedly tighten. She'd only been in the tower for a few days, but its silence was one she had quickly grown accustomed to. Lazander paused, sensing her hesitation and made a show of offering her his arm as if he'd planned to stop all along.

Eternity smiled, gratefully pressing her hand on his forearm as they walked through the training grounds.

She tried to enjoy the chaos, knowing it would vanish any moment now.

The noise dimmed, right on cue, starting just off to her left where three cadets in practice armor had been sparring. One elbowed another, and the whispers began.

"Is that…"

"… in the tower above, idiot."

Her name passed from one set of lips to another until the whole yard fell silent.

Lazander made no comment when the men and women of the Keep stood, sweaty and disheveled from a morning of drills. They pressed their fingers to their eyes and bowed their heads, the show of respect for Gallow's Chosen.

It had been the first body part the Tyrant had ripped from her namesake when the very first Eternity had refused to bow down.

Eternity wanted to call out that there was no need—that she wanted them to act as normal, but she said nothing. Nor did she try to smile and meet their eyes in a show of reassurance. She used to when she first came to Navaros a year ago.

Evergarden's time to host her had ended, and Navaros had made a grand show of welcoming her to their city-state with a three day festival in honor of Gallow.

She had been determined that this time—this time! —would be different. She would mingle with people. She would show them she was no different to anyone else, regardless of her abilities. Perhaps she would even make *friends*. The mere thought had made her beam.

But the Ivory Keep was no different.

It took weeks of awkward smiles and stilted small talk for her to realize the servants she tried to befriend were terrified of her. Or, more accurately, terrified that Gallow was watching them through her. Before her kidnapping, she'd been allowed to walk freely throughout the Ivory Keep, and she had forced herself to go into the local tavern, the Resplendent Farrow. The boisterous crowd, clapping hands, and roar of shanties would always quieten when she appeared in the doorway, replaced by small talk and lowered eyes.

It hurt more than the crushing loneliness.

So she stopped.

Soon, her world narrowed to the library, the gardens and the Gallowed Temple, and she told herself she was content.

The Gilded were the only ones who didn't seem to care she was Gallow's Chosen. She recalled her first day at the Keep, exhausted from the days-long festivities. Gabriel had appeared at her side like a shadow, bombarding her with a thousand questions about how she maintained her connection with Gallow and the cost channeling a god took on her person. Marito had to physically pry the mage away and had suggested that Gabriel at least give the poor woman a drink first before the lady wished she had never left Evergarden.

They snuck her away from the crowds to the Keep's gardens, and Marito had even managed to smuggle several large pitchers of sweet mead from the kitchens. Lazander had soon appeared, bereft of armor, his hair tousled from a visit to the Keep's wolfhounds.

They'd spent the night laughing at Marito's poetry recitals, teasing Gabriel about his most recent romance, and thrilling her with tales of their adventures. She'd felt like a normal person for the first time in many years.

Her hand tightened around Lazander's arm at the thought, and the red-haired knight looked down at her, brow raised in concern. She smiled, shaking her head.

Gabriel, Marito, and Lazander had probably forgotten that night—they were the Gilded, after all. They had no shortage of company, and a couple of glasses of mead beneath the stars was likely a boring evening to them.

But it was one of Eternity's favorite memories. She had never thanked them for it, embarrassed they would pity her. So she tried her best to be cheerful and happy in their company, hoping it would show how much they meant to her.

Valerius was the only exception. He had been her escort during her first few days in Navaros—the king and queen eager to have both a Gilded and their son at the forefront of the festivities. He had stood at the front of the parade—beaming and waving at the crowds while Eternity awkwardly smiled from a carriage. He was the most popular by far of the Gilded, and Eternity had been excited to finally meet him.

During the festivities he'd smile encouragingly at her and make a show of cheering. At night, however, he'd simply nod and present his back to her—the epitome of a dedicated knight. They'd barely exchanged a handful of sentences since. There was something about him that made the hair on the back of her neck raise, though if pressed she could only say he was standoffish and cold.

"Mabel's daughter, Delia, is pregnant," Lazander said, pointedly loud. "If Delia is anything to go by, her foal will be a steed fit for a knight."

Eternity smiled at Lazander's chatter about his horses, which judging by his shoes was where he had spent his morning.

"Mabel had a difficult pregnancy though, didn't she?" he asked.

Lazander nodded. "Good memory, Lady Eternity. But we are prepared this time—I've had the mages whip up a soothing balm for her. Oh, do you remember that beautiful, dappled stallion I brought from Freyley? The one with the temper? We've made *excellent* progress getting him used to other riders. Although he did kick one of the stable boys yesterday..." As Lazander chatted, noise around them resumed. The drill sergeant roared at her cadets to stop lollygagging, and the thump of wood on wood picked up as sparring continued. In moments, it was like Eternity wasn't even there—and for that she was grateful.

Soon enough, they left the training grounds, passed the palace barracks, and cut down the main road of the Ivory Keep.

It was the usual, the quiet and the stares. The reverent whispers. One woman even dropped her basket, apples spilling across the street.

A man, age creased into every line of his skin, caught her eye. It was unusual to see someone as old as him at the Keep—the fast pace of life meant retirees usually left for smaller, more coastal areas such as Ruanu or Vastin. He sat heavily on a wooden bench, his skin as thin as parchment, bruises from the simple chore of existing dotting his frail skin. His eyes were sunken and yellow. He raised his head—meeting Eternity's eyes dead on.

He pressed his fingers to his eyes and whispered, his words nearly lost.

"Judgment. I seek Gallow's judgment."

Her smile dropped, her heart sinking into the depths of her stomach.

She knew what she had to do.

With a gesture she asked Lazander to stay where he was as she crossed the road. Lazander's hand automatically went to his sword, more a sign of his discomfort than any real danger. She could sense the foot traffic stop as people froze in place, eyes on her—but she ignored them.

This was her duty as Gallow's Chosen. This was the task every Eternity had been given since the first. This was the price she had to pay to protect the world she knew and loved.

She only prayed the man would live through it.

The old man cracked a weak smile at Eternity's approach, dipping his head forward.

"Will you submit to his Judgment—even if you are not found worthy?" she asked formally.

"Yes," he whispered. "My bones creak with sickness—it spread to my heart. The mages say it's a matter of weeks before it reaches my brain—if I'm even alive by then. This is my one chance at life—and I will fight for Gallow. I will fight for this world—I *swear* it."

His voice carried an edge of desperation she'd heard more times than she could count.

"You know the price, if you do not pass?" she said, her voice a whisper. This wasn't part of the script, but she had to ask—it gave her a measure of comfort and helped ease the guilt.

"I do—and if he wills it, I will pay it," he said, closing his eyes.

Eternity nodded, pressing her warm palm to his cold forehead as her eyes shuttered closed.

The Void whispered to her, an empty space that sat just at the back of her mind—she needed only to let it in, and Gallow would find her.

"**Witness him. Witness his power. Witness his *Judgment*,**" she intoned, steeling herself.

Eternity's eyes rolled back in her head as light pooled about her feet, crawling up her body. Symbols, small and intricate, trailed up her skin, bathing her body in light so white it blinded all who looked at her. These symbols were engraved above every temple, on every prayer scroll, below every offering.

Honor.

Obedience.

Sacrifice.

The three guiding tenets of Gallow

Images appeared in her mind—slow at first. A kiss, full of shyness and excitement. A woman, her hair short, her smile wide. A stomach, belly heavy with pregnancy—the man's hands pressed against it. Tears, the woman pointing at empty cupboards, a suckling newborn cradled in her arms while another child clung to her skirts.

A tavern—noisy and full. The man clutched a glass, pawing the few coins in his threadbare pockets.

Just one more. He swore. *Just one.*

But it was never the last. Not until he was thrown from the tavern, drunk and stupid. He would crawl home to his sobbing wife. He would roar at her cries, asking what choice did he have when he had to put up with a sow like her?

Eternity looked at it all—letting her human judgment slide away.

Gallow did not care for the sins of your past. He did not look for kindness or compassion.

He looked for one thing only.

Champions.

Gallow sought people with courage and conviction—those brave enough to look a god in the eye as it ripped your own from your skull. People whose strength and determination would outlast the limitations of the body and mind. He pried the pages of your life apart, examining the clear scripts and messy blood-stained scrawl to see who you *truly* were.

Eternity was the speaker to his voice—his seeker of Champions. Yet even after all these years she could not predict which way his scales would tilt. To be found worthy meant receiving Gallow's favor, and a new life filled with his powers and gifts aplenty.

If you were not...

Eternity kept her face still as the pain began. The symbols on her skin vibrated, heat pouring from them as they raced across her eyes, down her cheeks, pooling above her heart before they spilled down her arms—straight onto the man's forehead.

"I'm sorry," she whispered, knowing what was coming.

Some of them fought when they realized Gallow had found them wanting. Those were always the hardest. But once Eternity's hand pressed to their foreheads, no force could remove it until the judgment was done. Not even her.

The symbols slid from her fingertips to the old man's, melting into his flesh. She knew it burned him, but he didn't say a word—merely gripped one hand in the other, shaking as his skin turned ashy and gray.

Lazander looked away, eyes on the street beyond, as if keeping watch.

Eternity locked eyes with the man—Malcolm was his name. It was a small thing, but she could be his comfort in his last moments.

It was something she had to do all too often.

"Gallow has passed his judgment," she said quietly, her skin clear of Gallow's tenets as the last slid from her palm—soaking fully into Malcolm. Taking a steadying breath, she lifted her hand from his head—stepping back.

His cheek caved in first—crumbling like ash. Nose and eyes followed, allowing a terrifying moment in which an eyeless corpse stared back at Eternity.

In seconds, he collapsed in on himself—leaving a small puddle of ash where once he sat.

"Gallow has found you wanting," she said as she dipped her finger in the pile of ashes and pressed it to her eyelids—hoping Malcom found peace wherever he ended up.

Chapter Thirty-Five

When Waylen had said H'tar village was close by, he had been *severely* exaggerating.

I had been forced to slow to a jog hours ago. For creatures the size of an SUV, the molger moved at blistering speeds. *Tithe of Beasts* was my guide, the scent of the molger clearer than any map, the pounding of their many paws a steady rhythm that let me stay close—but not too close. I found that while they charged like a wrecking ball, they struggled at basic maneuverability, coming to a near halt at fallen trees or stray boulders—allowing me precious minutes to catch my breath.

I filed that away—it would be helpful to know if I ever needed to run from one.

The trees began to thin, the lack of cover slowing my steps as I stuck to the increasing shadows of twilight. Creeping forward, I heard murmured voices rise to shouts, loud and furious.

"Use your damn nose, and tell me that's not vaxion!"

"Not now, Jerome! You had *no* right to—"

"You hear that folks? It's not enough that a blood-spiked mongrel kills our animals, terrifies our homes, and forces us to keep a moonblade in our pockets!"

There was a murmur of assenting voices, and I cautiously peeked through thick blue leaves topped with ivory flowers, praying no one would look my way. A crowd had gathered, twenty or so people at most, and they stood around two men who stood nose-to-nose.

"That's not enough for Chief here to raise a bloody finger!" a tall, well-built man roared. He waved a ragged piece of cloth in his hands, holding it at arm's length as his face scrunched in disgust. I recognized it immediately.

My old tunic! What is he doing with—

My cheeks warmed and I had to force my eyes to stay locked on his face when I realized the man was completely and utterly naked.

Neither him, nor the rest of the crowd, seemed remotely bothered by it.

The wind shifted, bringing a scent of soap and sweat—a scent I recognized. A low, feral growl escaped me as talons peeked through the tips of my fingers.

He was Waylen's uncle—the man who'd beaten Lenia unconscious the day before.

"Here I stand with just what Chief wanted—*evidence*. Irrefutable proof that Lenia is housing a *vaxion*." He spat the word as if it were a curse. "The scum who made us flee to this Gallow-forsaken spit of land! Who could be on their way right now—fangs at the ready. And what does Chief say?" He pointed at the exasperated man who faced him, the barest wisp of silver in his stark black beard. "'Not now.'"

The crowd murmured in agreement, though I noticed a handful of faces frowning—whether in disapproval or irritation, it was hard to tell. Most people looked to be between their thirties or forties, but I spotted a few kids poking out from behind protective legs.

I heard a groan—soft, as if the person was trying to stifle it.

Lenia lay on her side between the two men. One hand gripped her side as she winced, a fresh bruise gracing her forehead. Her dark blue dress had been ripped open, teeth marks circling the edges, revealing a gray undershirt.

Her teeth were gritted—her customary glint of steel in her eyes. But beneath that I saw fear.

Forcing myself to take a calming breath, I felt my talons recede into the smooth skin of my fingertips. I clutched at the pieces of information being dropped—a "blood-spiked mongrel" was on the loose in H'tar, Waylen's uncle and Chief were at loggerheads, and the vaxion were the reason the molger had fled the Moonvale Mountains—something Lenia had neglected to mention. Bits and pieces of the jigsaw puzzle that was H'tar and the molger were falling into place, but I had yet to make out the whole picture.

If I jumped in now I had a strong feeling, based on the furious faces in the crowd at the word "vaxion," that I would make everything worse.

Waylen's uncle grew loud, spittle flying as he claimed that animals had been the first to go missing. How long until the mongrel took someone? What if it killed a *child*?

That earned some gasps and mumblings from the crowd.

Chief watched all of this looking more tired than worried. The thick leather apron over his gray pants and shirt reminded me of a blacksmith. The tools in his front pockets hinted that he'd been in the middle of his work day when Waylen's uncle had shown up with Lenia, dumped her on the ground, and started shouting.

"Jerome, we have a town charter for a *reason*. When we founded H'tar we agreed on justice—on *fairness*. Showing up and waving a piece of cloth as you spew accusations is not the H'tar I know and love. We can discuss this, in depth, at a town meeting, but not—" Chief began, but Jerome cut him off.

"Do you hear yourself? Do you think we have time for this?" Jerome said, blue eyes wide, fists clenched.

"Our first mongrel in five years, right when a vaxion shows up—do you think this is a coincidence? What if they're working together? What if this is all part of their plan—to get us scared, to make us freeze with indecision—before they strike!" A vein in Jerome's neck pulsed, and behind his rage I saw fear—real fear. "Nine years. Nine bloody years we've fought fang and claw to make H'tar work. I love it as much as you do, you know I do! Which is why I won't let everything go to waste," Jerome hissed. "A vaxion is here, and Lenia knew about it. I'd bet my left claw she told them we were here."

"*What?*" Lenia exclaimed. She struggled to one knee but fell instantly. "This is ridiculous! My husband—your *brother*—died for H'tar! Why would I—"

"—a vote!" Jerome roared, drowning out Lenia's protests. "I call for a vote to expel her from H'tar, and to organize a party to find and kill the mongrel and its vaxion master before it's too late."

A whine erupted from the crowd, and Waylen waddled forward in his auburn molger form. A woman lunged for him, trying to pull him back but he was too quick—charging toward Lenia with a yipping bark.

"Don't! Peanut, stay," she cried, arm raised in warning.

Jerome aimed a vicious kick into Waylen's side as he reached Lenia. "Traitors both!" he roared. "After everything my brother did for you! You spit on him! On his memory—on his *death!*"

Lenia cried out, falling on top of Waylen as he shrieked in pain. Her limbs snapped together as she curled protectively around him, bracing herself as Jerome pulled back for another kick.

I snarled, about to charge—but someone else got there first.

Chief moved with the speed and grace of a man half his age. He sidestepped Lenia and Waylen with a half turn, his knee kissing the earth as he deftly pulled a hammer from his apron and drove it with swift and brutal force into Jerome's left knee.

The whole thing took less than a second. If I'd doubted these people weren't human, I didn't anymore—I'd never seen anyone move so fast. Not even Valerius.

Jerome howled, spewing words in a guttural tongue I didn't understand as he crumpled—clutching his knee.

Chief rolled a shoulder as he stood, replacing the hammer in his apron—even giving it a little pat to make sure it was secure.

"Let's make a couple of things absolutely Gallow-damned clear," he roared, fury and disgust sharpening every word. He stared every person in the crowd down, daring them to interrupt.

"We do not drag mothers through the forest in our jaws. We do not make wild claims about vaxion in the middle of town. And we do not—we do not—" He straddled the squirming Jerome, who winced in pain as Chief grabbed him by the back of the head and gave it a vicious shake. "*We do not. Kick. Children.*"

There was silence as eyes found shoes, the crowd refusing to look at Chief. Even Jerome looked chastised.

With a lurch, Chief dropped Jerome in the dirt. He gave a grunt but said nothing else. Chief stepped back, hands behind his back—the image of authority. "Accusations have been brought against the Doorin household that its members house a vaxion. As Lenia is the head of that household, she will be its representative. An argument has also been made that the beast that has been attacking our livestock is connected to the vaxion. These are accusations that must be dealt with swiftly and seriously."

Chief approached Lenia, bowing his head low. I activated *Tithe of Beasts* a second too slow, missing the beginning of what he said. "… housed in my shop. You'll have a bed and three meals, for you and Waylen both, until this is resolved. Is this fair?"

Lenia nodded stiffly, cradling a transformed Waylen in her arms.

"Tomorrow evening, we will have an emergency meeting to discuss our next steps," Chief said loudly.

Jerome grunted as he struggled to his good knee. Two men, one with dusty blond hair, the other balding, helped him up. I would have bet money they were the other two smaller molger I had seen at the lake.

"And finally," Chief continued, "I sentence myself to five days community labor for attacking another member of H'tar village. Is this fair?"

No one answered.

"Is this *fair*?" he roared.

Jerome tightened his lips but nodded.

"Excellent. Now, we're losing daylight and there's still chores to be done." Chief dismissed the crowd with a nod. They shuffled about awkwardly before drifting away. Ignoring them, Chief held out a hand to help Lenia up.

She favored her right side as Chief guided her to a large stone building with two chimneys, a workbench, and an anvil just outside. Wheels in various stages of repair, scraps of ripped metal, and even a half-torn saddle lay scattered in the greenery of his yard. He pushed the door open, gesturing for Lenia to go inside.

When Waylen toddled after them, his tiny paws kicking up dirt, Chief held out a hand to stop him, murmuring something. Waylen shook his head, yipping with a high-pitched whine I recognized as panic. Chief knelt, resting a hand on Waylen as he ran his fingers from his head all the way down his back in long, soothing motions.

I could have used *Tithe of Beasts* to listen in, but something stopped me. There was quiet gentleness to Chief as he tried to calm Waylen that I didn't want to intrude on.

Several minutes passed, but Chief stayed kneeling by Waylen, murmuring gently as his fingers dug into his fur, petting him. The boy shivered, and I gasped as his auburn fur thinned, turning dark in the waning light. Bone erupted from his back, rising and cresting as he straightened up, threads of muscles weaving around the exposed flesh. His jaw unhinged as his snout shortened, human teeth jutting out from the white bone of his changing skull. Bile rose in my throat, but I couldn't look away, fascinated and horrified by the transformation.

It took what must have been two or three minutes, but soon Waylen stood in human form, shivering and naked. Chief patted his shoulder, ushering him inside.

When Lenia had revealed they could change into molger, I didn't know what I'd expected. The smooth flow of flesh, a flash of smoke—or maybe even a snap second transformation? I didn't think it would be this slow, flesh-sliding, painful looking change.

I looked down at my own hands, thinking of my talons. It didn't hurt when they appeared—but then again, the only times it happened I was usually so high on adrenaline that, if it had hurt, I wouldn't have noticed.

I backed up, disappearing into the undergrowth as I moved away from H'tar village—trying to process everything I'd heard. While I wanted to kick down Chief's door, grab Lenia and run, it didn't sound like the molger had many places to go— H'tar was their safe haven for a reason. Chief, at the very least, wasn't breaking out the pitchforks just yet. Plus he had obliterated Jerome's knee with a hammer—that made him a good man in my book.

I recalled the "mongrel" they mentioned. That must have been the monster I saw in the forest—its jaws misshapen and painful, eyes white and milky in their blindness. It was killing and likely eating their livestock. The molger were huge in their beast-forms though—surely they could defend themselves against something like that?

I shook my head. The mongrel was terrifying, but it wasn't my problem—I needed to focus on Lenia. I wondered if I should knock on Chief's door, and present myself, but swiftly thought better of it. Lenia was in this mess because she'd helped me—if I threw myself into this headfirst it would be out of a selfish need to ease my guilty conscience.

I had to get her alone and see what she wanted.

I stepped back into the shadows of the forest and picked a large, towering tree at random, its branches thick enough to hold me for the night.

I climbed quickly and quietly, settling in the thick foliage at the top. Finally I opened the small bag Lenia had given me. There was bread, an apple, a bar of soap, and even a small clay canister of water. I gulped it down eagerly, inhaling the bread in-between breaths. My stomach gurgled, still hungry and despite knowing I should save it for breakfast, I bit into the apple, finishing it in three bites.

My nose caught the scent of warm spices and cooked meat, and I clasped my stomach at the smell. Three small cottages surrounded Chief's shop, and something delicious was clearly being cooked in at least one of them, judging by the aromatic smoke that drifted my way. I sighed, turning onto my side as I curled up, trying to get comfortable.

A few hours. I just needed a few hours of sleep. Then I would find a way to speak to Lenia, and I would fix this.

I had to.

Chapter Thirty-Six

The Menu appeared in my dreams as clear as if I had been staring at the arcade screen of *Knights of Eternity*. Its lines were a little sharper, the text a little clearer every night, making me wonder if there was a way to summon it when I wasn't asleep. I now knew how to use my abilities—the ones I'd unlocked at least. But I hadn't a clue about the Inventory, not to mention...

My thoughts trailed off, forgotten, as I spotted the "Miscellaneous" tab. In the arcade game, this led to the Bestiary, and I was delighted to see it existed here—even though most entries were gray blocks of hidden text. I scrolled until I found the "molger."

Bestiary:	**Molger**
Molger are midsized falslings.	

I thought of the giant badger-like creatures I'd spent hours chasing after—weren't mid-sized to me.

Bestiary:	**Molger**
Omnivorous by nature, when not in human form they are natural foragers. With curved toes tipped with claws as strong as steel, they are more comfortable digging than they are fighting. In addition, their weak eyesight and limited peripheral vision makes them vulnerable to attacks from above.	

Duly noted.

Bestiary:	Molger
However, they are not to be underestimated. With one of the most powerful bites of any falsling, they will lock onto their victims and refuse to let go—even in death. They used to share territory with the vaxion in the Moonvale Mountains, along with a host of other falslings, until the Mi'xan took control and decreed it for vaxion use only.	

That lined up with what Jerome had said in his argument with the Chief, although the more I learned about the vaxion, the sadder I became. Why had they driven every non-vaxion out of the mountains? Why did Zara leave them behind to "sell her soul", as Lenia put it, to Magnus?

My eyes caught on another tab, almost hidden behind the others. It was smaller and written in a tiny cursive.

"Origin." Curious, I mentally clicked on it.

My mind went completely blank at the words on the screen.

ORIGIN OF PLAYER CHARACTER: ZARA THE FURY. STATUS: AVAILABLE.

WOULD YOU LIKE TO SPEAK TO ZARA THE FURY?

Wait—what? I could *speak* to her? Zara herself?

Shame sparked, uncomfortable, at the thought. It hadn't even occurred to me to wonder what had happened to Zara when I took over her body—her life. I'd forgotten she was a real person—a terrifying one, but real. If I could speak to her through the Menu, did that mean she was trapped in it? Or was she somewhere else?

I had so many questions for her about being a vaxion, the Moonvale Mountains. About the aunt Magnus mentioned, about the deal Zara made—did he force her? Did she know I was going to appear? Did she agree? Does she hate me? Does she—

Breathe. You can't do anything about this if you're freaking out.

I took a breath—or the imitation of one, at least.

I should speak to her. And I would. But now wasn't the time. I had jumped the gun with the Operator and ended up burned alive beneath the dual suns of an alien desert. For all I knew, Zara could attack me or hurt me as the Operator had. If I was going to do this, I would go in prepared.

Light pulled at the edge of my vision, my mind pushing to wake up.

Another night—I promised. When I was ready.

***

I rolled onto my side, cracking open an eyelid—shocked at how good I felt. Zara had clearly slept in more than one tree in her time.

Brushing off several leaves that had fallen on me during the night, I spotted smoke already billowing from Chief's workshop. It was just past dawn, but H'tar was already buzzing with activity. A harassed-looking father balanced a child on one hip and bundle of sticks on the other. A woman wielding a wicked looking scythe headed for fields thick with a dark brown crop I didn't recognize, and a group of kids chased each other about to the cries of frustrated, but bemused, adults.

I looked at Chief's shop, finding the dark-haired man already outside—hammer in hand, completely focused on the scrap of metal on the anvil.

Now was my chance.

***

"I wanna go *home*," Waylen whined, kicking his heels against the bed frame where he lay sprawled out.

I smiled—he was still the same, at least.

"Read your book, peanut," Lenia replied. She was curled up in the corner, head buried in her knees. From the shadows that dragged at her lids, it looked like she had sat there the whole night. My guilt rose, refreshed and ready for another day, at the exhaustion and worry that pinched her face.

Chief's workshop was a chaotic mess. Tables groaned with scrap metal and tools covered every surface, centered around a black stove-like device in the center. A forge? I was surprised to see three beds shoved up against the wall closest to me, a tattered curtain strung by a piece of string separating them. How Chief lived in this mess, and no offence to the molger, utter filth was beyond me.

"Mom, this book is about how to break different types of *rocks,*" Waylen said, voice flat and unimpressed.

"Then you'll learn something new. Now, hush. I need to think." Lenia's hands gripped her hair, and my heart twisted. The woman I'd met in the cottage was strong and sure of herself—wielding a confidence I envied.

This woman looked like she wanted the whole world to stop.

Grimacing, I gently, oh so gently, slipped my fingers beneath the window's frame and shimmied it open.

To my surprise, it glided easily—Chief's house might be a mess, but the man oiled his window frames.

"But Mom, what—it's Zara!" Waylen shrieked in delight, leaping from the bed. Finger raised to my lips, I frantically shushed him, tripping in my haste to get inside. I landed in a tumble of limbs as the window slammed shut behind me with a satisfying *thunk.*

Oiled them too well, maybe.

"Ah, crap on a—"

Feet stomped into my vision. Even from the ground, I could tell Lenia was furious.

"What. Are. You. *Doing here?*" she hissed.

"I, uh…" I winced at how stupid I must look. "I came to… help you?"

"You're the entire reason I'm in here!" Her voice rose for the briefest second before she ducked down beside me, eyes dark with fury.

"I know—I'm really sorry," I rambled, choosing a spot on her left shoulder to stare at as I sat up. "I saw Jerome take you and I wanted to help."

"Zara!" Waylen yelled once more, flinging his arms around me—knocking me to the ground again.

"Hey, kiddo," I said, both surprised and pleased.

Lenia's gaze softened at Waylen's clear delight, and she sighed, rubbing her temple. "No. This isn't *entirely* your fault. Jerome's been looking for a reason to kick me out of H'tar for years. You just happened to be it."

"But why would he want that? He's your brother-in-law, right?"

"How do you know that?" she asked, eyes sharp.

"Oh, I ah…" I felt embarrassed, like I'd been caught with my hand in the cookie jar. "I might have heard the argument between Chief and Jerome."

She sighed. "All of it?"

"Well… not *all* of it. Just… most of it."

"Peanut, why don't you go—"

"Yeah, yeah." Waylen sighed, untangling himself from me. "Go and pretend I can't hear the grown-ups talking, I know." He grabbed a book at random, whistling as he wandered to the other side of the workshop.

I laughed, covering it with a cough when Lenia glared at me. Then she grinned, shaking her head. "He's going to be a nightmare as a teenager."

"I think you'll be able to handle it," I said.

She sat on the bed, gesturing for me to take Waylen's. "Only because he's so like me—stubborn. Defiant. He gets his kindness from his dad."

I said nothing, waiting for her to continue. "Rowan was his name. We grew up together, but I had *no* time for him. I spent my days running all over the Moonvale Mountains with my friends—ripping trees from the root, seeing who could crack the biggest boulder with their heads." She laughed. "Idiot kid stuff. Nights were little better. I'd get drunk with my friends on *glok* I'd robbed from my parents. Still shocked I never died from a hangover."

Lenia and I had very, very different ideas of what fun looked like.

"He, on the other hand, was quiet. He liked plants. And books. Then one day my mom got sick, along with a bunch of the elders. A bad batch of *glok*, we guessed, but we never found out what. Mama was vomiting day and night—couldn't even keep water down. I remember crying outside our den—and I *never* cry, when he showed up with this pot of black goo. Told her to eat it—that it would help."

"*Blackroot Cleanse?*" I asked.

"How did you know?"

I thought of the black pixelated potion bottle with a red lid on it from *Knights of Eternity.*

I shrugged. "Heard of it."

"Well, we hadn't. He saved my mom's life—and then acted like it was no big deal." She smiled, looking into the distance.

"That's what made you fall for him?"

"No. That's what made me notice him. *He* made me fall for him—how he listened so closely to everything I said. How he'd make necklaces for me out of my favorite flowers. How he'd trek to the nearest town, a trip that took a *week*, to buy fabric to sew me a dress." She shook her head. "He was terrible at sewing. The thing was covered in blood stains, and I had to bandage every one of his fingers."

Love softened her eyes as she smiled. "It was the best gift I ever got."

I remembered the men's clothes wrapped in a black ribbon at her house—and the baby blue dress underneath it, stained by droplets of blood. Waylen had said it was her favorite.

"He'd always wanted us to spend more time with humans. Pushed the elders for it—claimed he'd invented a soap that allowed him to move among them undetected, even by other falslings. But they brushed him off. 'We have everything we need at Moonvale,' they'd say. 'What use do we have for such a thing?'"

"And then the vaxion kicked you out," I guessed.

"You say that like you're not one of them."

I must have flinched because she crossed the room, sitting down next to me. She squeezed my hand—an apology, I knew. "They ordered us to leave," she continued. "We refused—it was our home as much as theirs. And then… the killings began." She looked away. "Rowan was one of the first."

"I'm so sorry," I said, gripping her hand back.

"So am I," she whispered. "Rowan had gone to the Mi'xan clan and asked them to let us stay for another few months—until Waylen was born. If I'd known, I would have stopped him. He always thought every problem could be fixed with words."

Her hand tightened on mine hard enough to hurt. "When they dumped his body outside my den, they left a note on it saying, 'Any woman worth her claw can raise a babe alone.' Jerome has blamed me ever since."

I gasped—trying to imagine how she must have felt. I couldn't even come close.

"That's… that's…"

"… the vaxion," she finished. "Ask for one thing and they'll take away two. You understand now why I wasn't the most… trusting of you."

"If I were you," I said, "I wouldn't have saved me. Not for all the money in the world."

She shrugged. "Waylen did. Not me."

"Waylen's not the one who patched me up and let me sleep on their floor," I said, nudging her gently with my shoulder.

"He's not the one who made you muck out Didi's pen either—especially as I *knew* she'd hate you." She smiled, nudging me back. "So maybe that evens it out."

"What now?" I asked when the silence stretched on—easy and comfortable.

"Now we wait for this ridiculous meeting. All Jerome has is a scrap of fabric and the sound of his voice. He can't prove we ever met or that I housed you." She shrugged. "I won't say I'm not nervous—I'd be a fool not to be. But I trust Chief. He'll keep Jerome in line."

I hesitated, arguments dying on my lips. I didn't want to leave them.

Her dark eyes softened. "Stop looking at me like a kicked dog," Lenia said, laughing gently. "I pray you never meet your vaxion kin—they'd eat you alive."

I smiled. "I'll take that as a compliment."

"Take it however you want because I don't regret kicking you out of my house." She stood, brushing down her dress—stern and in control once more. "But I don't regret helping you either. So stop looking so worried—I'll be fine. We both will."

"And so will Didi!" piped up Waylen, who had been slowly drifting back to our side of the room, his book long abandoned. "Not even Lukas will hurt her—I asked him nicely."

"Lukas?" I asked, the name familiar.

Lenia shot Waylen a look, and he immediately winced at his blunder, staring at his feet.

"Doesn't matter," she said, a warning in her voice. "Now—get out of here before someone sees you."

"Okay, okay," I relented. "But I'm staying in H'tar until the meeting."

Lenia opened her mouth to protest, but I shook my head. "If I leave now, I'll never stop worrying about you two."

"Fine. But *do not* be seen. I can't feign ignorance if you get spotted peeking through the damn windows."

Chapter Thirty-Seven

I spent the day in the trees watching the molger, munching on fruit and berries I'd picked on Lenia and Waylen's advice (they had disagreed on how edible a large purple berry was, and so I had decided to steer clear).

I peeled the small yellow fruit that had quickly become my favorite (their name escaped me, but I had been mentally calling them "sweet lemons"). Their skin was as tough to peel as a lemons, but the inside was as sweet and succulent as a grape.

H'tar looked, at first glance, completely ordinary. People tilled fields, laid out crops to dry in the sun, and tended to larger livestock. (I spotted several cows in a nearby barn with locks the size of my head on the outside. Protection from the "mongrel" I'd guessed.)

But then one of the women shirked off her dress, tossing it into the grass. No one batted an eye at her nakedness, nor did she seem even slightly ill at ease. I felt a blush rising in my cheeks, unable to imagine doing the same. I think I would curl up into a ball and die.

I stopped myself. What was the big deal? If they kept their clothes on when they transformed, they would rip every time—she was just being practical. I mentally repeated this but still couldn't look anywhere but her face as she cracked her shoulder, the people around her backing up.

I had wondered if Waylen's horrifying transformation was the product of his inexperience and young age.

It was not.

Her left arm snapped backward as it grew, fingers elongating into black talons. With practiced ease, she leaned forward, allowing her back to carry the weight of her new arm until the second paw sprang from her shoulder—her flesh ripping as it tore with the ease of parchment. There was a gurgle and a pop as her spine broke, widening and arching to fit her new arms.

She fell to all fours as her legs followed, but it was the skull that was the worst. Her molger eyes appeared first, small for her shifted form but huge for her human head. They bulged outward, pressing against the confines of her lids as her skull expanded to fit them.

My stomach turned, and I immediately regretted scarfing all those sweet lemons.

Her transformation was quicker than Waylen's, maybe a minute and a half. Her fur was a deep black with streaks of red, a twist of brown around her eyes hinting at the color of her human hair. She was smaller than Jerome in his molger form, a thought that irritated me for some reason. I didn't like the idea that a guy who thought it was okay to *kick a child* was the biggest and baddest molger in town.

The molger took a moment to shake out her limbs, rocking back and forth until she snorted—satisfied.

Two villagers, still human, called out to her, and she turned at the sound of their voices—blinking in the sunlight. As she followed their voices, she eventually closed her eyes fully until she hit the shadowed edges of the forest, easily dodging villagers and farming equipment along the way. I wondered if that was from hearing, memory, or both.

Minutes later, I heard a thump of something heavy being moved. A huge boulder rolled out of the forest, the molger driving it forward with the force of her shoulder. Two villagers called out directions as she pushed it into the center of H'tar. Moments later, several people went at the boulder with pickaxes—muscles straining as they fought to crack the stone.

I felt at peace watching them. I had no idea what the purpose of half their chores were, but how seamless they moved from human to molger form and how they used both to get through their days, amazed me.

Two falslings in molger form padded along until what I guessed was a female shouldered the male—laughing when he tripped. The male responded by latching his teeth around the offender's neck, shaking her viciously. Her wail was high and piercing, and he reluctantly released her when her paws tapped the ground furiously—the call for surrender.

Several watching molger let out a high-pitched bark that startled me until I saw those in human form laughing.

"That's what you get, Veema!"

"Toss her next time, Hoods!"

I bit back my own giggle. They were laughing—human and molger together.

There were other moments like that throughout the day. A human child cried in the street, and a nearby molger nuzzled her belly with his snout until her cries turned to laughter. When the boulder had been broken down fully, an exhausted woman held her hand out, palm first, to a molger. The molger gently headbutted her palm, and I realized I'd just seen this world's equivalent of a fist bump.

While I still wanted to kick Jerome's head in for hurting Lenia, I could see why he was scared of something happening to this place.

Despite watching for the whole day, I still had questions. I thought the molger's size when they transformed corresponded to their age or human form, Waylen's was tiny in comparison to the others, but that didn't seem to be the case. I'd seen both men and women in varying sizes and shapes transform into what seemed to be the average-sized molger. However, the woman who had rolled the boulder out of the forest, who couldn't have been more than three or four years older than me, had been the biggest I'd seen—beaten only by Jerome.

The color of their fur was also apparently random, with only occasional hints to their human coloring. Waylen had dark hair and yet his molger form was pure auburn, and I'd seen a range of colors so far, from midnight blue to a deep red.

As the sun dipped in the sky, people tidied up—stretching tight muscles and chatting idly as they walked the short distance to their homes. I caught only snatches, someone was going to forage later in the night for grubs (I shuddered at the thought), whereas someone else had set up several animal traps in preparation for a stew. No one, I realized, had mentioned tonight's upcoming town hall meeting.

Not until they wandered home.

"Do you think Jerome was spinning a yarn? About Lenia housing a vaxion?" a male voice asked, passing beneath me.

"Dunno. She's always been a bit odd—though I think living out in the shack would drive anyone mad. It's like she doesn't even want to be here," a female voice answered.

"That's true. She never comes here neither, not unless Chief makes her," the male voice said. "Wasn't Waylen friends with Lukas too?"

That name again—Lukas.

"Shhh." A thump followed, a slap on a shoulder. The man hissed an "ow."

"Don't talk about him—it's bad luck. What if *we* have kids and the same thing happens to them?" she snapped.

"Our kids will *not* be blood-spiked, don't be ridiculous. Also that bloody hurt."

"I'll kiss and make it better later. Now come on—I need to eat and wash before the meeting."

Their voices faded as they walked away, turning to what they'd eat that evening.

I grimaced as I leaned back. I had a sinking feeling I knew who Lukas was.

The sun began to sink, the light streaking with red, when I finally stood—brushing myself down. I didn't have to wonder where this town meeting was because people began to gather outside of Chief's workshop. I took a running jump, leaping from one tree to another as I moved closer, making sure to keep to the shadows.

I got as close as I dared, scowling from the coverage of trees as Jerome pushed to the front of the crowd. He was mercifully dressed this time in a roughspun, but durable looking blue tunic and navy trousers tucked into worn boots. He walked with a stick he'd fashioned into a crutch, a large bandage wrapped around his knee.

A not insignificant part of me was happy to see him grimace every time he walked.

A woman, her auburn hair tied back in a loose but elegant braid, stood by his side looking nervous. Her green dress hung past her knees and lacked the wear and tear of Jerome's. I did a double take and looked down at the dress I had borrowed from Lenia. A gift from her sister-in-law, she'd said.

They were almost exactly the same.

I leaned as far out of the tree as I dared, trying to get a read on her. I could tell little other than she clearly didn't want to be here—she looked around anxiously and was worrying the nail of her thumb to nothing. Jerome, on the other hand, was a ball of energy—stomping about on his crutch despite the obvious pain it caused him. After his eighth increasingly angry glance at Chief's door, I thought he'd try to force his way in. But Chief, timing impeccable, flung it open—stepping aside in a smooth motion.

Lenia walked out first, her hand gripping Waylen's tightly. She stood with her head held high, but I could see her free hand clenching and unclenching in a fist.

"Let us call the ninety-fifth H'tar town meeting," Chief announced. "Tonight we will discuss charges brought against Lenia Doorin regarding the housing of a vaxion. But first…" Jerome, mouth twisted in anger, moved forward, but Chief held up his hand. His other drifted to the hammer he still wore in his apron. "But first, we will discuss once and for all what to do about the 'mongrel.'"

Chief sighed.

"What to do about Lukas."

Chapter Thirty-Eight

Eternity knelt, eyes dry and heart heavy. The spiced incense of the Gallowed Temple, usually a comfort, seemed pungent today, and her nose twitched in irritation. She *should* be praying, but her focus was as fragmented as the corpse of the man she'd just turned to ash.

She had wielded the power of Gallow thousands of times—offering their souls up to the all-seeing god for judgment. More often than not, it ended as it had with the old man. The first time she had done it, she had been fifteen years old and terrified out of her mind.

The woman, barely older than Eternity at the time, had not survived.

She didn't sleep for weeks afterward, ashen faces reaching out to her in dreams that left her covered in a cold sweat. On those nights, she would light a candle and reread the letters her brothers sent her, telling her how proud they were of her. How amazing it was that their own little sister was Gallow's Chosen. And how they hoped she was doing all right.

She wished she could reach for those letters, but they were now so worn she kept them stored away—saving them for a truly dire moment. And she had felt far worse than this, she chastised herself.

Eternity wondered why the old man whose life was no more or less remarkable than any of the thousands she had judged preyed on her mind.

A laugh escaped her when she realized why.

Since her ascension, it was a rare week she hadn't needed to crack open the door between her and Gallow. That some soul had come to her, asking if they were worthy of being a Champion, hoping and praying for the power and gifts Gallow offered.

Yet because she'd been kidnapped, it had been over a month since her last judgment—something that had never happened in her life as Gallow's seeker of Champions.

A small, very small, part of Eternity was thankful to Magnus. Her heart had begun to grow numb to the pain of judgment. It was good to be reminded of it—it kept her sane.

Kept her human.

After the old man had keeled over in the street, his body crumbling, Gallowed disciples had appeared as if from nowhere—sweeping up the remnants as they whispered blessings of mercy. Lazander hadn't said a word when she rejoined him, nodding at her stiffly as he escorted her to the Gallowed Temple.

She couldn't blame him. If she, after all these years, still wasn't used to it, how could she expect him to be?

Still—it tugged at her heart. Lazander, Marito, and Gabriel were the closest things she had to friends outside of the other disciples. If she lost them, she didn't know what she'd do.

"I'm afraid I'll have to leave you here, Lady Eternity," Lazander said, bowing.

She panicked, afraid he'd come to fear her like so many, but his eyes were warm with determination when he raised his head. "The spymaster has finally caught wind of Magnus' location. With Zara gone, he is vulnerable. We'll catch him and make him answer for his crimes against you."

Eternity recalled seeing Zara mucking out a pigpen and said nothing, even as guilt reared its head—cold and unfamiliar. "When do you leave?" she asked instead, trying to keep the worry from her voice.

"Now." He smiled. "Myself, Valerius, Gabriel, and Marito are going after him."

Eternity's brows raised in surprise. "All of the Gilded?"

He nodded. "Magnus caught us by surprise last time. We won't make that mistake again. It is past time we find out why he kidnapped you, knowing that it would risk the wrath of not only Navaros but Evergarden too."

Lazander rested a hand over his heart and tapped it twice, the standard salute for the Navaros army.

The red-haired knight turned to leave, but Eternity reached out to stop him. To both of their surprise, she asked him to stay for just a moment.

Eternity took a deep breath. On Gallow's Eve, the biggest feast day in the realms, there was no door to crack open to channel Gallow. Instead it was like a dam broke, and she stood at the bottom of a thunderous waterfall, bathing in the tidal wave that was his godly power.

Any other time of the year, however, reaching beyond the veil of this world to where Gallow lay—a dimension of shadow and darkness—had a cost. To try twice in a day was foolish.

But today, she felt a little foolish.

She cracked open the door between dimensions—her mind expanding, the veins of the universe exploding into possibility and impossibility as the power of a god coursed through her. While Gallow's gifts were plentiful, she couldn't glimpse into the future and see what lay in store for Lazander. Couldn't see what Magnus, that vile worm of a man, would try to do to a person she called friend.

That didn't mean she couldn't try to guard against it.

Lazander stayed resolutely still as Eternity opened her eyes, knowing her sclera were pitch black—allowing him a glimpse into the dimension where Gallow lay, watching. Always watching.

With difficulty she raised a hand, her body moving like granite as her mortal form rebelled against the power she forced it to wield. She pushed past the pain, pressing a single finger against Lazander's chest. She pictured a shield surrounding Lazander, blades and magic crumbling against it as Gallow reached out a mighty hand and swatted them away. It was purely a visualization, but it helped focus her mind against the onslaught of magic she struggled to contain.

"Your heart sings with a Champion's spark. In your darkest hour, may Gallow see your worth," she whispered, struggling to stay upright.

Lazander gasped, and Eternity stumbled as she slammed the door shut between her and Gallow.

Lazander didn't touch her as she righted herself, his hand coming to his chest.

"Blessing of the Righteous," Eternity explained, gesturing to his chest. "I'm alive because of your bravery. I'm sure Gallow would approve of me offering you some protection."

"I—thank you, Eternity," Lazander said, eyes wide with wonder. He quickly adjusted his casual tone and straightened. "My lady. We won't fail you, Lady Eternity. *I* won't fail you." He strode away before she could answer, leaving instructions to the Gallowed Temple guards to escort her back to the tower when she was ready.

Eternity turned, hand cupping her nose where blood flowed freely, black spots dotting her vision. As she fell to one knee, a disciple in dark robes, Yolana she dimly recalled, rushed to her aid. Eternity was grateful that Lazander had left when he had.

She would hate for him to see her like this.

***

Nose clean, a dress of white cotton donned, she knelt before a bronze statue of Gallow.

Depictions of Gallow varied wildly—not even Eternity had glimpsed him in his true form. He'd been drawn as a giant with powerful arms and a horned helmet (a favorite of children's story books). A hooded figure with eyes like stars (houses of healing favored this). Even a single tower of darkness by Gallow's cynics, who claimed that by asking his followers to sacrifice so much, he was little better than the Tyrant he once triumphed over.

This statue was entirely different.

Standing at twice Eternity's height, his body was thin and pointed, clavicles sharpened to points that pierced his bandaged torso. His face was hidden by an elongated skull he wore like a helmet. The beak of the massive birdlike skull obscured his features but not the dark sclera that stared down at her.

It came to her predecessor, Eternity III, in a vision. She'd sketched it immediately, commissioning a sculpture of it. A bird's skull, hollow and scoured clean, was now his most common symbol—found in temples and taverns alike.

It had always resonated with Eternity. While she served Gallow, she never forgot what he was—a god. A deity that demanded as much from his followers as he gave. The alien form of the creature before her captured that feeling as it gazed down at her—accepting nothing short of perfection.

The sculpture had also sparked what would become the temple sages' favorite question.

What, exactly, is a god?

Gallow was not of this world—that was easy to see. They called him god because what else do you call a creature that descends from the skies and wields the power to split mountains and grant life? Like the Tyrant, he came to this world from the Void, a far-flung dimension beyond the realm of mortals. But where was it? *What* was it?

Eternity personally thought it existed alongside theirs, bound to their threads of time but not commanded by them. When she opened the door, she felt the touch of the alien marred by the familiar—like seeing an old friend you'd never met.

She'd tried to explain it to the temple sages once. They'd simply nodded and told her she was doing an excellent job.

She hadn't bothered them since.

Her knees ached but she leaned into the pain, letting her mind wander.

Gallow's origins had never particularly bothered her—she felt his gaze when she opened the door, felt his power when she carried out his will. He knew her, and she knew him—and that was enough for her.

What kept her up at night, however, was a far bigger question.

When?

When would the Tyrant return?

Eternity couldn't help but smile at the childish phrase—the "Tyrant." She'd become so used to saying it aloud that she now even thought it. She knew its name—all higher-level disciples did. But to speak it might awaken it from its slumber.

It seemed ridiculous, but she had seen the impossible too many times to think it was just a silly superstition.

One of Gallow's long spindly arms rested by his side, the other reached out—bony fingers splayed as if He were about to press his own palm to Eternity's head. To see her, to judge her as she had done to so many.

Guilt pulled at her heart.

She had told no one of her vision of Zara. As the queen's focus had turned to Evergarden, and now the Gilded focused on Magnus, people seemed to have forgotten about the fire-wielding falsling. Eternity assumed they thought her dead, but it was hard to tell—everyone was doing their best to keep her in the dark.

As always.

Yet Zara was only mucking pigpens. She was hardly conspiring with Magnus.

Or was she?

She shook her head. She'd seen the look in Zara's eyes when she'd faced down Magnus. Zara would cut off her own hand before helping that treacherous mage.

Lighting a fresh stick of incense, she placed it at the foot of Gallow's statue. Eternity had told the other disciples she needed "silent contemplation," her go-to excuse as a teenager when she needed space, and she was pleased to see it still worked.

One disciple however, Yolana—the girl who had run to Eternity's aid, didn't budge. Yolana wore only the half-mask of a novice, the dark lace veil obscuring her eyes but not her vision. While full disciples had to keep their hair short and simple, novices could style their hair as they wished.

Yolana took full advantage of that.

If Eternity tied her hair back in a single thick braid, Yolana would be wearing it the same way the next time she visited the temple. Same with two braids trailing down the front. Up high and coiled. Long and loose.

Yolana hovered nearby, even now, a pitcher of water and a platter of fruit in her hands—ready should Eternity show so much as a hint of hunger or thirst. Catching her gaze, Yolana smiled broadly, showing too many teeth. Eternity did her best to smile back. She made a gentle "backing up" gesture with her hand, and Yolana nodded—taking a single step back.

Eternity tried not to sigh, knowing Yolana meant well.

Kneeling, she bowed forward until her elbows and forearms met the cold stone floor. She had planned to meet with the Head Disciple and ask her to intercede on Zara's behalf. By the time Eternity had recovered, however, the Head Disciple had been called away to Neverwood—two days ride from here.

But that didn't mean she couldn't prepare herself.

She leaned forward, pressing her forehead to the ground, her elbows tucked in by her sides.

Gallow was not a god who accepted favors or indulgences. He sought demonstrations of iron will and fortitude. Obedience and sacrifice. This was a small gesture on Eternity's part, but she hoped it would be enough for Gallow to impart some of his strength and power to Zara.

Zara is worthy of you. She silently pleaded with Gallow, numbness spreading from her aching knees to her thighs and back. *She is worthy of your guidance and mercy—I stake my life as your Chosen on it. So help her, please.*

Four hours she stayed in place, still as the stone she knelt on. Four hours she prayed, hoping Gallow would hear her call.

When the bells of the temple sounded noon, she stayed four hours more.

Chapter Thirty-Nine

"**B**ut first, we will discuss once and for all what to do about the mongrel. What to do about Lukas," Chief said.

Jerome's face twisted in fury at the mention of the name, and I was surprised to see he wasn't the only one. The crowd's expressions were a mix of anger and pity. Jerome's wife looked on the edge of tears.

My eyes fell on Waylen, who clutched Lenia's hand tightly as his eyes welled with open tears.

Lukas was his friend, I remembered.

"Don't call that thing by his clan's name," Jerome said. "He's a mongrel—that's it. A deranged animal who can't even shift back."

Chief shook his head. "He *is* Lukas because I need you all to understand—if we decide to kill him, we're doing more than killing a predator. We're doing more than ending his pained existence.

"We're setting a *precedent*—a dangerous one," he continued. "The molger way is to ask the question 'Is this fair?' It is why, when someone shows signs of being blood-spiked, of being on the brink of losing control, that we offer them a choice. We can kill you now, at your behest. Or you can leave before you turn. This is our way—this is how we give them a choice when life has made one for them.

"But if we choose to kill Lukas," Chief strode before the crowd, his thumbs resting in the pockets of his apron as if he was simply chatting to a neighbor, "when his only crime is killing livestock that we can easily replace, then we take away that choice. Make no mistake, what happened to Lukas could happen to *any* of our children."

Chief spread his hands. "Is this what we want? Is this fair?"

"'Any of our kids?' You're bloody full of it," Jerome spat. "Lukas turned because his mom was a filthy vaxion. If your kid is molger through and through, you aren't turning into some abomination."

His wife brought a hand to her stomach, resting on its sloped bump. I belatedly realized she was pregnant.

"So five years ago when my son showed signs of turning," Chief said, his voice low but somehow louder in the heavy silence, "when he chose to die before becoming trapped in the mind of a beast, why was that? He had a molger mother and father, two parents who would have cut their own throats to save him."

Jerome smirked. "We don't know for sure that he had two molger parents. When your missus was still alive and kicking, she spent a *lot* of time traveling. Who knows what she got up to."

The change in Chief's stance was slight—a tightening of his shoulders, the shifting of one foot to the other, but in a second he went from calm and controlled to a man on the brink of violence.

Jerome smirked, handing his cane to his wife as he raised his chin to Chief—a clear challenge.

Bastard knew exactly what he was doing, I realized. I looked back at Chief, hoping he wouldn't take the bait—although I wouldn't blame him if he did.

Chief sighed, straightening. I couldn't read his expression, but even I could tell it cost him a lot to back down. "To argue the why is pointless. Lukas has committed no crime that would warrant his death. If we wish to kill one of our own, it will not be with my blessing."

"And I won't stand by and wait until he kills one of our own—just so you get to sleep at night. Let's vote!" Jerome called, turning to the crowd. "All those in favor of killing the mongrel before it kills one of us, one of our kids?"

Hands shot up into the air. I counted them, my heart sinking as the numbers climbed. Jerome glared, lip twitching with the hint of a growl, and several hands that once hesitated now rose.

"It is decided," Chief said, eyes closed in clear defeat. "Lukas will die."

"No!" Waylen called. "Lukas doesn't mean to, he doesn't know what he's doing!"

Lenia tried to pull him back, to turn his face into her skirts, but it was too late.

Jerome gestured to them. "And next—Lenia Doorin for housing a vaxion," he called. "This is something I raise with a heavy heart. She married my brother—Waylen is my family, my blood."

I noticed he didn't say Lenia was his family, and by the thinning of her mouth, she did too.

"But *something* is going on in that house. The mongrel has taken all of our pigs but Lenia's. And then I find clothes drenched in the stink of vaxion right by her house."

"They were by the *lake*," Lenia corrected. "And unless I'm suddenly responsible for everything that goes in and out of the water, this has nothing to do with me."

"So you deny having seen or assisted a vaxion in any way, shape, or form?" Chief asked.

"I do."

"Then why was a clean towel washed in our soap right by the clothes?" Jerome asked. The crowd murmured, and even Chief looked at Lenia in surprise.

Crap. The towel was missing when I got out of the lake. I had completely forgotten.

"We—we all use the same soap," Lenia said, her voice faltering. "That towel could have come from anywhere."

But her argument sounded weak, even to my ears.

"There's a river right by H'tar," Jerome said, gesturing off to the right. "You think the vaxion stole a towel from one of us, trekked through the forest—ignoring everywhere it could have bathed along the way—just to have the pleasure of washing in the lake right by your house?"

"Who knows why a vaxion does anything?" she snapped. "I can't read their minds, nor can you. And has anyone seen this so-called vaxion?" Hands wild, her gestures were as frantic as her words. Lenia was panicking, and nothing screamed defensive like panic.

"Where is the vaxion?" Jerome asked.

"I don't know."

"Lenia," Chief said, brow furrowed, sadness twisting his mouth. "The vaxion kill without conscience—you know this better than most. If one of them is here, if the Mi'xan clan has decided to send someone after us, then we need to know. Answer him."

"She wouldn't—it's not like that." Lenia winced at her blunder, but it was too late.

Jerome's wife stepped back, horror etched into her face. Several of the crowd murmured in surprise, any hope or belief in Lenia gone. The change in the air was tangible, from mild suspicion to anger directed at Lenia.

"*Where is the vaxion?*" Jerome roared, limping toward her.

"I-I don't—"

Jerome grabbed Lenia by the tunic, bunching it in his chest as he shook her. Chief stepped forward, but hands from the crowd, Jerome's friends, held him back.

"You fooling around with one of them, is that what this is?" Jerome spat. "My brother is dead in the ground because of you, and now you're whoring yourself out to one of those bas—"

His words were abruptly cut off by the fist I drove into his mouth.

He stumbled backward but didn't fall because I grabbed a fistful of his own shirt, hauling him to his feet.

"**I am death's mistress,**" I hissed. "**Bow before me.**"

Fury's Claw Activated.

Talons, inches long, punctured the thin cloth of his skirt, leaving bloody trails on his skin, but I was too angry to care. Fury gave me strength, and I lifted him off the ground with one arm, his legs kicking the air weakly.

I heard, rather than saw, several people simply run——their feet pounding on the dirt path toward the forest. Others fell to the ground, prostrating themselves and begging for mercy. Some simply stood in shock. The part of me still rational registered this but only as an aside. All that mattered was the fear in Jerome's eyes.

"Apologize," I said.

"Wha-what?" Jerome sputtered in surprise, pawing at my arm like a weak child.

"*Apologize to Lenia,*" I roared, my grip tightening.

Vicious Command Activated.

A chorus of "I'm sorry!" "Forgive me," echoed around the crowd, and I knew my voice carried with it the thrum of power—the threat of command. Jerome, to his credit, didn't flinch. HIs gaze sharpened like flint.

"I won't bow to you, vaxion. We did once—never again."

"*Apologize*," I yelled, shaking Jerome like a doll. It would be so easy, I knew, to rip his throat out. To feel the warmth of his blood on my skin, hot as summer's rain, as his eyes grew dim. They would know what it meant to cross me. To hurt someone who—

"It's all right," a voice whispered, and I looked down to see Lenia.

Eyes wide, she reached out, gently resting a hand on the arm that clutched Jerome. "Let him go. Please." She spoke with caution, watching me carefully but without a trace of fear.

Jerome looked from me to Lenia, and I could see his mind racing with questions—brow furrowed in disapproval. My anger spiked. I could kill him in an instant, and he had the *audacity* to be judgmental?

I sighed, abruptly opening my hand.

Jerome hit the ground with the elegance of cold spaghetti on a tiled floor, crumpling on himself.

His wife rushed to his side, but he held out a hand in warning, planting himself between us as he struggled to his feet. A small part of me admired his desire to protect his wife, not that it would stop me. He squared himself, taking a deep breath.

A whisper of power curled about him, his scent sharpening on the wind. A second later his right sleeve split open, cloth bursting as fur-lined flesh erupted from his shoulder—a fully formed molger arm, clawed and ready. Beads of sweat gathered on his forehead as he raised his new arm in a defensive stance, the rest of his body still human.

Part of me knew that a partial transformation was difficult—near impossible, in fact, for all but the strongest of falslings.

Good, I thought, letting him see his own death play out in my eyes. That would make this more interesting.

My gaze flickered to Jerome's wife, fear naked in her eyes as she clutched her stomach. The crowd was deathly silent as some stood, glaring at me with open hatred. Others knelt on the ground, cowering. Regardless of where they stood, the same undercurrent of fear ran through every falsling.

These people who could transform into beasts the sizes of small houses were scared.

Scared of *me*.

Abruptly my mind went blank. The anger and bloodlust that had left me itching for a fight vanished, leaving me hollow.

What happened? Why did I do that? I searched for Waylen and found him backed up against the door of Chief's workshop—eyes wide, shoulders hunched. The same fear in his eyes.

Oh, god.

Everyone was looking at me—Jerome with his molger arm, his wife, Chief, the entire village of H'tar. I was suddenly aware of how it looked, how I'd crashed into their meeting. How I'd threatened Jerome. How Lenia was going to be banned from her home because of me.

I'd ruined it. I'd ruined everything.

Abruptly my chest tightened, and my breathing increased. Panic flooded my brain as I stared at the ground, panic crashing into me like a tidal wave. My hands came to my eyes, human once more, as they welled with tears.

Oh god, please stop staring at me. Please stop.

Jerome looked from me to Lenia, confusion clear on his face.

"Zara?" Lenia said.

My hand went to my chest, my heart bullying my ribcage.

"Zara? What's wrong?"

"I'm sorry," I said. "I'm so sorry."

Why was I so bad at everything? What was the point of me? What—

Chapter Forty

"Well," I heard Chief say from outside the door. "You're right—she isn't like other vaxion."

"I wouldn't have helped her otherwise," Lenia said. "I'm sorry. For—well, for lying."

There was a beat, and then a heavy sigh. "The father in me wants to tell you I understand, but I'm Chief of H'tar for a reason. You know you'll have to serve some sort of punishment for this, but I'll see if I can swing hard labor plus extra additions to our winter supplies. Is this fair?"

"It is, Chief. Thank you."

"So what do we do… about…"

I could only imagine the gesture that was being made in my direction. Shame burned bright as I held my face in my hands. When everyone stared at me, my brain shot into overdrive, screaming at me to run away.

So I did just that.

Without a word, I charged into Chief's workshop, slamming the door shut behind me. Then I slid to the ground, covered my ears, and imagined I was in my room back home under a freshly laundered duvet, pillow clutched tightly in my hands.

I didn't hear much of what happened next but caught pieces of it.

Chief stepped in, trying to calm everyone down and telling them he'd deal with "the vaxion." There were disgruntled murmurs and even some arguing, but no one else seemed willing to approach me. I heard more than one exclamation of "Did she just say '*sorry*'? You heard it too, right?"

Not even Jerome seemed to know what to do, although he let off a choice couple of words in myself and Lenia's direction.

I could think again, although my chest hurt, and my breathing was frayed. I felt hollow and empty, and all I wanted to do was sleep.

"Should we, um, knock?" Chief asked from just outside.

You're being ridiculous, I told myself, *he shouldn't need to knock on his own door.*

Lenia gave a small laugh. "I have no idea."

I groaned. Better to get this over with.

"I'm coming out," I said, trying and failing not to sound embarrassed.

I opened the door a crack, and Chief immediately stepped back. Whether it was to be cautious or considerate, I didn't know—likely both.

Lenia gave me a small smile.

"Hi," I said lamely.

To my surprise, Chief held out a hand. "Ryland—head of H'tar village. Call me Chief, everyone else does."

I shook his hand, shocked at how warm it was. It was like clutching a mug of tea that was *just* bordering on too hot. I didn't know if that was a molger thing or a Chief thing—another question to add to the list.

"Zara," I said, purposefully ignoring the rest of my title. "Just Zara is fine."

"As much as I'd love to welcome you to H'tar, I think it's understandable that I have questions."

"That's fair," I said, and he smiled at the turn of phrase.

"But we can hardly do this on an empty stomach. I'm a better blacksmith than a cook, but I can make a mean stew thanks to my wife—Gallow rest her. What say we discuss this like civilized folk?"

I nodded. "Please."

***

Chief had vastly undersold his stew, or maybe it was because this was my first proper meal in this world, but I wolfed it down like I'd never seen food in my life.

I was on bowl number three before my pace finally slowed.

"Wow, you eat more than Didi. And she's *huge*," Waylen said.

Lenia lightly tapped the back of his head. "Waylen, it's not nice to compare someone to a pig."

"It's true though!" he protested.

"Sorry," I said, eyes down.

Chief laughed—a deep pleasant laugh that rumbled in his chest. "Not at all, I take it as a compliment." He took my empty bowl, tidying up the table briskly before settling back down. He passed out several whittled cups, pouring something sweet smelling and tangy into them. With a pleased sigh, I sipped it—spiced-warmth slipping down my throat.

This was the most relaxed I'd felt since I'd woken up in Zara's body.

"Now I have to ask, Zara. Where did you come from? Are you really the Fury as Lenia says? Or have you simply taken on her moniker?"

I looked at Lenia, who nodded. Chief deserved the truth. I thought of my mom's words—*when you tell the truth, good people listen.* Valerius hadn't listened. He'd left me half dead on a forest floor. But that didn't mean the truth was the problem, the voice in my head that wanted to lie said.

Trust goes both ways. I had to trust them, or why would they trust me?

I told Chief everything, aware Lenia and Waylen were hanging on my every word—about waking up in a prison cell, rescuing Eternity, burning Magnus half alive.

When I got to the part about leaping from the castle roof with Eternity in my arms onto Lazander's dragon, I thought Waylen's eyes would burst from his skull.

"You got to ride Galora? *The real actual dragon, Galora?*"

I did, I said, not sure how to tell him I'd also accidentally stabbed her with my claws several times. Or that Lazander had nearly skewered me for it.

"So, before your time in the cell, you have almost no memories?" Chief asked, rubbing his beard thoughtfully, when I finished my tale.

I nodded, not trusting my words to carry the half-lie. I hadn't told them about the game *Knights of Eternity*, the Operator, or that I came from another world. It sounded insane, and I wouldn't have believed me in their shoes.

"I've heard of you and Magnus both—I daresay there's a falsling this side of the Moonvale Mountains who hasn't. I confess, I thought you a traitor to your own kin as many of us do," Chief said.

Lenia looked down at his words, and I recalled her calling me just that.

"I'm heartened that you were able to get away from him," he continued. "That took courage."

"I thought mages were supposed to be smart?" Lenia said. "What idiot goes after Gallow's Chosen? The Gilded will be crawling up his backside in no time."

"Gabriel will wrap him in a shadow, hold him down, and then Marito will charge at him and chop his head off." Waylen mimed the action dramatically, adding a kick at the end for good measure.

"Waylen, peanut, calm down," Lenia said.

"But she met Valerius! And Lazander! What was Valerius like? Is his shield as big as they say? I bet it was even bigger. Did you see Lazander's hawk? Can she really cut a man's eyes out with a single claw? And what about…"

Waylen chatted on, not giving me a chance to answer any of his questions, for which I was grateful. I knew the Gilded because of *Knights of Eternity*, but I'd had no idea they were so famous. The way Waylen spoke of them, they sounded like this world's equivalent of celebrities or influencers.

I squashed a smile at the thought of a stern-faced Valerius on a "sponsored post," trying to sell constipation medicine—he certainly looked like he could use it.

"Your words have a cost to them, Zara—I can tell," Chief said, gently motioning Waylen back to his seat. "Thank you for trusting us with them."

"Unfortunately," he continued, "that doesn't change the fact that you being here is a problem," Chief said, bringing me back to reality. "We all saw your claws, and while hearing you apologize, something unheard of for a vaxion, bought me time to sit down and speak to you properly, people will still see you as a threat. You might not be a run-of-the-mill vaxion, but you're still a vaxion."

I sighed. I had tried to help, and in the end made things worse. "What can I do? Should I just leave?"

"Maybe. But then Jerome might argue that both Lenia and I are in your pocket—and the last thing I need is for everyone to start pointing fingers at each other." Chief rubbed his hands over his tired eyes. With a sigh, he glanced out the window, squinting at the darkness. "But we won't solve anything with a tired head as my wife used to say. Let's sort this out in the morning." He turned to Lenia. "And we *will* sort this out—you have my word."

Lenia hid her worry with a tired smile. Grabbing an extra blanket from a wooden chest, Chief said, "I'll take the floor, you can—"

"No," I said, more forcefully than I'd intended. "I've eaten you out of house and home, I'm not taking your bed as well."

Chief chuckled, giving me a bemused smile, "A polite vaxion? I'll be damned. Well, I won't insist—my back isn't what it used to be, anyway."

"Night," he called, drawing a thin curtain back so it obscured his bed. I heard the thump of clothes hitting the floor and then the whine of springs as he flopped on the mattress. He was snoring in seconds.

Lenia laughed quietly. "I wish I could fall asleep that quickly."

"Same."

Lenia spent the next few minutes trying to tuck Waylen into bed as he continued to pepper me with whispered questions. "Can Gabriel summon shadow creatures? Did Marito really take on half of Freyley's army? How about—"

"Waylen, I will ban Zara from answering a single question if you don't go to sleep—right now."

Waylen pouted, but seeing his mother's glare, abruptly turned onto his side. Lenia smiled at me. "Victory," she mouthed.

I stood awkwardly as she pulled off her dress, a simple shift underneath, and climbed into bed. She gestured to the floor beside her, and I made up a small nest of blankets that I could curl up on.

I thought she was asleep when I heard the barest whisper. "Jerome has always been a bully—ever since we were kids. He had to be bigger, tougher, and stronger than anyone else and couldn't handle it if you talked back to him. And I did. A lot. He hated that I married his precious little brother. Hated it more when I got pregnant."

Unsure what to say, I kept quiet.

"I think, deep down, he's still grieving. He misses Rowan desperately—we all do. And since he couldn't hurt the vaxion, I was the next best thing. I took it—the comments, the looks, the anger. I even moved farther out so he wouldn't have to see me. I thought I deserved it."

I suddenly desperately wished I'd beaten Jerome to a pulp.

"I'm sorry," I said lamely.

Lenia's breathing evened out, and her voice was barely a whisper when she dropped her hand over the side of the bed, squeezing mine gently. "Thank you—for standing up for me."

"Any time," I said, squeezing back.

Maybe I'd done some good after all.

I was just drifting off, the outline of the Menu hovering on the edge of my consciousness, when a bolt of terror shot through me. I sat up, clutching my chest as my heart pounded viciously. In an instant I was on my feet, staring into the darkness of the workshop.

Time had passed, I could tell by the pitch black that had descended, but something was wrong. Something was *here*.

I looked around, cursing eyes that saw enemies in every shadow.

And then the screaming started.

Chapter Forty-One

"What fondness, dark prince,

Bless me with thine sweet lips,

Oh saints, hear my wish,

Dare I steal a fateful kiss?

Low the darkest sorrow sleeps,

Where once the storied angel weeps,

My heart, my will, my faithfulness,

Dare I steal a fateful kiss?

Your breath—"

"Mari, I swear, I will tie you to a tree and leave you here if you do not stop," Gabriel hissed, yanking the reins of his horse in a fit of temper.

"This is why you're still single, Master Gabriel," Marito said. "No appreciation for beauty. For *romance*."

Lazander smiled as the familiar argument erupted between the two Gilded. Five minutes into what would be a day's long journey, and they had started arguing like an old married couple. Lazander turned to make a joke of it to Valerius, but the dark-haired knight was staring off into the distance, lost in his own world. He held the reins of his horse loosely in his hands, face cast in sadness.

"Lord Valerius?" Lazander asked. "Are you well, sir?"

Valerius blinked, then nodded—expression returning to its usual sternness. "I'm just thinking how best to tackle Magnus. Without Eternity as a shield, he doesn't have a chance against us. The problem is making sure we take him alive."

Lazander nodded, relieved to see Valerius acting like his old self. Marito, Gabriel, and Lazander had sprung at his offer to track down Magnus together. This was exactly the opportunity they were looking for—to watch Valerius and to build a case against him to bring to the queen.

Lazander felt a twinge of guilt for going behind Valerius' back. He knew something was amiss, and he planned to get to the root of it. Until then, their plan was to act like things were perfectly normal while ensuring Valerius was with at least one Gilded at all times.

"We know Magnus is due west, but did the spymaster give you any further information?" Lazander asked.

"None, but you know how he is. One of his shadows was waiting in my room, lurking like a damned wraith. They handed me an envelope and left without a word." Valerius shuddered. "I know he's the spymaster for a reason, but I could really do without the cloak-and-dagger nonsense." He reached into his cloak, pulling out a piece of paper and handing it to Lazander.

"Here. Now you'll know all I do."

Lazander took it, studying the contents intently.

A man matching Magnus' description has been spotted moving due west along the Barrow river. A shadow is on him. Pursue him. Updated locations will be sent to you along the way.

The dual rings of the Ivory Keep were pressed into the wax seal at the bottom. Lazander was quietly relieved. He'd considered the possibility that these orders were somehow fabricated, but there was no way Valerius could have faked the seal. Only the queen and her spymaster had access to it. Besides, the contents alone would have told Lazander this was authentic—only the Ivory Keep's elusive spymaster would send them on a mission with the bare minimum of information.

Lazander had never met him, nor even had a name for him. All he knew was that very little, if anything, passed by without his knowing.

"No updates since?" he asked, handing the paper back.

"Of course not," Valerius said, rolling his eyes. "He'll probably send a raven to crap on my head, and we'll find the location mixed in with the feces."

Lazander laughed aloud, more from surprise at Valerius' crass joke. It usually took several pints of mead to see Valerius so relaxed.

Gabriel spun in his saddle. "Kindly share it with the group, so I might be saved from yet another recital."

"Indeed, young masters—it is a delight to see you in such fine form!" Marito boomed.

"Lazander was wondering when you'd start exercising something other than your biceps," Valerius said with a wry smile. "He used the words 'chicken legs.'"

"Young Master Lazander?" Marito roared, looking stricken.

Gabriel laughed so hard he nearly fell from the horse. Lazander frantically protested his innocence, and even Valerius laughed aloud.

The four knights rode on into the evening, a troop of knights trailing after them. Several had also been in their retinue during their search for Lady Eternity, and there was more than one smile as the knights joked and laughed—glad the tension between Lazander and Valerius had subsided.

***

The scream was high-pitched—cutting off almost as soon as it began. I ran for the door, struggling with the lock before simply kicking it down.

"Sorry!" I yelled, mentally promising to fix it later.

Cold air kissed my skin. The light of the moon was obscured by fat, heavy clouds that promised rain. H'tar, vibrant and full of life only hours ago, looked silent and abandoned—windows dark, curtains drawn. I shivered—and not from the cold.

The thud of bare feet made me turn a second too late.

"Like a fly to muck," Jerome snapped, skidding to a halt next to me. He was shirtless, hair sticking up. Whoever had caused the scream, it wasn't him. "I was full sure I'd find you covered in blood, up to your claws in one of our own."

"There's only one molger on my hit list," I snapped, anger pushing past sense. "And I'm looking at him."

"Try it, vaxion." He snarled. "See what happens."

I didn't know if it was mine or Zara's, but I fought the desperate need to punch him in the face. Instead I squared my feet, closed my eyes as I let the world expand.

Tithe of Beast Activated.

Heartbeats flooded the air—mine and Jerome's. The grunt of dreams, insects chittering in the night, the snap of leathery wings, and then underneath that, so faint I almost missed it—the dull whimper of the frightened.

"The barn!" I said at the same time as Jerome.

"*Stay.*" He spat as if I were a dog. He took off at a limping run, not even checking to see if I'd obeyed.

I immediately chased after him, passing him easily.

"I said, stay! You damn—"

I increased my pace, pointedly kicking up dirt behind me. I was rewarded by a cough and curse from Jerome.

Chief's workshop was in the rough square that was H'tar's center. A dirt road worn by the tread of feet led to a small cluster of stables, outhouses, and a large wooden barn—one of the ones with a padlock as big as my head. Its thatched roof was tidy and well maintained, but the rust colored paint looked like blood in the dim moonlight.

People were steadily coming out of their cottages, half asleep and confused, but I charged past them—reaching the barn first.

A feeling of dread welled up in me. I hated horror films with a *passion,* but even I knew nothing good happened in a barn.

Ever.

The padlock was gone—snapped in two by something that left deep claw marks in the wood. I ran my hands over them, splaying my fingers—even at their narrowest, my thumb and pinky still couldn't reach the edges.

I thought of the monster I'd seen out in the woods. Its milk white eyes.

Not a monster, I reminded myself—*Lukas.*

I focused my hearing, my stomach sinking as my ears painted a picture within.

The smacking of lips. The tearing of flesh. The lapping of a tongue as it flicked out.

And the low, heavy thrum of breathing—each breath punctuated by a satisfied growl. A growl I knew all too well.

Stay away.

Stay away.

Lukas was inside. And he was eating something, or *someone.*

I took a step back, raising a hand in warning as Jerome finally caught up.

"Wait, Jerome," I said in a whisper. I knew Lukas would probably hear me anyway, but it felt wrong to shout. "Lukas is—"

"I know you're in there!" Jerome bellowed, panting slightly. "We can hear you from here. We won't run from some mutt. Not anymore!"

Jerome dropped to his knees, and I leaped back as his skin began to undulate like rocky waves against the shoreline. His trousers split, bone piercing the night air, followed swiftly by flesh that twisted into powerful legs. Dark mahogany hair followed, covering his pink flesh in a thick coat. His skull was the last thing to change, and I wondered if he did it on purpose as he called out, "Die like a man, Lukas. Die like a molger. While you have the chance!"

Jerome's voice cut off as his tongue receded, a long flat snout growing with his elongated skull. I looked away when his eyes bulged. Even after seeing it several times, it still made my stomach turn.

He was quicker than the woman I had seen earlier that day, but the change still took him a minute. Other than the crunch of bone and wet slap of flesh as Jerome changed the barn within was silent.

If Lukas had wanted to attack, now would have been the perfect time.

With a thump, Jerome landed on all four paws in his huge molger form—his transformation complete. He gave a low rumble—squaring with the barn door.

Nothing stirred within.

Jerome geared up to charge, but I stepped in front of him.

"Wait! The barn is small. You—you can't move well in small spaces, right?"

Dark eyes framed by a line of white fur stared back at me.

I tried to calm my pounding heart. "I'm here to help you, I swear it. So let me prove it—I'll see if I can draw him out. Better me than you, right?"

The molger growled but took a lumbering step back—the movement awkward. While a charging molger was like a bulldozer, they clearly weren't great at moving backward. Others had gathered around, whispering to one another, but no one else seemed to be transforming. I looked for Lenia and Chief but saw no one I knew among the growing crowd.

I was on my own.

I held out a hand, still half expecting Jerome to charge me. He watched me closely, dark molger eyes narrowed but made no move to stop me.

I cracked open the barn door, finding only a thick, heavy darkness. The tearing and chewing sounds from within had stopped, but I could still hear it—the low, labored breathing.

Trying to convince myself this wasn't the worst idea I'd ever had, I stepped inside.

Chapter Forty-Two

"Lukas?" I called out, knowing whispering was pointless. If I could hear him, he could hear me. While part of me thought I was insane for doing this, I couldn't stop thinking about him in the forest. The wounds that covered him, his growl as he warned others to stay away. How *scared* he looked.

I'd used *Vicious Command* on him once. If I could do it again, maybe I could stop Jerome and Lukas from slaughtering each other.

"Do you remember me?" I asked the darkness. "I saw you out in the forest. I'm not going to hurt you."

Trying not to spook him, I kept my pace slow and measured. Barely five steps in, my foot slid in something wet and sticky. I froze as it slipped between my toes, making every hair on my arm raise in disgust.

A sliver of moonlight peeked through the barn door, revealing a cloying puddle of blood mixed with coils of what looked like rope.

I knelt down, looking closer.

And clamped my hand over my nose and mouth.

Intestines, ripped and stinking, were curled in a messy pile. I spotted a bone, stained pink with blood and gristle, protruding from another pile close by. I tried not to gag—I had seen raw meat before, what difference did this make?

My churning stomach told me it was different—very different.

I jumped when I saw the severed head, sliding in the blood. The cow's eyes were frozen and unseeing, tongue lolling from its open mouth like a graying slug. It had been cut off at the neck, ragged flesh marking where its shoulders should have begun. I had to look away from its expression, so animal and yet so human in its fear.

Nauseous, I skirted the remnants of the corpse and found a torch, a barely glowing ember, off to one side.

The scream I'd heard was human. It must have come from whoever dropped this here. But where were they?

Bales of hay were stacked high, the floor strewn with rope, tools, and broken furniture. They could be hidden anywhere in this maze.

I struggled to calm my own heartbeat enough to listen. If I could focus, I could pinpoint where they were. Unfortunately it was difficult to hear anything beyond Jerome's growls from outside. Could he not shut up for five seconds?

As the thought finished, I realized I'd missed something vital.

I couldn't hear Lukas breathing anymore.

He hit me in the side, teeth clamping down on my forearm as his huge, muscled form barreled into me. I flew off my feet, hitting the ground like a ragdoll.

Flat on my back, I scrambled, screaming when fangs sank into my arm, rows of sharpened enamel burrowing into my flesh, tearing muscles and drilling into bone. All logic left me as I flailed, slapping uselessly at Lukas' jaw.

He slammed a huge, meaty paw into my chest—pinning me. My breath left in a *whoosh*, cutting off my scream as he pressed into my ribs, cracking them like dry spaghetti.

The whole thing had taken a split second—but that was all the time Lukas needed.

I stilled, trying to catch snatches of air as my own blood spilled into my face, dripping from Lukas' jaws. He stared down at me, eyes unreadable. In the forest, I'd thought they were milky white, but staring at them now, I saw the tiniest star-shaped pupil in their center.

His fur wasn't black either—instead it was flecked with a midnight blue that reminded me of my own hair. The jaw, on the other hand, was even worse up close. It looked like someone had taken a sledgehammer to the bone, shattered it to pieces, and left it to heal as it was.

A jaw that now held my forearm in its slanted grip. While he mercifully wasn't biting down anymore, he wasn't letting go either. He hissed out a breath, and I heard that same warning.

Stay away.

Air expelled from his mouth, spitting blood on my face like rain.

"Lukas," I tried, wincing as he growled. "Lukas, *stop*."

But my voice sounded weak even to my ears—the demand to be obeyed nothing but a whimper. I couldn't use *Vicious Command*—I was in too much pain.

Think, think! Before he rips you apart.

I raised my free hand. "Look, *look at me*," I said, showing him my splayed and very human hand. "No claws. I'm not your enemy." Slowly, oh so slowly, I rested my hand on the top of his huge head. I thought of how Chief had calmed Waylen down, how he'd helped him turn back to human.

Starting with two fingers, I gently stroked a patch of fur between his two curved ears. It felt surprisingly soft and downy.

"See? I'm a friend." My movement was limited, but I pressed all five fingers onto his head and tried to make the petting motion as long and smooth as possible.

A rumble began in Lukas' chest, and I grimaced, preparing for him to bite down. Instead he loosened his grip on my arm ever so slightly, and I smiled despite my fear.

He was purring.

I had imagined many things in my life, but lying on my back stroking a shapeshifted monster while it held my arm in its mouth was not one of them.

"That's it," I murmured. "I knew we could be friends."

His mouth opened another fraction, just enough for me to slip my arm out of his jaws. The puncture wounds, now free of Lukas' fangs, oozed like a blood-soaked sponge.

I cradled my injured arm against my stomach, breathing tightly as I tried to sit up—pressing against his paw. He moved with me and eventually lifted his paw from my chest and set it on the ground to my left, so I was cradled between his front legs. Ducking out of reach of his fangs, I pressed against his neck, murmuring words of encouragement.

He sat down with a plop that made me jump. He tensed, growling, but I resumed petting him instantly, and his growl turned to a purr that made my whole body vibrate. His chest was a furnace that made Chief's hand feel like ice.

"Good boy," I said.

Something wet slid down my cheek, and I leaned back—worried I was bleeding somewhere else.

It was only when I raised my head that I realized it had come from Lukas. Thick, fat tears spilled from his eyes.

He was *crying*.

"You poor—"

A yelp came from the corner, and Lukas growled, instantly on all fours.

"Wait!" I said, holding up a hand.

"Hello?" I called out. Lukas swiveled his head in the direction of a shadowed corner, and I heard a small voice whimpering, trying and failing to hold back a cry.

"Please, come out," I said. "He's calm now, but he won't be if you keep hiding."

There was a beat and then the shifting of feet on hay. A tiny ginger head appeared from behind a bale, a boy's head peeking out.

Lukas hissed, and the boy yelped, stepping back. I moved between them, keeping them both in sight.

"What's your name?" I asked, trying to stop him from panicking.

"... Tommy."

"All right, Tommy, I need you to walk to the door, but do so very, very slowly. You got that?"

Tommy nodded, his mussed up fringe almost touching his eyes. He moved from behind the hay bale, his oversized nightshirt nearly engulfing his whole body. Blood stained one side, but he walked unimpeded.

The blood must have been from the slaughtered cow—or I hoped at least.

As he drew closer, inching toward the door, his hands shaking as he stared at Lukas, I realized he was older than I'd thought. Maybe eleven or so. What was he doing out of bed?

"That's it," I said. "You're almost there. See, Lukas? It's all right. It's—"

Boom.

The doors of the barn burst inward, one completely flying off the hinges. It zipped past Tommy, missing him by a hair, hitting the other side of the room with a crash that made the whole barn shudder.

Jerome filled the width of the barn entrance. Slamming a paw on the ground, he let out a furious roar. Just behind him, I saw two more molger—the ones from the lake.

"*No,*" I said, all hope of everyone living through this vanishing.

Lukas' claws scraped the floor as he splayed his feet, muscles coiled. He threw back his head and screamed. The sound was as ferocious as it was overpowering, and it took all my will not to throw myself to the floor, cover my head, and cry. Spittle flew from his mouth and yet still Lukas screamed, the sound a hurricane to the whisper that was Jerome's battle cry. The molger behind Jerome stepped back, but to my sliver of admiration, Jerome didn't budge. He dropped his head low, squaring his shoulders.

Do it, his stance said. *Come for me.*

Caught between the falslings, Tommy dropped to his knees with a terrified cry.

My memory flashed back to the arcade—the gun. Noah. To the fear in his eyes as I prayed I would make it before the bullet meant for him.

"I am death's mistress—bow before me," I whispered.

Fury's Claw Activated.

Talons erupted from my hands and feet, dark and vicious.

I leaped forward with a new burst of speed, reaching Tommy instantly. I pulled him into my arms, rolling to the side.

The cold, wet splash of blood and guts coated me as I hit the ground. The barest hint of a claw scraped my back as Lukas leaped over me—missing us by inches.

Head buried in Tommy's shoulder, I heard Lukas and Jerome slam into each other.

And then there was chaos.

Chapter Forty-Three

S creams of terror and roars of fury mixed into one cacophonous wall of noise. I could barely make out who was who in the tangled mess of claws and fur that was Lukas and the three molger as I scooped Tommy up into my arms.

"Close your eyes," I said. "When I tell you to open them, you'll be safe. I promise."

Tommy complied, squeezing his eyes shut as he buried his head in my shoulder.

Jerome swung a mighty paw, barely missing Lukas as he twisted with catlike agility, dashing around the molger easily. With a growl Lukas planted his hind legs, swiping a paw upward—dragging it over Jerome's face and eyes. He grunted, stumbling to one side from the force of the blow.

I winced. I'd seen Lukas' claws when he'd first charged at me in the forest—Jerome had lost at least one eye, I was sure of it.

But when Jerome righted himself, he glared at Lukas with two eyes—looking dazed but intact. I looked at Lukas' paws.

He'd retracted his claws. I gripped Tommy.

I might still have a chance to stop this.

That was a big might.

One of the smaller molger, streaked with blonde, slammed into Lukas' side—the blonde sleazy sidekick who helped Jerome up when his knee was hurt, I bet. Unbalanced on his hind legs, Lukas toppled to one side with a whine, thrashing. The other molger, the bald man it must be, reared up, slamming his full weight down—straight for Lukas' skull.

He howled, twisting away like water through a sieve, but it was too late—one of the molger's talons caught him, dragging through his skin like a finger through butter. Lukas hissed as he righted himself, circling his opponents with a bloodied shoulder—the molger's claw marks wide and deep.

The fight was happening directly in front of the barn. I could hole up in here, but then Lukas or Jerome was going to end up dead, or I could…

Baldie charged, but Lukas slithered like a shadow, easily dodging it. Unable to turn in time, the molger slammed into the barn. It shook, creaking as flecks of dust and hay fell from the rafters.

Or I could end up buried in here when this whole thing came down. The barn was sturdy, but it wasn't built for a fight with creatures the size of small trucks.

I scanned the barn for a window, or another door I could escape through.

Nothing.

My taloned feet dug into the dirt, the edges of my toes the same midnight blue as my fingers. Last time I'd seen them had been on Magnus' castle roof—running with Eternity in my arms.

I'd been quick—blisteringly so. But Valerius, in a full suit of armor, had nearly caught up to me.

A growl rose in my throat. It wasn't enough. *I* wasn't enough.

More.

I concentrated on the fire of anger inside me, of the fury that sparked—mine or Zara's, I didn't know. But I needed it now.

WARNING.

APPROACHING CALAMITY SYSTEM LIMITS.

The pop-up flashed before my eyes, but I ignored it. My skin tickled with pain, bubbling like the surface of boiling water.

More.

WARNING. WARNING.

Black fur burst from my ankles, spiraling up my knees. The muscles of my legs pulled and stretched, reforming as my feet grew and my calves lengthened—my knees snapping with a wet crunch.

CALAMITY SYSTEM LIMITS BREACHED.

Fangs, long and elongated, grew from my canines as I growled into the night. "Untethered—the beast screams."

PARTIAL TRANSFORMATION UNLOCKED.

Panting, I looked down at my body—feeling no fear.

Only awe.

I was human until my thighs, then fur replaced flesh—black as night with hints of midnight blue. It curled around to my knees, which I had to twist to see—they pointed *backward* now, like a dog or cat's. My clawed feet had narrowed into sleek, pointed toes, and my talons were shorter—like they were built for speed.

Tentatively I pressed my tongue against my new fangs, wincing at the sting—the copper taste of blood filling my mouth. I hopped from foot to foot, expecting to feel unbalanced in this new form, but I felt stronger, faster—and in a bizarre sense I couldn't place, more like myself. Like I was closer to who I was meant to be.

Hot damn.

A roar brought me back to the present.

Baldie had Lukas' back leg in his jaw, snapping his head back and forth with a vicious jerk, dragging Lukas' howling form along with it. I recalled the Bestiary's entry on a molger's bite—not even death could force them to release their victims.

Lukas twisted his body like an eel, moving at an impossible angle as he reached for the molger—jaws wide. Instead of biting down on Baldie's neck, easily in his reach, he wrapped his jaw around his pointed brown ear.

And pulled.

Baldie shrieked in pain, jaw unlocking as blood gushed from the stump that remained of his left ear. Lukas leaped away, spitting out a goblet of flesh that rolled in the dirt like leftover gristle in the pan. He was limping heavily, blood dripping from his left leg and the wound on his shoulder, but he still refused to kill his fellow molger.

Jerome knocked his head against Baldie, who instantly stopped whining. The three molger spread out, surrounding Lukas.

I bent low, gathering power in my new legs.

Don't think. Just move.

I didn't run.

I was simply gone.

I blinked past Baldie, the molger closest to the barn, in a second—the only sign that I'd been there was a slight rustling of his fur. Lukas sensed me, snapping the air as I leaped over him, spinning in a graceful arc to land in front of Jerome. He didn't even see me, his wide-swinging paw aimed squarely at Lukas.

I threw myself forward, letting momentum pull me into a slide as I glided beneath Jerome's stomach—his fur tickling my cheek as I slapped a hand against the ground and landed squarely in the center of the crowd.

"Gallow's breath," someone whispered behind me.

I came to a standstill, breathing hard. The entire thing had taken less than two seconds.

Holy crap.

Several people backed up, but I heard a voice call, "Tommy? Tommy!"

Two women pushed through the crowd. One, with dark hair and stern expression, stopped short—hesitating. The other, curly haired blonde, barreled up to me—arms outstretched.

"Open your eyes," I whispered to Tommy, who had not only screwed them up but had slapped his hands over them for good measure.

Peeking from behind his fingers, he burst into tears when the woman wrapped her arms around him.

"Are you all right? What happened? Gallow help me, there's blood all over you!"

"It's from D-d-d-dandy," he cried. "I thought I heard her cry-crying, and I went to c-c-check on her, but I fell, and it was her b-blood and her head… and… and…"

His words vanished into sobs, and she shushed him.

"Thank you," the woman said, her eyes on mine, stroking his head as she rocked him. The dark-haired woman behind her merely nodded in thanks, her eyes straying to my still bleeding arm.

The crowd had backed up, watchful and silent. "You're welcome." I smiled, hiding my arm behind my back as I turned to the fight.

Blood dripped from Jerome's chest, four huge gashes ripping him open from his shoulder down—Lukas was done holding back, not that he was faring any better. One of his eyes was glued shut, a strip of flesh hanging from his forehead. The air crackled with rage and bloodlust.

I thought of the crying "mongrel" who had wept on my shoulder when I pet him. Of his growls as he warned people to stay away from him. Of his restraint, until now, when fighting three molger twice his size. There was a person inside that monster—I knew it, and I knew I had to help him.

I used my newfound speed to zip in front of Jerome, who was surprised enough to skid to a halt.

"**Stop this**," I roared, throwing every ounce of anger and power into it.

Vicious Command Activated.

The world grew hazy and I winced—between *Tithe of Beasts, Partial Transformation,* and now *Vicious Command,* I was pushing it. But I couldn't stop.

Baldie and Blondie stilled instantly. One had even paused mid-step, a paw hovering, freezing like water in a cold snap.

Jerome shook his head, dragging a foot forward.

"**I said** *stop*," I hissed, threading more power into the command, but he dragged himself toward me, his movements as slow and heavy as treacle.

Lukas growled at my back, but I couldn't afford to look. Jerome bared his fangs, blood vessels bursting in his eyes as he forced himself forward, inch by painful inch. My body shook, the world swaying in focus, but I forced myself to stare him down.

"**Enough, Jerome. You need to stop this, or one of you will die!**"

For an instant it looked like it was enough—that I'd gotten through to him. Then he snapped his head to one side, biting down on his own leg. I jumped in shock, breaking the *Vicious Command's* hold. His jaw opened as he charged.

I moved too slow, the air heavy, my vision blurry.

He swung a mighty paw straight at me.

Suddenly I was flying through the air, my back slamming into the wooden barn—the wall splintering from the force.

I saw stars.

The ground rushed to meet me.

Darkness.

Chapter Forty-Four

"**D**ue south, in the ruins of the old Captain's Barracks," Marito read aloud, flipping the parchment. Finding the back blank, he cocked an eyebrow at the lithe figure in black.

"The spymaster leaves us in a bind, Mistress Shadow. This is little enough information to mount an assault—especially as we intend to take Lord Magnus alive. Does he travel alone? Has he recovered from the injuries? Has he made use of the barrack's physical defenses or rekindled the magical ones?" Marito asked, his rapid fire questions at odds with his relaxed posture.

He rested against a log, long legs outstretched before the fire—axes on the ground beside him, always within reach. He'd stripped off his armor in the firelight of camp and had been enjoying the peace of the forest's nighttime chatter when the shadow had appeared.

Lazander and Valerius had already left with two other knights to take the first watch. The Gilded didn't actually need to participate, there were enough knights and spare hands to cover it, but Marito always insisted they take a shift. It was a show of good faith and trust, he claimed.

The shadow shook her head. She wore a plain mask the color of night and robes to match. Other than being short and lean, there was nothing to distinguish her from any of the other shadows the spymaster had sent the knights on their hunt for Magnus.

"You don't know, or you can't tell me?" Marito asked, trying not to sound annoyed. He had little time for tricks and subterfuge.

"None of the shadows are allowed to speak, Mari." Gabriel sighed. "For fear someone would recognize their voice."

The shadow nodded and made a complicated gesture with her fingers in Gabriel's direction. The mage nodded along while Marito stared, impressed as always by his friend's seemingly endless knowledge.

"She says he appears to be alone, but several magical barriers seem to surround the barracks," Gabriel said. When Marito opened his mouth to ask why this wasn't written down, Gabriel continued. "This, however, is only guesswork as until a mage arrives, they cannot confirm. I imagine you're waiting for me, then?" Gabriel asked the shadow.

She nodded.

"Then get out of here," Gabriel said brusquely. "The sooner you go, the sooner we sleep—we'll arrive by midafternoon tomorrow."

The shadow tapped her heart twice in the Navaros salute and left, disappearing into the night.

"Master Gabriel, there was no need to be rude," Marito chided.

"You get just as annoyed as I do when the spymaster feeds us these little paper trails—like corn to a flock of chickens," Gabriel replied.

Marito sighed but said nothing, knowing the mage was right. Instead he asked, "I cannot figure out what Lord Magnus is planning. Why the Captain's Barracks? It's barely standing since Captain Helm lost to Freyley decades ago. Has anyone even used it since?"

Gabriel shrugged. "If we'd known this was our destination I could have checked the Ivory Keep's records before we left, but no—not to my knowledge. It is on the border to Freyley though, maybe he's trying to flee the kingdom?"

"Perhaps, but the queen's treaties have cemented them as our allies, and after the trouble with Evergarden and Lady Eternity's disappearance, I highly doubt they wish to stir the pot—so to speak," Marito replied.

The Gilded sat alone by the fire as the rest of their company, barring those patrolling on the night watch, had retired to their bedrolls. Gabriel, however, was a cautious man. He stood abruptly, circling the fire to settle down next to Marito. With a whisper, he leaned in. "What did you make of Val today?"

Marito shook his head, braids spilling over his shoulder. "This is the lightest mood I have seen Lord Valerius in for months. He almost reminds me of his old self—before his... illness."

Marito stared at the flames, old memories twisting and writhing within the flames. "I knew something was amiss with Lord Valerius—he would disappear for days at a time and return with unexplained wounds. Not to mention killing those vaxion—but I chose not to look. Not to see. It took Lazander, a man only in the throes of his knighthood, to remind me of my own duty. I confess, my friend, I am ashamed."

Gabriel wanted to comfort his old friend, but knew it would only be a false platitude. "I feel it too. But tormenting yourself over what could have been isn't going to fix this. If Val purposefully let Magnus take Eternity or worse," he paused, not wanting to say it out loud, "if he helped kidnap her, that's treason. And if we see any hint of that in the coming days… you know what we have to do."

Marito nodded, brushing his hand over an axe. "As a boy, I dreamed of knighthood. I thought honor and a stalwart heart were enough to defeat any enemy. I never thought…"

Gabriel rolled his eyes, shoving Marito gently in the side. The man barely moved. "Spare the melodrama until after this is done. I'll even help you write a poem about it."

With a smirk, Marito shoved Gabriel, sending him face first into the dirt. "No thank you—you are a terrible wordsmith."

Gabriel rolled onto his back, pulling a shadow cast by the slowly dying fire and wrapping it around Marito. Surprised, the knight struggled for a moment before Gabriel snapped his fingers, the shadow spinning him around. He hit the dirt next to Gabriel, his breath leaving in a *whoomf*.

The giant laughed. "I suppose I deserved that."

"You did," Gabriel said, getting to his feet. He reached out to Marito, helping him stand. "We'll get answers from Magnus tomorrow—and then we'll plan from there. But we'll be worse than useless if we're half asleep on our feet."

"Well said. Goodnight, my friend," Marito said, waving Gabriel off as he strode away. The Gilded made a point not to sleep next to each other when making camp as it made them an easier target for an ambush, but Marito suddenly wished he was by his brothers-in-arms that night. He had lived too long and survived too many close calls not to trust the heavy feeling of dread that settled in his stomach.

What would they find in the Captain's Barracks? Just how much of a fight would Magnus put up? And were they up to it?

***

The outline of the *Knights of Eternity* Menu swam before my eyes, an exclamation mark flashing in the right hand corner.

Confused, I mentally clicked on it.

YOU HAVE A MESSAGE FROM ZARA THE FURY, it read. **WOULD YOU LIKE TO READ IT?**

In a daze, I nodded—grasping the significance a second too late.

The Menu vanished.

I didn't fall. There was no gut-wrenching shift of reality. Instead I was suddenly lying on the ground, grass tickling my bare arms and legs, the warmth of the sun on my face.

I got to my feet, feeling strangely at peace.

I was in a forest bursting with lilac and peach flowers in full bloom. The air was thick and humid—my lungs growing heavier with each breath.

Something brushed up against my fingers, and I leaped backward with an undignified shriek.

A small girl stared up at me, eyes wide. Dressed in a simple homespun shift, she had dark hair and large golden eyes. The tips of her fingers were a startling midnight blue.

I looked down at my own midnight-blue fingers then back at her.

It was Zara—*the* Zara the Fury. And she was about seven years old, judging by her size and her adorably puffy cheeks.

"Zara? What are you—what are *we* doing here?" I asked.

She took my hand without a word, tugging me gently. I followed, confused but intrigued as she brought me through low hanging vines and past a rushing stream. Fish, silver and quick, twisted in the shallows.

What in the hell?

"Zara?" I asked quietly. "What is this? Where are we?"

She said nothing, merely gripped my fingers, tugging harder.

A vicious roar cut through the forest, guttural and thunderous in its fury. I froze, but Zara pulled at me impatiently.

The peace I'd felt waking in this forest was gone—fear trickling like ice in my veins. I had an intense feeling of déjà vu—dread settling in my stomach as if I knew what was coming.

All at once we broke through the cover of trees to a large enclosure, and the roar came again—close enough I could almost feel the spittle. It was higher-pitched this time—and I knew the animal was afraid.

A black shape darted around the enclosure, snapping at the air with a misshapen jaw—surrounded by a dozen or so people wielding ropes and sticks, their edges blunted.

My heart leaped.

Lukas.

As it moved, however, batting away sticks and dodging lassos, I realized I was wrong.

This beast was larger—almost a third bigger than Lukas. Its jaw was bent at more of an angle. Squinting, I raised a hand to shield my eyes from the blistering sun.

No—whoever that was, it wasn't Lukas.

Chief said what had happened to Lukas could happen to any falsling. So was this a former molger? Or something else?

The people who circled the beast wore loose tunics and trousers under thick leather armor. Blades were attached to their chest plates and to a belt at their waists, but they didn't draw them, instead focusing on distracting the creature and directing it away from the forest. Several had gashes on their legs and arms, but they moved unimpeded—darting about almost as quickly as the creature.

They weren't human—that was obvious. But why were they keeping the beast inside the enclosure?

A woman emerged from the forest, mere inches from me. I jumped in surprise, but she didn't even glance in my direction. Standing head and shoulders above me, her hair was shaved at the sides, a thick braid trailing from the top of her head all the way down to her waist. Tattoos, ink-black and intricate, lined her arms, circling biceps the size of her head. Her skin was nutbrown, her eyes as golden as my own.

I looked from seven-year-old Zara to the woman and back again. They were the spitting image of each other—only their build and the curve of their jaws betrayed they weren't the same person. This woman was clearly related to Zara, but who was she?

Aunt. The word swam to the surface of my mind, triggering a mix of emotions—anger, hatred, fear. Beneath all that, hidden like hope in Pandora's Box, was the deep yearning that comes from seeing a loved one.

Zara's aunt strolled toward the beast at an easy pace—her hands at her side, the picture of ease. A strange tableau played itself out, and my eyes widened at what I saw.

Understanding dawned as I realized why Zara had chosen this memory to show me.

Chapter Forty-Five

My eyes snapped open, every muscle and bone in my body a heartbeat of pain. I was back in H'tar village, splinters of wood scattered all over me. Rolling onto my side, I forced myself to my forearms, knowing what I had to do.

It would be much easier, however, if the world would stop spinning, and whoever was swinging the iron bat against the inside of my skull would stop.

I had to give it to Jerome, I thought wryly. He hit like an articulated truck.

Lukas skidded past me with a whine, trying and failing to stay on his feet. He fell to the ground in a graceless flop, another wound bleeding freely from his side, inches deep. His fur was now a dark brown from the sheer amount of blood that covered him—both his and the molger's.

The molger I mentally referred to as Blondie was missing a sizable chunk from his shoulder while Baldie was shaking his head—the blood from his missing ear dripping into his eye, blinding him.

What had felt like hours in Zara's memory must have been seconds here. At least I hoped it was a memory. If it wasn't, then what I was about to do would kill me.

Jerome's massive molger form huffed a laugh as Lukas collapsed. Other than the deep cuts on his chest, he looked as fresh and ready as he had at the beginning of the fight—his teeth drawn back as he squared his shoulders, grinning.

Lukas was done—Jerome had won. And he knew it.

I got to my feet, unsteady as moonlight on water.

It was probably stupid bordering on insane to trust a woman whose body I had stolen, who inspired hatred and fear in everyone who heard her name.

But I'd never forgive myself if I walked away now.

Lukas' breathing was weak, his chest pumping up and down feebly. Eyes closed, he sheathed his claws.

Do it, he seemed to say. *Kill me.*

With a roar, Jerome charged—and so did I.

I leaped high into the air, arms outstretched as I spun like a top until I faced the ground directly above Jerome. He opened his jaw wide, fangs gleaming, unable to see anything but Lukas.

A small part of me was sorry. A larger part was delighted.

"**If the world will not yield—then I will break it**," I whispered.

Monstrous Strength Activated.

I spun in an arc, slamming my heel into Jerome's skull with a sickening crunch.

A lightning bolt of pain shot through my leg—it was like hitting steel, but I pushed through, driving Jerome's head into the dirt.

He hit the ground with an earthshaking thump, his entire body slack, six limbs splayed almost comically. I landed with a thud, my heel going out from under me.

Baldie and Blondie whimpered, looking at each other as Jerome lay still—both too chicken to make the first move against me. I peeled back my lip to reveal my fangs, hissing for good measure—a pure bluff.

They backed up instantly.

Relieved, I quietly thanked the Bestiary for the tip to attack from above. However, I wasn't done. I had to get to Lukas and…

Jerome groaned, rolling onto his side as his eyes fluttered feverishly.

Will this man not stay down?

"Jerome, stop!" I called out, panic and pain making me stumble to my feet "I know how to make Lukas human again! Let me try, ple—"

Courageous once more, Baldie charged for me, swinging wide as I desperately threw myself to the side. Blondie was on me a second later, and I scrambled between his legs, dodging and weaving with none of my earlier speed and grace as the throbbing in my ankle shot red hot needles of pain up my leg—each step threatening to be my last.

Jerome was on his feet, his massive girth swaying as he shook his head, struggling to stay upright.

I can't keep this up. They're going to kill me, then Lukas. I can't do this—I can't—

I didn't hear it. I didn't even see it coming.

A molger, the largest I'd ever seen, crashed into Baldie, his claws whisking past my face close enough for tendrils of hair to whip about my cheeks from the force.

With a roar, the colossal furry mountain that was the new molger drove its snout under Baldie's belly, flipping him upward.

Baldie didn't just go flying—he blasted toward the barn at speed, crashing through the flimsy wood as if it were paper. There was a *thunk, thunk* as his body skipped over the ground like a flat stone on water, hitting the other side of the barn.

The wooden structure creaked, swaying dangerously. For a moment looked like it would hold.

Then with a groan, it folded in on itself like soggy paper collapsing inward—directly on top of Baldie.

Mouth agape, I could only stare.

The gigantic molger was a familiar shade of auburn with dark circles around its eyes. It swiveled awkwardly on its six legs, planting itself between me, Jerome, and Blondie with a defiant roar.

The message was clear, the new molger was here to protect me. But who in the hell was it?

A diminutive auburn molger trotted up next to it, almost identical in coloring, and gave a tiny high-pitched roar—*Waylen.*

If the small one was Waylen, that meant the big one was…

Holy crap. *Lenia?*

Baldie swiped for Lenia, a clumsy blow she took on the shoulder with a grunt. Driving her head downward, she slammed her skull against Baldie—headbutting him viciously with a crack like thunder.

He hit the dirt and didn't move.

I quietly resolved to never make Lenia angry.

A squeak broke me out of my slack-jawed awe as Waylen shuffled over to Lukas, his tiny legs kicking out as he whined—worried.

Lukas, still on his side, growled in return, but it was feeble. He was hurt—badly.

Glancing back at Lenia, I watched her face down a furious looking Jerome. Pawing the ground, she snorted through her nose in a clear challenge.

Come and get me.

A challenge Jerome answered with a bellow.

Lenia was taking a huge chance on me. Not only had she been caught lying about me, she had now attacked three of her own. Best case scenario, she would be exiled from H'tar—Waylen too.

Unless I saved Lukas.

Trusting my gut, I ran for him—praying Lenia could handle Jerome.

Waylen was struggling with Lukas, dodging around him as he snapped at the small molger.

Stay away. Eyes wild, Lukas swayed. *Stay away.*

Blood poured from his wounds every time he moved—he was going to bleed out if I didn't get him under control. "**Stop!**" I roared, trying to infuse some power of command, but Lukas flailed and whined, snapping wildly in his pain. I doubted he could even hear me anymore.

Crouched low, I leaped forward, wrapping my arms around his head in a vice. My knee hit the dirt as he flailed, but I gritted my teeth and held on—determination lending me strength.

I thought of the woman in Zara's memory, her aunt. How fur had rippled down her right arm as it lengthened, partially transforming. With a single fur-lined arm, she'd held the beast in the enclosure easily—a lioness pinning a newborn cub.

I concentrated on the image, remembering the feel of the muscles in my legs as they snapped and grew, elongating like warm rubber.

"**Untethered**." I gasped, Lukas thrashing like a snake. "**The beast screams.**"

My arms grew hot, the surface of the skin boiling as the flesh turned liquid for an instant—sleek black fur trailing down from my shoulders like a waterfall.

Partial Transformation Activated.

Lukas yelped as I pinned him, forcing him face first into the ground. In a burst of anger, he got a paw free—swiping at me.

I braced myself for the blow, knowing if I moved he would get free.

There was a squeak as Waylen bit down on Lukas' paw, throwing his whole weight on top of it.

My heart warmed. He was a third of the size of Lukas, and yet here he was— throwing himself into the fight, doing everything he could to help his friend. If it had been any other time and place, tears would have sprung to my eyes.

I bit down on my forearm, my new fangs cutting through fur to find the hard flesh beneath. Blood burst into my mouth. I got notes of spice and warmth—something almost close to cinnamon.

I didn't have time to wonder what that meant as I spat—praying this would work.

"I give this to you freely and willingly," I shouted.

Lukas was near rabid, Waylen squeaking as he held on for dear life.

"I welcome you to the world with new eyes. I welcome you to the fire and fury. I welcome you to the *vaxion.*"

I released Lukas—he immediately shot up as I knew he would, jaws wide.

He jerked in surprise when I shoved my arm down his throat. Instinctively he bit down. *Hard.*

Suddenly, he stilled—just as the beast had done in Zara's memory.

I had watched in awe as the creature grew calm. Its furred flesh had bled away, like watercolor on wet paper, to reveal the form of a sleeping woman. The group swarmed about her, but Zara's aunt had shooed them away, pulling a rich red cloak from her shoulders.

Carefully wrapping the unconscious woman in it, she'd picked her up—cradling her as if she were a newborn babe. She turned, locking eyes with Zara and me as the memory faded—expression unreadable.

As far as I knew, yelling the words and shoving my arm in Lukas' mouth was all it took.

Little did I know that was only the beginning.

One moment Lukas was biting me while Waylen yipped in fear—clearly thinking I had gone mad. Lenia and Jerome rolled in the dirt, each fighting for purchase.

The next I was falling.

Chapter Forty-Six

"What do you see?" Valerius asked at Gabriel's back. They had arrived at the crumbling ruin that was the Captain's Barracks later than intended, heavy rains slowing their journey, and the sun's amber rays were now barely breaching the horizon.

Despite the oilskin cloaks they wore, the knights were soaked and miserable and had spent much of the final leg of their journey in tense silence—the kind that left Gabriel's patience frayed. He shoved down the stab of irritation he felt at Valerius' question—it was reasonable enough and focused on the shadows he had cast out into the hungry dusk.

The barracks lay at the top of the hill beyond, its dull outline an inky darkness against the brightening stars of the falling night. Valerius and Gabriel had decided to err on the side of caution, staying far enough back that no human eye could detect them.

After all, they had no need for human eyes.

Shadows pooled around Gabriel's feet, twisting outward into lengthening strands like a nightmarish web of darkness. They crept up the hillside, stretching to absolute capacity as Gabriel's mind traveled their lengths, studying the barracks and the surrounding area

While Gabriel could not "see" through the darkened strands, all living beings emitted a varying level of magic—from the simple rock beetles to knights like Valerius who could withstand immense levels of magic. Using his shadows, he could gauge magical defenses and even count the number of living beings within a certain space. It had saved his life more times than he could count.

Valerius crossed his arms, a single metallic finger tapping against his forearm, the *plink plink* of the noise increasing in tempo. Gabriel furrowed his brow as he struggled to ignore the noise and was successful until—

"I can't feel my own feet, Gabriel. Tell me what you see."

"I can see that you're being a giant pain in the ass," Gabriel snapped, opening his eyes. The shadows at his feet rippled, returning to form his own lengthening shadow. "You're the one who insisted on doing this without so much as a moment by the fire to warm up."

"Spare your whining for Marito. I need details—not misgivings," Valerius said, hands parked on his hips, chin tilted—daring Gabriel to argue back.

The mage almost did but held back at the last moment. Not because he was afraid of Valerius' wrath, but because he couldn't face the lecture he'd get from Marito about how "knocking your commander on his posterior is not knightly behavior."

"I couldn't breach the barracks itself—it's just out of reach of my shadows," Gabriel said, forcing a civil tone. "But the surrounding area is enough of a pain. He's set up expanding Calix Rings—starting from the center of the barracks. They'll trigger when we approach, giving Magnus our exact location. If I had the architectural plans of the barracks, we could map out his potential escape routes, but I doubt it would do much good. It's so dilapidated, there's likely countless exits we couldn't predict. We need to get in *without* him noticing us—or risk him running once more."

Valerius nodded as if he'd thought the same all along, and Gabriel had to think very hard about the nice warm fire that awaited him back at camp.

"Plus, if I was Magnus," the mage added, trying his best to remain professional, "I'd have cast a couple of rounds of *Fury's Touch* inside the boundaries of each ring— we step on the wrong spot, and *boom*—they'll be picking bits of us out of the trees for weeks." Gabriel frowned, eyeing the barracks. "How did Magnus do all this on his own? And in such a short amount of time?"

"Can you dismantle it?" Valerius asked, ignoring the question.

"I could, but it'll take me hours, and I'll be exhausted afterward."

"I'd rather have you fresh and ready to bind Magnus with your shadows. How would the other mages fare?" Valerius asked.

Gabriel placed a hand on his chin, tapping in thought as was his habit. "Kilin and Farah? They're talented, but this is beyond them. What I *could* do is freeze the Rings for a couple of seconds, allowing us to slip inside. So long as I stay in front, I should be able to guide us away from anything that'll melt us into puddles. But…"

"But?"

"*But* I won't be able to get the entire company through," Gabriel said, glaring at the crumbling ruins of the barracks as if they were personally responsible for his conundrum. "Six, *maybe* seven people at most, but that's likely pushing it. Holding the Rings will drain me. I should still have enough magic to bind Magnus, but we should bring another mage as backup."

Valerius rested a hand on his sword. "Make it six people. The Gilded will be four—choose the mage you think suits best. I'll choose a knight."

He strode away without waiting for an answer, mounting his horse and turning his steed toward the small copse of trees they had made their base. Gabriel ignored Valerius' abrupt retreat, opting to stay behind and study the barracks.

The land surrounding him was sparse in terms of coverage, scarred by the remnants of the battle that had taken place decades past when Freyley had invaded Navaros' borders. Ragged tree stumps littered the area, their fallen trunks slowly decomposing. Entire patches of earth were still scorched black—remnants from a mage's fire. The occasional rust-colored sword had been driven into the earth, a leftover from the battle or a marker for the dead. He wouldn't have touched them either way.

Gabriel knew the God of Judgment did not look kindly on those who disturbed the dead—and if he knew it, that meant Magnus did too. So why had he chosen a barracks so riddled with the dead to hide away in?

He thought of the mage as he often had since reading Lazander's report on Eternity's abduction. While Lazander and Marito were focused on Valerius, Gabriel's mind kept turning back to the mage who could freeze a speck of dust and an oncoming tsunami with the same ease.

They were not friends—acquaintances at best. However, when the gift of magic affected only one in ten thousand people, you quickly learned the names and the talents of people who could blast you into the sun.

Born of a minor noble of a border town, Magnus was privately educated at home and only appeared in court once his magical abilities began to manifest at ten years of age—a late bloomer. While that was often a sign of little talent, Magnus was the opposite—quickly mastering elemental magic although his affinity lay in its wintery brethren.

Magnus was fifteen, Gabriel ten by the time they met—and Gabriel had not been impressed. Constantly clinging to nobles of more import, Magnus took every opportunity to showcase his magic—from chilling a lady's tea to making snow fall in the middle of a toast (which ruined a young Gabriel's favorite cloak). He seemed incapable of telling any anecdote that didn't end up being a drawn-out brag about himself, and when pressed on why he had never joined the palace mages (thereby doing something useful for the first time in his life, Gabriel had thought), he'd simply said, "I couldn't possibly—I have far more important things to do."

The Magnus Gabriel had known was like a strong perfume—better in small doses. Also, exceptionally irritating but ultimately harmless.

Then he met Zara the Fury.

It began as court gossip—the flames shaped like dragons that lit up the sky around the Moonvale Mountains. The whispers of a falsling who could walk through fire unscathed so complete was her control of the element. The court soon turned to other affairs (quite literally, Lord Harcourt was caught with his butler), but Magnus seemed unable to let the falsling go.

Gabriel recalled the mage trawling the court every day, asking people for news of Zara. They refused him politely at first, but when he became more insistent people took to simply turning their backs on him and pretending he didn't exist. While Gabriel didn't necessarily approve of the tactic, he also didn't blame them. There was a glint in Magnus' eyes that spoke of madness or obsession—Gabriel couldn't tell which.

As a palace mage, Gabriel spent hours in the library—quite happily in fact. He was also used to being the only one there. To his surprise, Magnus began to join him among the stacks and shelves, but he was only ever interested in three things— vaxion, falslings, and the Moonvale Mountains.

Then one day, Magnus packed up a cart and two horses and left without a word for the Moonvale Mountains.

The gossip mill churned for weeks after—claiming the mage was drunk on his own ego or had even gone insane. More than one person who had once called Magnus friend now used the words "fool" and "country hick" to describe him.

Things moved on as they always do, and Magnus was forgotten.

Until he appeared at the Ivory Keep months later.

Gabriel only saw him by chance from a window on the palace's third floor. He was pacing angrily, hands behind his back in the muddy courtyard of the stables. Gabriel did a double take at the sight—both at seeing Magnus alive and well but also at the state of the mage who had once preened over his appearance like a prized peacock.

His clothes, once a brilliant robe of red velvet and soft leather boots, were ragged scraps that clung to a body marred by burns and bruises. If not for his telltale shock of blonde hair, now tangled and matted, Gabriel would have thought him a beggar.

There was something animalistic and frantic about the mage as he stalked around the muddy courtyard, stopping occasionally to run his hands nervously over a large trunk—bound and padlocked and never far from his reach. It took four men to tie it to the back of a carriage. Gabriel had no idea how Magnus had transported it to the Keep by himself, and then Magnus hopped up onto the driver's seat and snapped the reins—fleeing as if the beasts of the Void were on his heels.

That was ten years ago.

Gabriel was a newly christened Gilded Knight when next he saw Magnus who was a far cry from the performative hot air balloon he'd remembered. Instead he was cold and arrogant—snapping barbs at every turn and taking every moment to drunkenly boast about his betrothed, the very fire-wielding falsling he'd once obsessed over.

A falsling who'd burned Magnus' arm to mere charcoal, if Lazander's report was accurate.

Gabriel shuddered at the thought. Without his arms, he couldn't use his shadow magic. In Magnus' shoes, he'd have preferred if Zara had simply killed him.

He was missing something, he knew—a key to the puzzle that was Magnus. What if Eternity's abduction wasn't politically motivated as the queen assumed. What if it was nothing more than the same obsession that had driven him to the Moonvale?

He sighed. Sitting out here in the rain wasn't going to get him answers—besides, Marito would likely send a search party if he wasn't back soon. The man could fell a tree with his bare hands but had the softest heart.

Gabriel pulled his cloak tighter around him as he made his way to his horse. A patient gray stallion hand-reared by Lazander, the horse hadn't so much as budged from where he'd tied it to a fallen tree.

He mounted it easily—pleased Lazander's riding lessons were paying off. The mage had never been the most confident rider, and the Gilded's newest member had been working to change that. In seconds, he was charging back to camp—thinking of the fresh clothes and warm fire that awaited him.

***

From the shadows of *Whisper of Darkness* Valerius watched Gabriel ride off—his hand gripping his sword tightly, the naked blade catching the falling dusk. Biting the inside of his cheek, he sheathed his sword—his heart beating wildly.

Stepping out of the shroud of the spell, he dismissed it as he forced himself to take a breath and begin, once more, to run through the fighting styles of the Gilded and what made them so formidable.

Gabriel's magic was unparalleled as was his command of his shadows—the only way to beat him in a fight was to separate him from the rest of the Gilded, and even then it would be a close call for any knight. His magic, however, was only half of what made him such a terrifying opponent—his mind and his cold, tactical approach to every situation, big or small, was what had earned him a place among the Gilded.

Lazander wielded a bow with the ease of breathing but struggled in close combat—his archer's mind was so focused on finding the perfect strike he sometimes became overwhelmed by a flurry of strikes. His attunement to the natural world and the animals he had bonded with, however, was his greatest strength, allowing him to scout an area and travel great distances—beyond the abilities of most knights.

Valerius, however, had insisted that Lazander only bring his hawk, Merrin, on the journey. He'd said a dragon was too obvious and required special food or travel accommodations—neither of which they had time to prepare. Lazander had protested, of course, but Valerius had stood firm—and as he surveyed the barracks he was glad of it.

Finally there was Marito, who lacked the magic of Gabriel and the range of abilities of Lazander. But then, he'd never needed either. He was the brawn as well as the optimistic backbone of the group—when it came to a straight up fight, he always led the charge.

And he *never* backed down.

Valerius felt himself calm as he weighed up his fellow knights' strengths and weaknesses—it was par for the course of being a leader. On this mission, however, he'd been borderline obsessive about it, spending almost every waking moment weighing them up in his mind. This mission would define the course of his life, and he had a single chance to pull it off—there could be no mistakes.

Chapter Forty-Seven

"**B**astard."

My eyes snapped open at the voice, and I shot up—soaking wet from the puddle I lay in.

"You're blood-spiked, kid. You'll turn *mongrel*—no doubt about it."

I leaped to my feet at the voice, vaguely registering that my wounds from my broken ribs to the fang marks in my forearm were gone.

Lilac flowers trailed from vines that surrounded me, the floral scent of the molger's soap thick in the air. I recognized this part of the forest—it was between Lenia's house and H'tar. Instead of being comforted, however, my nerves were ragged—like I stood on the precipice of a cliff.

Was this a memory like Zara's?

"His mother is a *vaxion*. What is Chief thinking, letting that thing in here?"

I spun, searching for the voice that echoed through the trees—it was different from the previous two, older and more feminine. Where were they coming from?

"Disgusting."

The vines swayed, even though the heavy air was still. I frowned, realizing the vine flowers were growing bigger, their petals blossoming.

"Letting a mongrel near the other kids? Gallow above, what if he hurts them?"

I stepped closer, watching the petals flutter with every word. Brushing them aside, I recoiled as a human face glared at me from within the flower.

"Do the honorable thing, Lukas," spat an older woman with a scar on her cheek. "Kill yourself before you kill *us*."

***

I found a dozen in total—all faces I'd seen in the village. The woman who'd transformed into the molger, pushing the boulder into H'tar center told Lukas that if he even looked at her kids, she'd rip out his throat. The father who I'd seen balancing a child on his hip told him to get back to Moonvale Mountains where he belonged. Then there was the woman who told him to kill himself. I'd seen her laughing with an older man, their hands intertwined—nothing but love in their eyes for each other.

The quiet, almost idyllic life I'd seen in H'tar shattered like a broken mirror. All I'd seen were hardworking people, who—while afraid of the vaxion—would protect H'tar with their lives.

Yet they treated Lukas like this?

The voices grew louder until they were a single, hateful roar—spewing abuse until I wanted to rip them from the vines and pop each one like blood-filled ticks.

Disgusted by the violent image, I slapped my hands over my ears, shoving through the forest at a reckless speed.

Was it all a lie? I didn't see Chief or Lenia's faces, but they must have known. Did they even try to stop it? Did they join in? What if...

I stumbled, tripping over my feet. With no time to brace myself I hit the ground hard, air bursting from me with an audible *whoosh*. I groaned, winded.

My eyes fell on a pair of bare feet in front of me with long, dark talons.

I looked up to find Zara's aunt staring down at me—golden eyes alight with rage.

"Choose, boy," she said, voice cold. She looked much the same as she had in Zara's memory. Tall, imposing, her tattoos straining against her crossed arms. Her single, thick braid fell forward as she glared at me—casting her face in shadow. Two scars marred her face, one on her chin, another on her cheek, but they only framed her powerful gaze.

She was as beautiful as a storm—one whose lightning could split a stone with a single bolt.

"Mom?"

A high voice made me turn to find a small boy with a crown of blonde hair behind me. His small hands gripped a loose sack slung from his shoulder. Tiny fingers worried the strap as he looked from a blonde woman by Zara's side I had missed to a man with graying temples behind him.

"Do not look at your parents, boy," Zara's aunt snapped. "The molger are not welcome here, so now you must choose. Stay and become vaxion or leave and remain *molger.*" The ice in her words made it clear which she thought the better option.

"Mom, but why—"

The blonde woman, the image of the little boy with his big blue eyes and a smattering of freckles across dimpled cheeks, covered her face with a sob.

Tears welled in the boy's eyes as she walked away. She didn't look back once.

"Her place is here. Now choose, or I will make the choice for you." Her talons, already inches long, grew slowly—stretching into pitch-black tips.

"It's okay, Lukas," the man with the gray temples said, voice breaking.

Like the young boy, he had a sack hurriedly tied around his back—heavy and bulging with contents. He was also wrapped in several layers of clothes despite the warm weather. He stepped back up, smiling broadly even as tears streamed from his eyes.

"I love you, son. Look after your—your mother, okay?" He turned without another word, walking briskly away. I could hear his choked sobs with every step.

"What do you say, Aerzin?" Zara's aunt said. "Be you the molger, Lukas? Or the vaxion, Aerzin?"

I gasped at the name—*Aerzin.* The quest the Operator had given me flashed in my mind.

Stop Aerzin.

The boy squeezed his eyes shut, shaking his head.

Then he spun on his heel and chased after his dad, calling for him. The man stopped, tear-stained face flushed with disbelief as the boy leaped into his arms. With a gasp of delight, the man scooped him up, hugging him close. He risked a fearful glance at Zara's aunt, who flashed a smile—her canines sharp and elongated.

"Run along, little Aerzin." She laughed as the man clutched Lukas close, nearly running from her. "Come back when you wish to see who you truly are!"

Stop Aerzin.

Stop him from what? Hurting people in H'tar? Or did it mean…

Do I have to kill him? Was saving him the exact opposite of what the Operator wanted? How the hell was I supposed to tell?

A laugh brought me back.

Zara's aunt waved the blonde woman over—Lukas' mother. Her braid was frayed from where her fingers were excessively tying and untying the end of it, and she stared at the horizon—a look of intense longing and sorrow on her face.

"Do not cry, *chara,*" Zara's aunt said, wrapping a hand roughly around the woman's shoulder. "Our children's destinies are their own—as I know all too well. Zara's fate will plague me until the day I die."

"Zara? What happened to her? Why did she go with Magnus?" I blurted out, knowing they couldn't hear me.

"While I may never see my niece again, that is not your fate. Aerzin will return."

She pulled Lukas' mother into a tight hug, and as she turned I saw a giant tattoo, the flesh still raw and healing on her back. It looked deep and bloody—like it had been done with a knife.

"Your boy will return—I feel it in my bones."

A crack sounded, the ground sinking beneath my feet. I moved a second too late as the ground crumbled.

Suddenly I was gone.

***

"One song? A ballad, even!" Marito protested.

"Do you *want* Magnus to hear us and go running into the night?" Gabriel said, even as his lips crooked into a smile.

"Unless the mage has suddenly developed the ears of a wolf, we are perfectly fine," Marito said, pointing at Lazander. "What say you, Master Lazander? I gifted you *Fiery Ballads for the Stalwart Heart,* I seem to recall. No doubt you have them all memorized."

The knight smiled, feeling suddenly shy. "I—I did learn a few of them..."

"You *did?*" said Gabriel and Marito at the same time.

"Then let us sing the opener, *Courage for the Ages!*" Marito stood, cup in hand (water, at Gabriel's insistence, despite Marito's claim that no successful mission began with anything but wine). Lazander spotted Farah, the mage Gabriel had chosen to come with them during their assault on the Barracks, and Corym—Valerius' pick of the knights. They hovered on the edge of the fire, looking unsure.

"Join us, join us," Marito called. "For tonight, you are honorary Gilded. And it is customary for us to have a little song before battle."

"Since when?" Gabriel protested.

"Since now. Come!" He poured water from a canister into several cups he'd whittled himself, passing them around. Farah, a small slip of a woman with mousy hair and a timid smile, ducked her head in gratitude. Corym, a short barrel-chested man a year or two younger than Lazander nodded—doing his best to look stern.

"Master Valerius, come! I insist."

Lazander had almost missed the shadow of their leader up against one of the trees just outside the light of their campfire. No Gilded was on watch that evening— they were under orders to rest before the assault, which would take place in the dead of night. The breaching of the Calix bindings would take some time, Gabriel explained, but if they timed it right they would reach the barracks as the sun rose. This would allow them the cover of darkness on the approach and the advantage of dawn if it came to a fight within the barracks itself.

"Of course," Valerius said, smiling. A smile, Lazander noticed, that didn't reach his eyes. "We must commemorate the night—it is only proper."

Marito raised his cup and said, "May we best Lord Magnus as we always do, with style and panache!"

The group clanked cups as they yelled, "Cheers!"—even Corym's stern expression relaxing.

Taking a deep breath, Marito began the opening lines of *Courage for the Ages,* a ridiculous and dramatic tale about a knight going weeks without food or drink as he chased a villain across the realms. Lazander joined, quieter than the booming Marito, but his eyes kept drifting to Valerius. The knight was smiling and singing along in a melodious baritone that kept perfect time, but every word seemed an effort.

"How about *Magic and Merriment?*" Farah asked as the song came to a thunderous close—Marito slapping his chest like a drum.

Lazander felt a rush of nostalgia at the suggestion. Suddenly he was a child again, laughing from atop his father's shoulders as he watched a traveling carnival troupe perform this very song.

Marito roared in approval. "A fine choice, good lady!"

"That takes me back." Gabriel sighed. "It wasn't a festival without it."

"While I belted it out with my mother," Corym laughed, "I would sneak some mead from her cup."

"All together now!" Marito yelled, arms waving dramatically.

Laughter, lies, and lucky days!

Copper and coin for drunken ways,

They started off pitch and off-key, but it added to the revelry, stirring up memories of late nights and summer festivals.

Gallow look not upon mine deed,

Of bellies full of delicious mead!

Valerius was the only one who didn't join in.

"That's enough," he said tightly. "We should get some sleep."

Marito was belting too loud to hear, wrapping one huge arm around Farah, the other around Corym. Even Gabriel sang along, his voice surprisingly high and melodious—together, they wove a beautiful harmony that seemed to make even the stars above brighter, the night sweeter.

"Enough," Valerius said loudly, to no avail. The anger in his voice made Lazander cut off mid-note, and he raised a worried hand to catch Marito's eye, but a cup flew across the campfire, hitting Marito square in the chest.

He broke off singing, staring down at the water that spilled down his shirt.

"Do you ever get tired of listening to yourself, you bloody oaf?" Valerius hissed.

Marito's jaw dropped, and while it moved, no words came out of his mouth.

"And you!" Valerius snapped, gesturing at a wide-eyed Gabriel. "Pissing and moaning about how annoying 'Mari' is, and then you act as big an idiot as him. Make up your mind!"

The mage froze, hands mid-clap. Then his brow furrowed—eyes as dark as a storm. "Says the man who walks around with the realm's biggest stick up his ass," Gabriel snapped, getting to his feet.

Farah gasped, hands coming to her mouth in a way that would have been comical if not for the crackle of anger and violence in the air.

"Now, sers, we're all just a bit wound up," Marito said. "Why don't we—"

"No, no—if Val here wants to have it out, I'm more than happy to," Gabriel said, stepping around the fire as he squared up to Valerius. "The past few days, you've been in the best mood I've seen you in in *literal* years and then we arrive here and you act like a pissy child. The hell is the matter with you?"

Valerius raised his chin, the fury in his eyes making him appear to tower over the armored knight despite being a head shorter.

"Perhaps I was simply doing my best to forget how utterly aggravating you all are," Valerius said, fists clenched. His anger was cold—to an outside observer he might have looked annoyed, perhaps even irritated.

To Lazander, however, he looked furious.

Gabriel's anger was the opposite—bright, hot, and gleaming. The mage jabbed a finger into Valerius' chest plate, punctuating his words.

"Years. For *years* Mari and I have picked up your slack—covering you when you vanish to do Gallow knows what—well, no more," Gabriel said. "You're a spoiled, self-centered, egotistical *brat*."

Like the steps in a dance, Valerius moved—hand going to his sword. Gabriel spun in answer, shadows twisting around his hand—threatening to erupt.

Chapter Forty-Eight

Valerius and Gabriel faced each other down—the air crackling with violence. Valerius' sword inched from his scabbard as shadows darted from Gabriel's fingers.

Lazander knew he had seconds.

He leaped in front of Valerius, wrapping his hands around the knight's sword arm. Some would argue that turning his back on a mage was unwise, but Lazander didn't even glance behind him.

Marito appeared behind Gabriel, dropping arms around the mage in a bear hug. He lifted Gabriel as if he were a toddler, walking backward.

"No, Mari—stop it." Gabriel spat, kicking the air. "I will knock your teeth out—I swear it."

"No, you won't, Gabriel," Marito said, and Lazander had to stop himself from turning around. He'd never heard Marito address anyone by their first name, not even Magnus, without saying "Lady" or "Master" before it. "You shall not harm me, for I am your comrade and friend. To hurt me is to hurt yourself, and you will regret it afterward."

Gabriel kicked feebly, then sighed, flopping his head on Marito's shoulder. "Could you at least threaten to squeeze my head like a lemon or something?" he asked.

"Very well. Stop this at once, Master Gabriel, or I shall squeeze your head until it pops—like a lemon."

"*Fine.*" Gabriel sighed.

Lazander kept his grip tight on Valerius' arm, but he finally raised his gaze. A part of him hoped for the heartfelt moment he'd just heard between Marito and Gabriel.

At the look in Valerius' eyes, however, all hope of that was gone.

The knight's anger had dissipated, but so had everything else. His eyes were glazed, a cold stillness enveloping. He may as well have been on the other side of the continent—and Lazander had no way to reach him.

"My lord, why don't we—" Lazander began but was cut off by a sharp pain in his arm. Surprised, Lazander released Valerius and the knight strode away, cloak whipping about him.

How had Valerius broken his hold? He hadn't even seen him move.

Lazander winced as he flexed his hand—the pain sharp but duller than the sight of his leader walking away without a word. In that moment, he felt like something had broken between the Gilded—something that no word or deed could ever repair.

A mantle of dread settled about his shoulders.

"Really, Val?" Gabriel called out. "You're going to stomp off like a *child*? The minstrels will be singing songs about your anger management skills."

Marito swatted Gabriel on the back of the head. "Master Gabriel, for one of the most intelligent and tactical minds I have ever had the joy of conversing with, you have the temper of a petulant twelve-year-old."

"Please, the temper of a fourteen-year-old at least," he said, gesturing at the disappearing figure of Valerius. "There's your twelve-year-old."

Marito frowned, pinching the bridge of his nose. "I, for one, have suddenly found myself in desperate need of a bedroll and silence. What say we turn in for the night?"

The group grumbled in consensus, Farah and Corym stepping away awkwardly, their heads dipped in whispered conversation. The rest of the company would know what happened by morning, Lazander knew. Which meant it would be all over the Ivory Keep by the time they returned.

He sighed. Gabriel and Valerius had needled each other in the past, but it had never exploded. Not like this.

"Well done," Marito said, clapping a hand on Lazander's shoulder. "It is no easy task to face down Master Valerius."

Lazander shrugged, pleased at the praise, but sad at what had sparked it. "It just seemed to make him angrier."

"No, Master Lazander." Marito sighed heavily. "Anger like that can only come from within. I'm afraid that, regardless of what occurs tomorrow, I must speak to the queen about him. Son or not, he is the leader of the Gilded and heir to the throne. To see him lose his temper over a childhood ballad is… well, it is cause for concern."

***

Valerius strode through the darkness, letting everything go—the anger, the fear, the worry. He started with the feelings that made him want to run screaming into the night—the Operator and his quest be *damned*.

He didn't stop there. Joy, happiness, admiration, *affection*. He shoved them down, down, to the base of his feet, stomping them into the dirt with every step.

He had tried. He had laughed with his fellow Gilded on the road. He'd taken command when they arrived, making camp and preparing for the assault tomorrow with confidence and ease. His temper had slipped with Gabriel when they scouted the Captain's Barracks, his mind jumping ahead, but he'd reined it in—determined to make up for it by the campfire that night.

He wanted to be like the old Valerius one last time—to be the one loved and admired.

Until that damn song—a song filled with childhood memories of fairgrounds and laughter. He had memorized the classics over the years in order to play his role, including the stupid songs in Marito's *Fiery Ballads for the Stalwart Heart*. He was Valerius—the heir to the throne. The educated prince. Yet he didn't know *Magic and Merriment*.

It was in no book. Instead it was passed from town to town along the carnival trail. It was a song the real Valerius would have known, would have sung as a boy. But he didn't know the words. Had no memories of carnivals and games.

Because he *wasn't* Valerius—and all the pretending in the world wouldn't change that.

He didn't know his real name, not anymore. That had been the first thing to go. The names of his mother and father had followed, but that had been no great loss. His brothers were harder. He knew he had some, although how many, he couldn't remember.

It had all slipped away—seeping down the festering drain that was this world.

Because none of this was real. It was just a playground where the Operator reigned supreme. If he wanted to leave, he had to obey the Calamity System and finish his damn quests.

And playacting as a heroic knight wasn't going to help that.

He sat with a thump, leaning against the trunk of a tree.

All it had done was make things harder.

It's just a quest, he chastised himself. *A quest like any other—just finish the damn thing.*

But it wasn't just a quest, he knew, and if he didn't hate himself before this...

He would by the time it was done.

***

I screamed as I fell—at the beginning at least. But when you've been falling for ten minutes, the novelty wears off.

Now I lay on my back, the air forcing my long hair to whip about my face like a cat o' nine tails. I had tried turning in midair to face what should have been the ground, but the speed of the air made my eyes water, blurring the darkness further.

So I stretched out with my hands behind my head, like I would on a couch, and let myself fall.

"Lukas?" I called, growing bored. "What's next?"

The darkness didn't answer. I couldn't even see my hands in front of my face, yet I rubbed them over my eyes—hoping *something* would change.

"If you have any more traumatizing childhood memories, now would be a great time to show me."

Minutes passed. I thought back on what I had seen. The people of H'tar fearful of the half-vaxion in their midst. Lukas' own mother turning away from him, unable to bear the choice. His dad calling out that he would love him no matter what.

Zara's aunt—and her claim that Lukas would return one day.

No, not Lukas. That was his molger name.

"Aerzin?" I called out.

Abruptly the scene changed, and I had all of two seconds to appreciate the blue, cloudless sky above me before I hit the water.

Hard.

Every part of my body felt like it had been slapped by a thousand ice-cold palms. Unable to tell up from down, I panicked—spinning helplessly.

Light sparkled—pointing me to the surface. Kicking hard, I swam upward, shocked at how deep I'd gone.

I burst out of the water, wet hair clogging my mouth as I sucked in lungful's of freezing air.

The light disoriented me, blinding eyes that had grown used to inky darkness. As the world swam into focus, I saw I was surrounded on three sides by open water—but on the forth there was a scattering of trees along the shoreline.

Not having much choice, I swam hard, each stroke slower than the last as the icy cold of the water crept into my bones—threatening to freeze me.

By the time I made it to the shore and crawled out of the water on all fours, I was shivering, tiny ice crystals forming from every breath.

I took several long, ragged breaths before I could even look up. Blue mountains towered above me. They had been mere smudges when I'd seen them from Magnus' castle and the trees near Lenia's home. I didn't know them then, but my gut knew them now.

The Moonvale Mountains—home to the vaxion. Home to Zara the Fury.

Their peaks pierced the clouds, and even with my head craned back I had no idea how big they were. Definitely bigger than any skyscraper I'd seen.

The thought jolted my mind, feeling foreign and alien—skyscrapers. I knew what they looked like and had even lived in plenty. But the memory felt like a phrase I'd read in a forgotten book.

I shook the feeling off. I might know I was in the Moonvale Mountains, but that didn't help me figure out what I had to do. And I was getting very, very tired of being thrown from creepy talking flowers to terrifying control freak aunt to freezing cold mountains while *barefoot*.

"Aerzin?" I called out. "Could you *please* come out and stop tossing me about like a ping-pong ball?"

To no one's surprise, my words echoed into the distance, unanswered.

I sighed—and the voice began.

Chapter Forty-Nine

"*Stupid, useless, ignorant human.*" It was a woman's voice, each word barbed with fury, echoed in the forest.

I rolled my eyes. "It's my turn to be tormented now, is it? Great. Just great."

"*What I would give to have the joy of tormenting you. Would this moronic path kill only you, I would bask in delight. But your unfettered idiocy shall drag me down with you!*"

The words dripped with an anger and disgust that sang of the familiar—a familiarity that made my skin crawl as a horrifying thought dawned on me.

"*I know not what Magnus has promised you for wielding his whip, but he has led you astray. This is no magical playhouse—this is a vaxion's tul'gra. You will lose yourself to it long before you save the mongrel!*"

"Zara?" I whispered.

"*Who else, shek? Now leave—I command it!*"

My mind flooded with questions, drowning my brain with possibilities—how was Zara *here*? Had Zara been awake and aware this whole time? Why did she mention Magnus? Did that mean she didn't know what I had done? What was a "tul'gra"? Had she been in one before? Did she know how to save Aerzin?

"*Ah! Stop it. Your mind is a festering quagmire—each question dragging you deeper into its depths. You grab every pointless thought and feast on it 'til you feel sick—a glutton! Quiet your mind, human. Not even my aunt could save the mongrel, he is too far gone.*"

My fists clenched as I fought to calm down—*not* because Zara had told me to, but because I needed to think.

"If you think Aerzin can't be saved, then why did you help me?" I asked. "You showed me a memory of your aunt turning a…" I paused at the word, "mongrel." It had felt bad before, but worse here, for some reason. "… a *hybrid*, human again. It's how I got here in the first place."

"*I showed you no such thing, human—I awoke to find us here and you on the brink of killing us.*"

Frowning, I filed that away for further thought.

"Look," I said, pacing in a circle. "I know this is a lot. I freaked out too when I woke up in this world. But I'm not your enemy, all right? Let's figure out this… 'tul'gra' and then we can—

"No! You will turn back, miserable shek—*this instant!"*

When I wanted to be obeyed, I used *Vicious Command.* It was an ability— something I had to activate to force my will on others.

Hearing Zara now, I knew what was a special ability for me was simply natural for her. She had no need for magic, or spells—her simple presence was a force of nature unto itself. One that brokered no argument. No dissent. No resistance.

I stiffened, my body turning of its own volition toward the lake. My legs itched with the need to do as she said, to please her—all I had to do was give in.

"No…" I hissed, my knees crumbling beneath me as I dug my hands into dirt— refusing to move.

"You dare? You, a vile, bottom-feeding—"

"Shut up!" I yelled, slapping my hands over my ears. "Shut up—shut up!"

I waited for retaliation, my blood pumping—hands trembling with the need to flee from the enemy within.

Zara was silent.

For now.

I couldn't believe it. She was here—*the* Zara the Fury. While I'd learned some snatches about her life and had seen the option to interact with her in the Menu, I hadn't thought about what it would be like to *actually* speak to her. Hadn't thought every word she spoke would be filled with bile and hatred—all directed at me.

But then, why wouldn't she hate me?

I had stolen her life, after all.

I sighed—I already had one voice berating my every choice, my every move, my every *thought*—my own. If I had to deal with her spewing insults at me on top of that, I might actually go mad

Which meant the sooner I found Aerzin and got out of here, the better.

"Aerzin?" I called out, suddenly utterly exhausted. "I would very much like to get out of here, so if you could just—"

A whining, high-pitched cry sounded—echoing among the skeletal sticks of the forest.

It was a sign I'd adapted, at least somewhat, to this world since that sound didn't make me jump—because after spending time in H'tar, I knew that whine.

It was the cry of a molger.

I scanned the trees around me, which were little more than sparse, frozen sticks bursting from frozen soil, but they provided enough coverage I didn't immediately spot the molger.

Then a flash of brown caught my eye as a six legged beast the size of a car charged through the forest in the distance—heading straight toward me.

I couldn't tell if it was the hunter or hunted, but my fight with Jerome had taught me I didn't want to take a molger head on. I picked a tree off to the side, one with a spattering of gray foliage near the top, and scaled it quickly.

The molger began to slow, its raspy breath a grating sound in the silence of the lake. It stumbled, the snap of bark echoing as it knocked into several trees, snapping them in two.

What now? If I have to deal with a drunk molger, I swear I'm going to…

The molger staggered under my hiding place, banging into the tree so hard I had to grip the branches with both hands and legs to stop from falling.

With a grunt, the molger collapsed, hitting the ground with a thump. A skittering of birds fled a nearby bush, the snap of their wings echoing in the silence that followed. The air was thick with tension. My claws began to tear through the flesh at the tips of my fingers.

Something was wrong with the molger. Very wrong.

To my shame, I hesitated—Zara's warnings fresh in my mind. I hadn't been able to interact with any of the other memories here, why would I be able to do anything about this one? I was frozen, my thoughts scattered until the molger let out a dull whine, making my decision for me.

I jumped from the treetop, landing quietly. The hair on the back of my arms raised as I crept forward, scanning the trees. Nothing moved in the forest but me, but instead of quelling my sense of dread, it only increased it.

The molger's fur was unusual—a deep brown with patches of inky black in parts as opposed to the usual streaks and stripes I had seen. Its breath wheezed like an accordion struggling to find the right note.

It was only when I tiptoed around to its front that I abandoned all caution. The dark patches that covered its body wasn't fur.

It was blood.

Claw marks, thick and deep, covered the molger from neck to back to hind legs, like something had grabbed it from behind and tried to shred its flesh from its bones.

The molger's eyes were closed. Breath ragged with pain and fear.

"*It's already begun,*" Zara said, her voice thick with disgust. "*You have damned us both.*"

Ignoring Zara, I pressed a hand against the molger's cheek. "Aerzin?" I whispered. "No—Lukas? Is that you?"

He cringed, trying to drag his massive body away from me—blood pouring anew from his wounds as his six legs scrambled.

That was a yes, then.

"Woah—woah. I'm here to help, all right?" I pressed a hand against one of the largest wounds on its neck, my fingers disappearing among the fur and blood.

He quietened at that, cracking a single bright blue and very human eye.

"I'm here," I whispered, blood seeping through my useless fingers. "It's, ah, it's going to be—"

Something dark and huge flew over my head, hitting the lake with a slap. A wave of water sprayed me and Lukas. I instinctively covered him—my body hunching over his head, leaving the rest of his huge body open and exposed.

A shadow moved beneath the surface of the lake, powering toward the shoreline at full speed. Images of serpents and sea monsters flashed through my mind as a shadow erupted out of the water.

Six paws hit the dirt with grace and ease. Ink black fur soaked, his misaligned jaw let out a growl.

"Lukas?" I called out, looking from the wounded molger I still covered to the beast in front of me.

His head twitched, ear flickering at my voice, but Lukas' hybrid ignored me—staring into the trees ahead. Shoulders hunched, he dug four paws into the dirt, claws snapping out. He'd clearly heard me, but something else had his attention.

I followed the direction of his gaze into the forest beyond—and all hope of saving anyone left me.

When I'd been scared in this world, Zara's anger and power, terrifying as it could be, was a comfort. Her magic and strength had surged through me—the promise of safety within my grasp, if I was just brave enough to take it.

Now, icy blue eyes locked onto mine from the depths of the forest, glowing like ghostly sprites. There was no hope or humanity in those eyes—I saw only my death replayed over and over as claws ripped my stomach open and teeth crushed my skull. I shook as terror flooded my body, the adrenaline that had made my claws erupt and fueled my battle instincts vanishing.

"Now you see," Zara's voice whispered in my head, softer now in its disappointment. *"This is* tul'gra—*our innermost selves. Our hearts. Our minds. The mongrel's is fractured—broken. His true forms fight for dominion—and you, whose mind is as riddled with doubt and fear as his—have damned us to a fight we cannot win. Death awaits us."*

The icy blue eyes that stared into mine echoed the same promise. Someone would die today.

Me.

Chapter Fifty

"Be ready to move—we'll only have seconds," Gabriel said. It was dark still, the whisper of dawn two hours away.

Farah stifled a yawn, and a tuft or Corym's hair stood up, one buckle of his breastplate slowly coming untied. Gabriel had roused them only minutes before, hoping to give them as much rest as he could.

None of the other Gilded had slept a wink, Lazander could tell. He was glad at least Farah and Corym had.

Gabriel slapped his hands together, whispering a guttural chant that thickened and solidified the darkness. Expelling his breath, he drove his hands forward like a blade, his fingers disappearing into the night. With a grunt, he began to separate his palms, forcing them outward, his teeth gritted in effort.

"Amazing…" Farah whispered, and for a brief moment Lazander was jealous. While some magic was visible to the naked eye, certain spells, such as the Calix Rings that surrounded the barracks, could only be seen by a mage. Whatever Gabriel was doing, however, was powerful enough that Lazander couldn't just feel the magic—he could taste it. Smacking his lips, he winced at the copper tang that filled his mouth like blood.

For the brief second after Gabriel flung his arms wide, Lazander saw the faintest silver outline of a huge dome that towered above them, encircling the barracks. It was gigantic—he could hardly imagine the sheer amount of magic it had taken to create.

"Stop gawking and move," Gabriel barked, holding his arms wide. His muscles shook as if the air itself threatened to compact around him.

The company moved quickly, single file as they had planned. Marito went first, as always, ducking under Gabriel's arm. He had to crouch so low he was nearly crawling.

Farah went next, followed by Lazander. Then Corym with Valerius bringing up the rear. As he disappeared under Gabriel's arm, the mage let out a gasp and stepped forward. A spark of silver, like a match in the darkness, hovered where Gabriel had been a moment before. The mage grimaced, holding up his cloak. Several inches had been sliced clean off, the edges still smoldering.

"A little quicker next time, if you don't mind," he said.

"Well done, Master Gabriel," Marito said. "Only five more to go."

"Your pep talks remain as inspiring as always, Mari," Gabriel said with a slight grin. He turned, almost colliding with Valerius who stared at the crumbling remnants of the barracks, looking lost.

"Watch—" Gabriel snapped, and then let out a sigh. "Pardon me," he said instead, sidestepping the knight.

Valerius nodded, eyes downcast.

Farah and Corym exchanged a look, the air heavy with tension. Gabriel and Valerius hadn't said a word to each other beyond cursory greetings, and seeing Gabriel force out a pleasantry was borderline physically painful.

Lazander almost preferred it when they were yelling at each other.

They were traveling light—all knights had donned magic-resistant armor, although to varying levels. Marito wore the least, simply because he didn't need it— he could withstand spells that could crumble a troop of knights. His leather brigandine was a deep russet red and built for flexibility, allowing him to charge enemies with the agility of someone half his size. His axes were crafted with dragon scales that Galora herself had donated (although Lazander was forced to bribe her with the promise of many tasty goats to get her to agree). It meant that while Marito's axes could slice a man's head from his shoulders, they could also absorb magical attacks just like Valerius' shield—*if* the knight timed it right.

And he always did. Lazander had seen Marito fight countless times—he'd never so much as stumbled.

Gabriel's robes stood out next to the giant, wearing cloth designed to enhance magic rather than suppress it. While Marito's blades were made using dragon scales, Gabriel's deep purple robes were woven with the hair and fur of the most magical beings in the realm—falslings. Gabriel swore up and down he'd convinced a vaxion from the Mi'xan clan to supply the fur, but given the mage's mysterious smile as he told the story, Lazander wasn't sure if he believed it.

Lazander wore a mixture of leather bindings that allowed for speed and dragonscale for limited protection. His shoulders and forearms were braced with Galora's dragonscale as well as his chest, whereas almost everything else was covered in leather. He preferred to rely on his bow when it came to battle, drawing his blades only as a last resort.

Valerius, on the other hand, stood out even amongst the Gilded. Dragonscale offered the most protection from both magical and physical attacks but was notoriously heavy—tiring even the fittest of knights.

Valerius was covered in it from head to toe.

Lazander had helped pack his commander's armor on many occasions and was always shocked at the sheer weight of it—the breastplate alone made his arms tremble. Yet Valerius moved with Marito's ease and Lazander's speed.

The royal family's crest, a six-winged farrow, was engraved into his breastplate and shield. In certain lights, it had even been enchanted to move. That Gabriel had managed to infuse magic into the most magic-resistant metal in the realm was still talked about in the Ivory Keep. He had done it as a gift to Valerius for his birthday, the two men hugging each other tightly in thanks while Lazander, a mere soldier on guard duty back then, had looked on in admiration. Seeing the two knights now, walking with stiff backs and sternly ignoring the other, tinged the memory with sadness.

Sudden guilt pulled at Lazander's chest as Gabriel approached the next Calix Ring. Lazander had worshipped Valerius as a teenager, driving himself to become a Gilded so he could fight at the side of the man he called hero. Now, he suspected Valerius of treason.

He didn't know what would happen when they cornered Lord Magnus in the barracks, but he knew every single Gilded would be watching Valerius like a hawk. His actions today would potentially define his future in the Gilded, and the thought of Valerius no longer being his brother-in-arms brought an unexpected prickle of tears to his eyes.

When Lazander had sworn an oath to protect Navaros, the kingdom he now called home, he hadn't realized that would mean turning on someone he once considered a friend.

"Get ready," Gabriel said, coating his hands in darkness once more. The Calix Ring that surrounded the barracks' ruins flashed as Gabriel forced open the sliver of an opening. The knights hurriedly dashed through.

Four more to go.

***

Lazander ducked under Gabriel's forearm, who held the final Calix Ring open with two shadowed hands.

"Quickly," the mage hissed.

Valerius brought up the rear, the last in their small company, and as he passed the threshold Gabriel let out a strangled gasp, falling forward. Marito was at his side before the mage's knees hit the ground, wrapping an arm around his shoulder.

"Mari, don't even think about picking me up like some maiden," Gabriel said weakly, sweat peppering his brow.

Marito smiled broadly, helping him to his feet. "Nay, Master Gabriel, that shall be for when we return to the Ivory Keep. With Lord Magnus over one shoulder and you cradled in my arms, it would be fitting to commission a painting, do you not think?"

Gabriel rolled his eyes, a hint of a smirk on his lips as he steadied himself, waving off Marito's arm. "We're here," Gabriel said, gesturing upward. It was clearly a change of subject, and Lazander graciously looked away from the mage who was breathing weakly to the towering Captain's Barracks.

In the distance it had looked like crumbling ruins. Up close, Lazander could hardly believe it was still standing. Scorched stone dotted the three remaining walls while one tower leaned heavily against the easternmost side. It looked like a stiff breeze would bring the thing down on their heads. The entrance was little better—a dilapidated beam blocked a solid third of the doorway, and Lazander could spy gaps in the broken stairs leading upward.

"I see no sign of sentries," Corym said, scanning the ruins. "But the condition of the building makes it difficult to tell—we should be on our guard." Corym glanced at Valerius, who nodded approvingly. The young knight struggled to keep the grin off his face.

"Farah, can you sense anything?" Gabriel asked.

Farah closed her eyes, stretching her hands outward. She shook her head a moment later. "The only magic I can sense is the Calix Rings behind me—that doesn't mean the barracks itself isn't booby-trapped, but the way inside is clear."

"Then the plan remains the same," Valerius said, his back to the group. "Remember—we need Magnus alive."

In a rare moment of solemnity, Marito glanced from Gabriel to Lazander—his eyes saying what words never could. The Gilded four had become the Gilded three—and they were in this together.

Now all they had to do was navigate a crumbling ruin that might collapse on them at any moment and take a powerful mage alive.

Chapter Fifty-One

The icy-blue eyed monstrosity was nothing I'd ever seen before, but my blood hummed, answering the call of its power.

I knew what it was. But I didn't want to say it. Didn't want to even think it.

It was larger than Lukas' molger form, its fur undulating as if it had been threaded from shadows, bending them to its will. It stalked with grace, its four legs corded with muscle. From the neck up, however, only horror awaited. Its face was narrow, jaw wide, and while no teeth poked from its upper lip like Lukas did, I knew razor sharp fangs lay hidden beneath its lips. It had no nose I could see, just a row of four narrow slits that looked as if they had been carved into its very flesh.

But that isn't what made my heart stop.

Tendrils of fur or flesh, I couldn't tell, coiled around its head, trailing along its back. They moved and twisted in the twilight, each seeming to carry a life of its own as they swayed in a hypnotic dance that made my stomach turn.

A vaxion.

A spark of light as blue as its eyes trailed along the vaxion's tendrils.

Lukas growled, and the vaxion, no, *Aerzin*, gave a low, choking rumble in return—a staccato sound that punctured the air.

It was laughing.

"*What's wrong, human?*" Zara hissed, her voice low and mocking. "*Why do your lips tremble, your hands shake? Make haste, for you must butcher the molger and mongrel, then feed their still beating hearts to little Aerzin! But you knew this, did you not? You knew that you would have to slaughter the fragments of his broken mind—so that his vaxion form might fly free. Why else would you drag us into this hellscape?*" She laughed, a maniacal, vicious sound like claws scraping against metal.

"*Little Aerzin has even tenderized the molger's flesh for you! My dear auntie, the leader of the Mi'xan, the conqueror of Moonvale, is the only one I know to have reforged a broken tul'gra. Since you so clearly think yourself her equal, then go ahead, human.*"

I heard her spit, and my cheek stung as if she'd struck me in the face.

"*Finish what you started.*"

Aerzin growled, light sparking between his tendrils as he took a step toward me—eyes alight with the promise of death. Lukas' hybrid risked a glance at me, his fangs bared, gaze flitting from Aerzin to me. And at my back, the molger wheezed, every breath a fight for survival.

I couldn't do it.

I couldn't choose who lived and died. I couldn't murder the parts of someone whose only crime was desperately wishing to live. Which meant I was going to *die*.

My mind screamed as I fell to my knees.

Stupid—stupid! *Spilled guts in the dirt, vaxion teeth at your throat, eaten alive. Dying— screaming. Alone.* Dead. Dead. DEAD.

"*Argh,* stop it! *You useless* shek," Zara hissed. "*If we are to die, it shall be with our claws unsheathed and fury in our eyes!*"

Her voice was distant as panic overwhelmed me. My soft, fleshy fingers dug into the earth as I struggled to retain my grip on reality. I could only grit my teeth as tears blurred my vision—my body frozen.

The hybrid screamed, a high-pitched noise of rage.

He leaped forward, claws unsheathed, scarring the earth as he charged Aerzin.

The vaxion ducked his head, coiled tendrils of flesh snapping outward—a shadowy crown. Blue light danced between them, picking up speed. Lukas leaped— jaws wide, ready to crush Aerzin's head with a single bite.

Aerzin grinned.

Electricity burst from his coils, streams of light and power colliding with Lukas—catching him midair. The hairs on the back of my arms rose in answering static.

Lukas hung, levitating as electricity flooded his body, shocking him over and over again.

As abruptly as it began, the sparks vanished. Lukas hit the dirt, limbs flopping, slack-jawed. The air was tinged with the smell of burnt flesh and hair.

"Lukas?" I said, my voice small and pathetic.

He lay on his side, foot twitching.

Slowly Aerzin turned his gaze to me.

***

Gabriel nudged Marito, nodding toward Valerius. The giant sighed, then whispered, "Master Valerius, can you repeat the spymaster's instructions?"

Valerius said nothing, merely handing a slip of paper to the pair before making his way to the entrance. Gabriel flipped open the letter. "Our spies have spotted at least one figure in the upper floors of the Captain's Barracks, but there has been no movement for the past three hours. This suggests Magnus is alone or in the company of no more than one other person."

The mage sighed. "That doesn't give us much."

"Upper floors, Master Gabriel—that is more than we had for other missions. Remember Jasmine the Lithe?"

"She coated herself in oil and kept threatening to set herself on fire—yes, I remember," Gabriel said, chuckling. "She kept dropping the match because her hands were too slippery."

"Had we naught but the word of a drunk and a lock of her hair to find and capture her?" Marito continued. "Steady hands and a steady heart are all we need."

Gabriel nodded while Farah and Corym exchanged a horrified look at the thought of an oil-soaked woman with a match. Lazander hid a grin at their expressions.

With a single hand, Valerius shifted the huge beam that blocked the entrance to the barracks. The hallway beyond tinkled with the sound of falling rocks but held steady. He gestured to the company, pointing upward. "Marito leads, Lazander at the back, Corym and Gabriel in the middle."

"What about you?" Gabriel asked, a brow arched at Valerius.

Lazander hoped he was the only one who heard the mage's suspicious tone.

"I'll circle the back with Farah and see if we can find an alternate entrance." Valerius' reply was sharp. "Search every room for both reinforcements and magical defenses. If we time this right, we can drive Magnus toward the easternmost wall and corner him from both sides—we cannot afford to let him slip through our fingers."

A few months ago, Lazander would have nodded and gone along with this plan without a second thought. But the trust he once had in Valerius, like the ruins they now stood in, was scorched and broken and on the edge of collapse.

"Why don't I go with Farah?" Lazander said, surprising himself.

"Excellent suggestion, Master Lazander," Marito replied as Valerius opened his mouth to argue. "The young hunter is unmatched in terms of stealth, Master Valerius, and the element of surprise is key to this endeavor."

For a moment a shadow passed over Valerius' face, but then the expression disappeared, and he simply nodded. "Easternmost part of the barracks—go," he whispered before disappearing up the stairs. He didn't even check to see if the others were following.

Lazander, Gabriel, and Marito shared a look—all unsure of what to say before they went their separate ways.

"Good luck," Lazander said awkwardly.

"Luck is not needed, Master Lazander," Marito said, placing a gentle hand on the knight's shoulder. "We have everything we need right here." He tapped his own heart with a wink while Gabriel rolled his eyes.

"Yes, yes, valor, stalwart heart, etc. Can we go kick Magnus' head in now? Please?" Gabriel said, but he reached out a hand, squeezing Lazander's forearm in quiet reassurance before turning away.

The mage gestured to Corym, who was nearly vibrating with the need to follow Valerius—be that from nerves or a desire to impress the leader of the Gilded, Lazander couldn't tell.

Lazander watched his fellow knights disappear up the stairs. Dawn was breaking over the horizon, warming Lazander's back—but a stab of cold cut through him, a sense of foreboding he couldn't shake.

In the library where he, Gabriel, and Marito had first discussed Valerius, the inevitable had come up—what to do in the case their leader turned on them. Lazander ran through those details now, taking comfort in the fact that while Valerius was the best swordsmen of the Gilded, he couldn't stand against Gabriel and Marito combined. They would restrain him and Lord Magnus both if need be, but Valerius took priority—the spymaster's shadows had found Eternity's kidnapper once and could do so again.

It would be all right, he promised himself, his hand touching his heart as Marito had.

With a sigh he gestured to a nervous-looking Farah, who kept looking between him and the disappearing Gilded—it was easy to see which group would have been her first choice.

"Slow and steady," he said to her.

She nodded, lids drifting closed. With a sigh, her eyes snapped open, now ringed in yellow light. She turned without a word, hands outstretched as she approached the back of the barracks.

Farah had been chosen to accompany them for a reason—her affinity lay in illusion and obscura—two branches that specialized in magical traps and trickery. Lazander had seen Gabriel using the same spell before, *True Sight,* but it exhausted him—shadow magic was his true calling.

Farah on the other hand could maintain *True Sight* easily, but as sharp as her eyes were, Lazander knew someone else who could give them an edge.

He gave a low whistle.

Chapter Fifty-Two

Farah turned at the sound, confusion clear on her face. He simply smiled and pointed at the sky.

A tiny black dot appeared, growing steadily larger as it dove toward him. As the shape grew, wings of a deep gray ending in threaded silver took shape, picking up speed.

At the last possible second the hawk snapped out her wings, talons extended. The air yanked at her feathers, yet she kept her wings locked and steady as she slowed dramatically. With barely a tilt of her body, she landed on Lazander's waiting arm—gripping it tightly.

"Show off," Lazander said with a smile.

Merrin chirped in reply, nuzzling Lazander's chin affectionately.

"She's beautiful," Farah said in surprise, and Lazander realized he'd never introduced them. He closed his eyes, focusing on the sigil on his left wrist.

Like most knights, his body was trained to resist magic—meaning he had to rely on abilities instead. These were honed through a combination of wits, stamina, and experience, often taking years to master. The sigil he bore, however, was a unique version of both.

A year or so before he'd become a member of the Gilded, Lazander had volunteered to take part in a magical trial run by Gabriel. It took weeks of nightly spell-working sessions for Gabriel to tattoo a beautiful series of interlocking marks on him as well as Galora his dragon, Mabel his horse, and Merrin—creatures he considered family. The goal was to find a way to grant magic-resistant knights an additional edge in battle—and what better edge than the claws and senses of beasts they trusted? The knights who participated volunteered everything from pet cats to childhood steeds.

Galora, Mabel, Merrin, and Lazander were the only successes.

The knight took a breath, opening the connection between himself and Merrin. The hawk stilled, closing her eyes as she opened her mind to him.

Finding the best way to communicate with each individual creature had been the most difficult part of the bonding. Mabel responded better to emotional cues—the two passed on feelings of courage or fear to communicate their wants and needs. Galora, on the other hand, could use entire words and phrases, each learning the other's language in a slow arduous process that Lazander took great pride in.

Merrin, being the hunter that she was, worked best with images. Lazander concentrated on the image of Farah, her purple mage coat and short brown hair—her nervous laugh, and how she cocked her head to one side whenever she used magic.

"Farah," he said aloud, "meet Merrin."

Image received, Merrin chirped, bobbing her head toward Farah.

The mage grinned. "It's a pleasure to meet the brave and heroic Merrin. I've heard you've saved Lazander countless times."

Merrin cocked a head at Lazander, and he sent an image of the hawk swooping in to distract an approaching enemy and another of her warning the Gilded of a hidden ambush.

Merrin squawked, nuzzling Lazander—sending a picture of her as an eyas, barely hatched, and the hours he spent feeding and caring for her.

Family, her eyes said.

He smiled, rubbing a finger under her beak.

"I have a job for you, Merrin," he said seriously. He concentrated on Valerius and the others disappearing up the stairs and then sent her an image of the easternmost wall.

In response Merrin thought of him and Farah, wondering what they were doing out here alone. He imagined the back of the building, his sword drawn as he crept inside, Farah behind him.

Merrin chirped, knowing instinctively what Lazander wished as she pictured herself flying high above the Captain's Barracks, patrolling for any sign of movement.

"Clever as always," Lazander said, giving her a gentle kiss on the head.

Merrin clicked her tongue affectionately and stretched out her wings—eager to begin.

There was no need for a count between them. Lazander simply lowered his arm and thrust it upward, giving Merrin a slight boost as she snapped out wings, dipping slightly before soaring into the sky.

The connection between them faded as the distance grew. Some, such as Galora, Lazander needed to be in constant physical contact with. However, Merrin could be twenty or so feet away and still send limited information. They had developed a system in which she would swoop low enough to pass on what she'd seen before flying up again. If she had to land every time, it would exhaust her and put her directly in the line of fire if Lazander was in the midst of a fight.

While Galora's claws and wings were unmatched in battle, Merrin had been by Lazander's side since he was a boy, and it was a comfort to have her now. With the entire sections of Captain's Barracks caved in, she would have a better line of sight than even the spymaster's shadows.

As if on cue, Lazander heard Merrin's cry from above. She swooped low, sending him an image of a partially hidden entrance around the back of the barracks—its opening almost entirely hidden by crumbling ivy.

"Good girl," Lazander said, sending her an image of the juicy mouse he would give her later in thanks.

She squawked in approval.

Lazander was hacking vines and undergrowth moments later, Farah watching his back—eyes alight with *True Sight*. He was grateful for Merrin—it would have taken him hours to find this otherwise. Peering into the darkness he stepped inside and found himself at the base of a tightly wound staircase.

Servant's entrance, he guessed, judging by the cramped space. Drawing one of his short swords he tested his weight on each step before pressing onward, and while some creaked ominously they all held. He signaled for Farah to stay close.

As they traveled to the floor above, signs of Freyley's attack on the barracks grew more pronounced. Doors were ripped from hinges, tables overturned, and even a skeleton or two lay, slack jawed and staring from dust-filled rooms. Farah would stand in the doorway of each one, checking for signs of magical entrapment. At her all clear, Lazander would then enter—searching the room thoroughly. It was slow work, and while they had seen no signs of Lord Magnus' presence, or anyone else's for that matter, Lazander had learned not to trust his eyes when it came to magic.

It was Gabriel himself who had taught him that lesson—albeit unintentionally.

A month after Lazander had joined the Gilded, the mage had drunkenly masqueraded as Marito, kicking down Lazander's door in the dead of night as he loudly bellowed about wine and attractive looking horses. He was pouring a casket of wine over a confused and sleep-deprived Lazander when the real Marito had appeared, apologizing profusely to Lazander as he threw the fake Marito over his shoulder, claiming he'd explain it all in the morning.

He never did—and Lazander had never asked.

As he passed a window, the glass and frame long gone, he saw the briefest shadow of movement as Merrin shot past, sending an image of Valerius and the others creeping through the barracks in much the same manner as him on the opposing side of the building.

He relayed their position to Farah, making sure to hide the relief he felt. A palace mage by trade, this was her first mission with the Gilded—she didn't need to know there was more at stake than just finding a rogue mage.

He moved to the doorway of the next room and found a dusty collection of splintered wood and torn cloth that might have been a bedchamber. Gesturing for Farah to examine it, he put his back against hers, blade at the ready. As he scanned the silent hallway, Merrin sent him another image.

It was a snapshot of a hooded figure taken from high above the barracks. Part of the roof had caved in, the edges scarred from mage-fire. At its center sat a figure in a rickety chair—a single arm lying still on the armrest while the figure's other sleeve hung loose and empty.

The memory of the last time Lazander had seen Magnus struck him like a slap. Magnus holding Eternity by the hair, yanking it sharply as she cried out, pressing a blade of ice to her neck. The cold arrogance in his eyes, the fear in hers.

A rush of anger flooded his veins, surprising him.

Setting it aside, he tried to be practical. Maybe the figure was Magnus, maybe it wasn't—but sitting out in the open like that, directly in line of Merrin's sight? It was too convenient.

His instincts screamed to tread carefully.

Lazander drew his second blade, keeping them loose and ready at his side. Steadying his heart, he thought of Lady Eternity, her blue eyes wide and earnest as she cast *Blessing of the Righteous* on him. He remembered the blood that spilled from her nose that he pretended not to see.

He would do this, not just for Navaros, but for her. A flush up his cheeks denied that the feeling only came from a duty to protect Gallow's Chosen, but he shook it off. Now was not the time for distraction.

Lazander and Farah moved quickly but efficiently through each room, finding nothing more than dust and skeletons. They were both sweating and smeared with grime, the noonday sun high in the sky, by the time they reached the easternmost side of the building where Merrin had seen the hooded figure.

A slight creak of wood and the shifting of metal over metal made Lazander hold up a hand—stopping him and Farah both.

Someone was up ahead.

He knew it wasn't Marito—the knight wore leather. Nor was it Valerius—even in his bulking armor, he never made a sound when he moved. He gestured to Farah to stay put.

She nodded, tension making her shoulders crowd around her ears.

In a single step he rounded the corner, blades at the ready—to find Corym leaning heavily against the stone wall, his back to Lazander.

He frowned—Corym should have been in the middle of the search party. Valerius' place was at the back.

"Corym? Why did you break formation?" he asked, remembering at the last moment to keep his voice to a whisper. He poked his head around the girth of the knight's armor and saw the knight was alone. "Where is every—"

Corym spun, swinging his sword with terrified abandon.

Lazander brought his blade up just in time, parrying the blow as he stepped back. "Corym! It's me! Stop…" But the words died in his mouth as the knight clattered to his knees, grasping at his throat. Blood spurted from a wound, gushing in time with his slowing heart.

Lazander looked at his own blades in shock, terrified for a moment he'd hurt the young knight—but the dragonscale steel was polished and clean.

Farah screamed.

"Hel—" Was all Corym managed before he fell to his side, eyes glazing over as the torrent of blood slowed to a stop, pooling around his head like a crimson halo. Lazander swiftly sheathed a blade and slapped a hand over Farah's mouth, cutting off the noise.

"Breathe," he said quietly.

Farah shook her head, tears welling in her eyes.

"I can't let you go until you breathe."

The mage pressed a hand to her heart, forcing her shoulders down. After a moment, she nodded. Lazander removed his hand and Farah hid her face, dragging her robe across her eyes.

Guilt and fear fought for purchase as Lazander knelt by Corym, examining the wound in the young knight's neck—it was thick but precise, that of a sword rather than a dagger.

Lazander dragged his gaze back to the unseeing Corym, closing the knight's eyes as he whispered a quiet prayer to Gallow. He spoke of Corym's bravery, of the fact that he was discharged with honors from the army at just sixteen, and had hopes of becoming a Gilded. That he was worthy of becoming a Champion of Gallow—an eternal protector of the world.

Lazander's offering to Gallow quickly ran dry as did his memories of Corym—other than the previous night's sing-along, he'd never actually spoken to the young knight.

Guilt won the battle—the boy had clearly wanted nothing more than to be part of the Gilded, and Lazander had never spared him a moment.

"I'm sorry," he whispered, standing up. He'd have to deal with the body later—and for his own sanity, it had to be "the body" until this was all over. While Gabriel or Valerius might have left to pursue an enemy, Marito would never have abandoned Corym—especially when he was injured.

Something was wrong.

Lazander wanted nothing more than to throw caution aside and charge forward, but that was a surefire way to blunder into a magical trap and get blown to pieces.

"Are you—" Lazander whispered to Farah, but she cut him off with a raised hand. Her bloodshot eyes shone with *True Sight* as she strode forward.

"We need to find the others," she said, grief sharpening her tone.

Lazander nodded, impressed by the mage. He drew his blades once more, knowing whoever killed Corym might be just ahead.

Chapter Fifty-Three

Marred by patches of still burning flesh, Lukas lay unmoving. Then his chest shuddered, stuttering like an engine as he took a long, trembling breath.

He was alive—but in no position to fight. Neither was his molger form at my back.

I was alone.

Aerzin laughed, a low vicious sound as he padded toward me. Sparks haloed the vaxion, zapping between the coils of flesh that encircled the beast's skull. My mind screamed that at any moment they would cover the space between us in an instant, burning me alive until my insides shriveled like overcooked meat. I had to run, had to get out of his range.

But I couldn't move.

My body was stone. My mind a frozen lake—the waters beneath churning with fear.

"… Control."

The word echoed, ricocheting in my skull as Zara's presence grew in the shadows of my mind.

"Give me control, useless human. Cower like a swaddled babe, and you will kill us both!"

"But how—why?"

"Now. Relinquish unto me."

My eyes rolled back into my head as electricity shot through the air.

But I was gone, my limbs moving of their own accord. I rolled to the side, fur bursting from my shoulders and shooting down my arms.

"Untethered—the beast screams." I laughed, a glorious rush of adrenaline flooding my body as I dodged the lightning touch of death's kiss.

Talons, twice the length of any I'd conjured before, flexed as a smile not my own lit up my face. Reality began to slip away, vision and sensation tunneling, narrowing inevitably into oblivion.

I was gone.

***

"The vaxion is Aerzin, is it not?" Zara asked, sniffing the air. The world came alive with the scent of burned flesh—an aroma as familiar to Zara as a beloved perfume. The iron-slick flavor of blood followed as she smacked her lips—tasting the air.

"The twitching bundle of intestines and lard is Lukas," she said, cocking an eyebrow at the fallen molger—who watched her from where he lay bleeding with wide eyes and flared nostrils. She smiled, enjoying the fear that dilated his pupils—the feel of it sending a shiver of delight down her spine.

"And then there is the *mongrel*." At this, her smile vanished. Everything from the creature's crude cut of a jaw to the pine cone stub of his tail made her lips twist in disgust.

"I hate many things in this world," she announced, her conversational tone at odds with the deadly talons she flexed. "Some would even call the list endless."

Zara strolled toward the mongrel as Aerzin watched, unmoving. He had been hunting prey—prey that cowered, the acrid stench of fear overpowering. In an instant, that fear had vanished—leaving behind a woman whose every step promised pain, every word whispered of death.

A predator—one his instincts warned him to be wary of.

"But I hate one thing more than any other." She gripped the back of the mongrel's head. Barely conscious, he whined—a sharp cry that made her grit her teeth.

"Cowards."

Zara slammed Lukas' head into the ground.

Again.

And again.

Each blow was punctuated by hissed rage.

"Wake. Up. You pathetic. *Stain*."

Lukas' eyes flew open. He growled, snapping at Zara's throat with relish.

But she was already gone, dancing away on newly fur-covered feet. Lukas hadn't even seen them change.

"Better—but not good enough, little mongrel!" she called. "We're here because of *you*. Because you straddled the line between two worlds—vaxion and molger. Too scared to choose. Too scared to *live*."

The mongrel's eyes dropped in shame.

Zara rewarded his downcast gaze with a kick to his ribs. Her taloned feet caught flesh, ripping a shallow wound along his side.

With a howl, the mongrel recoiled in pain.

"Your fear, your doubt, your *shame*—that is what polluted your *tul'gra* in the first place! Rid yourself of it, or die," she hissed.

Lukas growled but faced Aerzin—teeth bared.

"Better." Hands on hips, Zara faced Aerzin, rolling her eyes at his vaxion form—his coils were pathetically short, his fangs barely longer than a newborn's. The fact that the human had been struck dumb in fear by such a mediocre creature was nothing short of embarrassing.

Not that Zara knew what her own vaxion form looked like. Not anymore.

It had been over a decade since she had transformed. When she had left the Mi'xan clan, her aunt, and the Moonvale Mountains behind, she had sworn she would never again assume the beastly shape her family was so proud of.

Proud enough to betray her. To sell her like cattle to the highest bidder.

She would use fire, claw, fang, fist—whatever it took to take down her enemies. But she would never transform into her vaxion form again.

Never.

"As for you," she said, finally addressing Aerzin. "I imagine Magnus has need of you—why else would he trap me in this wretched *tul'gra*? But Magnus isn't in charge." Zara smiled—showing too much teeth. "*I am.*"

Her feet sank into the ground as she crouched low, muscles coiled.

"And I will die before letting a vaxion cub, one who dared raise their lightning against me, go *unpunished*."

Zara's fangs elongated as she charged forward—eyes wild.

***

Lazander scanned the empty corridor ahead. The thick layer of dust that coated the rest of the barracks was broken by a flurry of footsteps the knight knew meant a fight. He spotted Marito's thick heavyset foot, Gabriel's light step, and the pattern of Valerius' sabatons—as well as a fourth he didn't recognize. They came this way, then doubled back, but it was impossible to tell who went through and when.

Frustrated, he touched the sigil on his left wrist once more, sending out a call to Merrin—praying the hawk was in range. He focused on images of Valerius, Gabriel, and Marito as she knew them best, but in truth he didn't want to upset her. She took her duty as his eye seriously, and if she learned someone had died on her watch she would take it to heart.

Merrin responded instantly, sending back sky-high pictures of the top of the crumbling barracks. The section they were in still held its roof, and while she had circled the ruins, she couldn't see any of the Gilded. Despite his care, she sensed something was wrong—images flashed in Lazander's mind of him being wounded. He hurriedly reassured her, and he sensed her resolve as she quickened her pace— wings flapping frantically as she did another pass on the ruins.

"Magic," Farah said, stepping back so suddenly, Lazander had to jerk his blades above his head to avoid skewering her.

He bit back the urge to chastise her. The mage had just seen her friend die. Snapping at her to be more careful wouldn't help either of them.

"Someone is using magic. Not Master Gabriel—I know what his feels like. Perhaps Lord Magnus?" she said, frowning at the unseen.

They were in a long corridor lined by gray stone, narrow enough that Lazander's dual blades would spark along the rock if he swung them carelessly. The dim light of barely burning mage-fire lit the path—encased within glass wall sconces. While every second or third one lay shattered, crunching beneath their feet, Lazander was glad of them—they would be in total darkness otherwise.

"If you can't tell who, then how about where?" Lazander asked. No less than eight doors split off from the corridor, including one directly at the end of the hallway—a nightmare if it came to an ambush.

"Close, I think. But I can't, *damn it*, I can't see," she said, sweat peppering her brow. The yellow rings of her *True Sight* flickered, slowly fading.

"Release your *True Sight*."

"I'm fine. I can still—"

"I need you fresh and ready for a fight. Release it—that's an order," Lazander said, not unkindly.

Farah blinked, her eyes fading to their usual hazelnut brown. Though she tried to hide it, Lazander noticed the hand she pressed against the stone wall, steadying herself.

"Stay behind me," Lazander said. "I'll check the—"

Boom.

A patch of stone wall three feet ahead of them burst—exploding outward as something crashed through it, hitting the opposite wall with a vicious thud. The wall to Lazander's right cracked but held—a cloud of dust and dirt erupting, covering everything.

Lazander pushed Farah behind him, blades raised.

The dust settled, revealing a dirt-covered figure on the floor.

"Marito!" Lazander called, crouching by the groaning knight. "Are you all right? What happened?"

The giant coughed and grabbed Lazander—shoving him roughly away.

With a roar, a huge barrel-chested man charged through the hole left by Marito. Clad in the crimson armor of Freyley, Lazander's homeland, he wielded a sword as long as Lazander was tall. Marito rolled to the side as the blade sparked against the stone where both Lazander and Marito had lain a second before.

Using the momentum from his roll, Marito dashed forward, snapping his leg into a kick that caught the soldier in the back of the knee—forcing him down. With brutal rigor, Marito drove his knee into the soldier's face—the crunch of bone and blood echoing in the narrow hallway.

Lazander had seen him do this move countless times—his opponents would stumble, often going slack. In that split second, Marito would draw both his axes, decapitating his enemies with a single, deadly strike.

The Freylen fell back. Marito reached behind him, the tips of his fingers gripping his weapons.

The soldier's eyes snapped open, and he shot to his feet, his greatsword coming up just in time to block Marito's axes. In a shower of sparks, the soldier spun his blade around him in tightly focused circles with a precision Lazander would have been in awe of in any other circumstance.

Marito was forced to back up, his eyes flashing briefly with something dangerously close to panic.

"Farrow, north!" Marito barked. The knight's usual smile and charming demeanor was gone—replaced by cold determination. "Lock box—purple!" He charged forward with a flurry of strikes, eyes locked on the soldier.

"Tree-topper?" Lazander called out, fighting not to jump into the fray.

"Hurt. Unknown!" Marito grunted, barely parrying the soldier's blade. "Farrow—go!"

Lazander grabbed Farah's hand. "What—" she started, but he dragged her forward, running straight for the soldier and Marito, who were locked in a deadly dance of blades and speed.

While the meaning was lost on Farah, Marito's orders were clear as a summer day to Lazander. Farrow was Valerius' codename in a fight—the symbol of the royal crest. He was in a "lock box"—some kind of trap, one that could only be disabled by a "purple"—a mage. A tree-topper was a small many-legged mouse that flew from tree to tree and Gabriel's codename after he lost a bet with Marito.

Lazander's heart clenched at the thought of the mage. He was hurt—badly enough that Marito was left fighting alone. His instincts urged him to find his injured comrade, but Marito was barely holding off the Freylen soldier—something that should have been child's play for him.

The giant had faced down armies with nothing more than his axes and a belly laugh. Who was that soldier, and what Void-spat pit had he crawled out of that he was strong enough to go toe-to-toe with Marito?

Something was wrong. Deeply wrong.

Lazander picked the closest northerly door, the first to his left, and kicked it down—dragging Farah within. Marito had ordered him to get to the "Farrow"—to Valerius. He would have to trust his friend knew what he was doing.

He'd barely stepped foot inside the doorframe when he heard a shriek of warning from above—Merrin.

Lazander tightened his grip on Farah's arm and threw her forward with all his strength. In the same movement the knight spun…

… Just in time to catch the full weight of the soldier's greatsword between his blades.

The soldier growled, pressing down on Lazander. With a gasp, the knight buckled, falling to one knee.

Lazander couldn't believe the man's speed and strength—his limbs were shaking from the sheer weight of his sword. Teeth gritted, he met his attacker's eyes. Scars edged the man's features, one splitting his cheek in two. Brown eyes, hardened from experience, stared down at him with cold indifference.

But beneath that he saw a spark of—sorrow? Regret?

"Hold, brother," Lazander said, switching to Frell, a local dialect spoken in the outer rings of Freylen. As a soldier, there was a high chance this man had grown up like Lazander—among the tanneries and bars, the slaughterhouses and the seamstresses of the city-state. "We're not here for you," he said, unable to stop himself from trying to end this madness. "We seek an enemy of Navaros. Lay down your sword!"

The soldier didn't even blink at Lazander's words. The knight tried once more—arms aching from the strain. "I am your brother-in-arms, do not do this."

The soldier frowned, head cocked. For a split second, Lazander thought his pleas had worked, but a panting Marito appeared in the doorway behind the Freylen, blood dripping from a fresh wound on his forehead. With a roar, Marito leaped forward. The soldier kicked Lazander in the stomach, sending him flying as the Freylen swung his sword backward—catching the full force of Marito's incoming axes. The blades sparked as they parried, the *sching* of steel cutting through the air.

"Your fight is with me, beast," Marito called. Lazander saw he favored his left leg, but the knight's face betrayed no hint of pain as he grinned. "And a beast you are—for only Valerius has ever squared up to me. Come—face a stalwart heart true!"

As Marito charged, *Heroic Strength* lending him a ferocious burst of power, Lazander grabbed a dazed Farah, grateful for the seconds his fellow knight had purposefully bought them with his theatrics.

Ahead there were no windows and no exits but for a single door that seemed an eternity away. Lazander and Farah sprinted for it, adrenaline lending them speed. The knight heard the clanging of blades and a cry of pain from behind him, but he refused to look—trusting Merrin and Marito to watch his back.

Farah made it to the door first, feet nearly tripping on her mage robes. Lazander immediately followed, kicking it closed behind them. It would only gain them a second, maybe two, but sometimes that was all it took to turn the tide of a fight.

Blades at the ready, Lazander examined the room. Dust-filled and dotted with broken furniture, the smell of human waste nearly overwhelmed him. He spotted a chamber pot in the corner, filled to the brim. Scraps of food, half-eaten, littered the room.

Two things, however, made Lazander's heart stop.

The first was a dome that lay in the center—gold and gleaming like a newly polished chalice. Aptly called *The Cage*, even Lazander could see the sheer force of the magic that powered it. Able to contain even a full-fledged knight, this must have been the "lock box" Marito was talking about. Nearly impenetrable to magical and physical attacks from the *inside,* its weakness lay in its vulnerable outer shell.

There—Valerius must be trapped within.

He should tell Farah to disable it, he knew. But his eyes were locked on the man in the corner of the room.

One arm was tied to a chair by thick corded rope while the sleeve of his other hung loose and empty. His blond hair, usually meticulously clean and styled, was streaked with grime and dirt. Gagged, his gray eyes stared at Lazander, begging and pleading as he thrashed, frantically trying to say something.

It took a split second to recognize him—Lazander was used to seeing him dressed in crimson finery laced with gold, glaring at the room with cool arrogance. To see him bound, gagged, and terrified out of his mind made Lazander blink in shock.

It was Lord Magnus.

Chapter Fifty-Four

azander didn't have more than a second to register the pleading look in Lord Magnus' eyes before the Freylen soldier burst into the room.

"*The Cage!*" roared Lazander as he readied his blades.

Farah stood mouth agape, staring at the soldier with the flickering yellow eyes of her *True Sight*.

"Disable *The Cage!*" Lazander barked, thinking her frozen with fear. "Free Valerius!

"Wait!" she yelled. "But that's—"

Her words were lost as the Freylen darted left at the last second, out of reach of Lazander's blades. He brought his greatsword down in a wide arc—aiming straight for Farah.

While this might have been Farah's first mission, Gabriel trained his mages to treat magic as the knights treated their swords—weapons of instincts. Her eyes flashed iridescent blue as her hands glowed.

She gasped, throwing her hands up—a shield of light erupting from her fingers. It was sloppy and thrown together, her specialty lay in illusion not defense, but it would block the soldier's blade, Lazander knew—giving him the opening he desperately needed.

But the Freylen's greatsword cut through Farah's light like paper, slicing Farah open from chest to hip. Blood sprayed from the mage in a crimson arc—her eyes comically wide.

"No!" Lazander cried. Ducking low, he got to one knee, darting beneath the soldier's arms as he drove a blade upward with a single, sharp jerk. He was rewarded by a grunt of pain as his dragonscale blade slipped between a gap in the soldier's armor, just above the hip.

He gave it a vicious twist, anger overriding caution.

The soldier lashed out with his greatsword, nicking Lazander's forearm as he leaped back—barely avoiding the man's blade.

The soldier pressed a hand to his wounded side, staring in shock at the blood-soaked fingers that came away.

A curious expression crossed his face as the regret and sorrow Lazander had seen in his eyes trickled away—replaced by cold determination. Spinning his greatsword, the soldier ignored the steady flow of crimson from his side and settled into an attack stance.

The fading sun peeked through a crumbling slit of a window, the light catching the greatsword.

Lazander tensed at the telltale flash of gold along its silver edges—dragonscale, the only metal in the world that could have cut through Farah's magic like that. A soldier from Freyley was easily overpowering the kingdom's finest knights, *and* he wielded the rarest metal known to man?

The knight gripped his blades, mind snapping to a decision.

Merrin. Lazander tried to keep his mind calm as he opened the sigil between them, but he knew the hawk would sense his fear and panic. He sent images of the base camp and the knights who waited there, pictured the single mage who remained placing his hands on the Calix Rings.

Get help. Get help, Merrin.

It would take them hours to break in, if not days, Lazander knew. But it was all he could think of to do. Merrin shrieked in his mind, scared for him, but he sent images of her diving, swift and true for the camp.

Hurry.

Farah whimpered, and Lazander risked a glance at her. Her eyes were closed, but her chest fluttered like an injured bird's—she was still alive.

Determination blossomed in Lazander's chest—they still had a chance. If he could protect Farah until Marito arrived, they could…

The thought died, lost in an aching chasm of grief as he stared at the door he'd just come through.

Marito lay on his side, his back to Lazander. Blood pooled around him, a crimson almost as rich as the leather brigandine he wore—now shredded from a gaping wound, inches thick, down his back. Streaks of blood trailed after him from where he'd dragged his ruined body—forcing himself to crawl toward his companions even in the throes of death.

Lazander's gorge rose when he spotted Marito's hand still tightly gripping one of his axes.

A hand that lay about three feet away from his body—cut off at the wrist.

Lazander had seen dark days. The hopeful story he'd told the servant boy back in the Ivory Keep had been true—he had once worked in a castle in Freyley and had come to Navaros as part of the new peace treaty, working his way through the army's ranks to join the Gilded.

It just hadn't been the whole truth.

As a boy, he'd had no interest in knighthood. He'd dreamed of following in his mother's footsteps and becoming an apothecary—one who specialized in the treatment of animals. He'd grown up surrounded by cats, birds, pigs, horses, and every beast in-between. When his mother volunteered to go to Navaros and work at the Ivory Keep, he'd been nervous.

A new life, a new kingdom… it was scary to an eight-year-old.

But his mother's excitement was like her smile—infectious. As the days passed, and he helped his big sister pack up the small room they'd shared, he began to dream—mainly of the birds he'd see. Entire species were native to Navaros that he'd only seen in the black-and-white sketches of his mother's books. The royal crested farrow with its six wings and vicious temperament was number one on his list to see—perhaps he could even *pet* one.

When their two caravans, loaded with people and animals alike, set out for Navaros, a weeklong journey, he'd been happy.

His happiness was short-lived.

To this day, he didn't know how the fire started. He just knew that one moment the night air was crisp and clean, the next it stank of burnt flesh. The screams and howls of his dying family were nearly indistinguishable from those of the animals.

Lazander and a small hawk, mere days old, were the only survivors. She was tiny—the runt of the litter, rejected by her own nest. Lazander had insisted on making her a small home of straw and rags by his bunk in the caravan as he nursed her back to health, waking up at all hours to feed her.

It was the only reason he'd survived.

He'd been walking with her, holding her bundled up close in his arms as she cried out—unable to settle despite the worms he'd fed her or his soothing words.

Lazander liked to think that, even then as a hatchling, she was watching over him—protecting him. He'd later name the hawk Merrin after his mother.

He didn't know how he made it to the Ivory Keep. Memories of that night were fragmented—he recalled armored hands around him, a thick cloak shielding him from the sight of the wreckage, and a deep, rumbling voice that promised he was safe now.

A knight had found him—one of the Gilded returning from a mission in the Moonvale Mountains. It was pure luck he happened to see the smoldering remnants of the caravans in the distance.

Large, bombastic, and kind, the Gilded was Marito's father—Essam.

Lazander thought of Essam now—how he'd taken him into his own home until bed and work could be arranged for him in the Ivory Keep. How, when seeing how lost and alone Lazander was, he had insisted on introducing him to his own son, Marito.

Marito made it his personal business to stay by Lazander's side. He would cheerfully fill the silence of Lazander's grief, telling him how he was going to be a knight—a Gilded like his father. How he was going to look after the whole kingdom—all by himself if he had to. Mostly he told Lazander that he didn't have to worry about anything anymore.

Marito, the soon-to-be greatest knight ever, had his back.

The chasm of grief that had threatened to overwhelm Lazander as a child now reared its head as he stared at Marito's unmoving body.

Lazander was a hunter at heart, a dutiful man who moved with the beat of the forest.

But now he roared, grief and fury granting him strength as he dove at the Freylen soldier. His blades were a blur that took the man by surprise, his eyes wide as he frantically parried and dodged Lazander's blows.

A line of blood appeared on Lazander's cheek, his left thigh, his right shoulder—shallow cuts as the soldier began to keep pace with the knight's frantic attacks.

Lazander knew he was a single misstep away from getting cut in two, but he didn't care. A bloodlust had consumed him, one that wanted to split the Freylen soldier in two as he'd split Marito.

The castle rumbled—a dark, foreboding sound.

Shadows crept along the walls, filling the corners, closing up the holes in the roof, and trickling up Lord Magnus' terrified legs—blocking out all light as it caged them.

The soldier saw what was coming a second too late.

Inky black darkness sprang from the walls, wrapping around him. It dug into his arms and legs, squeezing his body like a hissing viper. With a vicious wrench he was dragged to his knees—locked in place by the darkness.

A dark portal appeared at Lazander's feet, and he leaped back in surprise as a bloodied hand reached out.

The dark head and deep purple robes of Gabriel emerged from the portal as he rose from its depths. A vicious bruise marred his forehead, and he bled from dozens of shallow cuts that covered his body. But Lazander's eyes were drawn to the vicious gash at his neck—wide enough to have sent his heart's blood pumping from his body, killing him in minutes.

It was threaded by a line of shadows frantically knitting it together in a startling demonstration of control.

He knew Gabriel was unmatched in shadow magic—but he'd never seen him like this. Never seen his eyes as dark as night, his breathing ragged as he summoned every shadow under his command.

Never seen the promise of murder in his eyes.

"Gabriel, Marito is—"

The mage held up a hand to silence him and turned his head a fraction, closing his eyes briefly at the sight of Farah. Her eyes, one bright yellow with *True Sight*, lay wide and empty. Blood pooled around her.

Lazander started—he hadn't even noticed she'd died. He'd been too wrapped up in his own revenge. Shame fluttered in his heart.

"Where is Valerius?" Gabriel asked in a quiet voice. It was almost a whisper in the darkness of the room, but it carried the fury of a roar.

"He—he's in *The Cage*," Lazander said, surprised at the spark of fear he felt. It was *Gabriel*—he wouldn't hurt him.

"Are you sure?' Gabriel asked, turning his gaze back to the soldier.

The Freylen stiffened, mouth thinning to a tight line.

"I—what are you talking about, Gabriel? Where else could he be?" Lazander's brow furrowed. Something was wrong.

"Exactly," Gabriel said, pointing a shadow-coated finger at the dome.

The Cage didn't dispel—it simply exploded as an arrow of darkness split it, fragments showering the room like gold dust.

"Valerius?" Lazander called, carefully stepping around Farah's body as he stalked to the center of the now vanished trap. "What is this?" he snapped at the bound Freylen. "What's going on?"

The scarred man didn't look concerned by the shadows that forced him to his knees or the fact that two Gilded now turned to him—fury in their eyes.

Instead, he looked resigned.

"Indeed, *Freylen*," Gabriel spat. "Where is he? Where is Valerius?"

The Freylen's form shuddered in a hazy glow of muted light. The man's scarred face and crimson armor disappeared, revealing an intricate ivory chestplate decorated with Navaros' wildlife. Lazander recognized them all—the poisonous rake, the whipped tail of the clipper, and the creature he'd dreamed of seeing when he first set out for Navaros.

The six-winged farrow—the emblem of the royal family.

Valerius knelt before them in the soldier's place. He looked at them, now not with sadness.

But with pity.

Chapter Fifty-Five

Zara's memories were shadows on the wall of a dimly lit room. If she focused, she could see rough details of the past few days—running down Magnus' prized little corridors, the ones coated by an illusion a child could see through. The feel of the night sky and wind against her skin as she leaped from the castle roof—something she'd dreamed of in her darker moments. A dragon, a beautiful beast of such power and elegance her stomach churned at the thought she'd hurt it, had driven her sharpened claws into it.

The rest was dimmer—a woman and her son. A squealing pig. Molger—whining and cowering as they so loved to do. However, as she studied the shadowed form of her memories, larger gaps emerged.

Magnus was behind this—of that she had little doubt. How he managed to cage her mind and trap her in the *tul'gra* of a blood-spiked falsling, she had no idea, but every brush stroke, every detail of this torment spoke of his cruelty.

The girl child who wielded her body with the grace of a newborn foal was a particularly creative choice. Her thoughts alone were a torment—the frantic panic, the ceaseless questioning, the endless fear.

It was as pathetic as it was weak. If the girl had been a real vaxion, she'd have been culled at birth—and it would have been a blessing.

The vaxion had a saying—" Refuse death." A man could be on his knees, bound and gagged. His children could be held hostage as his captors made a single demand—his life in exchange for his children's.

In any other culture, sacrificing his life for his children would earn him posthumous songs of praise.

Not the vaxion.

They would curse the children first, for hiding behind tears and wails. Even tottering babes had teeth, and they were expected to use them. The father would be mocked for allowing his family to be captured, and most heinous of all, for taking the *easy* way out—for accepting death rather than standing on his own two feet. For refusing to fight back.

If his children survived, they would be turned away until they returned, the heads of their captors gripped in their tiny fingers.

It was with this in mind that Zara, in control of her body for the first time in days, viewed her situation. Knowing that her body had been puppeteered by another's hands would cause panic and fear in anyone else, but Zara did not so much as blink.

Magnus wished to break her. He wished for her to bow her head and kiss his boots, begging for more.

Instead she would do as she had always done.

She would refuse.

Every inch of Zara was scarred, from the inside out. It was proof that she was *strong.* That she was *unbreakable.* She'd survive this punishment, adding the scars to the broken art gallery that was her body. Then she'd take something of Magnus'— his prized steed, his favorite minstrel, another of his beloved paintings of blonde, doe-eyed women, and she'd destroy it. Rip it apart. Taunt him with their ruined remains.

Zara's claws twitched at the thought, a smile spreading across her face. She was trapped in the *tul'gra.* The mind. The most sacred place of a falsling—one tormented by the duality of his nature. The vaxion cub before her had probably expected a quick meal and a new life in the real world.

He could never have imagined he'd meet *her*—the monster under the beds of little falslings. The scourge of human flesh. The claws that never missed their mark.

She smiled. This might be her favorite punishment yet.

Aerzin hissed as Zara charged, lightning building in the undulating coils that haloed his skull, but she wasn't worried. For all Aerzin's mewling and bluster, he looked barely out of his cub years—and the little ones could call down the lightning twice, maybe thrice a day.

He'd used it twice.

There wouldn't be a third.

Zara laughed as she slid gracefully beneath his snapping maw. "**If the world will not yield, then I will break it!**" The words were foreign to her, yet as natural as breathing, and she did not question the power that dripped from them as her muscles expanded. Strength flooded her body, and she drove her fist upward in a perfect uppercut.

The vaxion's jaws slammed shut as his head snapped back, bone rattling his skull as his entire body jolted from the force of it.

Zara grabbed him, slapping her hands on either side of his head as she hissed, "My fury is but a whisper of the flames to come."

In the past flames would burst from her fingers, cooking her victim's flesh like meat on a spit.

But nothing happened.

Confused, she faltered—giving Aerzin the second he needed to snap out a paw, dragging his talons down her side.

Blood gushed from a wound along her ribs that was far from shallow. She cackled as she slithered away.

"Magnus has bound my fire, has he? No matter." A bloodthirsty grin threatened to split her face in two. "Come, little Aerzin. Refuse death! Refuse to yield!" she roared, slapping her chest with joy.

Their battle wore on, both fast and unflinching.

Zara *reveled* in it.

***

With weak eyesight and struggling to keep up with the fight, the mongrel looked on. *No, not a mongrel*, his mind whispered. *Lukas. Lukas!*

Something was happening to him. His mind, once a shattered mirror, was coming together piece by piece. He remembered a boy—neither vaxion nor molger. Remembered terror the first time he'd changed into a monster. Remembered Chief offering him a choice—stay and die or flee and live.

But there was something else—a whisper in his ear, a thought that danced away like smoke in the wind. If he could just grasp it, maybe this would all make sense.

Maybe he would finally be whole again.

***

Zara punched through a massive oak tree as Aerzin danced out of the way, snarling. She gripped the tree trunk, muscles bulging as she watched the vaxion crouch down, preparing to pounce—thinking her open. *Defenseless.* She grinned fiercely, wrenching the tree free from the ground with a roar.

Aerzin's eyes widened with realization, but it was too late. She swung the massive tree, slamming it into him. There was the sharp crack of shattered bone as the vaxion went flying, skipping over the dirt like a stone on water until he hit the lake, sinking beneath its depths.

Panting, Zara dropped the tree with an earthshaking thud. She grinned as Aerzin burst from the water, frantically paddling to its edge like a cub in a shallow pool.

Blood mixed with water as he emerged, favoring his left side. Bark-encrusted puncture wounds decorated his body alongside Zara's claw marks—a hundred cuts from shoulders to hindquarters.

Zara fared little better. She had less cuts, but each were inches wide, splitting her skin so bone met air. Yet while Aerzin swayed, Zara stood upright and at ease—her expression one of casual amusement as if she were taking a stroll on a summer's day and not bleeding out.

It was in this moment of blood-soaked stillness that Zara saw the truth shine in Aerzin's eyes, a truth she had known since the moment she had taken back control from the girl child.

He couldn't win.

Clearly panicked, he crouched low, the air crackling as he screwed his eyes closed, struggling to call down the lightning that lived in his heart and in the heart of every vaxion. Now would be the perfect time to strike him, she knew. Instead, she sheathed her claws, her fur melting into her bare skin. Stained by blood and sweat, she raised her arms, opening them wide in welcome.

"Do it, boy. Strike me down!"

Aerzin's eyes roved over her, searching for the trap—the ploy, she knew. But he would find none.

She smiled, her teeth showing. "Do it!"

Lightning, ice-blue and electric, began to build between his tendrils. The hair on Zara's arms raised in answer—this would be no half measure.

Good, she thought fiercely.

The mongrel whined in warning behind her. She merely spat a growl without looking. She felt the mongrel's ears flattened at her rebuke as he backed up.

Her aunt, if she could see Zara now, would call her mad. Stupid. *Reckless.*

Zara's muscles vibrated as she forced herself to stand still—she could do this. She was better than the Mi'xan, better than her aunt—better than any of the bastards who'd cursed her to a life as a deranged mage's pet.

She might not have her freedom, but every god be damned, she'd have her strength. Her pride. Her *fury.*

The lightning snapped between Aerzin's tendrils at blistering speed, the air crackling with power.

He let loose, electricity snapping from his body in a thousand spiderwebs, closing the distance between Zara and Aerzin in a split second. There was no dodging this, no escape.

Zara closed her eyes, head thrown back in ecstasy as it struck.

Chapter Fifty-Six

"Why?" Gabriel said, his fists clenched.

Bound by shadows, forced to his knees before them, Valerius was silent—his face schooled in its usual cold indifference.

Gabriel snapped his fingers.

Lazander said nothing as a shadow slithered up his leader's back, grabbed a fistful of his hair, and yanked it hard enough to make Valerius grunt in pain. Nor did he say anything when Gabriel gripped Valerius by the jaw, forcing him to meet his eyes. "*Why?*" the mage roared.

"I thought only Farah would see through it," Valerius said quietly. "I should've known you would as well."

Gabriel slapped him—the sound echoing in the quiet of the mage's shadows. He raised his hand for another blow, but Lazander grabbed his wrist.

He was shaking with grief and rage, mind flashing to Corym's slit throat, Farah's lifeless body sprawled like a doll, Marito's decapitated hand still gripping his axe. Never in his darkest, most cynical moments would he have thought Valerius capable of this.

He thought of Marito—how the knight never panicked. Never forgot his duty.

Lazander would do the same. He would treat Valerius like any other prisoner. Because if he didn't, he would drive his swords into the their of the throne and not stop stabbing him until Valerius' corpse was skewered meat on his blades.

"Have you been working with Lord—with Magnus this whole time?" Lazander forced himself to ask.

Valerius laughed, a harsh barking sound.

"Look at him—does he seem particularly fond of me?" Valerius asked. Indeed, Magnus was glaring at the knight with pure hatred, shaking his head viciously.

"No—he played no part in this. But..." He trailed off, looking at Lazander with a mix of sorrow and pride. "I will give it to you, Lazander—you were right. Zara didn't break into the Gallowed Temple alone. *I* killed the guards. *I* disabled the magical defenses. *I* stood by and let Zara take Eternity."

"Damn you to the Void," Gabriel cursed, shaking off Lazander. "*Why*? Why would you do this—to *us*? To Marito!" His voice broke as he looked away. Me... me, I could understand. We haven't exactly seen eye to eye these last few years. But Marito trusted you—*loved* you like a brother. He... he didn't deserve this, Valerius. Not from you—not from his family. Just... just tell me why."

Valerius shook his head. "Even if I told you, you wouldn't believe me. I know this isn't a comfort, but I wanted to make this as easy as possible for you. I wanted you to die fighting a nameless Freylen soldier, not Valer—not me. Not a friend." He sighed, looking ancient.

The shadows tightened around Valerius' throat, but he didn't struggle.

"You are many things to me, Valerius," Gabriel spat, hate dripping from his words. "A friend isn't one of them."

"Gabriel, I sent Merrin to the camp, but it will take them hours to get here. We—we need to signal them somehow," Lazander said, unable to look at Valerius any longer. If he stared at his leader, he feared the pain and grief that dug into his mind like vines would render him useless. "The queen and spymaster should know what—

"You know what we planned to do if it turned out you'd betrayed us?" Gabriel asked Valerius, cutting Lazander off. "Marito would overwhelm you, I would bind you, and Lazander would knock you out. We ran through different scenarios, of course, but that was it—that was the grand plan. It had never crossed our minds to *hurt* you. But it's starting to sound like a great idea."

Gabriel's fist clenched, and the shadows around Valerius' throat tightened in answer—but still Valerius didn't make a sound.

"You deserve to be flayed by Gallow for all eternity," Gabriel said, his fist tightening, his shadows answering in kind. "And I think it's past time you met him."

Lazander wanted to jump forward, to stay Gabriel's hand, but he couldn't move. Instead he looked away—staring at Marito's body and the pool of blood that surrounded him.

"For what it's worth, I'm sorry," Valerius said. "I really am."

Light flashed in Valerius' palms, eradicating the shadows that bound him with a *whoosh*. Blinded, Gabriel stepped backward, raising his hands to shield his eyes...

… and jerked as two blades, long and bloody, punched through his stomach and out his back.

Gabriel gasped, a horrible rasping sound. Blood dripped from his mouth as he pawed feebly at Valerius, who now stood head and shoulders above his fellow Gilded—gripping the blades' hilts.

He bent low, dark hair brushing Gabriel's as he whispered something in the mage's ear. Then he yanked the blades free in one smooth movement—blood spraying the walls, ceiling, and Lazander.

Abruptly shadows that once caged them vanished—dissipating into the twilight.

The entire thing took seconds—an eternity to the frozen Lazander who could only watch in horror as Gabriel's body went slack. He fell to his knees—a puppet whose strings had been cut, hitting the wooden floor with an echoing, lifeless thump.

This isn't real, Lazander thought, staring at the puncture wounds in Gabriel's back, edges rimmed by torn flesh. *Please, don't let this be real.*

"Blades of Radiant Sun," he said simply, nodding at the dead Gabriel. "These and another mage are the only things that can negate shadow magic."

Memories skittered through Lazander's brain like a nest of spiders. Nights laughing with Gabriel and Marito, the pair's infamous arguments, their smiles when they nominated him to be a Gilded.

How they never failed to make him feel like one of them, despite his youth and inexperience.

He did this. He'd told them his suspicions about Valerius. He'd encouraged them to turn on their leader. Valerius had said Lazander was "right" about him—he'd somehow found out about their plotting.

Now his brothers were dead—because of him.

Valerius stepped aside, Lazander blasting past him like a sigh of air as he slashed at the Gilded leader. "Bastard!" he roared, grief lending him strength as he struck out at Valerius. He should be tactical, he knew—aiming for the throat, under the arms, the back of the knees. But he couldn't—all he saw were the dead bodies of the friends he'd failed to protect as his blades moved with reckless abandon.

Valerius sidestepped him, sweeping his leg under Lazander's. The red-haired knight fell forward, expecting a blade through his throat any second, but Valerius gripped him by the back of the neck and *threw* him.

Lazander flew across the room—far beyond a regular human's reach. Wood cracked and bones snapped as the knight hit the ground several times, body flapping like a ragdoll until he finally slowed.

Valerius' turned to Lazander—his expression as cold and uncaring as marble as Lazander forced himself to one elbow.

"I knew…" Valerius said, shaking his head. "I knew it would be you, in the end. But it doesn't matter. I can't… I won't let you stop me."

His sword and shield reappeared as he strode toward Lazander with the care and ease of an evening walk.

"How did you—how are you—" Lazander said, staring at the vanishing weapons in Valerius' hands. His mind swam with questions, and for some reason this was the one it locked on.

Valerius glared at his sword as if it were a viper, poised to bite him. "The Inventory—I've collected nothing short of an armory since coming here. It's one of the only benefits of the Operator—and this stupid, pointless world."

Most of what Valerius said was pure gibberish, but it did prove one thing to Lazander.

He forced himself to his feet, his dislocated shoulder sticking out at an awkward angle. Taking a breath, he gripped it with his free hand and yanked it back into place with a jerk. His breath expelled in a hissed burst, the only sign it had hurt.

The Valerius he knew and admired—the leader of the Gilded, his brother-in-arms, was no more. The man who stood before him would never have butchered innocents, wouldn't spout pure nonsense about "Inventories" and "Operators." This man was insane.

A danger to be put down.

Slowing his heart, he pictured himself in the woods, face-to-face with an unknown predator. He gave it claws and fangs, adding the tendrils of the lightning-quick vaxion and the body mass of the charging molger.

When he stared at Valerius, Lazander the knight was gone.

Only the hunter remained.

"Don't," Valerius said, a hint of desperation in his voice. "I'll make it quick, I swear."

But the hunter ignored the predator's words. One of his blades lay near Valerius' feet, the second lay on the other side of the room.

No matter—he was an archer by trade.

He drew his bow, nocking an arrow tipped with Merrin's starlight plume.

"*Fine,*" Valerius said, bringing his shield up in front of him as he spun his sword in lazy circles—the dragonscale sharp and deadly in the waning light. "But I know your every weakness—I've finished *Knights of Eternity* with you as my main hundreds of times." Valerius' words were rapid, his eyes wild. "You're just a *character*, a bunch of code in an arcade game. This isn't my fault—I'm just doing what the Operator wants!"

The hunter ignored the predator's nonsense but did allow, for the briefest second, the real Lazander to speak.

"You killed Corym, Farah. Gabriel. *Marito,*" he said, drawing back his bow with every name, the steel-tipped arrow ready to fly. "I don't know if you're evil or insane—and I don't care. You're a *traitor*—and I'm going to put you down."

He let the arrow fly.

Chapter Fifty-Seven

Aerzin's lightning stuck Zara in the chest, her skin crackling as it dove into her heart and lungs, her stomach and intestines. It left nothing untouched as it raged through her, threatening to cook her alive from the inside out.

She gritted her teeth—her long, midnight-tipped hair whipping around her.

I will not bow. I will not break. I will not be beaten!

Aerzin grinned, sure he had won.

Fire was her true calling—when the flames licked her skin she felt at home. She felt *safe*.

Cupping her hands over her chest, she gripped the lightning—a wild, rabid animal, much like herself, she thought wryly. Inch by painful inch, she dragged it from her chest, forcing order on the feral beast as she added her own magic to it.

For what was lightning, but fire's sister? Her warrior-in-arms, nature's fury made real.

It grew in her hands, an ice-blue sun that threatened to erupt from her locked fingers.

"**Death**," she hissed, "**has no dominion over me.**"

Words flashed behind her eyes:

VENGEFUL REBUKE UNLOCKED.

Zara snapped her hand to the side—yanking a long whip of pure lightning from her chest.

It curled around her, the air crackling as Aerzin's magic and hers became one, bending to her will.

To her disgust, Aerzin tried to run—the apex predator of this world turned to cowering prey.

Death scorned his cowardice as her lightning followed, wrapping around his hind leg as she snapped it toward him, sizzling through the fat of his flesh—straight to the bone. He shrieked, a horrible, pained cry that mingled with Zara's laugh as she yanked on the whip—dragging Aerzin toward her.

His claws scrambled in the dirt, frantically trying to get away, but she wrapped the lightning around her arms like rope—bracing herself.

"If the world will not yield," she roared. **"Then I will *break it*."**

Drunk on her newfound strength, she dragged the vaxion toward her, laughing at how light he felt. Her vision swayed, and she knew she'd pushed herself too hard, but she didn't care. She wasn't finished with little Aerzin.

She molded the lightning whip, adding sharpened barbs as she wrapped it around Aerzin, his flesh bubbling at every touch. He flailed and screamed like a wounded babe—all his bluster gone, a wounded pup in his place. She ignored his whimpering as she bound him from head to toe.

"Did Magnus think you would pull on my heartstrings?" Zara mused aloud. "My 'fellow vaxion'—trapped and tormented? Or did he bring me here to save your host's broken mind?"

Aerzin only howled, the lightning that bound him burning him alive.

"Either way—I have a grander idea," she said. "Why don't I cut out *your* heart, *and* the molger's—and feed them to the abomination? That will be a delight, won't it—a *tul'gra* purged, only for its owner to be trapped in the body of a mongrel."

She leaned forward, flicking the beast in the nose. "I quite like the sound of that."

***

Lukas' hybrid form stared in shock. He'd watched their entire battle without moving a muscle—too afraid of the woman's hissing command to do anything else.

But her words stirred something in him, cutting through the muddied pool of his mind.

He looked to his molger form—the other part of him, he now understood.

The six-legged beast still lay stretched out and bleeding, his mahogany fur matted and torn. He hadn't moved since he'd collapsed, nearly shredded to pieces by Aerzin. Yet the molger's eyes were wide and alert, and Lukas knew he'd heard Zara's every word.

An entire conversation happened between hybrid and molger—silent and unspoken.

The molger nodded, grunting as he forced himself to all six legs, blood gushing from his side.

Lukas bowed his head in thanks. Their plan was stupid, reckless—suicidal, even. But as he turned to face Aerzin, who screamed in pain and fear, determination crystalized in his heart. Yes, he was probably going to die.

But he'd do it on his own damn terms.

***

"**I am death's mistress,**" Zara whispered, her talons lengthening slowly. "**Bow before me.**"

Snapping her fingers together, she flattened her palm like blade—aiming it directly for the vaxion's heart. Aerzin whined, fighting against the waning lightning that held him, his every move causing it to dig into his flesh.

So focused was Zara on her prey that she made a mistake.

A single, vital mistake.

She didn't look behind her.

The hybrid bit down hard on her extended arm, stopping only when his fangs met bone. Snapping his head to the side, he shook it—yanking her back from Aerzin and throwing her to the ground with a thud.

The lightning that bound Aerzin vanished.

"You stupid, ignorant, useless mongrel!" Zara screamed, scrambling to her knees as she raked her claws down Lukas' neck—catching fur. "Do not—"

A molger's thick, heavy skull struck from behind, charging into her at full speed. Her breath was pulled from her body like a loose thread, and she was pitched forward, hitting the dirt in a graceless heap.

Winded, she could only watch as the mongrel and molger approached the panting Aerzin. They would murder the vaxion, she knew, then turn on one another, stealing the joy of the kill from her. She gritted her teeth, furious with herself. How could she let two pups best her like this? Getting to her feet, she vowed to make them *scream*, to—

Thoughts of vengeance fell away, replaced by horror as the hybrid turned his back on the fallen, vulnerable vaxion and planted himself between Zara and Aerzin. The molger followed but not before side-eying the vaxion, grunting quietly as he limped into position.

"Have you lost what little sanity was left in your *sick, polluted mind?*" Zara shrieked, unsteady on her feet. Dirt marred her cheeks and face, her tangled hair falling into her eyes. "Only *one* of you can leave here alive! You gain nothing by this storybook showing of *valor.*" She spat the word as if it were a curse.

With a whine, Aerzin got to his feet—swaying. The molger stepped up beside him, and the vaxion leaned against him—grateful. The hybrid stared at Zara, and she saw his eyes were clear, free of the fear and confusion she'd beaten him for

I'd rather die, a thousand times over, his eyes said, staring into Zara's furious gold ones. *Than kill as you do.*

A piece of Zara from before—before Magnus' beatings, before the blade, before the punishments, shied away from the judgment in the hybrid's eyes.

She screamed, near frothing at the mouth as she charged forward in a rage—her claws begging to dig into their blood-soaked flesh as she bathed in it.

"... stop... said... stop."

The voice was small—a mere whisper in the towering inferno that was Zara's fury. The hybrid limped forward, one paw clutched to his chest. He growled, a small, feeble sound, but the message was clear.

Stay away.

The words made something in Zara's heart tighten, and suddenly her fist clenched of its own accord—driving directly into her own face, breaking her nose instantly.

"Stop."

Her head snapped back, and she skidded to an unsteady halt—palms bleeding from where her own talons had pierced her skin.

"That's enough, Zara." It was the girl child's voice in her head, ricocheting in her skull as her presence grew, an infectious disease she couldn't escape.

"How *dare* you," hissed Zara. "This is my mind, my body. You are a *parasite*. An invader who has stolen my very life. I banish you. I refuse you!"

She reached for the vaxion, who whined in fear, but found her arm being redirected—a puppet on a string. Suddenly it was clutching her own throat, but this time she was ready. Grabbing the rebellious hand in a vicelike grip, she struggled against the shadow of the invader who grew in her mind, towering above her.

"*Leave them alone,*" the girl child ordered, an edge of steel in her voice Zara had never heard.

"I thought fighting for my life in this wretched *tul'gra* was Magnus' punishment," Zara hissed. "But it wasn't. It was *you*."

Fueled by hateful rage, she bit down on the rebellious hand.

The invader screamed, loosening her hold.

"I will cut myself to shreds to keep you out, child!" Zara roared, her words almost incomprehensible as she bit down harder.

"*You are weak. Small. Pathetic.* Stupid," she thought at the invader, rage and venom spiking her words. "*Your mind is a festering quagmire of doubt and pain. Lukas will die. Aerzin will die.*

"*And you will die with them.*"

"*No,*" the girl snapped.

Zara's free hand reached behind her, yanking her hair back so hard she fell on her back. She kicked out, fighting an invisible enemy.

"*You're right—my mind is a mess. I wake up every day scared, feeling like there's a hole in my chest. Feeling useless. Helpless. Wishing someone would tell me what to do. Tell me how to live, so it doesn't hurt anymore.*" The invader's voice grew louder, becoming a burning pyre in the center of Zara's mind, matching Zara's anger with her own. Memories flashed, scenes Zara didn't know yet felt as familiar as her own claws.

Humans shoving a girl child on the ground, laughter as they walked away—*school.* A man with a kind smile charging forward, his body prone and bleeding on the ground—*Jacobi.* An armored man throwing her from a... blessed fang, a dragon! Zara's awe at the beautiful, scaled beast was cut short by the name the memory whispered—*Valerius.*

"*But no more,*" the parasite raged.

While Zara's anger was sharpened to a knifepoint, the girl's fury was a wildfire—chaotic. Savage. Uncontrollable. At another time, in another life, Zara would have found it beautiful.

"I am not weak. I am not stupid. And I won't let you hurt them."

And just like that…

… Zara the Fury was gone.

***

I blinked and was aware of two things.

One—I was flat on my back, and everything hurt. *Everything.* Lying down and simply breathing made the world spin so hard I thought I was going to vomit.

The sheer amount of blood Zara must have lost… that *I* must have lost, was staggering.

As a child playing *Knights of Eternity,* I'd thought Zara the Fury was a cool if incredibly difficult boss. While she had corny one-liners, "Die, little hero!" she was just an overpowered bunch of pixels who served Magnus—the *real* villain of the series.

But she was so much more than that. She was angry and cruel, of course.

She was also painfully, breathtakingly sad. It was buried deep in the barbed wire that was her mind, but I'd felt it in the brief moments when she wasn't furious.

I shivered. My mind might be anxiety-fueled and panicked. There were days when I'd do anything to be "normal."

But I'd take my mind over Zara's any day.

The second thing I noticed was that two very large monsters crowded around me—staring down at me intensely.

Aerzin leaned heavily against Lukas' molger form, who looked like he was barely standing himself. They both blinked at me with wide, terrified eyes. Me—lying on my back, barely able to move.

It was almost funny.

"It's okay," I said, struggling to one elbow. The world spun—*nope, bad idea*—and I flopped back down.

I raised a hand instead. "She's gone. She's not going to hurt you—I promise."

Huge feet padded heavily toward me. Lukas' hybrid form appeared, fur sticking up at odd angles from Zara's lightning.

Remembering him from the forest, my whole body tensed. If he wanted to kill me—if any of them did, I'd be helpless to stop it.

Lukas dipped his head, sniffing me.

Sated, he dragged a thick tongue as rough as sandpaper over my cheek, nuzzling me gently.

I laughed, my ribs aching in reply, reaching up a hand to scratch the side of his head. "Hey, Lukas. And, also Lukas," I said, nodding at the molger who dipped his heavy head in reply. "And... Aerzin." The vaxion locked his star-shaped pupils on mine for a long second, then bent his head—pressing his nose against mine.

Kin, I heard in my head.

Knowing what little I did of vaxion, I guessed that was as close as I was going to get to a "thank you."

"Well, the big question is," I said, looking at the giant mahogany form of the molger, the sleek predator that was the vaxion, and the crooked jaw of the hybrid— each part of Lukas' mind.

"What do we do now?"

Chapter Fifty-Eight

Lazander's arrow shot straight for Valerius—his aim true, but the Gilded leader brought up his shield. The arrow's steel tip dinged against it harmlessly.

Dropping the shield, Valerius readied himself to charge.

But the red-haired knight was gone.

Valerius knew this technique—*Hunter's Shadow*. It was unique even among knights and Lazander's iconic ability from *Knights of Eternity*. Lazander would blend into the environment, near invisible to the naked eye, and then strike an opponent from behind.

Valerius waited, timing his breaths.

One.

Two.

Three.

He drove his sword behind him—to exactly where Lazander's heart would lie.

His blade met open air.

He felt the arrow before he saw it—the steel tip finding the miniscule gap between his pauldron and breastplate, driving into his shoulder. He gasped, bringing his shield up as he rounded, searching for his opponent.

The next arrow found the back of his knee.

The third his left foot, chipping bone as it drove into his ankle.

Valerius grunted, falling to one knee. Pain, a rarity for him, clouded his thoughts. *What is going on? How is Lazander doing this? Think—think!*

He had to heal himself, *now,* he knew. But if he did, he'd be wide open.

The Inventory, for all its uses, had a very irritating limitation. If something was part of a "set"—a sword and shield, a suit of armor, you could only materialize and vanish them as a *whole.*

Which meant that if he summoned a health potion, he'd need to dismiss both the sword *and* shield in his hands—leaving him defenseless

Valerius tried to ignore the steel-tipped arrowhead digging into his shoulder and arm, grinding into bone with every move—but he couldn't. He couldn't fight like this. He had to chance it.

Light enveloped his hands as his sword and shield vanished. He'd summon the potion in one hand and the greatsword he'd used in the guise of the Freylen soldier in the other. He'd be weaponless for a split second, he told himself, less time than it took for a heart to beat.

That was all the time Lazander needed.

There was a saying in Navaros—" There is no greater fury than that of a gentle man." It was something Valerius had heard in passing over the years, but he'd never given it much thought. He had brushed it off as peasant nonsense, right up there with using leeches to bleed out evil.

Until Lazander appeared in front of him, an arrow gripped in a tight fist, the promise of death in his eyes.

The dark outline of a greatsword appeared in Valerius' hands, but he was too slow. With a snarl, Lazander drove the arrow into the dragonscale armor's most vulnerable spot—the armpit. He forced the steel tip into the precious artery he knew lay beneath the skin, jamming it in with all his strength.

Valerius roared in pain, nearly dropping the potion bottle as he swung his newly materialized greatsword, but Lazander was already gone.

Blood instantly soaked his armor and the thick leather padding beneath it as if he'd been plunged into water. It came in fountainous spurts in time with his rapidly beating heart, and Valerius felt a terror he'd solely reserved for the Operator.

Move, damn it, move!

With shaking hands, he forced his teeth around the cork of the purple-ringed potion bottle, yanking it open. The smell of rotten eggs flooded his nose, but he forced himself to choke down the chunky, slimy contents.

He threw the empty bottle away, the glass smashing against the far wall, and felt the arrow wounds in his shoulder, knee, and ankle begin to fade.

Blood still poured down his side. The room spun as blood loss plunged his head into fog.

Please, work. Please, please, please…

He gasped in relief when he felt the arrow in his armpit shift—the thick metal head forced out of the tender flesh by the potion. With aching slowness his wounds began to close. Valerius shook with the realization that if he'd been even thirty seconds slower, he'd have been lying dead on the ground.

Knights could withstand intense magical attacks—but it came at a cost. Healing magic, a rarity even among mages, had limited effect on them. The exception to the rule was *Healing Void*—the potion he just drank.

Not only was it not bound by the rules of this world, it simply didn't exist here— it was a gift from the Operator, one of his rewards for finishing his quests. He'd earned only a handful over the years and couldn't afford to use anymore of the precious potions.

Nor could he kill Lazander with magic—his mana was drained from maintaining the illusion of the Freylen soldier and his rapid casting of *The Cage* when Lazander skewered his plans by going with Farah.

He'd adapted, of course. But then, his plan hadn't changed drastically. Gabriel, Marito, then Lazander, with Corym and Farah struck down when opportunity presented itself. It was a kill list he'd fallen asleep picturing ever since the Calamity System had ordered him on this damned quest. He'd planned to kill Gabriel and Marito first for good reason. They were the real threats, he'd thought.

He'd been wrong.

Anger blossomed in his chest. He hadn't survived the Operator's quests and that savage, red-hot alien desert only to be killed by an *NPC.*

Valerius activated *Swiftness,* an ability that increased his speed and agility. His mana might be gone, but his abilities as a knight had ballads dedicated to them for good reason.

He dodged Lazander's next arrow easily as *Keen Eye* sharpened his vision—the darkness of the shadowed room exploding in detail. At the slightest creak of a floorboard behind him, Valerius threw himself forward, hitting the ground with his shoulder as he rolled. An arrow hit the floor where he'd been a second earlier.

Valerius leaped to his feet, activating *Iron Strength,* his greatsword suddenly light as a feather as he dismissed it, summoning Twin Strike—one of the rarest weapons in the game. It was a gigantic crossbow lined with thick, blackened steel. The weight alone made it impossible to wield without the use of a strength-based ability.

It looked both cruel and wicked, but that wasn't why Valerius had summoned it. It had one very unique feature—something Lazander would never expect.

Valerius raised the crossbow, stilling as he watched the room with sharpened eyes. *Keen Eye* caught a sliver of movement to his right, and Valerius swiveled—letting a bolt fly.

Lazander dodged the bolt as Valerius knew he would, materializing out of the darkness as *Hunter's Shadow* faded—twin blades in hand once more.

Valerius grinned, teeth showing, as he aimed for the red-haired knight's heart— and fired.

Unlike a regular crossbow, which had to be painstakingly reloaded after every shot, the *Twin Strike* lived up to its name. It came loaded with not one, but two iron bolts nearly as long as Valerius' arm.

One of which buried itself in Lazander's left shoulder—inches above his heart. The powerful crossbow hit like a ballista. His legs went from under him as he was knocked backward from the force—hitting the stone floor with a satisfying thud.

Breathing hard, Valerius vanished the Twin Strike, greatsword appearing in his hands once more. Cautiously he approached the groaning Lazander, who had rolled onto his side, his fingers trying to grip the feathered end of the iron bolt.

"Don't bother," Valerius said. "It's gone straight through the other side—you're not getting that out without a vice grip and two men."

Lazander lashed out with his right hand, blade glinting, but Valerius simply let the wild swing drag over his armored shins. Almost lazily he kicked Lazander in the face, the knight's head snapping back as blood shot from his nose.

"Congratulations are in order," Valerius said, gaining confidence as the knight twitched in pain. "That is the closest anyone has ever come to killing me—other than the Operator that is. There was a reason you were my main in *Knights of Eternity*."

Lazander ignored Valerius, pulling at his bracer and the blade Valerius knew he kept hidden there. He backhanded Lazander with a meaty slap, punching him once. Twice. Three times. Finally Lazander lay still and groaning—barely conscious.

Valerius had done it, he'd beaten the Gilded. He'd *won*. Now all he had to do was finish the job.

He gripped his greatsword with both hands, angry they shook. His plan had not gone perfectly. He was supposed to enter with Farah alone, kill her, then appear as the Freylen soldier and slaughter everyone but Corym. The boy knight would then go running back to camp, crying for help. This would buy Valerius time to drag the bound and gagged Magnus to a safe location, and then reappear, appropriately injured of course, and filled with grief for his fallen Gilded.

Everything went off the rails after Lazander had insisted on pairing with Farah. He'd had to improvise. *The Cage* had been a stroke of genius, if he did say so himself. The acrobatics required to make it appear as if he was trapped inside mere seconds before the Freylen soldier appeared were nothing short of spectacular.

The problem now was that he had no witnesses—no one who could back up his claim that a Freylen soldier had massacred the Gilded. It was only a slight wrinkle, he told himself. In fact, this would make an even better story. The sole survivor of Freyley's horrendous attack, he'd be due a hero's welcome. The spymaster would be suspicious, as he was of everyone, but he'd bought off several of that idiot dog's shadows—with violence when needed.

He'd been running circles around every idiot *NPC* in this world for years—and this wasn't going to change that.

So why, as Lazander kicked feebly beneath him, did his greatsword shake?

He's not real—none of this is. Just kill him—do it!

"You really were my favorite character," Valerius whispered, driving the blade downward, deep into Lazander's heart.

Chapter Fifty-Nine

In H'tar, a tiny auburn molger desperately clung to the paw of his friend. Waylen, living on the edge of molger society with only his mom, didn't have a lot of friends. He hadn't minded too much—he had Didi the pig and his rock collection. He had the books his father had left him and his mother's make-believe games. She was funny when she let herself be.

He did, however, have one friend—Lukas.

Lukas was older than Waylen. By how much, Waylen didn't know, but it didn't really matter—all grown-ups were old to him. But Lukas wasn't like the other grown-ups. The grown-ups always went drinking at Uncle Jerome's, or played bone-drop and gambled away their chores behind the barn, or went dancing at the half-moon. Lukas didn't do any of those things.

Maybe that was why the other grown-ups didn't like him—which Waylen thought was dumb. They would make weird faces when talking to Lukas, or even pretend they hadn't seen him when he waved. It didn't take long for the kids to notice and begin copying their parents—some even running away when Lukas showed up.

Waylen never understood why. Lukas was his second favorite person (after his mom but before Didi the pig, although he would never tell Didi that.)

"What are we feeling, big guy?" Lukas would ask, stretching out beneath the big blue twilight blossom tree. "Is it a 'Marito versus the *entire* Freylen army' kinda day, or maybe a 'Lazander tames the ferocious pyrions'?" He'd rub his hands together eagerly, like a magician about to dazzle an audience.

Waylen would furrow his brow—Lukas had so many stories, it was hard to choose from! There was the time Gabriel used his shadows to part an entire lake and save a drowning kid or the one where Valerius saved a village from a *xandi*—a giant beast with horns that even the vaxion ran from. That was one of his favorites.

When, inevitably, he couldn't choose just one, Lukas would sit with him until it grew dark, arranging pebbles on the ground to paint a picture of the battlefield, waving his hands in the air for spells, and even doing voices. Marito's big booming voice always made him laugh.

One day, Lukas started to smell funny. It was a strange smell—something coppery and rotten. It wasn't very nice. The other grown-ups got really worried about the smell and started whispering behind Lukas' back. Some even yelled at Lukas to go back to the Moonvale Mountains, even though Chief told them to stop.

When Waylen asked his mom why, she said, "They're scared. When people get scared, they get mean." Then she did that annoying thing where she said she'd explain when he was older.

A couple of days later, Waylen went to the twilight blossoms to meet Lukas as usual. Instead of waiting for him beneath the blue leaves, Lukas stood facing the waters, his hands in fists.

"This is goodbye, big guy," he'd said in a strange, sad voice Waylen had never heard before. "I have to… go away, for a little while."

Waylen asked why, pulling at Lukas' sleeve when he refused to answer, until the man knelt—holding Waylen's hand in his own. "The—the Gilded need my help. Marito contacted me—that's right, *the* Marito! Valerius didn't want him to, of course—you know how he is. But the Gilded are fighting a *huge* xandi to the north, and they need backup. I know, right—a real xandi! I'll make sure to count how many horns they have. No, I don't know how long I'll be, but this is the Gilded, buddy. I can't exactly say no, can I? I'll be… I'll be back before you know it, yeah?"

Waylen knew he was lying. Grown-ups thought they were really good at it, but they did this sad thing with their eyes whenever they lied about something bad. His mom did it whenever he asked about what happened to his dad. Lukas was doing it now.

So Waylen just hugged him and gave Lukas his favorite rock, a super cool purple one he'd found when he went diving, before running off.

He didn't want Lukas to see him cry.

He didn't get far before he heard a huge crack, like the thunderstorms Didi hated. Looking back, he saw Lukas had his hands wrapped around the biggest twilight blossom tree. With a roar, he ripped it out—throwing it at the lake so hard it skipped along the surface.

Then Lukas was gone.

Weeks later, Waylen couldn't sleep. It had been happening a lot since Lukas had left, and people started pretending he'd never even existed. So Waylen did what he always did—he went to play with Didi.

His mom told him they had to sleep inside for a little while. Waylen hated sleeping in his human form, he'd no fur or anything to stay nice and warm. She even started locking the door—something they'd never done before.

He waited until he was sure his mom was fast asleep before slipping out the window—the wet grass cold and tingly under his feet. Didi and Gibi were both fast asleep in the pigpen but jerked awake the moment they heard Waylen's feet on the fence, climbing it as he always did (using the gate was boring).

Didi nuzzled him with her big pink nose, eager for scratches under chin—her favorite spot. Gibi just glared—shaking her curly tail as she showed them her backside before flopping back down to sleep.

Then Gibi was gone.

Waylen didn't see it happen. Didn't hear it either.

One second she was there, her round pink belly rising and falling with her tiny snores. Then she vanished with a flash of blood and a cutoff squeal echoing in the night.

White eyes, brighter than the full moon, stared at him from the darkness. Waylen had heard the stories—the older kids told them that Gallow came for bad molger, twisting their bodies and turning them into horrible monsters. He hadn't believed them.

Until now.

Gibi's shredded carcass hung from the monster's jaw. With a hiss, it tossed Gibi to the side. Her body made a squelching sound as she hit the ground, one of her eyes hanging limp and useless from its socket.

Waylen knew he should call his mom. His mom would stop the monster. His mom could do anything.

But he couldn't move.

Blood-streaked, the monster crept toward Waylen. Didi squealed, a tiny, terrified noise, and the monster's head swiveled to face her—its thick tongue hanging from its mouth, saliva dripping in thick goblets.

."No—not Didi. Please, no!" Waylen grabbed the pig, burying his head in her shoulder. He could hear the monster as it padded toward him, growling deeply. "Not Didi, not Didi," he whispered frantically into her neck.

He felt the monster brush his hair with his snout, sniffing him. Instinctively Waylen sniffed in return—catching a coppery, rotten smell mixed with a scent he knew as well as his mom's.

"Lukas?" he said, head snapping up. At once, Waylen's fear vanished. It was Lukas—Lukas was here. He stood, excited. "Lukas, you're back!"

The monster stiffened, shaking his head as he stepped back. "Lukas? It's me—it's Waylen? Mom said I grew lots, so maybe you don't recognize me?"

The monster growled as if in pain—then leaped the gate and slipped into the shadows.

Waylen kept seeing Lukas after that but only ever from a distance. He would watch Waylen and his mom from the dark, his eyes glowing like lanterns. But he never came close again. His mom never saw Lukas or at least pretended she didn't. Not even when Uncle Jerome showed up, demanding to know why every single pig in H'tar had been slaughtered.

Every pig, that is—except for Didi.

Waylen didn't tell him it was because he'd asked Lukas not to hurt her. He didn't tell him Lukas wasn't a monster—that his friend was still in there. He didn't tell anyone because he was scared, he'd get in trouble.

Which was why he clung so hard to Lukas now, his monstrous body cut to pieces from Uncle Jerome's claws. Why he held on even after Zara had shoved her arm into Lukas' mouth, and the two of them stood as still as rocks.

Because he should have told people—he should have helped his friend.

Lukas would have done the same for him.

***

Lenia was a big believer in keeping her mouth shut. It was why she'd moved to the outskirts of H'tar. Why she hadn't kicked Jerome's head in when he turned half the village against her. If she'd interfered, she'd just make things harder for her and Waylen, she told herself.

It was a lie. The truth was she thought she deserved it. Rowan was dead, and she couldn't help but lie awake at night and think of all the ways she could have saved her husband. After all, isolation and the occasional slap was a small price to pay for failing the love of her life.

It was why she'd held Waylen tight as she watched Lukas fight for his life. Why she had stood by and said nothing as Zara frantically dodged and weaved between them, trying to stop Lukas and Jerome from killing each other. If she interfered, she'd just make Jerome angrier and make things worse for both her and Waylen.

Then, in the middle of the fight, Zara had claimed the impossible—that she could turn Lukas back, that she could make him human again. Waylen's eyes had lit up, his hand gripping hers.

"Please, Mom," was all he'd said.

Those two words were all it took.

She drove her molger skull into Jerome's, headbutting him with years of pent-up anger, grief, and loneliness. He hit the dirt with a vicious thud, breathing heavily.

He didn't get up.

She huffed—his skull had been as thick as she'd suspected.

Chief, harried and gray, emerged from the crowd, looking scared for the first time in her memory. Turning awkwardly in her molger form, Lenia knew she'd probably ruined her life. She'd be exiled from H'tar, along with Waylen.

She looked at Waylen, her precious boy, holding on to Lukas for dear life. At Zara, that mysterious, confusing woman who had stood between her and Jerome. Who was willing to risk everything for Lukas—a total stranger…

She found she didn't regret a damn thing.

She smiled, knowing that Rowan would be proud of her.

Lukas yelped, snapping out of whatever trance had held him.

Lenia charged forward; exhaustion forgotten at Waylen's yelp of fear.

With a jerk, Zara ripped her arm from Lukas' gaping jaw. She must have lost several fingers, if not her whole hand, Lenia knew—a mongrel's bite wasn't as strong as a molger's, but it was damn close. Yet Zara's arm didn't have so much as a scratch on it—in fact, it was entirely free from blood and gore, at odds with the rest of her battered body.

"Back—everyone get back!" Zara yelled, pulling Waylen away. The crowd froze, and Zara hissed at them—the villagers suddenly leaping to her command. Lenia waited until Waylen was tucked safely between her front paws, dipping her head to give her son a good lick, and then shuffled back to join them at a safe distance.

Lukas was on his side, so still Lenia thought he was dead. The air was thick with the tension of waiting as she leaned in, feeling the crowd do the same.

Then his skin began to ripple, fur undulating in the telltale sign of the change. Lenia held her breath as Lukas' body elongated, doubling in size. His skull split open, and thick black tendrils sprouted from his head, traveling down the length of his body in a waterfall of darkness.

Lenia's heart sank.

Lukas was what the villagers had cursed him to be, had spat in his face for all these years—a vaxion.

She should be happy, she knew—he was no longer trapped in the body of that awful, bloodthirsty monster. But if he wasn't hated before, he would be now. Not even Chief would be able to stop the others from running him out of H'tar—the only home he'd ever known.

A woman screamed, and the crowd murmured in discontent. Before Chief could step in, Zara turned on them—growling fiercely.

"He's not done."

Lenia smiled when the crowd shut up instantly.

Lukas' flesh shivered once more as he grew larger again. His snout lengthened, talons becoming thick and short as coarse mahogany fur sprang from his body. Tiny ears popped out from the sides of his head like daisies in springtime as his tendrils shrank, fading into his fur.

A molger. He turned from a vaxion into a *molger*.

"Impossible," whispered Chief. The crowd stood, stunned into silence. For the first time in her life, Lenia found herself speechless. Only Waylen, nestled between her legs, gave a squeak of joy.

Zara stepped forward, kneeling by Lukas' side. Head bent, she whispered something into his ear.

His molger eyes fluttered open, and he grimaced, shaking his head—but Zara's whispering grew more insistent, and she gripped one of his huge paws in her two hands.

With a grunt, his fur began to recede, yanked into his skin in patchy clumps. There was a crack as his spine broke in half, shortening. His eyes shrank within his skull and his head soon followed. Blonde hair streaked with blood and dirt grew where coarse fur once sprouted.

Until finally, hands free from claws and talons gripped Zara's.

"Told you." Zara laughed, hugging a very human, very surprised looking Lukas.

Waylen waddled forward, chirping happily, and Lenia felt tears prick at her eyes.

No—she didn't regret a damn thing.

Chapter Sixty

L azander was about to die.

He'd failed them. Corym. Farah. Marito. Gabriel. He'd failed them all. He'd buried arrows in Valerius. He'd even severed an artery. Anyone else would have been dead in seconds, but Valerius simply drank from a bottle he'd summoned with his strange magic and then was moving again as if fresh from a good night's sleep.

It was like Lazander had never even touched him. Not even Gabriel, with his salves and balms and endless magical remedies, could have done that.

Now Valerius stood above him, greatsword gripped in his hands. He whispered something about "favorite character"—the meaning lost to Lazander, but the words carried the finality of a goodbye. The traitor's sword moved, plunging downward…

… as a furious roar rent the air.

Something huge and heavy struck Valerius, knocking him away. Lazander heard metal on metal and the sounds of a struggle—but he couldn't see from where he lay sprawled on the ground. He forced himself to roll onto his side, the bolt that skewered his shoulder bursting with a pain so intense he nearly blacked out.

A knight, a behemoth of a man, grappled with Valerius—his dark braids whipping about him.

"*Marito?*" Lazander gasped.

Bleeding from a vicious wound in his back, one hand a mere bloody stump, the knight rammed a knee into Valerius' stomach. Valerius gasped, doubling over—allowing Marito to slip behind him, dropping his arms around Valerius in a crushing bear hug.

"*You were the best of us,*" he snarled, lifting the knight clean off his feet. "The hero of Navaros!"

Valerius wheezed in pain, kicking the air wildly, and Lazander heard the unmistakable *crack* of armor.

Marito was breaking dragonscale armor, the toughest metal in the world, with his *bare hands.*

Then Marito's eyes flickered to Gabriel—his pale face, death's unmistakable touch painted on his skin. The giant stilled, all color draining from his face, and for a second Lazander thought he would drop Valerius. But Marito roared, an agonizing sound of pain and grief, squeezing Valerius with every ounce of his strength. Light flashed in Valerius' hands.

"Watch out!" Lazander yelled. "He can—he can summon weapons! Don't let him—"

Lazander's warning was too late—two daggers, small and agile, appeared in Valerius' hands. Arms pinned to his sides above the elbows, he managed to spin them in his fingers—driving them backward, deep into Marito's stomach. "Let go, let me go, you bastard!" Eyes wild, spittle flying from his lips, he looked nearly demonic with rage and panic.

The giant merely grunted, unwavering in the face of pain Lazander could only imagine. Still, Valerius stabbed him, again and again, his legs kicking wildly.

"There is—there is nothing you could have done, Master Lazander," the giant forced out, his words broken by the blades that slid in and out of his guts. "I can think, ah, I can think—*argh*." He stumbled but righted himself—blood poured from his stomach, dripping down his armor, leaving crimson footprints with every step. "I can think of no one better to lead the new generation of—of Gilded!"

Lazander frowned, his clouded brain and injuries stealing understanding from him.

Marito bumped against the crumbling window frame, and Valerius' eyes went wide in panic. He frantically summoned different weapons—a spear, an axe, a sling—but with his arms bound by Marito's strength, he could do little.

"It's been an honor, Lazander," Marito said, grinning broadly—his face serene and free from the pain Lazander knew he felt.

Marito threw himself and Valerius backward, through the window—and into the open air beyond.

***

For a long time, Lazander could only stare.

Then the shock began to wear off, making room for the pain. His nose was a ruined mess, his left arm numb from the shoulder down.

After a time, minutes, hours, he couldn't tell, he forced himself to one knee, breathing deeply through his mouth as his head spun, his stomach threatening to vomit up its meager contents.

When the dizziness passed, he wobbled to his feet, concentrating on putting one foot in front of the other—each step a heroic effort.

He had to look.

He had to see.

Reaching the crumbling window frame, he gripped it tightly—leaning forward.

Marito lay on his back, a mere dot at this distance. Valerius was crumpled next to him, his white cloak spread out like a flag of surrender.

Neither moved.

"I have to—I have to get…" Lazander swayed, falling to one knee. A squawk made him raise his head, and he saw Merrin, flapping and chirping with panic. She flashed images of the camp and her shrieking at the day guard, even biting an ear or two, until the entire company was armed and heading this way.

Help. She was saying. *Help is coming.*

"Good girl, Merrin. Good… girl," Lazander said, the words thick and slow in his mouth. Why was it so hard to speak? A tingling numbness began in his shoulder where Valerius' bolt still skewered him like a roasted pig at a summer festival. The numbness was spreading, its tendrils creeping up his back and shoulders.

He knew this meant something bad, but he couldn't remember what—the answer danced on the tip of his tongue, just out of reach.

A hand lay on the floor in front of him—deeply tanned. It was clear the owner had spent his days out in the sun. Two of the nails were split, and speckles of blood dotted it. He stared at the hand and saw a layer of golden dragonscale began at the wrist. He followed it, frowning when he saw it led to his own shoulder.

He stared at his hand in confusion, a heavy haze stopping him from moving so much as a pinkie.

It was only then that the answer came to him—fear cutting through his mind with startling clarity.

"Merrin…" He croaked, his throat a raspy desert. "Merrin, I've been *poisoned*. A mage—a mage needs to—" Lazander's eyes rolled back in his head as he collapsed on his side, frothing at the mouth—Merrin's frantic cries fading into the distance.

***

"Lady Eternity, are you sure—"

"Yes, I'm sure," she snapped. Yolana recoiled, clutching her hands nervously, and Eternity regretted her tone.

"Novice Yolana," she said gently. "I just need the Heart for a minute—and if anyone takes issue with that, you can direct them to me."

She'd been so close. It had been days since Lazander and the other Gilded had left, and there had been no word since. While that wasn't unusual, the Ivory Keep thrummed with nervous energy. Guards were stringently checking the papers of everyone who crossed their path—even friends and family. Champion Imani, with her ebony armor and one word answers, had been glued to Eternity's side—unwilling to let Gallow's Chosen out of her sight.

It had taken a desperate plea that the constant rattle of Imani's armor as she patrolled was making meditation an impossibility for Eternity to *finally* have five minutes to herself. She'd used the time well.

The Gallowed Temple's meditation rooms were not built for comfort—most were simply four walls with an icon of Gallow at its center. Cushions were provided for novices, the injured, and older initiates—but that was it. The benefit of the meditation rooms, however, was they were built to be easily accessible. Which meant it was a simple thing for Eternity to sneak out the side door, leaving the pacing Imani alone in the corridor.

She'd felt guilty, of course. Imani had been on edge ever since the kidnapping, and while she'd never say it, the brusque woman clearly felt guilty she wasn't there that night. However, Eternity was done sitting on her backside while Zara's name was smeared at every turn.

So, she'd decided to take matters into her own hands.

She'd made it so far—past the kitchen, clattering with activity. The sleeping chambers, her heart twisting at the memory of the many nights she'd spent there, even if some were spent cursing the snores of her fellow disciples. Finally, she reached a long corridor, at the end of which lay a sign above a hollowed-out bird's skull—the traditional symbol of Gallow. The sign read:

"The Heart. Do not approach without permission from the Head Disciple."

Eternity had almost reached the skull and the thick cord of rope that cordoned it off when Yolana appeared at her back. The ever helpful, ever attentive novice had noticed Eternity had left the meditation rooms and had decided to follow her.

Unfortunately.

"Lady Eternity, I—I would never question the will of Gallow's Chosen, but the Heart is only to be used in times of great need. If the temple were under attack, or a Champion was injured, for instance. I cannot condone this, I must tell the Head Disciple—"

"Yolana! Yolana, *please*," Eternity said, snapping a smile on her face. She gently unhooked the golden ties that cordoned off the nondescript dark marble wall. Taking a hand, she pressed it against the wall, right beneath the skull.

"I wouldn't do this if it wasn't important—of that you have my most solemn vow." Fingers splayed, she let her mind grow still. Gallow was only a whisper away within the temple walls, but here, in this most sacred of places, she didn't have to open the door to him. He was simply there—a whisper in her lungs, a pulse of her heart. The marble beneath her fingers thrummed with his power, calling out to those who followed him. The stone shivered, tendrils of darkness spreading out from her fingers—forming a large, undulating circle.

Before Yolana could protest, she stepped into the portal, sighing when she heard the novice's quick step behind her.

The Heart was stored in a room that wasn't of this world, nor was it of the Void where Gallow and the Tyrant had hailed from—and where Gallow had ultimately sealed away the destructive deity.

Rather, it was a space in-between—a pocket of time and space that hovered between the two realms. It had no beginning and no end, and regardless of which

373 | Rachel Ní Chuirc

direction you walked in its star-glittered darkness you would always end up at its center.

While that alone was enough to make the jaws drop of the precious few who ever saw this room, that wasn't what made it so special.

In front of Eternity stood a glass box on a simple stone pedestal.

"Righteous judgment, know my heart is eager. My need great," she intoned. Behind her, Yolana dropped to the floor and began chanting the eighth mantra—a prayer for forgiveness.

The air grew cold, her steps heavy as she approached the box and reverently lifted the glass lid. Within lay a clump of wizened muscle and sinew the size of Eternity's fist. It twitched ever so slightly—throbbing in time with her pulse.

It was a heart—the Heart of the first Chosen, the one who'd impressed the God of Judgment so much he'd left the Void to grant her his power. It was the Heart of Eternity—*the* Eternity.

Yolana gasped at the sudden weight in the air, the spark of magic that burned through her lungs. Eternity barely noticed—it was a whisper compared to what it felt like when she wielded Gallow's Judgment.

Including Imani, only three Champions had been born from her touch. While it had been through her that they were granted his power, that didn't mean they answered to her. They walked this world alone, obeying only Gallow's will. She never knew where they were or what they were doing.

That didn't mean she couldn't speak to one.

The First's Heart was kept locked away for good reason—if all of those blessed by Gallow were threads, then the Heart was the needle, connecting them across time and space. Its powers were many, but Eternity was only interested in one. Through it, she could speak to those blessed by Gallow, no matter the distance. An impossibility for even the most talented mage.

Malik had been her very first Champion. He'd been by her side since she was but a fledgling Chosen, back when her powers were new and frightening to her. If she used the First's Heart and told him about Zara and how she'd saved Eternity, then Malik might agree to find the vaxion—he *had* to.

It was a mad idea, she knew. Zara had fled from Magnus, had *saved* Eternity—and what had she done with her newfound freedom? She'd mucked out a pigpen! The woman was no threat to anyone. Eternity knew this.

The problem was, not everyone agreed.

It was only a matter of time before someone discovered the vaxion was alive—be it the queen, spymaster, Gilded, it didn't matter. They would strike first and ask questions later.

Which was why Eternity had to get to Zara first.

The Chosen sighed, thinking of the lecture she would get from Imani. Especially as she was going behind the Champion's back. She'd tried asking her first, of course, and had been shut down so quickly she'd—

"CALAMITY."

The word pounded her skull, her blood freezing in her body.

Yolana screamed, clutching her head.

Years of practice kept Eternity standing. The first time she'd heard that voice, it had felt like an ice pick being driven into her skull with a sledgehammer.

Flashes followed. She saw a blonde woman, barely older than her—her hands cloaked in light. A flash of swords, the thud of bodies. The woman's eyes burst from the sockets like overripe tomatoes. Blood dripped down her face, but she didn't make a sound.

Four soldiers, clad in dark armor—the blonde woman lay at the center of a circle.

"CALAMITY."

Suddenly the Heart vanished. As did Yolana and the room of glittering darkness.

Sun kissed her skin, and Eternity felt warm and safe—happy even. She opened her eyes to find herself in an open field, the sky above blue and free of clouds. Confused, she spun—wondering what Gallow wanted her to see, wanted her to know.

There was a thunderous crack, and the sky darkened—the sun was dragged across the sky by an invisible hand. Magic, crackling hot and near overwhelming in power, threatened to choke Eternity where she stood.

The Chosen had thought she had been scared when she'd awoken in Magnus' castle, bound and unable to use all but a sliver of magic. But that was nothing compared to the terror she felt as the darkened sky split in two. A shriveled graying hand the size of a city emerged from the darkness, blocking out the sky as it reached for Eternity.

She realized now this wasn't a vision. It was a memory. A memory from the First Eternity, the one who had stood alone and unafraid against the Tyrant who'd threatened to destroy the world.

"CALAMITY," Gallow intoned. "HAS RETURNED."

END OF BOOK ONE

REVIEWS

You made it to the end! (Unlike some of my characters...) I started this book during a stressful time in my life when the imposter syndrome was at an all-time high, and I really didn't believe in myself. This book was my light in the dark, and I hope you enjoyed reading it as much as I enjoyed writing it. If you did, please, please consider leaving a review on Amazon—it makes a *huge* difference. In fact, if you want to go do that... I'll wait!

...

...

...

Welcome back!

Knowing that you've got my book in your hands makes me so happy. If you happen to know anyone who might be interested in stocking my books, please reach out.

Thank you, and see you in the next book!

Love,

Rachel Ní Chuirc

DESECRATE

By Rachel Ní Chuirc

Trapped in the body of the murderous Zara the Fury, our hero might not know her real name, but she knows how to play a game.

Or so she thought.

The world of Knights of Eternity is no simple dungeon-crawler with damsels in distress. The tyrannical god Calamity treats the world as his chess board, a knight is faced with the chance to change his fate, and cryptic quests promise our hero overwhelming power.

But the real Zara the Fury wants her body back. And she'll do whatever it takes to get it.

Welcome to the world of Knights of Eternity—a LitRPG adventure where power has a price.

https://mybook.to/KoE_Desecrate

WANDERING WARRIOR

By Michael Head

Punishment for the guilty is coming – carried by the armored fist of Judge James Holden

He's reached the limits of his power, and in the process, he's brought justice to nineteen entire worlds. But now, cast across time and space to his twentieth planet, something's wrong.

The darkness runs deeper than ever before, those in power corrupt those beneath them, and the concept of honor is twisted and long lost to those who should know better.

James has had enough, and as the chosen weapon of the gods, he'll bring balance to this world again, or die trying.

If somebody needs to be sent to their gods for that to happen? Well, that's a sacrifice he's willing to make.

It's time for judgement.

https://mybook.to/WanderingWarrior

QUEST ACADEMY

By Brian J. Nordon

A world infested by demons.
An Academy designed to train Heroes to save humanity from annihilation.
A new student's power could make all the difference.

Humans have been pushed to the brink of extinction by an ever-evolving demonic threat. Portals are opening faster than ever, Towers bursting into the skies and Dungeons being mined below the last safe havens of society. The demons are winning.

Quest Academy stands defiantly against them, as a place to train the next generation of Heroes. The Guild Association is holding the line but are in dire need of new blood and the powerful abilities they could bring to the battlefront. To be the saviors that humanity needs, they need to surpass the limits of those that came before them.

In a war with everything on the line, every power matters. With an adaptive enemy, comes the need for a constant shift in tactics. A new age of strategy is emerging, with even the unlikeliest of Heroes making an impact.

Salvatore Argento has never seen a demon.
He has never aspired to become a Hero.
Yet his power might be the one to tip the odds in humanity's favor.

https://www.amazon.com/Quest-Academy-Brian-J-Nordon-ebook

ARISE ALPHA

By Jez Cajiao

When you steal a hundred grand from some very bad people, the best way to survive is to stay small and quiet...

Possibly its not to save a pair of drowning girls, not go 'viral' on social media and certainly not to let the local police take your passport, trapping you on a small 'party' island in the middle of the Mediterranean Sea.

But Steve isn't the average guy, he's ex-military, ex-enforcer and ex-human. He's a one-man nanite fueled nightmare for those that cross the line, and he's decided that it's time to clean up his act. He's going to make up for the things he's done, and save 'the little guys'.

It's a nice fantasy, but even he has to admit, it's really just a justification, because he's a very bad man, with horrifying abilities, and he's only just learning what he's capable of. He needs a reason to not go to the dark, and if that's hunting down the creatures of the night and beating them to death with their own femurs? Well, he's just the man for the job.

Stolen money. Greek Islands. Werewolves and Enforcers...
What could possibly go wrong?

https://www.amazon.com/Arise-Alpha-Dark-LitRPG-Adventure-ebook

SOMNIA ONLINE

By K.T. Hanna

Discover the class you were born to play.

Wren, a seasoned healer, is dismayed when Somnia Online automatically assigns her character, Murmur, to the Enchanter class. Determined to overcome the unexpected setback, she assembles her guild, intent on the coveted #1 spot. Twelve keys stand between her and victory but finding them is only part of the puzzle. Armed with telepathic abilities, Murmur rises to the challenge. However, old rivals have followed her to Somnia Online desperate for revenge. Intricate quest lines become more dangerous as NPCs absorb powerful artifacts, and Murmur begins to wonder just what sort of AI controls the world.

Murmur questions her sanity as the real and virtual worlds mesh together. Everyone is keeping secrets from her, even the AI, and Murmur's determined to uncover them.

https://www.amazon.com/Initializing-Somnia-Online-Book-1-ebook

FACEBOOK AND SOCIAL MEDIA

I have a very fancy author page if you'd like to reach out and chat! I can't promise you witty banter, but I *can* promise you terrible memes:

OR

There is an FB group where I often lurk, like Valerius in a library. It's dedicated to two very simple rules;

1; Lets spread the word about new and old brilliant LitRPG books.

2: Don't be a dick!

Come join us!

www.facebook.com/groups/litrpglegion

There are also a few really active Facebook groups I'd recommend you join, as you'll get to hear about great new books, new releases and interact with all your favorite authors!

www.facebook.com/groups/LitRPGsociety/

www.facebook.com/groups/LitRPG.books/

www.facebook.com/groups/LitRPGforum/

www.facebook.com/groups/gamelitsociety/

LITRPG!

To learn more about LitRPG, talk to other authors including myself, and to just have an awesome time, please join the LitRPG Group

www.facebook.com/groups/LitRPGGroup

LITRPG LEGION

I am published by The Legion Publishers, a fabulous (and wonderfully chaotic) trio. Jez, Chrissy, and Geneva are taking on new authors, as well as experienced ones, focusing primarily on the LitRPG. They are guided by one simple rule:

Don't be a dick.

That's it. They're also up front and open about their contracts, which you can find here:

www.legionpublishers.com/legioncontract

Got a LitRPG that's been sitting on your desktop, looking for the perfect home? Well, look no further. Submit here!

www.legionpublishers.com/contact-and-submissions

Printed in Great Britain
by Amazon

45244215R00215